PENGUIN BOOKS

BREAKTIME

Bernard Lefkowitz, author of *The Victims* (with
Kenneth G. Gross), is a free-lance writer and a
consultant to the Ford Foundation. He was a reporter for the New York *Post* for six years. He
has taught journalism at Duke University, the
New School for Social Research, and City College of New York and has written for *Esquire*,
The Nation, *Look*, and *The Village Voice*.

BERNARD LEFKOWITZ

BREAKTIME

LIVING WITHOUT WORK
IN A NINE-TO-FIVE WORLD

PENGUIN BOOKS

Penguin Books Ltd, Harmondsworth,
Middlesex, England
Penguin Books, 625 Madison Avenue,
New York, New York 10022, U.S.A.
Penguin Books Australia Ltd, Ringwood,
Victoria, Australia
Penguin Books Canada Limited, 2801 John Street,
Markham, Ontario, Canada L3R 1B4
Penguin Books (N.Z.) Ltd, 182–190 Wairau Road,
Auckland 10, New Zealand

First published in the United States of America by
Hawthorn Books, Inc., 1979
First published in Canada by
Prentice-Hall of Canada, Limited, 1979
Published in Penguin Books 1980

LIBRARY OF CONGRESS
CATALOGING IN PUBLICATION DATA
Lefkowitz, Bernard.
Breaktime: living without work in a nine-to-five world.
Includes index.
1. Retirement—United States.   2. Occupations
—United States.   3. Self-actualization (Psychology).
4. Dropouts—United States.   I. Title.
HQ1062.L39   1979b   301.43'5   79–23968
ISBN 0 14 00.5547 9

Printed in the United States of America by
Offset Paperback Mfrs., Inc., Dallas, Pennsylvania
Set in Janson

For my mother
In memory of my father

CONTENTS

ACKNOWLEDGMENTS

First and foremost: Jessica Nelson. Her kindness, wisdom, wit, and enthusiasm sustained me from beginning to end.

This book was supported in part by a grant from the Ford Foundation. People sometimes think of foundations as faceless bureaucratic institutions. That hasn't been my experience. The staff at the Ford Foundation has always been compassionate, concerned, and forgiving. I am particularly grateful to Robert Goldmann, who personally supported and encouraged this work although it didn't exactly coincide with the foundation's policy interests. I am also deeply indebted to Mitchell Sviridoff and Robert Schrank who, for some unknown reason, suffer my idiosyncrasies year after year.

Daniel Yankelovich was enormously helpful. His ideas and advice clarified my thinking and provided direction when I was going around in circles. He also took time to read the manuscript and make a number of thoughtful suggestions.

Johanna Johnston always asks the right questions and never lets me get away with a dumb answer.

Someday we'll both figure out an easier way to pay the rent.

Without Martha Fay's support I might have given up before I started. Ann McCracken reminded me of my chauvinism and helped me with my early research. Three students at the City College of New York, Mary Ann White, Holly Klokis, and Vickie Hardison, contributed to the research, pounded out transcripts, listened to my sad stories, and bought me beer.

Louise Tropeano and Sharman Everett typed patiently and waited patiently to be paid.

My deepest thanks go to the people all over the country who welcomed me into their homes, who told me their stories, and who believed in what I was doing. They are anonymous in this book, but I will never forget any of them. At each stop there were people who were generous with their time and hospitality. I want to thank, particularly, Chapin Day of the San Francisco *Chronicle* and Susan Schwartz, who was then a reporter for the Seattle *Times*.

And then there's Gut. Every writer needs a friend who chases the blues. In my life, Ralph Gut is that person.

AUTHOR'S NOTE

Most of the people I interviewed did not ask ano-
nymity in return for their candor. They believed
that the transition from work to not working had
taken courage. They felt that if I disguised them it
would imply some guilt or shame on their parts.
Against their wishes, I decided to change some of
the identifying details of their lives. Their experiences involved many other people apart from themselves, including their friends, parents, families, co-
workers, and former employers. I was concerned
that by naming the people I interviewed I might ac-
cidentally identify the others. To spare them all possible harm or pain, I changed their names, situated
them in different but similar communities, and associated them with other work organizations in their
previous occupations and trades. In some instances,
I have used the names of actual companies and corporations because they are similar in size and organization to the real employers. They are stand-ins
for their actual employers. The remarks and observations of the people I interviewed were not directed toward them and should not be construed as
criticism of them.

BREAKTIME

INTRODUCTION 1

It is one great task of social studies today to describe the larger economic and political situation in terms of its meaning for the inner life and the external career of the individual, and in doing this to take into account how the individual often becomes falsely conscious and blinded. In the welter of the individual's daily experience the framework of modern society must be sought; within that framework, the psychology of the little man must be formulated.

—C. Wright Mills, *White Collar*

I always thought there was more to work than a paycheck. I believed that how you treated the public and the people you worked with set the tone for the way you treated people in the rest of your life. I suppose I got that idea from my father. His vocation and his personal life were so closely woven together Pierre Cardin couldn't find the seams.

My father sold ladies' hats. Millinery. Thirty-eighth Street. He worked on the same block in Manhattan for forty years. When I was very young, he would occasionally take me to The Street with him.

He'd begin with the waitress who served him coffee every morning.

"Doris, you know my boy."

She'd slide into the booth and pinch my cheeks. "Why, Eddie, he's gotten so b-i-i-i-g."

Crossing the street between the double-spaced vans and the hit-and-run hand trucks, he would pull me over to a paunchy guy carrying a sample case. "Sam, I want you to meet my son."

"A boy to be proud of," the man would say. "He'll grow up to be a *mensch*. Like his father."

Then to the back of the shop where he worked, to meet the black woman who sewed the hat bodies. "Alberta, I brought Bernie down today."

One fast glance up from the veil she was working on told her all she had to know about my future. "A lawyer, definitely. A politician, maybe."

My father seemed happiest at work. He was part of a community there. A friend of mine often reminds me of my father when he talks about *shmoozing* on the job. The freedom to shmooze is what he believes distinguishes boring, thankless labor from a tolerable job. On the assembly line, the pace of work doesn't allow for much shmoozing. In an office, in most white-collar jobs, an employee can pick up the phone to talk to a friend or a relative. There's plenty of time to banter with other workers and sometimes with supervisors. Shmoozing is a relief, a diversion from the repetition of typing letters or balancing the books. In my father's job, shmoozing was the core of the work. He shmoozed before a sale, during

a sale, and after a sale to set up the next sale. Sometimes the shmoozing had nothing to do with the
hats he was peddling. It could be about politics or
gossip—who was shafting whom, who was buying
out whom—but it cemented the work relationships,
it reinforced his position in the work community.
The quality of the shmooze probably had more to
do with a sale than the quality of the hats.

Late in his life, when he had to put a nitroglycer-
in pill under his tongue every morning to make it
up the subway steps, when he realized finally that
he wasn't going to buy into a gold mine in the Yu-
kon, he thought up a very salable conceit. It was a
broad-brimmed shapeless hat. The customer could
shape the body any way it pleased her. It fit in perfectly with the casual styles of the late 1960s—non-
fashion fashion—and it made some bucks for his
boss. The profit for my father came in a different
kind of shmooze. His new hat was very popular in
the East Village, a highly politicized neighborhood
then. Every day he dragged his sample case down
there to sell his nonhat hat and to shmooze, to
shmooze about the antiwar movement, about Jerry
Rubin and Abbie Hoffman, and about what was
happening on the campuses and on the streets.

In a sense, his life had come full circle. When he
was younger, he talked mostly about the depression,
about the union struggle, socialism and commu-
nism, about Roosevelt, about McCarthyism. Now
there was Columbia and Berkeley, black power and
white hippies. I'm not sure he completely understood the significance of what was happening or
where it would lead. Who did? But it lit up his eyes.

Work was at the center of his life. He was sustained by the community and fellowship he found there, and he was deeply loyal to most of the people he worked with. But not to the people who paid him. He couldn't feel much loyalty to employers who paid him $100 a week, max, for most of his life for a sixty-hour week. And he couldn't feel much loyalty to a union after going out on strike for two years during the depression only to be told that there weren't enough employees in his shop to make it worthwhile for the union to organize the place.

Of course, my father knew he was trapped. Most of the discussions at home were about money. How do you stretch $75 or $100 to buy groceries, to pay the rent, to see a movie on Sunday, to buy clothes, to take a vacation? There was one way out. One way out of the endless, ulcerating arguments about money. Sam Goody's.

Sam Goody's, the record chain, the chimera, the Willy Loman gold strike. He had once met an executive at Sam Goody's who had offered him a job. In the most desperate times, he would remember the man at Sam Goody's.

"Of course, if I made a move, there'd be a trial period."

"But you were always such a good salesman," my mother would say.

"What difference does it make, records or hats? It's all selling," I'd say. What difference did it make to me what he did; I was halfway through college, one foot out of the house.

"You don't understand there are different people in the record business. On Thirty-eighth Street they know me. Fifth Avenue is different."

"Suppose you don't make the trial?" my mother would inevitably ask.

"I'm out on the street."

"*We're* out on the street."

He stayed put. It was inconceivable to him that a responsible father and husband could choose to be out of work. Beyond work, there was only the abyss. Poverty. Disgrace. Humiliation. At least with work you could make the payments on the Household Finance loan. Second-generation Jew, raised in a cold-water tenement, he was a man who started family life during the depression, and his job, no matter how mean or dispiriting, was preferable to risk. Rationally he knew that if Sam Goody's didn't work out, he could always find a job back on 38th Street. But leaving a job and the uncertainty of a new job were not subjects he or my mother could discuss rationally.

He finally got out. One Sunday morning he and my mother were standing on a street corner waiting for a bus to take them to a wedding. My mother cracked a joke, he smiled, the smile froze, and he died. They closed the store where he had worked for half a day. "Out of respect for the passing of Eddie Lefkowitz," the sign in the window said. His boss gave my mother two weeks' pay, which represented his entire pension, death benefits, and final severance. That was his payoff.

I have worked all my adult life. Work was important to me in a different way than it was for my father. Security, or the fear of insecurity, didn't motivate me, as it did my father. The sense of community he found at work was not as significant, especially since I have free-lanced for a long time, which is a kind of lonely business. It was the nature of my work that gave me pleasure. Reporting satisfied my curiosity, educated me as no college could, and challenged my intellect. It also brought out the ham in me. It provided a sense of drama that regenerated me at the bleakest moments. To be in a strange place, surrounded by strangers, not all friendly, and to figure out what was going on—that was my living theater. I never wanted to walk off the stage. My life and my work were inseparable.

About four or five years ago I began to meet people who had stopped working. They seemed to be people who had shared my values. They had been relatively successful; at least the people they worked with and for thought they were talented. On the surface their jobs seemed interesting: They edited magazines, illustrated books, reported news for television stations, made documentary films.

What confused me was that there was no clear reason for their decisions. They were not all angry at their employers; they did not find their work distasteful; they were not always contemptuous of the organizations that employed them. In the early 1970s, I had met a number of people who had left their jobs to do political organizing. That I understood. I felt they were working. They put in long hours, they pushed themselves hard, and they were seriously committed to what they were doing. Just because they weren't getting paid didn't mean that they weren't working; a salary is not the defining characteristic of work.

I was meeting people now who hadn't left for political reasons. They hadn't left their jobs to pursue another career or another kind of work. Frank, the accountant, said his true love was archaeology. He would spend his vacations exploring the digs in Mexico and Peru. When he quit it wasn't to become an archaeologist. It was, as he said, because he didn't want to work. Carol edited a magazine. She was well paid; she did a good job. She was also a gifted writer and a painter of some promise. She didn't leave her job on the magazine to paint or write. She said she didn't want to work. Michael ran a highly profitable, quite creative business renovating and refurbishing homes. His customers thought his work was terrific. He had always felt a little cheated because he had to leave college in his sophomore year when he ran out of money. When he closed down his business, I thought it was because he wanted to finish his college education. I was wrong. He said it was time to retire. He was thirty-one.

At first I tried to explain their decisions as a rebellion against "the system." I was comfortable with that interpretation. Sometimes when my anxiety about their unemployment surfaced, they tried to reassure me with an airy reference to starting a gourmet restaurant—"small, charming, and really good food"—or auditioning for a play—"written by somebody with ideas that wouldn't sell on Broadway." Now I thought I understood: They were artists manqué, a condition which had always intrigued me. I made them into latter-day versions of Joe Gould, that romantic Village eccentric who was so marvelously celebrated by the *New Yorker* magazine writer Joseph Mitchell. In a profile for the

magazine, he described Gould as a "blithe and ema-
ciated little man who has been a notable in the cafe-
terias, diners, barrooms and dumps of Greenwich
Village for a quarter of a century. He sometimes
brags rather wryly that he is the last of the bohemians. 'All the others fell by the wayside,' he says.
'Some are in the grave, some are in the loony bin,
and some are in the advertising business.' "[1]

My friends lived a little differently. They had
nicely furnished apartments and lofts. They had ste-
reos and well-stocked bars. Some owned cars. They
traveled. They weren't stealing ketchup from diners, and they weren't sleeping in three-dollar-a-
night flophouses. I assured myself that they were
romantics, too, just with bigger stakes. They had
quit to give themselves a little time to do what they
wanted to do, which was to start that charming restaurant, to act in that aesthetically worthy play.

Mitchell had been careful to point out that Gould
had done an "immense amount of work during his
career as a bohemian." He was writing a book
which he called, "An Oral History of Our Time."
Every day for twenty-six years, he told Mitchell, he
had spent several hours on a park bench or on a
cafeteria stool scribbling in the massive portfolio he
always carried with him. That was what he told
Mitchell; that was what Mitchell wanted to hear.
Except when Gould died, Mitchell found out it was
all a hoax, a sham. There was no "Oral History of
Our Time." The portfolio was a prop that Gould
used to rationalize his life. So, too, my friends gave
me restaurants and plays, props to rationalize their
decision not to work. After all, they knew it made

me feel better, and being good friends, they didn't want me to be uneasy.

As time passed and the restaurants didn't open and they stopped talking about auditions, we drifted apart. We were living in separate worlds. In their world, there were no deadlines, no assignments, no work responsibilities, no alarm clocks, no bosses to please, no editors to cultivate, no office gossip to pass on, and no sardonic, epigrammatic critiques of the foolishness of the world that for so long had been an end-of-the-work-week ritual for us.

The separations came about slowly. I would get a midnight call from a not-working friend. "You want to come out and play," she'd say. Silence. Then: "I'm at the typewriter, sorry." Or: "Love to, but have to get up early in the morning." Sorry, again. Maybe next time.

The next times were less frequent and when they did occur, the conversations were always awkward. I would have to remind myself to start with "How's it going?" instead of "How's the work going?" Another forbidden subject was *my* work. Mention an article I was doing, a study I was researching, and an instant attack of eyeglaze would overcome my friends. I became adept at the art of the fast switch. A sentence that began with something connected to work would end with "Anyway, so what did you do on your trip?" I was always searching for neutral turf.

One night my discipline slipped. I was having dinner with Charles Braithwaite, a friend I had known for fifteen years, a journalist who hadn't worked in a year and a half. He looked a littl over, a little dissipated. The fixer in me surfaced. I told him about a job opening I had heard about, something at a radio station, not very demanding.

He listened for a while and said, "You don't understand, I'm not interested."

"But it's light stuff, really part-time, just a way to get back in," I said.

"You still don't understand," he said, "I don't want back in. I don't want to work."

"But, Charles, why? I mean, what's the payoff?"

"I'm not ready to talk about it. Sometime. But not now. I can't explain. It's not that I can't explain. I just don't want to. I don't think the way you live, what you want, that you'd understand the payoff." He pushed his chair back, stood up, and said, "Later." He left me with the check. I stared at it for a second and then yelled after him, "Hey, Charles, charm'll take you just so far. You can't stretch it forever. It's gonna run out."

That was January 1976. I didn't see Charles for a long time after that. I was busy traveling around the country looking for the answers to two questions. Why? And what's the payoff?[2] I spent the next two years talking to and living with people who had decided to stop working. They were not second-generation welfare recipients and they weren't millionaires. In life-styles and in economic terms, they were somewhere between lower middle class and upper middle class. They lived in cities, suburbs, and rural communities. They rented apartments; they owned their own homes. Some were married, some were single, some were divorced. They were older than college or graduate-school age, and they hadn't reached their traditional retirement age. Some were planning to stop work. Others had stopped working. A few had gone back to work. Some had been fired and refused to look for another job; some had just walked out.

It came to one hundred people. I stopped at one hundred; it could have been one thousand or ten thousand or . . . Most of the time I spoke to them in their homes. There were more men than women. The majority had held white-collar jobs. They had been bill collectors and carpenters, construction workers and economists, keypunch operators and laboratory technicians, teachers and liquor store owners, deputy sheriffs and thieves, machinists and politicians, lawyers and day laborers, salesmen and nurses. For the most part, they looked like the neighbor next door. Lawns, churches, neat apartments, and digital watches.

The payoff. When I started I knew what the payoff had been for my father; I knew what the payoff had been for me. When I was done, I understood what the payoff was for Charles.

BREAKPOINT 2

> Older than all preached Gospels was this un-
> preached, inarticulate, but ineradicable, forever-en-
> during Gospel: work, and therein well being.
>
> —Thomas Carlyle, *Past and Present*

> We seem to be working more than we wish and liv-
> ing lives that are less than they should be, to con-
> sume goods and services that we really don't want.
> For increasing numbers, the activities and goals of
> today's work conflict with their hopes for a better
> way of life, which seems possible but ever elusive.
>
> —Fred Best, *The Future of Work*

NAKED IN AMERICA

In 1970 Cliff Jones stopped working as an investment counselor for the Bank of America in San
Francisco. Later he was asked how he felt when he
made that decision. Answering quickly, he said, "I
felt naked."

His response was not surprising. Jones was an early enlistee in the massive conflict of values and expectations that would transform the social landscape of America in the 1970s. By comparison with the cultural and political shocks of the past decade, this was a quiet revolution. Tear gas canisters did not explode on college campuses. The streets were empty of demonstrators. There were no love-ins in San Francisco. The revolution of the 1970s was personal, internal, and individual; it was waged in the silent confessional of the human psyche. Yet in the next ten years it would reach to the marrow of the American character.

In 1970 there were only the faintest stirrings of the coming struggle. That year Daniel Yankelovich, the social psychologist, conducted a survey of college students.[1] Among the questions he asked was: "Do you believe that hard work will always pay off?" Three years before, seven out of ten students said yes. But in 1971, 60 percent said no. More than half expressed strong self-doubts about their ability to make money. Asked what influenced their choice of careers, they listed as most important the opportunity to make a contribution, the challenge of the job, and the ability to express oneself. The influences considered least important were money-making potential, the chance to get ahead, job prestige, and what their family wanted them to do.

The era of traditional optimism about work and career was ending, but Cliff Jones was not alert to it. He, and most of the others I had interviewed, had worked long and hard during the past twenty years. As a group, they were not rebels. For years they had identified themselves by their trade or occupation: Billy Morgan, policeman; Lucille Roberts, laboratory technician; Carl Reiter, office manager for a finance company; Charles Braithwaite, journalist.

They had been ambitious. They remembered what they wore when they appeared for their first job interview and what their starting salary was— "Forty-five dollars a week. Imagine, forty-five dollars a week." They could list the dates of their promotions and how they celebrated. They remembered the night on the town the company gave them when they finished installing the new telecommunications system; they remembered the date on the bottle of champagne their wives bought when their annual sales broke the $500,000 barrier.

Memory wounded them. Not to go on. To *choose* not to work. At first, the idea brought a guilty flush. It was as if they had been caught whispering a blasphemy in the cathedral. They had subscribed to sociologist Peter Berger's belief that "to be human and to work appear as inextricably intertwined notions. To work means to modify the world as it is found."

Through work, they had modified their worlds. They had achieved some degree of economic security. Their efforts had been recognized, not only financially, but with elevated status on the job and at home. Their work kept their families together and gave their children a start in life. Whatever frustrations they experienced at work, they suppressed in their pursuit of the conventional symbols of success.

In the years that followed, their values began to change. As Yankelovich observed, "Self-fulfillment became severed from success." They had joined what he describes as "the New Breed," although they did not necessarily surrender all of their traditional beliefs. "They have come to feel that success is not enough to satisfy their yearnings for self-fulfillment," he writes. "They are reaching out for something more and for something different. . . . Somehow, the conventional systems no longer satisfy their deepest psychological needs nor nourish their self-esteem, nor fulfill their cravings for the 'full, rich life.' "[2]

If Cliff Jones had decided to stop working in 1978, he would not have felt as naked as he had in 1970 because he would have had company. By 1978 a Yankelovich survey of adult Americans found that a majority could no longer be wholly satisfied through conventional success. A striking measure of the change that took place during the previous eight years was that only one out of every five said that work meant more to them than leisure. A majority said that work was no longer their major source of satisfaction.

If you wanted to position Cliff Jones and his non-working compatriots in America's value spectrum, they would be the *advance scouts, the trail blazers.* Their dramatic break with work has carried them some distance from the working community. But their conflicts and discontentments with work, what they expected and what was denied them in their work lives, are not atypical or unusual. Their protest resounds in our own lives. They are different only because the strains have reached the surface and they cannot tolerate the idea of indefinitely continuing the nine-to-five. They have acted on those attitudes and concerns that trouble the majority of working Americans.

Yet because they acted while others they knew complained but kept working, they felt a sense of loneliness. They were solitary travelers in a strange terrain. What follows is a journal of their exploration, an account of what made them take that first dramatic step, what they discovered, and how their discoveries affected their lives.

When I began my research, I was troubled by a search for the definition of work. If I could not define work, how could I describe its antithesis, the experience of not working? I ran across one definition, in a study of working in America, that was appealing in its simplicity. The authors had defined work as "an activity that produces something of value for other people."[3] Despite its agreeable simplicity and the obvious desire of the authors to broaden the definition of work beyond the wage or income it produced, it seemed to leave a lot out. The man who mows his lawn once a month produces something of value to his neighbors and to his family. Not many people I met regarded mowing the lawn once a month as their life's work. Reading a book and describing it to someone else has a certain value: Not many people I talked to—even those who were teachers—would say their career consisted of reading a book.

As I thought more about work and talked to more people, I built on the foundation of work as an activity that produces something of value. Working allowed you to grow up. It marked the passage from adolescence to adulthood. Working initiated you into a fraternity; it brought you into a life-minded community. Work inculcated a sense of responsibility; it meant that you had to deliver, to honor your commitments and discharge your responsibilities. Work had varying forms and structures, depending on what you did and for whom you worked. Work required discipline, at one end to respond to the alarm clock, at the other end to stick to the typewriter when the leaves blossomed in the park outside your window. Work provided continuity. You might switch jobs or occupations; you might take time off; but there was always a time when you returned and resumed the work. The longer I reflected on work, the more subclauses I added. I felt lost in the myriad of possibilities.

To find my way back to solid ground, I did two things. The first was not to impose my own definition of work on the people I met. However they defined work was the most important thing. They knew best what work was; it was their lives, their work, and I did not want to distort their experiences. I let them tell me what work was for them, and I accepted that. Second, I tried to discover what they had in common—what myths and values cut across class, ethnicity, geography, and upbringing. I found that most of them shared one core fantasy. Very early in their development they had been taught that work was achievement, progress, and active struggle. In Harvard psychologist Samuel Osherson's phrase, work meant "rising up"; the alternative to work was "sinking down."[4] For them there was no middle ground.

Work, at one time in their lives, represented a "coherent web of expectations." In work they would find the essence of their humanity. It was the means by which they would not only "modify the world," but shape their own world. No surprise then that Jones says he felt "naked" when he stopped working. The web of expectations—to find the right occupation and the right job, to marry, to raise a family, to earn acknowledgment and respect, to evolve, to rise up in the world—had come unraveled. Without it, what was there? What would take its place?

Work makes you human. It was the one verity almost all of them absorbed in their childhood. In the barn where they helped their fathers milk the cows. In the kitchen where they baked the Christmas fruitcakes with their mothers. In the bedroom where their parents put them to sleep with the warning, "If you don't improve your report card next time, if you don't keep your mind on work, if you let your mind wander, you'll wind up fixing old cars like us." Wherever they grew up, Wichita or Boise, Yakima or Greensburg, McAllen or the Bronx, Alexandria or Arcadia, the expectations were roughly the same: You made something of yourself through work.

Implicitly their parents imbued work with religious meaning. They did not all believe, as the Puritans had, that hard, unsparing work was a sign that a man or woman had been chosen for salvation. Work did have religious significance in the sense that it was a source of renewal. Their parents' generation believed that even when work had been demeaning and unrewarding it contained the seeds of regeneration. For them work had been a reenactment of the myth of Prometheus. "To work is no light matter," Berger wrote. "To work is to mime creation itself."[5]

This they were told, this they believed. The lesson was taught first by their parents and grandparents and repeated as if by rote by their classmates, teachers, and commanding officers, by their wives, husbands, friends, and bosses. The lesson became a pledge, solemnly sworn, and the pledge became a contract. It was their original contract, the most binding contract of their lives. By honoring the contract to work, they would redeem their pledge to their parents and families, to all those who had sweated and suffered for them. In turn, they would sweat and suffer for them. Until the dreams of their past would become the fulfillment of the present. *You will be a mensch, like your father. A lawyer, definitely. A politician, maybe.*

When they first thought about stopping work, they felt a loss of the bond between them and their past. And they felt fear, too. Not so much fear of the future, but the more powerful feeling that they had done something wrong and that fearful sanctions would be imposed on them for breaking the bond. Paul Goodman, an earlier and much more committed defector from traditional American values than most of the people I met, once recalled asking young men, What do you want to work at? "The terrible answer," Goodman wrote, "is, 'Nothing.' The young man doesn't want to do anything. I remember talking to a half a dozen young fellows at Van

Wagner's beach outside of Hamilton, Ontario; and all of them had this one thing to say: 'Nothing.' I turned away from the conversation abruptly because of the uncontrollable burning tears in my eyes and constriction in my chest. Not feeling sorry for them, but tears of frank dismay for the waste of our humanity."[6]

This is what they feared most: By not working they would waste their humanity.

This is a great fear, that by leaving work we will become something less than human. It was this stricture, more than anything else, that bound my father to his job. If the people I will describe have overcome this fear, it is because no longer are they *required* to work. They have received a new social message: You will not be disowned by society if you stop working.

The break from work occurs then at the crossroad of external culture and inner yearning. The reordering of ethics, values, and standards of achievement in the external culture can catalyze the nascent quest for a different personal perspective. Similarly, as individuals redefine what they mean by self-fulfillment, they also claim a cultural environment that will nurture and support their process of redefinition. "So central is the work ethic to American culture that if its meaning shifts," Yankelovich says, "the character of our society will shift along with it."

The breakpoint is the moment of decision, but not necessarily a time for action. It is the moment when they decided their lives were incompatible

with their work. Some people waited a long time between their psychological separation from work and
their actual disengagement. Others took their leave
soon after they began questioning the value of work.
The accounts that follow describe the events, the
environments, and the different states of mind that
led to the decision to disengage. Their attitudes at
the breakpoint are at once revealing of their social
and psychological histories and premonitory of
their experiences beyond the work ethic.[7]

FIRST PERSON SINGULAR

It will take us a long time to assess fully the impact
of the social and cultural and political upheavals of
the past twenty years—of the assassinations, the
Vietnam war, Watergate. All we know is that we
are a little less trusting. We are less willing to commit ourselves to institutions of all kinds and more
concerned about protecting our private lives against
the encroachments and claims of the outside world.
On my travels I met a twenty-eight-year-old law
graduate in Chicago, whose brother lost an arm in
Vietnam, whose father lost his job during the recession of the mid-seventies, who had been married
and had been divorced, whose parents had split up.
I wondered how it had all affected him. The word
he used was "detached."

"Since law school," he said, "I've had three jobs in
three years. I'm working for the state now. Titles
and searches. You know what it's like when I get a
job? It's like when you're about to move out of an
apartment. You let it run down. It begins to look

like shit. You're making sure that you don't get attached to it, so it doesn't bother you when you leave. That's what I do when I get a job. I don't get involved. I'm on the outside. I'm always planning for when I'll leave."

Martha Gorham, Robert Stern, and Frank Morse were raised in relatively secure if not affluent households. Stern, in his early thirties, is younger than the other two, and he was more directly involved in the storms of the sixties. Gorham and Morse began the traditional upward climb in the early 1950s; up they climbed, getting their college degrees, rising on the career ladder, securing themselves in their family and community. What they share is a common attitude of icy detachment toward work. While they have held jobs and worked hard at them and sometimes derived pleasure from their work, they no longer measure their personal development by their occupational status. As they look back on the times they worked, it's as if they were watching strangers. Work was a temporary way station, a phase they passed through, a necessary expedient.

Their primary commitment is to themselves, not to any trade, job, or organization. They have secondary alliances with their families, parents, and friends. First and foremost is their singularity. They have emerged from the work cocoon as post-industrial freemen, set loose to roam through the jerry-built structures of what sociologist Warren Bennis calls our "temporary" society.[1] The only "permanent" structure they inhabit is their own personality. They have learned, not always easily, that "the world will require us to rely most heavily on our own resources. . . . We die alone and to a certain extent we must live alone, with a fidelity to ourselves."

This is how Frank Morse came to that understanding.

Frank Morse: The Zone of Indifference

Frank wears a faded red sweatshirt these days and salt-whitened jeans and paint-splattered sneakers. There are deep squint lines at the corners of his eyes from staring into the sun. His skin has become a permanent red blister. He doesn't look and dress as he did when he came to San Francisco from New Jersey twenty years ago. In 1957 he had just received his graduate degree in architecture from Yale, and before settling in, he decided to take a trip west. He landed in San Francisco, picked up a part-time job with a small architectural firm, and never left the city. A job opened up with General Dynamics; they were building parts for the B-52 bomber then, but for some reason they felt they could use an architect who could redesign the various offices and work spaces in the plant. The degree from Yale helped. So did his flair. He commuted to work on a Lambretta and wore a war surplus poncho and an orange-painted pith helmet. Underneath was a tie and a jacket and gray flannel slacks. Apart from architecture, Yale taught him the difference between chateaubriand and tournedos, between Montrachet and Beaujolais, and that was fairly high-class stuff for a twenty-five-year-old junior architect in San Francisco then.

At first he didn't want to work for G.D. He thought it would be dull working for a large corporation. He had enjoyed a part-time job with a one-man architectural firm. But G.D. offered him an incentive. They said they would tell his draft board that he was working on essential government services. Which wasn't true. In return he had to promise that he would work for the company for two years.

"When they hired me they told me about the kinda work I'd be doing. I got very excited. The way they described the advantages of working for a large corporation like that was there are so many different aspects of architectural work in helping to control the whole environment, to make it a better place for working, to get more efficiency, more relaxation. And I thought, wow, that's a field that really sounds interesting—working with light and color and sound. First of all they gave me a big desk to work on, not a drafting table, but like an executive desk. And I had a telephone on my desk and In and Out baskets. But I had to punch in. And then there was very little for me to do. I kept saying, 'Well, what do I do next?' And they kept telling me you have to get the feeling of this, learn the vocabulary, read the reports, and go wander around the shops. So I did a lot of wandering.

"I discovered hardly anybody there works a full day except the riveters on the plane assembly because they had a foreman right over them. And I would go up on these little catwalks and look down on them, and I discovered even they could go in these little end sections of wings and tails and things like that and take a nap. There was a tremendous time wastage there, and what bothered me was that I was wasting time and it was very hard for me to make myself look busy. And I talked to my supervisor about it, and he'd say, 'All right, Morse, pretty soon we're gonna give you a job to do, but we still want you to get the feeling.' And they'd call me into meetings and talk about projects that I'd never even heard about, and my thoughts kept saying, gee, why don't we get out of here and get to work and stop writing reports and seeking further comments and doing all these dumb things.

"Plus, we'd start work at about seven in the morning and we'd be off at four, and at the end of the day, about three-thirty, I noticed the slow pace slowed down perceptibly, and by about three-forty-five, everybody was packing up. They're sitting at their desks squaring up the piles of paper, and by three-fifty their coats were over their arms, their lunch boxes were packed, and they were poised at the edge of their chairs. And when that bell rang, bam, they just ran. And these were people who were professional people, engineers and architects and technical writers and draftsmen, and they were acting like a herd of animals. They were rushing to be the first guy out in the parking lot to get their car out. And I really thought that was so degrading. There was no pride of work, no incentive to do anything. Every Friday after lunch everybody would get on their desk a sheet that would show the pecking order of their division. I noticed every week my position would get higher and higher, just because I was there. I never did anything.

"All that promotion in the group was from the top supervisor, and his prestige came from the number of people he had working for him. And the higher up I got, the more positions were open to hire somebody else lower down. It was just building up this wider and wider pyramid. My supervisor took me aside one day in his office and told me, 'We're all countin' on you to do big things. We see the value of your talent.' Which I couldn't understand because he never asked me to do anything. Meanwhile, the most important thing for me to do was to come every day on time and leave on time. Nothing in between was important. When I got there I'd been all excited about potentials that I'd never imagined. But there never was the opportunity to get into those things. They weren't concerned with the efficiency of the workers. And that crap about light and color and sound and clean air and health and safety, nothing happened.

"Later I thought about the workers there. What was the philosophy of the place? Mainly they wanted to create as little waves as possible, do their job, and get the hell out of there as quickly as possible. They were all looking forward to their paid vacations, their sick leaves, and then their retirements. I wasn't ready for retirement."

After Frank's first year, he smashed up his Lambretta and had to spend a couple of months in a hospital. "When I was in the hospital I told them I was gonna quit. After that they would constantly call me up and they would write me, and even the head of personnel came to visit me twice to beg me to come back. And the incentive was, 'You're gonna be a supervisor, we're gonna give you an orange badge. An orange badge means that you're parking inside the plant grounds instead of in the parking lot across the street, so you don't have to run so far for your car.' I told him, 'Gee thanks, but I find the work boring.' And he said, 'Well, what do you want to do?' I didn't see anything that I wanted to do, there wasn't any work to do."

Morse might still have returned to General Dynamics rather than risk being drafted. But his doctor at the hospital happened to be on the board of examining physicians for Selective Service. Morse described his dilemma: He didn't want to go back to the company but wanted even less to go into the army. The doctor wrote a letter to his draft board which said that Morse's injuries had made him unfit for military service. The day he received the notice classifying him 4-F, he wrote a letter of resignation to General Dynamics.

Once he left the company, he made another move. He discovered Sausalito, that lovely wonderland across the bay from San Francisco. Today it's a very fancy place. The higher you drive on the winding roads leading to the peak of the hill that dominates the island, the higher the prices of the houses. Toward the top, a modest house can run well over $100,000, if you can find one. But it was at the bottom of the hill, the dock and the community of houseboats anchored there, that enchanted Frank Morse.

After working as an architect for a year, Morse saved $1,000 and bought a houseboat. "I guess I was always seeking something unique, trying to get

away from the standard run-of-the-mill kinda life-
style. It was a different kinda culture then than it is
now. Now we're all more or less middle class, and
there are plenty of rich folks here. With the exception of a few people like me, they all work and com-
mute. Then it was filled with more of a mixture of
people, the only common denominator was that
most were poor. Some were poor because they were
students, some were poor because they were bums,
some were retired, some just didn't want to work."

Frank Morse, although perhaps he didn't see it
that way then, had moved into a zone of indifference, into a community where work and salary and
consumption were not all-consuming values. A
great many services were bartered: Fix my sink and
I'll cook you up a stew that'll last you a week. After
a while Frank said to himself, why should I expect
to be Mr. Hero Architect of San Francisco, much
less the whole country. "That's what they taught
you to be at Yale. That's what I untaught myself on
the houseboats of Sausalito. I recognized the big dollars were impossible to get without luck. The ones
with the terrific talent were not making the big
bucks, and they'd been practicing for ten years."

He figured there was something else he could do
with the next twenty years, aside from putting in
time with General Dynamics. He got married,
raised a couple of daughters, admired his wife's
paintings of Sausalito, and when money became a
problem he rented houseboats. It helped that his
wife was a high school teacher. Now he spends his
time caulking and sanding and mending the sails.
He never became the chief architect of General Dy-

namics or the Hero Architect of San Francisco. But he did become head of the Houseboat Association in the land of no-work. Now that things in the Sausalito boat basin are getting richer and creamier, the boats go for $50,000 and up; he may have to find a new zone of indifference.

Frank Morse is anchored more firmly than many of the others. Work never engaged him, but Sausalito did. There he found his psychological home, a place where he wasn't judged and he judged not. When his sphere of interest shifted from General Dynamics to the houseboat community, he had begun a process that sociologists and psychologists call *differentiation*. He was differentiating his needs and values from the expectations of his contemporaries and his parents and Yale. The important thing is that Morse had a pretty clear idea of what he wanted. Later he sharpened his self-image, filled it out, and molded his life to it. In Sausalito he achieved legitimacy. He moved from something that did not engage him—work—to something that did—the houseboat world.

Dr. Harry Levinson makes a living counseling business organizations and businessmen. When he meets a businessman who is unhappy in his job, he often tells them what he told me one afternoon in his office, "Given the rate of organizational change, you really can't count on organizations to do much for you anymore. You can only count on yourself. If an organization is merged or acquired or sold, if it changes its product line, you have to be in charge of yourself. When the chips are down, the person has to act on his own behalf. After thirty-five, you should be preparing yourself to move at your own wish."[2]

Dr. Levinson was referring specifically to work organizations, but some people have broadened the definition of *organization* to include marriages, parenthood, and religion as well as work. Their affiliations with those social institutions are temporary. Their first separations trigger chain reactions of comings and goings. They are always on the move, from one reality to another, from an old role to a new role. Work is like any other convenient shelter. You stay as long as it's comfortable. When things begin to break down, when the paint starts to peel, when roaches invade the kitchen, you move. Sometimes you purposely let things fall apart. That way you avoid attachments, and it's easier to persuade yourself that you *have* to move to survive. Movement is more important than destination.

In this light, work is only one in a series of changes. Like the experiences that precede it and the ones that come after, work is approached with hopefulness and optimism. First: Work is going to make my life better. Then: Stopping work is going to make my life better. This attitude suggests that human development is not an accretion of experience in which the understanding gained at one stage, youth, prepares one for the next, maturity. Life isn't an integrated whole; it's an escalator. Up and down.

Martha Gorham adheres to a psychological construction that has become very popular in America.

She is a human machine, a technological product of a scientific age. Later in the book I describe adherents of this view as "technicians." Although they often describe themselves as humanists or romantics, they really believe that psychological growth and emotional change can be orchestrated with scientific precision. If Martha, the life machine, is wearing down, redesign the machine; invent a new high-octane fuel; replace the engine. The machine will work better than ever.

Except, as Martha has learned, change doesn't always mean progress.

Martha Gorham: Moving On

A woman who once had theatrical aspirations, she was a good storyteller. Tall, red haired, and with a voluptuousness that bordered on the Junoesque, she would stretch languidly, drop her voice two octaves, and spring the next surprise. And her biography had more twists than a Hitchcock movie: In the first half she is teacher, school administrator, actress, organizer for Hadassah, suburbanite wife and mother; in the second half, she's divorced from her husband and separated from her children, estian and Esalener, a resident in a communal house in Boulder, Colorado. That accounts for only the first forty-eight years.

For hours I had followed her biographical maundering without much interruption or prodding. Then I broached an indelicate subject. Adultery. Specifically, the adultery practiced by a woman who was raised in a household where such practice was considered only slightly less shameful than marrying a Protestant. This was a woman who once seemed to have a "good" marriage, as those alliances are measured by outsiders; who had two kids and a few other goodies, such as a nice job and a nice house in a comfortable suburb. So, I asked, "Why adultery?"

Her response was the technician's credo: *I was responding to my needs.*

"When I started having affairs, I remember I ran to a psychiatrist. I was filled with guilt. The Ten Commandments, I had broken them, and I told the doctor that the circumstances were such that it was because my sexual needs were not being filled. . . . The doctor was a wise man. . . . He said I was doing it out of need, not just to be mean or whatever. He blessed me and said it's all right, he absolved me, and I went on my merry way."

This was her first significant break with a moral code that had subordinated her immediate needs to the all-inclusive ethical system in which she had been raised. It prefigured many other departures. Once she had stepped outside and found, not damnation, but absolution, her priorities shifted. Her needs came first now.

Martha Gorham grew up in a Jewish family in a gentile neighborhood in St. Louis. Her home life was a mixture of Jewish immigrant culture (with the emphasis on striving) and kitchen debates on Zionism. Her father sold supplies to cleaners and tailor shops. Her mother kept house. Martha went to the movies.

"My fantasy was to be a movie actress, but I didn't have the faith in myself or support from anybody, so I really didn't put it out there.

"To my parents that was foolishness, that was silliness, laughable. Real people didn't do things like that. What did real people do? They got a college education and found a man and got married and had children and had a house in the suburbs and were active in the local social service number and participated in their children's activities and had friends. And that was it and I did it. I made it happen. I was a terrific success.

"I had a degree, I had graduated from college, I was teaching, I was twenty-five years old—and I was a failure. I wasn't married. That was the curse of death! The only reason I got married was because my mother finally found me a husband. She courted him. He was a traveling salesman—ladies' underwear, bras, girdles. I had met him a few years before when I was in college. He was on the road in St. Louis for a weekend and he called me but I was away. My mother took him in and gave him a bed to sleep on, cooked for him and made him feel at home . . . she wanted me married so she got it done. *She* was a failure if I didn't marry. I don't think she cared who he was or what. It was just my image, so I'd have a label.

"So I finally married this guy who was my mother's choice. The image, the image. That was *so* important. That he look good. He was big and tall and handsome. He looked like Vaughan Monroe. Mr. Nice Guy, easygoing, not too bright, pleasant, very devoted, loyal, all the Boy Scout qualities which I used to put down but I don't anymore. I married up, I escalated. I married a man whose parents were American born, who had status—his father was making $10,000 a year during the depression. He had famous relatives—one was a mayor in Michigan, another was a talent agent. This was what life was made of.

"Martin was two-dimensional. I think of myself as three-dimensional. He was an average kind of guy and he didn't think about anything. He just got married 'cause he wanted to get married and I was there and why not? We both agreed it was not the great love affair of the century, and neither of us met each other's expectations. He was thirty-one, and that was old for a guy back then to get married, so he was ready. And I was ready: I was twenty-five and an old maid.

"He was a homebody. He just wanted to work and get a paycheck. He had no goals for himself. He just wanted to come home and watch TV and that was it. Movies once a week and watch TV sports. He was just a nice guy. How could you not like him? Even when I got divorced, my brother and sister-in-law said, 'He's such a nice guy,' you know, as if that was really all there was—a husband that was good to you. Why the hell would you ever leave him? He made a living wage. They couldn't understand that anybody would have any other needs."

Coming apart.

Three things fulfilled her in her first five years of marriage. She continued teaching. ("I was good at my work. I taught speech and drama, and I did a lot of creative stuff with the kids.") She had children. ("A boy first and then a girl. I was madly in love with that boy. I mean he was a perfect baby . . . God knows, I needed a positive—he never cried, he was the happiest, most-loving, gorgeous child in the world. We had a mad love affair going on. Then two and a half years later there was a little girl, and I felt, gee, well, I've already done that. I was tired of being home—I'd stopped teaching when the boy was born. I was bored and ready to do something else.") She acted. ("Almost every weekend I'd be in some theater thing. I'd write scripts for women's clubs. I'd do things for the religious school. My strength was I could do such diverse roles: I was acting, I was teaching, I had the kids, and I had the house in the suburbs.")

Martin's job changes. He isn't traveling as much, he's home a lot. Martin is losing confidence in himself as a salesman. Martin, at Martha's urging, takes a government job in Wilmington, Delaware, a job he gets through a family connection. Martha, meanwhile, is spreading out. She's teaching and acting, and that means that Martin has to stay home at night with the kids. She's out a lot of nights. "He resented that I'd leave him home with the kids and I'd go and do my thing. It wasn't that he resented what I did. He resented my not being home with him. And when I was home and we had people over, they always saw me as part of a package, a couple. It was boring as hell. I'd fall asleep. Men would talk about cars and women would talk about homes and children, and I'd fall asleep."

Coming apart.

First: Try to satisfy the sexual need. If Martin doesn't make it, try somebody else. "I was getting nothing from him, and he was not willing to do whatever he had to do to work it out. I could have stayed there forever and had another life outside of him, but I wanted to have a complete relationship. I wanted to be married with someone who I could share my whole life with. I never did find anyone who that could work with."

Second: Satisfy the need for a separate life.

"I made the conscious decision to divorce him when we were in Wilmington. He was really upset with my life-style, and I saw that there was no way I was going to continue in that marriage. We separated amicably. He went home to ma and I escalated in the school system. I had more time and energy to fulfill the job requirements; I wasn't distracted by the marriage obligations. So I started out as an elementary school teacher and then I went on to administration and I just kept escalating. Yeah, I was up to about eighteen-five, as an administrator, by the time I left, which was 1969. That was a lot of money in 1969."

Next: her mother.

"My mother excommunicated me. (My father had died before my first child was born.) The typical Jewish mother. You would not believe it. I said, 'Ma, I'm gettin' a divorce.' She said, 'Vat, are you tryin' to kill me?' She never spoke to me again. I had broken the code."

Then: the kids.

"I let my kids go live with their father, who had remarried. Then that wasn't a very popular idea. It was all getting too heavy for me. The kids were nine and eleven; my son was starting to know how late he could stay out. I saw drugs and sex and all kinds of problems with teenage kids, and I didn't really believe I could handle those problems by myself. I was beginning to be emotionally affected by the frustrations in my life. My needs in terms of relationships weren't being met. I began to see the writing on the wall—I'd reached the peak, I was about thirty-nine, and I was starting to go downhill.

"When I make these changes, the need is there. I don't have a choice. I'm at a point in time where I have to survive. I waited as long as I could and I couldn't wait anymore. I had to leave the kids. It was survival.

"It was terrible later. At the point I left them, it wasn't painful because it was such a relief! The kids didn't protest. No, they were good li'l conforming kids. They did what they were told. They never even thought they could have an opinion. Nobody really asked their opinion.

"Intellectually, it wasn't such a heavy break. Later I paid a high price emotionally. My mommy's guilt machine got reactivated. But at the time, intellectually, I could handle it because my identity has never been heavy in the female, homemaker, mother thing, even though I adore the kids. If you had said, Who are you, Martha Gorham? I wouldn't have said, Wife and mother. I would have said, Educator—or a woman, or something like that. All I knew when I left the kids was I had to get out of the pain. I didn't think ahead."

Last: work.

There were problems. Stiff, scared administrators blocking her efforts to introduce innovative programs. Officials who made promises they didn't keep. Colleagues who draped an arm around her shoulder at a convention and pretended they didn't know her in the corridors of the board of education.

Supervisors who told her, yes, they would support her attempt to pry dollars loose from the feds and backed down at the last minute when their positions were at risk. Parents who were never fully appreciative of what she was trying to do for their kids.

"Everything was wanted from me and I wasn't getting renewed. The last year I just limped along until summer. I mean the guy told me he wanted me to come back next year, so I must have done a minimal job. In terms of my standards and expectations, I was doing awful. You know, hiding so nobody would see me. I was just in bad shape emotionally, but I guess nobody else must have noticed. As long as I stayed out of their way, they were happy."

In the summer of 1969 she went back to St. Louis and then to New York, with a stop at Woodstock for the Celebration of the Century. Exegesis Unlimited. She met a woman at Woodstock who would serve as a model for the image that Martha would eventually adopt, the one she had been inching toward for the past ten years. "She was a Jewish middle-class gal who was into the arts and not too happy with her kid and engineer husband. We struck up a friendship and then I heard from her six months later that she was running off with her lover. She played a very important role in my life."

To use one of Martha's favorite words, the woman *validated* her secret life. Remember this was a few years before the watershed, a couple of years before the I-left-my-husband-and-took-the-train-to-Barcelona-and-sitting-right-next-to-me-was-this-parachutist-who-set-me-free novel. If you were traveling on the underground railroad in 1970, it helped when you met a kindred soul.

Reinforced by her role model, having just landed a new job as a West Coast coordinator for Hadassah, Martha was riding high. "It was dynamite. The organization was a manifestation of me as a person. All my interests were there—social work reform, senior citizen programs, day-care. They were always in the forefront. They were really highly respected among liberal organizations. They would fly their women to Washington to testify in Congress. I was working with *them* and I was as bright or brighter. I was in heaven. This met my needs unbelievably. Every skill I had, everything I learned, I was able to use. It was mostly human contact. When I went out to visit a chapter, they loved me. They were little babies who wanted to be stroked. I'd calm them down. I'd get them featured in magazines. I was wined and dined. I was the one who sent in the reports to New York to rate them, so they couldn't be nice enough to me. I'm telling you, what a job! I adored it."

And then the fall.

"Yeah, so what happened? A bureaucracy is a bureaucracy is a bureaucracy." Budget cuts derailed new programs. "You can't do this, you can't do that." Leadership struggles undercut her power. Women she considered her friends didn't support her when it came to a showdown. The paperwork increased. But what blew it in the end was the familiar mixture of one quarter guilt, one quarter boredom, one quarter anger, and one quarter disillusionment. "I was tired of it. I like new challenges . . . it wasn't fulfilling. I think also the guilt thing came up. They say that when you have a big shock in your life, sometimes it takes a couple of years for

it to work through your system where you really begin to feel it, and the guilt over the kids started to
come out, even though I had gone back to see them
very often. And then there was the power game. I
don't like to play those games. I'm an idealist. I'd
have faith and I'd be so shocked when people would
sabotage it or reverse themselves or not hear what I
was saying. What I learned was that working with
organizations, you get stabbed, no matter who they
are. And this was supposed to be the most humanis-
tic . . . you know, doing good things for people. I
didn't want to look for a job. I was burned out.
Everytime I'd gone through this pattern, I'd pick
myself up and go on to something else. My feeling
was that I couldn't do that again 'cause it's gonna
happen again."

Other women feel they're drowning as they try to
raise their children alone while holding down a demanding job, but they keep swimming. Other people suffer injuries when their intimates hurt or
(worse still) ignore their feelings, but they don't sev-
er their relationships or move into another social
world. They call in sick, take a couple of aspirins,
watch a soap opera, gorge themselves on a caloric
delight, and pick up the next morning where they
left off. Martha's problems are played as tragedy.
Their resolution becomes a matter of survival.

Victims, whose very lives are at risk, are justified
in rising up against their tormentors. Martha's
moves are justified because if she stood still she'd
perish. She had persuaded herself that she has no alternative but to make a change, both in her personal

life and in her work life. She refuses to accept the proposition that it's man's fate to suffer. She believes she's *entitled* to happiness. If others don't provide happiness, she will secure it for herself. I-have-been-screwed is fused with I-am-entitled-to-happiness. This Siamese connection of persecution and entitlement will not dissolve when work ends. It will carry over to her not-working life, and it will sanction a certain amorality. In an unjust world, one is left with no choice but to hustle for what one should be entitled to in the first place.

Bob Stern was working at a full-time job when I met him. I thought it was important to include his story because it affords a glimpse of the thinking and calculations that go into the decision to stop working. All of the others have already stopped. Their retrospective accounts are influenced by what they have gone through. To varying degrees they are defending their decision not to work. Bob is moving toward the exit.

Slowly. Deliberately. Cautiously. Calculatedly. Indeed, he is unusual for his deliberateness and for his cold-eyed planning. Bob is planning his departure with a draftsman's attention to detail.

In Bob Stern, we read the future. A future where the average American works when he absolutely has to and stops when he can. A future where the work life is no longer a continuous pattern but a sequence of stops and starts; where the stops grow ever longer. In the past we believed that people worked because it provided challenge, interest, excitement, continuity, and a sense of achievement. Bob also works to achieve. What he wants to achieve has nothing to do with his work. He works to gather the resources that will enable him to stop working.

Robert Stern: The Planner

Bob Stern is a poker player. He's been playing since he was fifteen, and he's pretty good. The game he's playing now started seven years ago. He figures it will take two more years before he can pick up his winnings. March 15, 1980, to be precise. That's when he plans to leave Xerox. Nine years to the day he began selling office equipment.

He wants to leave with a cushion. With enough money, he can have four, five, six years without scraping, without food stamps, unemployment insurance, or Christmas jobs in Macy's. "It's a matter of honestly looking at a long-term solution," he says. "In a poker game if you put all your chips in one pot, chances are you're gonna lose at the end of the night. A lot of people who just got up and left Xerox weren't looking at the end of the night. For me it's not just winning the pot. For me it's more of a question of playing for the final result, which is my whole life."

With such high stakes, he is able to postpone gratification. He lives in a relatively low-rent, sparsely furnished apartment in Manhattan. He is articulate and introspective without being solemnly profound. Casual, but well put together. Poised in the turtleneck and jeans he wears in the apartment; poised in the three-piece he wears on the job.

Bob lives on a tight budget and banks most of his monthly commission, which comes to about $500.

He's been doing that for three years, he'll be doing it for two more. Sometimes he travels on his vacations, but not very often. Before he goes to a play or a movie he thinks twice.

Working for Xerox is not hell; he is not driven to leave. He is planning his departure carefully because he has seen what happens to people who don't plan carefully. Like the secretary who decided to become an actress. "She was just a year older than I am now, thirty-two, and one day she left. She'd been with the company since she was nineteen. She never thought about what it means to live an alternative life. Suddenly she confronted that as a life experience. You know, first she's Xerox, then she's an actress. She's saying to herself, I'd better be a damn good actress because I've given up one life. I'd better make it in the other life.

"When you think that way you can do some pretty crazy things. You start to think, Oh, my God, what have I been missing all these years? And she acted in a way that could be understood in a nineteen- or twenty-year-old, but in a thirty-two-year-old woman, it's a little bananas. Two years later we heard she committed suicide. The shock of having to become an actress, of *having to*, or else she was nobody, I don't think she could take that.

"Me, I have to understand what the probabilities are. I don't like pipe dreams. I need a real life plan. I know I could have five reasonably good years now. But I'm going to wait until the pension is vested, so I know what's going to happen to me after sixty, until I've got all the stock options together, until my investments are at top dollar. I'm not looking at five years, I'm looking at a lifetime. The financial aspect is very important because it binds you to a job and you can't always fit the material needs to your heart. The more you can be free of that material requirement by being more independent, the more you can live according to your heart. I learned that nine years ago."

The breakpoint came when he was twenty-three and had finished his first year of law school. "I was reading Socrates and Plato and J.D. Salinger, and I just couldn't see how those values applied to law school. There wasn't any breathing space. You were just pushed along and along, and all of a sudden you're sixty-five and you're retiring. In high school and college I'd do as little as possible; now I had to go to classes, I really had to do this stuff. I was studying a case on the meaning of chickens in a contract, it went back to 1780. Broilers and chickens. It seemed like I was concentrating on such inane things. I wanted to think about the nature of man. At the end of the first year I had it up to here."

Pack the bag and off to Vegas. "I was winning a thousand a year playing poker all through college. I didn't want to take any money from my parents because I didn't want to have to listen to them. So I thought I'll take my poker winnings and go to Vegas and make some money, and maybe I'll only have to work one day a week."

Not so easy. "They were professionals. I bugged myself too much. I'd play on two, three hours of sleep when I didn't have to. I played a game where the stakes were too high for the stakes I had. After a month I left."

West to Los Angeles for a few months and then to

Berkeley. Berkeley: 1969. Living on garlic bread and coffee. Dropping fifty pounds in six months. Working for an antipoverty program, hosing down the streets from two to six in the morning, thirty dollars a week. Hoping the woman he was living with could bring in enough money to feed and house them.

"I met guys there who thought they were bohemians. They were standing on a street corner six hours a day, begging. They were in their thirties and they were losing their teeth. I found that living the bohemian life was not the answer. You didn't have any sense of direction; it was all hand to mouth. If you had any long-term goals, you couldn't achieve them that way. You worried too much about your next meal. I was dependent on the gal I was living with. What if we had a breakup? This wasn't the way of accomplishing what I wanted to accomplish. I had freedom, but I wasn't free."

Back to New York. Shave off the beard. Gain some weight. Buy some suits. Meet a guy at his father's country club. Shake hands. Why don't you come in Monday at nine for a talk, maybe there's something we can work out. The something is sales representative for Xerox.

Now seven years later there's Xerox and there's the plan.

"For me there's a difference between idleness and educated idleness. Idleness is my friend who's never held a steady job, who moves from job to job, lives off women, stretches unemployment insurance to the end. He has no desire to do anything. I'm different, I don't want to leech off someone. I want to live a life of educated idleness, to read what I want to read, to be where I want to be, to write if I want to without selling what I write. You could say there's more pride in me. My pride is in not taking from other people without contributing to them in some way. But that takes planning."

When I met these three I was struck by the absence of passion in their divorce from work. There is no great feeling of loss. (Martha Gorham is a possible exception, but I suspect that she grants herself dramatic license when she recalls her job frustrations.) I think they would have been more saddened by the death of their pet dog or cat. What stirs them is their singularity, their unincorporated selves. It is literally their self-interest that absorbs their minds and hearts. It would be wrong to say they *left* work; emotionally, they were never engaged by it. It was never an article of faith for them or a cause to be won. They worked for a while because they were curious about it, because they were expected to, and because they didn't feel they had a choice. Once they perceived an alternative to work, they left to pursue their interests in themselves.

There have always been people who were more interested in their personal realms than in lives of labor. But they didn't have a choice. They had to work or end up in the poorhouse. Now they don't have to choose between poverty and working. Now they only have to decide whether or not working is worth a modest reduction in consumption. That decision has been made easier for them because in the

1970s they had plenty of company. As they looked around, they could find many others like them who had already decided that their self-interest lay outside of work. This decade will be remembered as the time when the mythology of the work ethic surrendered at last to the personal-ethic myth. While our consciousness rose, our industrial output fell. Thus, the old order passeth.

THE PASSING OF THE WORK MYTH

In Western cultures, there have always been questions about the staying power of the work ethic. For example, in Bavaria in 1851, the royal bureaucrats were extremely nervous about the consequences of the breakdown in the traditional relationship between employers and journeymen workers. Previously, the workers were expected to live in the homes of the master craftsmen; their pay came in the form of room and board. Early in the nineteenth century, this system began to change; workers asked for cash in payment for their labor. They preferred to live on their own, cook their own meals, and buy their own clothes. This meant that their employers no longer controlled their personal lives. They could not tell them when to go to sleep or whom to sleep with; they could not restrain the workers' "licentious" interest in dance and drink; and they could not demand obedience and reverence toward the master's family. This change upset the Interior Ministry in Munich so much that one official proposed an ordinance to restrain the dangerous self-indulgence of the working population. He said the ordinance was necessary because of "the danger which threatens the entire social order," adding:

> increasing impiety, widespread laziness and plea-
> sure-seeking, the growing disregard for law,
> good-breeding and morality, the widening lack
> of domesticity, the ever-growing overestimation
> of self, the newly rising indifference to the inter-
> ests of the community when a question of per-
> sonal advantage is involved—all these are
> phenomena which, the more they emerge, the
> more emphatically they reveal that the basic pil-
> lars of the social order are deteriorating.[1]

That deterioration was also visible to the nine-teenth-century mill owners and empire builders in the United States. They complained that their straw bosses had to pull the workers out of the saloons every Monday—"Blue Monday"—to get them back on the job. There were too many holidays, too many feast days; at work, the spinners and tracklayers tended to daydream and chatter. It was increasingly difficult to get a full seventy hours of work out of them every week.

"At all times in American history—when the country was still a preindustrial society, while it industrialized and after it had become the world's leading industrial nation—quite diverse Americans," the historian Herbert Gutman wrote, "made it clear in their thought and behavior that the Protestant work ethic was not deeply ingrained in the nation's social fabric."[2]

As the collar turned from blue to white, as America passed from an agrarian to an industrial to a

postindustrial society, some skeptics did question
the force of the work ethic, but even the most insis-
tent skeptics did not challenge the assumption that
the vast majority of Americans wanted to work.[3] In
some periods there just wasn't enough work. At other times the jobs offered were just plain lousy. The
most innovative social reformers, the most progressive politicians, and the most committed union orga-
nizers directed their efforts toward generating more
jobs and improving the conditions of work. A
shorter work week. An end to child labor. A minimum wage. Pensions. Health plans. Each advance
offered further proof of the theorem that a better
job equaled a richer, more fulfilling personal life.

The price of a rich personal life was high. Everything cost. Leisure became big business as more
Americans spent their higher wages on travel,
amusement, and popular culture. The price of education went up. The price of owning a home went
up. The price of a car went up. Ultimately Americans worked harder to earn more, not only to finance immediate pleasure but future gratification.
Along with everything else, the cost of retirement—
the camper, the second home, the trip to the sun-
belt, and that new, dread institution, the nursing
home—was rising.

The equation became an iron law: You worked to
pay for pleasure. The notion that work could be
pleasurable in itself, that it contained intrinsic rewards not to be found in the pay envelope, became a
footnote, then seemed to fade from the pages of
American social history. In their monumental study
of the social fabric of a midwestern American com-

munity in the 1920s, sociologists Robert and Helen Lynd found that the pleasures of craft, skill, and achievement had declined, and that with the abandonment of an apprenticeship system the distinction between skilled and unskilled workers was fuzzy.

"For the working class both any satisfaction inherent in the actual daily doing of the job and the prestige and kudos of the able worker among his associates would appear to be declining," they observed.

Turning to the satisfaction of the work itself, the Lynds found:

> For both working and business classes no other accompaniment of getting a living approaches in importance the money received for their work. It is more this future, instrumental aspect of work, rather than the intrinsic satisfactions involved that keeps Middletown working so hard as more and more of the activities are coming to be strained through the bars of the dollar sign.[4]

The relatively mild caution voiced by the Lynds was noted in America without great alarm. Work must mean more than just the dollars it brought in. If not, why did so many people say they would go nuts without a job, that they would sink into depression, that their wives would kick them out of the house, and that they would immediately take up residence in the nearest gin mill?

In 1955, the same year that a new edition of the Lynds' book appeared, two sociologists, Nancy Morse and Robert S. Weiss of the University of

Michigan's Survey Research Center, published the results of a study of more than four hundred men. They had asked them, "If by some chance you inherited enough money to live comfortably without working, do you think that you would work anyway or not?"

Eighty percent said they would keep working. Among the most important reasons they gave for continuing working were that they had to keep occupied and that work is "healthy, it's good for a person." Interestingly only 9 percent said that they would stay on a job because they enjoyed their work. Without work, significant numbers said they would "feel lost, go crazy" and "not know what to do with my time, I can't be idle." But only 2 percent said they would "feel useless" without work. Generally, they would most miss the "feeling of doing something," and specifically, they would regret the absence of the "people I know through work, the friends, the contacts."

Morse and Weiss concluded: "For many of those in the middle-class occupations working means having something interesting to do, having a chance to accomplish things and to contribute. Those in working-class occupations view working as virtually synonymous with activity, the alternative to which is to lie around and be bored and restless. . . . Life without working becomes life without anything to do."[5]

The unanchored man. The dangling man. The purposeless man. It was as if no time had elapsed at all between the classic depression-era unemployment studies and the optimistic decade, the 1950s.

One of the most notable of these studies was Mirra Komarovsky's analysis during the depression of the effect of unemployment on men in fifty-nine families.[6] She found that the settled family life of many male breadwinners had been transformed into a wasteland.

Family conflicts that were disguised or suppressed before the husband lost his job surfaced during the period of unemployment. Many wives blamed their husbands for being out of work at the height of the depression. Komarovsky finds that the father is no longer able to exercise control over teenage children when he isn't bringing money into the house. The social life of families where the father isn't working often deteriorates: Some families are bitter because their friends who are working have deserted them; others are ashamed of their shabby clothes or that they have no money to invite friends to dinner. Sexual relations decline. Love is withheld. Expressions of tenderness are as rare as a $1,000 bill.

This is what some of the husbands and wives told her:

"When you are not working, you do not get so much attention."

"She gets mad at me when I tell her I want more love."

"How can you love a husband who causes you so much suffering?"

"The children act cold toward me. They used to come and hug me, but now I seldom hear a pleasant word from them."

"If I only had money I could make the girl do things for me. Now that I cannot offer her a nickel for helping her mother with the dishes, there's always an argument about it."

In general, Komarovsky discovered that when the husband lost his job, his authority was undermined. There were exceptions where the family made accommodations—even tried to protect the husband and father's wounded ego—because of the love they had for one another, but that was uncommon. It is a crude simplification of her complex study, but not a total distortion, to summarize it as: The power of most men in their families depends on their money-making ability.

Anxieties about the work ethic were epidemic in the early 1970s.[7] Discussion of job dissatisfaction became a cottage industry for journalists, politicians, sociologists, psychologists, for almost anybody who had ever written or reflected on the meaning of work in contemporary America. Computers spawned a mountain of tape on job turnover, mental illness among workers, absenteeism, alcoholism at the work place, and industrial sabotage.

Washington reacted. President Nixon established a special task force to study work in America. A Senate committee held hearings on worker alienation, and Senator Edward Kennedy sponsored a bill to fund research into "the problem of alienation among American workers in all occupations and industries."

Around the country various enlightened employers, sometimes over the muted objection of unions, began to experiment with programs to humanize the work place, to include workers in decisions that had been previously reserved for management, to reorganize the work force into smaller teams and "support groups."

The response was predictable. When work jitters broke out, the reflexive response was to reexamine the working life, to experiment with work relationships, to alter the work setting.[8] Washington in the early 1970s reacted as the Bavarian ministry did in 1851. It focused on work. The experts seemed much less interested in what was going on outside of work, in the claims, inducements, and sanctions of the social order, in the stirrings and rumblings below the surface of *la vie intime*. Against the weight of his academic training, against the weight of historical evidence, Craig Little got sucked in.

It started innocently enough. In the winter and early spring of 1972, Little was doing the field research for his doctoral dissertation in sociology at the University of New Hampshire. His subject was the response of one hundred technicians and engineers who had been laid off from their jobs in the electronics and aerospace industries.[9]

The setting was Route 128, the highway that loops around Boston. The area was studded with defense and electronics plants. Little knew what to expect. These were not men who had elected to stop working. They had been bounced. He was familiar with the literature of unemployment, which maintained that unemployment was threatening for American males because of the high value placed on occupational achievement. It said that unemployment damages self-esteem and morale; it disrupts and may mortally wound family life. What he expected to find was alienation, depression, and despair. He found something else.

"I assumed that being out of work had to be stressful, had to be frustrating," he says. "These guys had been into their work for some time, they hadn't changed jobs recently, they weren't particularly early in their careers. I was sure they would see unemployment as blocked opportunity. But they didn't. They saw being laid off as an opportunity to escape."[10]

Escape? Escape from what? First, the tension. "Their businesses were extremely competitive, very tight. They had to do everything to the letter, there never was a second to waste. They'd say to me, 'I was in a pressure cooker and I now realize that I can't handle that.'"

Second, the trivia. "There was more of the pressure cooker than the trivia, but the trivia was important. 'You know,' the guys would say to me, 'I did more at home today than I'd do on a morning at work. You know how much time I used to spend on trips to the water cooler, on conferences that were called to use up time, to make it seem we were busy? You know how many three-hour lunches I had that nothing came out of?'"

Third, an objection to the end product. The number who expressed this objection were less than the number who complained about the trivia and the pressure. But their objections were more vehement. They protested the lack of social concern and questionable purposes of their employers.

Little was not jarred by these criticisms. He knew, from his reading, that the unemployed often rationalized their position by accentuating their criticisms of their last jobs. When they were working they might have griped; once they had been fired, they inflated their complaints until they became an absolute condemnation of what they had been doing and the organizations for which they had worked.

Every morning Little would show up at the state's Professional Service Center. He would watch the men scan the computer roll of possible jobs, shake their heads, sip coffee out of plastic containers, and chat among themselves. They didn't look dejected. After a month, Little was antsy. He knew he would have to defend his dissertation. His research methods would be closely scrutinized, even more so than usual because what he was hearing, what the men were telling him, didn't agree with what he had expected.

The first time he heard it, he dismissed it as an exception. By the tenth time it had become a pattern. "They were saying that they were not living much differently than when they were working," he says. "I was expecting them to be devastated after three weeks or thirty weeks. But they weren't. They were saying life was going on, and life wasn't bad at all. Some of the guys who really had guts said to me, 'Actually I've looked forward to this for a long time.' That's when I knew I had something different. I was hitting a vein that hadn't been touched before. It scared me. It excited me."

To check his findings, Little asked roughly the same question that Morse and Weiss had asked in 1955: Did these men have a lot of extra time since they were laid off and was that a problem? The answers he got were very different from what Morse and Weiss had reported. Almost half the laid-off engineers and technicians said they did not have extra time on their hands. And almost 70 percent said that what extra time they did have was not a serious problem. The men in this survey weren't going nuts without a job.

Little went back to the University of New Hampshire and reported that approximately half the men he had interviewed had a positive attitude toward losing their jobs; that those in the middle of their careers had more positive attitudes toward not working than those at the beginning or end of their careers; that positive attitudes toward not working do not decline with the duration of unemployment but actually rise for the long-term unemployed.

"It seems reasonable to speculate that changes in the broader aspects of American culture between the Great Depression and the early 1970s," Little wrote, "might account for some reduction of the stigma attached to unemployment regardless of social class. It is probable that the motivating pressure of the Protestant Ethic has eased somewhat since the studies of the unemployed done during the Depression. And, in a society with increasing institutionalization of leisure, enforced leisure may not be very punishing if basic financial needs can be met."

Five years later Little and I are sitting in a restaurant in New York. Everything has turned out fine. He now teaches at the State University of New York. His dissertation was accepted; he was awarded his doctorate. He is a charming man, quite unprofessorial in his ski jacket, and not easily given to academic jargon. As we're about to leave, he makes one more point touched on only briefly in his study.

"If I were redoing it now, I would make much more of the structural changes in society that affected the values in our culture," he says. "What those guys in Boston were being told was that it was okay not to work. The federal government, the state government, that Professional Service Center were sending them a message: Don't worry about it, there's nothing wrong with being out of a job, we're all into this together. Not only the government, everybody was telling them this: their friends, their families, the local banker, the local grocer. They were saying: Don't sweat it."

After Little completed his study, he had one caveat. Unlike the people Komarovsky had interviewed, his subjects had been professional men. They had fairly broad interests. If they chose, they could probably find jobs in different occupations or in work related to engineering. They had the resilience and inner confidence that comes with being white, middle class, and professional in American culture. "My findings might have been very different if I was dealing with a working-class group," he says.

Professor Kenneth Root was dealing with an emphatically working-class group in work-ethic country. He was talking to meat packers and other blue-collar workers who had been fired when Armour and Company closed its meat plant in Mason City, Iowa, in August 1975. His study was more comprehensive than Little's. He interviewed workers just before the plant was closed, then eight months later, and then again five months after that. He spoke, not only to the men, but also to their wives.[11]

He found that 60 percent of the men and their wives had adjusted quite well to the firings. Particularly striking was the reaction of the wives. Many of them, for the first time in their married lives, had gone out to work. "You have to remember," he says, "that this is a community of thirty-five thousand people with bedrock American values. The surrounding area is primarily rural, farming country. There is a very tight, conservative family network here. That was a big change for them—to find a job—for them, and their husbands."

The anxiety of the unemployed workers was eased because their wives did not blame them for being out of work, and their family network—their parents, grandparents, relatives, children—were generally supportive. Their support was based in part on a widespread hostility toward the plant management. Over the years Armour had closed down a number of its plants, consolidating operations and firing more than fifty thousand workers. The Mason City plant had been purchased recently by the Greyhound Corporation, and many Mason City residents resented this: The plant had been removed from local control. "For five years people had been expecting the ax to fall," Dr. Root says. "When it did, it was no surprise."

Rather than break up the family, the firings seemed to bring it closer. "Sure, there were some divorces. But in the overwhelming number of cases, the attitude was that this is a time when the husband and the wife sit down and talk, when they hadn't really done it before. The wife really feels a part of the family decisions: This is something we *both* have to overcome [Root's italics]. Suddenly, a whole new life is open to them. It's a new challenge and they must do it together."

Before the firings, husbands rarely discussed their work with their wives and children. It was, as Dr. Root describes it, "dirty, unpleasant, self-centered repetitive work." The Armour plant was the major industry in Mason City. It was a job that was passed down from one generation to another, and until the shutdown, many of the younger workers had never considered alternatives to processing and packing animals' carcasses.

"All of a sudden, new possibilities about what you should be doing with your life started to come out," he says, remembering especially one man who had worked alongside his father at the plant for eight years. "I always wanted to get out of there," the meat packer told an interviewer. "But at seven bucks an hour and three bucks fringe benefits I couldn't do it."

Once out, this man found that he could survive. "My wife took a job, and we just learned to budget our money better," he said. "At Armour I got closer and closer to the final penny, and I never had anything left over at the end of the week. When I stopped working we cut out credit cards. We just said to ourselves: We can't buy everything we want. We're really happy we changed that element in our lives."

When Dr. Root sifted through the more than one hundred interviews, he was almost as surprised and excited as Little was four years before in Massachusetts, perhaps more surprised because his study concerned blue-collar workers in a traditional community. He found that:

- In overwhelming numbers the husband adjusted to not being the primary breadwinner in the family.
- There was little peer pressure to find another job.
- The unemployed men refused to take other work when it paid less that what they had been earning at Armour.
- It was much more "normative," acceptable, to be unemployed than he or other researchers would have expected.
- "All the things we've assumed about the intrinsic meaning of work, the value of productivity, have to be adjusted."

There's one remark by the wife of a former Armour worker that sticks with Dr. Root. "We're really liking our marriage now," she said. "Without work, we've found a ray of sunshine."

In the spring of 1977 the idea that somebody would choose not to work was no longer radical. Public opinion surveys, academic studies, numerous television and print interviews had challenged and perhaps demolished that most cherished belief that the average American would prefer work, any kind of work, to not working. Air controllers, firemen working as househusbands, social workers, college deans had all weighed in with their own body blows against the work ethic. What remained to be answered was: Did these defections from the work ethic amount to a temporary aberration, a blip on the chart, or did they represent a fundamental and enduring change in values? There was a related question. Why were the values changing? What was happening structurally—in the public policies and programs implemented by government—that allowed and may have encouraged the new attitudes toward work? And what was happening in the interior life of the individual and in the culture that made the once unacceptable now acceptable?

Two researchers at Fordham University in New York City thought they had some tentative answers. Susan Gray, an assistant professor of sociology, and Louis Henri Bolce, an assistant political science professor, spent much of their time between April and July 1977 supervising a random survey of 600 New York City residents.[12] Projecting their findings in New York nationally, they estimated that from 25 to 37 percent of the unemployed in America were choosing not to work. The primary reason, they found, was that "they cannot find the type of job that suits their skills and interests. . . . If they cannot find work that is acceptable to them [they] will opt, when they can, to be supported by government, family or savings."

Some of those they interviewed were working at "highly attractive and good-paying jobs but they form part of a growing number of persons who see working to support oneself, regardless of the type of job, as an undesirable life option and who believe that each individual has a right and perhaps an obligation to himself to avoid spending most of his working hours in disagreeable activities, provided that there are alternate means of support."

For both the disadvantaged and the middle-class population, various structural elements built into American life "result in a weakening commitment to any kind of work, no matter what the individual's class is.

"Three overriding characteristics of American society," they write, "are middle-class affluence, the scarcity of desirable jobs and the expansion of the government's role in providing means of support that are alternatives to work. In an age of affluence a person need not work to survive.

"The increasing visibility of middle-class affluence and leisure, along with the greater responsibility assumed by the public and parents to support those not working, has contributed to the erosion of the ethic that an adult is fundamentally responsible for his own support."

Gray and Bolce make two telling points about the middle class. "This is perhaps the only country and period of history in which a substantial number of people can reach 30 years of age without having stable employment and still maintain a comfortable apartment, car stereo, and color television set. The middle-class youths' attitudes toward work grew out of the experience of not *having* to work and have been reinforced by the counterculture ideology of the 1960s, which questioned the desirability of work as an end in itself [Gray and Bolce's italics]."

The second point: "The affluence and success of their parents exact another toll from the success/ work ethic by making it difficult for a middle-class youth to ... better himself materially over his parents ... it is next to impossible for him to top a successful lawyer, doctor or businessman or to equal their material success. He therefore sees himself condemned as a failure relative to his parents [and is] likely to be susceptible to the ideology that repudiates the value of striving to get ahead because it provides a solution for his perceived predicament."*

Robert Schrank, a project specialist at the Ford Foundation, has held a variety of jobs in the last forty years: machinist, city official, union organizer, and sociologist.** After all these years his ardor for the human qualities of work is undiminished. But Schrank recognizes that in his enthusiasm for work he is an endangered species.

"In this country there is an option to working, which is not working," he says. "I'm not a believer

---

*This hypothesis is supported by a number of studies. To cite one, in 1970 approximately seven hundred students at the University of Wisconsin in Madison were interviewed by the Wisconsin Survey Research Laboratory. Since it is a state university, it might be expected that a majority of the students came from working-class or blue-collar families. This did not turn out to be true. The fathers of more than half the students had at least some college experience. The fathers of two out of every five had graduated from college. Most of the students had fathers who were in higher-status occupational groups. Three out of every ten fathers were professionals; roughly the same percentage were managers, officials, or business proprietors. Only 22 percent of the students had fathers in blue-collar occupations, and in a state where agriculture was still a major occupation, only 6 percent of the fathers were farmers.

**For an evocative description of the human side of work read Schrank's book, *Ten Thousand Working Days* (Cambridge, Mass.: M.I.T. Press, 1978).

that intrinsically we want to work. Intrinsically, we want to have a good time. I'm convinced that the pursuit of pleasure in this country has become the focus of a lot of people's lives and more and more so. We used to think that working was kind of basic. The Freudian notion *arbeiten* and *lieben* were the two basic things that made you a healthy human being. My own feeling is that between Saint Paul, who said if you don't work you don't eat, and Luther, who said if you don't work you'll fry in hell—both of these guys' popularity is at a new low."[13]

THE FAMILY BUSINESS

The sounds and smells of work are as homely and comforting for some people as a pot of chicken soup bubbling on the stove or a plate of ravioli simmering in tomato sauce. These are people with two families. One loves and fights, succeeds and fails, matures and dies in the office, the other at 127 Shady Nook Drive. It is often difficult to tell which dominates the affections, but not infrequently a divorce from the work family is more wrenching than a break with the domestic family.

The rise of massive business bureaucracies has taken away from the family feeling of work, but in the cells and arteries of the most impersonal corporation, there are clusters of workers who venerate seniority, who respect skill and ability, and who honor promises.

In the 1950s Dr. Harry Levinson, the psychologist, undertook an extended study of a Midwest power and light company.[1] He found that for many of the employees it was more than a place to work; it constituted an extended family. And like all families it had certain secrets.

Two things happened at the company that no workers, supervisor, or executive would talk about. One night a manager of the company was staying at a motel during a business trip. He walked out of the motel totally nude, the police picked him up, and he was fired. His co-workers interpreted this as an expression of his grief at the death of a vice-president of the utility who had been very close to him. The second incident involved an executive who had been having an affair with a secretary in the office. The affair became known and the woman was dismissed. Dr. Levinson learned about both incidents from sources outside the company. "People in the company would talk to you about everything else," he says, "but not about these things. It became clear that these were skeletons in the closet. The relationship between the employees and the company was very emotional. In many ways it was a recapitulation of the family. People don't talk easily about family skeletons."

Another tie to the company is the concept of service. It means more than just being a good worker and getting paid for the work. It means that the worker has a responsibility to the outside community, to the external world as well as to the company. One New York City fireman who lost his job during the city's fiscal crisis has not looked for a job in two years. He remembers how he drove through the impoverished Lower East Side of Manhattan to work and could imagine the people on the streets saying, We need you, we depend on you for our sur-

vival. In his five years with the department he had
never saved anyone's life; he had never rescued
anyone from a burning building. It was the possibility that someday he might have to that made his
work important, that imparted a heroic quality to
his job. It made him feel indispensable. He has since
learned that when City Hall says he's dispensable,
he's dispensable. He chooses not to work until he
finds something that gives him the same feeling.

When Dr. Levinson was conducting his study he
would ask workers what they liked about their job.
"They'd say: 'You see all those lights down the road.
I had a hand in putting them there.'" They would
tell him about how they stopped their trucks on the
highway to help motorists fix their flat tires. "There
was really a heroic quality to some of this," he says.
"Some of the work was dangerous, the guys who
worked on high tension wires, and the people who
went out in tornadoes and blizzards to restore current. These people needed to be loved. And they
were loved. That's what giving service gets you."

Betty Tallgood's farm combined both qualities of
family work described by Dr. Levinson: It was a
family business, a testimony to her parents' will,
and at the same time her social legacy. The farm
was her mission: the next chapter in the Tallgood
saga.

Sam Mcyers's magazine was not handed down to
him by his parents. For the emotional claims it
made on him, it just as well might have been. It was
the only business for which he ever worked. It was
his second home. When it died, it could not be re-

placed any more than a father or mother could be replaced.

Neither Tallgood nor Meyers would associate the word *labor* with their work. Labor sounds too much like punishment. Their work was hard, but it provided pleasure. The pleasure of belonging—of belonging to something they cared about. This is a rare experience in this culture where so few people belong to anything and so many people believe they can count only on themselves. The brilliant social anthropologist Jules Henry wrote:

> Contemporary man suffers from the certainty that when dead *he will mean nothing to everybody* and from the anxiety that even while alive he may come to *mean nothing to anybody*. For this reason he allocates his emotional resources to those to whom he wants to mean something and he is torn between his commitments to them and the demands of those who want to be significant in his life but who are not important to him. . . . With *abundant emotional resources* one can be relatively sure of a personal community, for one has much with which to bind other people; otherwise, it is difficult, for then one is emotionally stingy and every heartbeat is a major investment [Henry's italics].[2]

Tallgood and Meyers gave generously, and in their work lives they meant a great deal to others. They were assured of a personal community. And then they were displaced. Later they faced the problem of restoring their legitimacy, for themselves and for their families, who for so long had regarded them as inseparable from their work communities.

Betty Tallgood: Close to the Earth

Betty Tallgood is something of a legend in the delta country of Mississippi. She became a prime target of the night riders when she organized the voters' rights league in Tallahatchie County in the 1960s. In Sharkey, the white men would meet in the back room of the general store to plan how they were going to drive her out of business. "Let her load those damn cukes on the truck," they'd say, "but that damn truck'll never get to market. There's gonna be an accident." In Twilight, the talk was rougher. The white farmers, piling their bales of cottons onto their flatbeds, would say, "Somebody's got to stop that snake woman. Stop her for good."

Betty went about her business. She drove the dirt roads in her pickup with a member of the local civil rights group, stopping from house to house to tell the other black farmers in the county that they'd better get their asses out to vote in the election or nothing would ever change in Tallahatchie. Communication wasn't always easy. In that part of Mississippi, the white county government had never bothered to put up telephone lines where the blacks lived.

Many nights she would wait for the night riders to come out after her. She'd sit in a ladder-back, cane-seated rocking chair rocking, rocking slowly as the setting sun turned the old plantation master's house a dusky orange. The shotgun always rested in her lap. She was never without it, and a couple of times she had to empty it when a stranger came within shooting distance of the house. She was not much for welcoming unannounced strangers.

Really, the only thing she wanted was for her son Roosevelt to come back home. He had left when he was in his teens to go to Chicago, where she had family. Roosevelt had promised to come back and help her work the farm. The letters she got from him now were filled with excuses; she could read the guilt between the lines. Roosevelt was married and he had a kid and a job driving a bus. His wife didn't think much of living a hick's life, wearing an old cotton housedress every day, slapping at the mosquitoes, living some place where you couldn't even get decent reception on the TV.

The farm meant a lot to Betty Tallgood. Her father had worked this land as a sharecropper. In the late 1930s and early 1940s, F.D.R. made good on his promise to break up the large white-owned holdings. He gave many of the sharecropping families forty acres and a mule. The complaints of the local politicians quickly put an end to this, but not before the Tallgoods got their land and their mule. Only right that they name their firstborn Roosevelt.

Charles, her husband, was killed in Italy, and she buried him a few hundred yards from the house. Her parents were getting too old to work every day under the delta sun. The children had gone north. So she planted and harvested the forty acres on her own. In the good years, she could afford to hire some of the local men to help out; most of the work she did alone. It wasn't easy. The Tallahatchie banks wouldn't give her credit, and the big pickle companies didn't see much profit in establishing a credit line for her. When she brought the pickles in, she couldn't keep an eye on all the sorting machines by herself. She had harvested those pickles, and she knew how many number ones and how many number threes she had; it always did seem, though, that there were more number threes than number ones when the white sorters got through counting.

Except when the hurricane hit, there was enough money for a woman alone to get along. And even then her folks helped out at harvest time so she got by. "I never did think I'd ever give the land up," she says, sitting on the porch, fanning herself, and offering me a lemonade. "It was the first time the Tallgoods had their own land. I always figured I owed Mr. Roosevelt that much. To keep the land and show 'em colored folks could do a better job than the white people did. No question, I made that promise to him."

From 1959 to 1976 the number of family-owned farms had declined from more than four million to less than three million. In the thirty years since President Roosevelt had awarded the Tallgoods forty acres and a mule, the number of farms in America had been cut in half, and almost all of them were farms that had cash sales of less than $10,000 a year. The most important statistic for Mrs. Tallgood was that in five years in the 1970s the number of self-employed black farmers dropped from 53,000 to 37,000.[3]

Mrs. Tallgood wasn't paying much attention to agricultural statistics through the 1950s and 1960s. She didn't have to. Just looking around she knew how many black kids were leaving the county to find jobs up north, and she knew that the ones that stayed didn't have much mind for farming. When

she drove over to Sardis, she could see them standing around the record store with their purple pants
and high-heeled shoes and their wide-brimmed
green hats. They didn't look much like farmers. If
Roosevelt didn't want to come home, at least he was
a good husband and a good father and he kept down
a good job. No sense talkin' people into somethin'
they didn't want to do.

Her son leaving the land, going up to Chicago, it
made her think. "When he left, it hurt me, right
then, I can't lie to you. I thought he was desertin'
the family. Then I got to think on it. He was a good
boy, he was supportin' his family, he wasn't stealin'
and killin' people the ways you always hear. Why
was he wrong doin' what he was doin' an' me right?
I tell you, sometimes it was hard, the river was bad
an' I was tempted an' I says, 'Betty, whyn't you become a school teacher or a movie star,' an' I'd laugh
an' say, 'You jes' gettin' foolish, old lady. What else
you fit for but raisin' pickles.' I jes' couldn't think of
nothin' else."

On a hot July day in 1975, Mr. Simpson from the
pickle company came by for a visit. He told her how
Mrs. Williams over in Flora had sold her place last
month and how Mr. Dempsey in Twilight had giv-
en up his farm, said he couldn't take it one more
time the Tallahatchie flooded. Would she listen to a
proposition? "I wanted to be polite," Betty Tallgood
says. "After all, he was the man who bought my
pickles. But I wasn't paying him no mind, 'cause I
couldn't 'magine me away from the farm. I been
workin' that farm since I was six. What else was
there for a woman who had forty-eight years on her,
livin' here in Sharkey, 'cept the farm?"

Mr. Simpson came back three times. The last time she accepted his offer. The company would pay her $30,000, plus $12,000 a year for the next five years because it was good "customer relations," as he explained. She could keep her house and a nice garden patch in back, so she'd have fresh vegetables for herself. Not only that: This white man would make a $1,000 contribution to the new black farmers' cooperative association in the county. "I guess if they were goin' to be that generous, this dirt was worth somethin' to them. I was thinkin', if I don't take him up, they'd buy somebody else out, and after a while there wouldn't be many folks holdin' out, and the price wouldn't be so good. I did feel a little strange. Knowin' I'd look out the window in the morning and see my land out there and knowin' it wasn't my land and knowin' I wouldn't be lookin' up at the moon anymore to know if the river was goin' to flood on me, 'cause without my land what difference if it floods or not."

The sun is dying now. The air is warm and sweet. The fried chicken and sweet potatoes are delicious. "You come back, ya hear," Betty Tallgood is telling me. "Don't be no stranger, you hear. 'Cause we're all strangers now. I feel like a stranger when I take the truck into town. They tell me about the new poisons they usin' to speed up the crop, and they tell me about the new tractor they're buyin' with air in the cab. 'Magine, drivin' a tractor with air in it. What do I have to tell 'em? The house is gonna need a new paintin' next year? Not much I can tell 'em. My son keeps on writin' that they have an extra room up there, for me, anytime I want it. I think 'bout that sometimes. Maybe I'll go and stay awhile.

Sure do wish he had a garden patch back of his house. Give me somethin' to do. Don't feel right, not growin' your own. I don't know. Maybe next time you c'mon to the delta, Miz Betty'll know what to do. Maybe she be a picture star."

Sam Meyers: Cultivating the Garden

Sam Meyers was fifty-three when *Look* magazine folded in 1971. It was no great surprise. He had seen it coming for a couple of years, and in his last six months as the bureau chief in London, he had the painful job of paring down the payroll. Sometime during the last few weeks he said to his wife, Frances, "Look, I've spent thirty years with the company. We've lived in ten different cities all over the world in that time. I fought in one war and covered four or five. We traveled everywhere and we did it in a manner that was absolutely marvelous. So do I want to start it all over again with a new organization? Do you want to dig in and be expatriates any longer? Aaaah."

Sam is sitting in front of his fireplace in his house in Kitty Hawk, North Carolina. It is an uncluttered place with lots of windows and lots of open space. Early spring in Kitty Hawk, and the fire doesn't completely chase the chill. Sam is comfortable in his flannel shirt, but noticing I'm cold, offers me a brandy. Sam is a trained observer; he made a living for a long time watching other people. "I'm not sure if I would have stopped if we hadn't built this house in the 1960s. That meant we had a place to go to. I wanted more than anything else to stay put. I just didn't expect to move in quite so soon."

Sam leans back in his rocker, closes his eyes, better to hear Joan Sutherland singing in the background. "I think really what it all added up to, being absolutely honest with myself, is that I really was tired of working. I really hated the idea of packing another suitcase, getting another mode of transportation. I've traveled all my working life on every goddamn thing there is. Dogsleds, everything. I said, 'I can't think of anything in the journalistic world exciting enough to go through that again.' Literally, I couldn't think of anything."

Later that afternoon while Sam is outside inspecting his garden, fretting over his new strain of radishes, Frances says, "When we left London, he didn't even want to get on a plane. His hands were shaking. The idea, just the idea of going anyplace, terrified him."

For Sam Meyers *Look* was a family and his job was to manage it. He made sure stories got covered, assigned reporters and photographers, occasionally wrote text blocks. He had seen his share of action: Vietnam, the Hungarian Revolution, Suez, the 1967 Mideast War. His name wasn't a household item, but in the *Look* household, he was respected, the stern but kindly father.

As Sam would say, though, that's not the whole story. Another factor was that he was fifty-three and no longer feeling invincible. The mortality factor. "In 1968 I was working out of New York and two of my friends died of heart attacks. One of them just dropped dead, sitting at his desk and typing something and dropped dead. He'd been a heavy drinker and smoker—he had all the symptoms of being about to drop dead. He was the same age as I was then, forty-seven.

"The other guy was in very good shape, I thought, and he looked good. He took a vacation to go on a ski trip, and two hours after he got off the plane he had a massive heart attack. The next year the guy who took my place in New York when I went to London had the same thing happen to him. What was interesting was those three guys and I all started out in the same office at *Look* the same year. They all dropped dead: forty-seven, forty-nine, fifty.

"A man is a reporter and smokes three packs of cigarettes a day and drinks and stays up late and gobbles down corned beef sandwiches ... I don't know, it's the tension and the bad eating. To this day I don't eat breakfast. You start that way and you're out on a story and you don't eat lunch either. You grab a hot dog. I can't believe that's good for you. Anyway I told Frances, 'It's incredible the way these three guys died.' *I was shaken by it.* I said to her, 'Now, I'm the only one left.' What I didn't say was, 'I want to come out to this house before it's too late.' "

Sam and I passed the afternoon by rolling up our pants and walking out to the dunes and driving out to the marshlands and watching the skimmers swoop low over the water hunting their lunch. Then we read the 150-year-old tombstones in one of the oldest English settlements in North America, guffawing over the statue commemorating the Wright Brothers' first flight, and ate overcooked hamburgers in a restaurant that advertised, "Your meals served by a beautiful barefoot coed." We stopped off briefly to visit the studio Fran rents in Kitty Hawk.

At dinner that night Fran and Sam talk about what his decision to retire has meant to both of them; what it means to differentiate, to evolve separately, and yet to honor the bond between them.

Fran recalls how when she met Sam she gave up her own newspaper job to marry him. "It wasn't a sacrifice for me," she says. "I was giving it up for something more exciting. I was interested in traveling and seeing the world."

"I got her to admit once," Sam says, "that she married me because I traveled a lot. If I were an insurance salesman, she never would have married me. I thought women married people—not jobs."

"Sam keeps saying that the kind of job you have tells what kind of person you are."

"That's nonsense," Sam says, stabbing the steak with his fork.

"Sam keeps saying, 'You would never have married me if I were a shoe salesman,' and he's absolutely right because he wouldn't have been someone who interested me."

"My God, I was young. How do you know how I would have grown up? I might have been a very interesting shoe salesman. That's a real incredible thing to say."

"It's true," Fran insists. "Why were you attracted to me? I was a girl reporter. That made me interesting."

"You see," Sam says, pushing his chair back from the table, folding his arms across his chest. "That's the attitude again. People are their jobs. When people ask me what I'm doing, I say, 'Absolutely nothing.' If it's during the growing season and they really care, I tell them what I'm growing in the garden. The work ethic is so strong in this country most people can't understand why a healthy man— I'm not an old man—a man who's fifty isn't working full time at something."

"What I miss," Fran says, "is the talk with your old buddies, being there when a government is falling. I miss the excitement of feeling you were in on things. Or having a real grandstand seat for history."

"*You* miss it. I think a man is perfectly entitled to cultivate his own garden. I see nothing wrong with making your first priority cultivating your own life."

"Intellectually, I can understand it perfectly. *But* if I see him sit down on the couch at ten in the morning and do the crossword puzzle and know really all he has to do is go to the post office and get the mail and come back and put on an opera, there's nothing wrong, as I say, intellectually—but it bothers me emotionally."

"Why does it bother you? I never understood why it should bother you."

"I don't know. For a long time I didn't really think it was decent to sit down a read a book until after dinner when your work was done."

"She worries about me because I shave once a week. Later on, she thinks, it'll be once a month. I change my winter underwear every two weeks. Later on it'll be once a month."

"He deserves whatever he wants to do at this point. He's worked hard."

"At any point. Why at this point?"

"Well, it's the reservoir of whatever's left over from the Protestant work ethic."

"Then *you* work," Sam says.

"I *do*. Sam's retired, but I haven't retired. I have more meals to cook, more dishes to wash with him home. And I'm painting and I can show my paintings here. If you're interested in your job, if you're doing something you like, something you get a kick out of—that excites you—then I think it makes you a more vibrant person because of what you're doing, what you're involved in."

"She comes home from the studio and says, 'What'd you do today?' And I say, "Dear, I canned ten quarts of tomatoes, I listened to Joan Sutherland, I read a little of Robert Penn Warren's new book, I put away the clothes you left on the washing machine, I went to the post office, I took the dog for a walk on the beach, I fingered my seed catalog.' That's quite a day. Why was what I did with Jack Kennedy any more interesting?"

"Well, I'm a square. That's what it boils down to. I can understand intellectually, but emotionally . . ."

"No, what it boils down to is this: Remember what happened in Naples? There was an American tourist, he was sixty-five, seventy, and he saw all the kids lying on the deck doing nothing. He walked over to one of the kids and said, 'What are you doing? You oughta be ashamed—you oughta be in school studying and working hard so that when you're sixty-five you can travel and lie in the sun.'

"When you get to be my age and if you haven't figured out what you want from life, you might as well forget it, 'cause you're never going to work it out. I always liked the idea of gardening. The idea. But I never had a chance to do it; I was always on the run. I don't ordinarily soul search, dear. But I always felt how nice it would be to spend some time doing one thing and watching something happen as a result. That's what gardening is all about. Look, if it makes you feel better, don't tell people I'm not working. Tell them I'm cultivating my garden."

Fran's restiveness is understandable. Sam may argue that there are a thousand human qualities he possesses, always possessed, that have nothing to do with editing a magazine. But the fact is that for more than thirty years his entire life had been intertwined with work, all their travels, their time apart from each other, their closest friends, the American community abroad—they were all tied to his job. After all those years, he had a right to be weary. The fatigue came more, I think, from the death of the magazine than the strain of the work. If you spent many years of your life trying to make your parents proud of you and they die, you feel like the air has been taken out of you. What's the point of going on? Who's left to affirm your success?

I think this is why the imagery of death recurs so often and so consistently with men and women who were deeply committed to their work. Work has been their family; when their work ends, they hear footsteps. The sound of their own approaching mortality.[4] They would describe how their parents, knowing they were terminally ill, worked until the last day at their tailor shops or out in the wheat field or carving meat in the butcher shop, worked until they dropped dead at their jobs. When I heard this the first or second time, I thought they were identifying work with death. What I have come to understand is that they were mourning the loss of work. They were asking, Is there anything more for me, but a slow procession to the grave?

The common wisdom is that each generation goes its own way. The wisdom is flawed because we take more from the past than we like to admit. When offspring go into the same field of work as their parents, it is not only because they are attracted to their parents' occupation. They might enjoy something else more, but they don't give themselves a chance to find out because they want to live as their parents did. They admire their parents more for the way they conduct their total lives than for the work they do. But they understand that work is an organizing force. They believe that the pleasant, supportive home life they enjoyed was attained through a satisfying, productive job. They also know that unrewarding work can poison a person's private life. In a desire to recreate for themselves the environment in which they grew up, they follow in their parents' path. It's the only model they have. But suppose the model doesn't live up to its promise? Although they may do well in their work, they may not be happy in their private lives. Cliff Jones went into investment banking. His father had been an investment banker. Joe Browne went into real estate. His father had sold real estate. Their choice of occupation was totally natural. The hard decision came later—when work let them down, when it did not assure them of a happy marriage, when it didn't provide the emotional security and ease that their parents enjoyed.

Jones & Browne, Inc.: The "Right" Thing

It wasn't the income that Joe Browne's father earned that drew Joe into the real estate business. It was the tone and style of his parents' life which he admired and which he hoped to duplicate in his own life.

His dad ran hard when he was closing a land sale. Later there would be time to relax, to ease off, to dabble in politics in Seattle, to build a little weekend hideaway in the country, to manage the Chamber of Commerce, to spend time with his son.

Joe was ready to sell real estate when he was seventeen, but his father persuaded him to go to college. "My mother had a degree, he didn't," Joe says. "He thought that would enable me to better myself economically. My motivation to go to college was more to satisfy his desire than mine."

College was a digression. By his junior year he was paying his tuition by selling soap to supermarket chains. By his senior year he was married. Two years after he graduated he was pulling in $20,000 selling lots and houses for a real estate developer. "I was right on the track, full steam ahead, living his life-style: married, a kid on the way, working hard when the big squeeze was on, making the big deal, then taking a lot of free time off. I felt so lucky.

"I never thought about changing my vocation. I loved it. There was nothing more thrilling to me than closing a real estate deal. The elation, it was a fantastic high. The money was secondary. The kick came in making the deal. I've talked to other people who've said they hate their boss and their job, but not me. I was a workaholic, but I dug it."

Cliff Jones is the former banker who told me that he had felt "naked" when he stopped working. Perhaps he felt so vulnerable because he grew up assuming that working and banking were as natural as breathing—things he'd be doing all his life. He got into finance without thinking. Jones's father was a successful banker in Portland, Oregon. A few days after Jones graduated from college, he got a call from his father's firm. They understood he was going to move from Portland to San Francisco. Would he drop in at the San Francisco branch office for a job interview?

"Hell, I didn't give it much thought," Jones says. "I went to the office, and they gave me the test they give to prospective security salesmen. After I took the test, the personnel guy said, 'What are your goals?' I had no idea. I hadn't looked at different things. He was surprised I didn't come to him with some pretty firm goals: municipal bonds, Oakland office, then run a branch office, and then be promoted. It occurred to me that that was the kind of people he was used to dealing with. I couldn't understand how the fuck people were making these decisions at such a young age."

Jones didn't aggressively seek out the job, but he accepted it. He was about to get married, his father had done very well, he admired his father. "I'm twenty-two, I didn't know what the hell I was supposed to be doing except banking was what I was supposed to be doing." Jones pauses, lights a cigarette, shrugs. "I don't know if that was good or bad. Lots of kids nowadays hang loose, smoke dope, and pick up their welfare checks once a month. I think that's kind of too bad. Maybe you have to learn responsibility first before you can get rid of it."

Jones progressed. Two years with his father's firm, a summer with a Wall Street brokerage, back to California, and three years with Bank of America. The bank was computerizing its operations in the late 1960s, and Jones taught himself what he had to know about computers. He set up a statewide telecommunications system, won a promotion and a raise up to $25,000. By way of commendation, the company awarded him a night on the town.

"Before the big night, I asked around. One guy had a night on the town and went to Howard Johnson's and spent ten bucks. I said to myself, Hey, you can't do that. I thought, fuck, do I go to Vegas? No, that costs too much. So I went to dinner, to a show, and then cocktails at Top of the Mark. I spent about seventy-five dollars. The next day my boss called me in. I thought, I guess I didn't spend enough. He said, 'You were totally out of line, you just spent too much.' I said, 'What do you mean by night on the town? You just ruined my dinner; I'm gonna pay for the sonuvabitch out of my wallet.' Well, he called me back in and said, 'No, we'll pay for it.'

"That was the first time I thought work was bonkers. What the guy said to me, that I spent too much, may have been rational in the corporate frame of reference, but the frame of reference was bonkers. I've worked in places where the partners wanted to make a helluva lot of money and pay the workers as little as they can. Maybe that makes sense in the corporation. To me, that's bonkers."*

The company was very straitlaced, and Jones liked to tease his bosses. He wore his hair a little below the collar line and forgot to wear a tie some days. (Remember: This is the late sixties, and the company was circulating memos on proper dress and tonsorial style.) The company treated him fairly—they put up with his games, they listened to his complaints and sometimes even went along with his recommendations. "I was thinking, I want to get out. I want to step back and watch the world spin." But back of his mind, another thought: "My mother's parents were immigrants. My father was two generations away from that. My father's father was a blacksmith. My parents had to quit school to go to work. Finance was my father's ideal. Finance was the natural thing for me to do. I didn't know what else to do. I'd always been very close to my parents,

---

*This view of management decisions, which appears rational within the corporation but seems irrational in a larger context, was expressed interestingly by Richard Cornuelle, who quit his job as an official with the National Association of Manufacturers. In his book, *De-Managing America*, Cornuelle writes, "All managed institutions are more or less like the Army. Their essential error is that they adapt the plausible principles of engineering to human enterprises, defining roles or tasks for people or institutions which are based on false or incomplete notions or prejudices of what they could be or do. But engineering deals with inert, largely predictable ... material. Management deals with people. And there is an elemental difference between a person and a bar of iron which management must ignore in order to 'work.'"

and I didn't want to do anything overtly to cause them discomfort. So when I thought about quitting, I tried to tell them, 'Just for a while ... Maybe I'll come back.' "

Cliff couldn't bring himself to quit outright. He needed an issue, a clash with the company that his father would understand, that would give Cliff a justification for leaving and would also give him something else he needed if he was going to do the thing right—money, severance pay. Even if he could find the issue, Cliff wasn't sure this was the right thing to do. Walk out. Quit. Leave ten years of work behind him, just because the benevolent, kind, reasonable corporate godfather made him restless.

Sometimes people verbalize forbidden thoughts in passing, and they suddenly become thinkable. One afternoon Cliff is having lunch with an accountant in his office. The accountant is having a technical problem with his work. Cliff makes a few suggestions. The man listens, thanks Cliff for his advice and sympathy, and says, "Cliff, you're an odd. You're playing it even, why don't you accept the fact that you're an odd."

Well, now. So I'm an odd. Why *can't* I accept that. Who says you have to be an even. I mean, I'm not an ax murderer or something. I don't have an irresistible desire to commit incest. So I don't want to work. Cheeeeez. Is that so bad? Is that a crime. Say it a few times: "Cliff Jones, the odd; Cliff Jones, an odd fellow." Rolls right off the tongue.

There's a recession going on and the company is holding back his scheduled salary increase. Cliff walks into his boss's office and asks, When am I going to get my raise?

"Well, we can't do it right now, not until we get past the rough period," the boss says.

"Bullshit," Cliff says. "My work's been fine. You said so. Why do I have to wait?"

"Sorry, we're going to have to wait. Company policy."

"Why don't we cut down my work," Cliff says. "I'll take off every Monday."

His boss laughs. And laughs. And laughs. "Cliff, come on. You don't always have to kid around, do you?"

"No, I'm serious. You can't afford the money—I understand. But I'm entitled. I just won't work as much."

"No, Cliff, we couldn't do that. It'd be a precedent. . ."

"I think we have an impasse," Cliff says, and leaves.

Three weeks later Cliff Jones gets his severance. It is 1970. It will be the last time (as of this writing) he holds down a steady job.

Interior breakpoints.

1967. Cliff Jones gets divorced. The attractive, intelligent woman from Grosse Point, the two attractive, intelligent children, and Cliff Jones are no longer a unit.

1968. Cliff Jones sells his station wagon.

1969. Cliff Jones sells his house, moves into a cheap apartment in San Francisco.

1970. Cliff Jones grows a droopy mustache, wears sun glasses indoors, becomes extremely adept at a barroom game called Liar's Dice, is, in fact, crowned the King of Liar's Dice, and begins to sell a little grass to some of his businessmen friends at the downtown bars, right out of his attaché case.

"It seemed to me that the work ethic was a diversion. Something to keep you busy. Pretty soon you get so many gottas; then the job becomes the most important fuckin' thing in your life. For my parents, finance was a gotta. For me, finance became a gotta. Then marriage became a gotta. After I was divorced, I saw that all of this was a don't-gotta. Divorce was a change. After that I was susceptible to all sorts of changes."

Interior breakpoints.

Joe Browne's father dies, three years after Joe picked up the college diploma his father had wanted so much. Two years later Joe's marriage crumbles. A year later he goes broke in a disastrous real estate deal.

"I contemplated suicide—very seriously," Browne says. "I'd done everything the world said I was supposed to—be good, go out, work your ass off, buy a big house, have a family. And then I lost it all. I didn't have the kids, I didn't want the family, the money was all gone. I asked myself, What am I doing this for? I could build it up again, I thought, if I get over this one. I just wasn't sure I *wanted* to do it again. I thought I'd pass this time and blow my brains out."

Instead, he took his boat out and made for Pago Pago. He got about one hundred miles and turned around. "I had a spiritual experience. It was the most intense the first two days, and then went on for another two weeks, less intensely. It was joy, an ecstasy I'd never experienced. There was no question I couldn't find the answer to. I had zero fear on any level. I had gone from the lowest to the highest. It changed my life."

I wouldn't want to challenge the intensity or meaning of Joe's spiritual "unfolding," since my own spiritual understanding and empathy is minimal. But I suspect that there is also a psychological explanation for his feelings of exultation and fearlessness. He had jumped the track; he was no longer required to live out the legacy of his father's life. Joe was free to establish his own yardsticks for success, achievement, and happiness. "For the first time in my life I wasn't doing the 'right thing,'" he says. "In a way, it was a relief."

In the late sixties, inspired by his spiritual experience, feeling that his life had value, despite his broken marriage, Browne built up his business again. By 1970 he was taking home more than $100,000 a year. He was in love with Ellen, a registered nurse whom he eventually married. He ran a business with more than seventy employees.

That year he met Jones at a sort of spiritual camp meeting. Externally, it was not a match made in heaven. Browne was the accomplished executive, neat, systematic, meticulous. Jones was casual, sardonic, undriven. Browne felt comfortable at a board meeting, closing the big deal. Jones took his pleasure with a well-timed roll of the dice at a friendly saloon. But they liked one another, they shared the same spiritual bent, and they had traveled the same track: father's occupation, early marriage, divorce, and the discovery that there was something out there in the limitless cosmos that shone more brightly than work.

Browne folded his business. Jones was already out. They merged their interests and formed a collaboration in not working. The first act of the corporation was to purchase some land. Their second act was to buy a peacock.

Jones and Browne had once regarded the striving, acquiring, and consuming cycles of work life as their birthright. When they began to dismantle that structure, they experienced a sense of rebirth. Jones and Browne had gone along for years, their future mapped out for them. Now for what seemed to them the first time, they were making a conscious choice. Terrifying in a way because now they had to answer to themselves; the compass that guided them from childhood was missing. They had to find their own direction.

For no one was the breakpoint more difficult than for Norm Walters. Norm didn't go into his father's business. Norm didn't try to simulate his parents' life-style. All he tried to do was live by the social catechism that he was taught at the age of six. It took him thirty-eight years to question it. And doubt crept in in the oddest place—in a cell in the federal penitentiary in Illinois.

Norm Walters: A Killing Business

The street that fronts the waterfront in Long Beach, California, is lined with benches. Old men and women pass the last years of their lives on these benches, soaking up the sun, cooling themselves with cans of Pepsi, holding down their straw coolie hats and golf caps against the tonic breezes coming off the water. Norm Walters is a lot younger than the other people on the street, just turned forty-four, but he, too, is retired.

In the contemporary corporate world, he performed an important function. He was an analyst and evaluator. His supervisors asked him to assess the strengths and weaknesses of the corporation, to recommend promotions and reassignments, to rate the efficiency of department heads and regional managers, and above all, to probe the loyalties of the employees. When he found a weak point, he would sometimes suggest dismissal. Sometimes when the weak point posed a danger to the entire corporate structure, and particularly to members of the board of directors, he would be required to take direct action. To kill.

Since he was eleven, he had been affiliated with organized crime. Since he was eleven, he had used heroin. It was not the work or the life-style you would expect of the young man with a 180 I.Q. who stood before the ark on his bar mitzvah day, drew his tallith around his shoulders, and intoned: "And they shall beat their swords into plowshares."

Although he is out of the business right now, there is still a quality of menace to him. It comes not so much from the slinky grace with which he glides between the tables in a sidewalk café or the soft command in his voice when he orders a glass of wine or the compressed strength in his muscular body or even in the cool emotionless look with which he sizes up the restaurant crowd and the waitress and the busboy. It is his voice, the voice of a detached, disengaged corporate analyst, that scares the hell out of you.

That flat voice: "I always considered myself strictly a professional, a businessman. The type of work I was engaged in was not always killing, don't get that idea. It was a lot broader. I would give evaluations which would determine policy. I would attribute certain values to people and their work effectiveness and recount these values, and from my recounting some decision would be made. You can understand it best if you think of a junior executive at General Motors. He's one of the boys. But he's not really one of the boys. He's only a junior executive in title. He's really a hatchet man. He's an investigator, and there are many of them in business and many of them in organized crime at all levels. What he is is an information seeker. He's seeking out weaknesses, he's looking for opposition, but more precisely, he's looking for any weak link, anything that could hurt the organization. This is his primary function: a glorified troubleshooter, a hatchet man."

The voice is harder now: "I never had to rationalize what I did. I never had to justify my work. Never once in my life did I worry about what I was doing. I have a good reputation to this day. I had a lot of freedom in organized crime. I was told to do something, and how I did it was my own thing. My life depended on how I did it and most of the time I did it very well. I became a very valuable property. I had certain qualities that other men in my line of work lacked.

"From the start I had an incredible ruthlessness. An incredible lack of conscience. And a superior intellect. The intelligence is very important because it allows you to be superb at rationalization. To me it was like: You have to do something, you know how to do this good. I never felt that somebody didn't deserve what I gave to him. Some of the deadliest human beings, they're machines. I was a machine when I was at my best. The thing you have to understand about me was, even when I was a kid, I was different. I established my own rules for living. There were no rules that meant anything to me. The books, the moral commandments that restrained everybody else, didn't restrain me. They were just pieces of paper."

Only once did his voice break. I had pressed him to explain why he was different, why the conventional rules of social behavior did not apply to him. He steepled his fingers and stared at me for a long time. Then, uncertain whether to entrust this scrap of psychohistory to a stranger, he said, "Understand, I'm telling you this because, first, you're a *landsmann*, second, because you're not in the business and you can't hurt me, and third, because I never unloaded this before and maybe it's time." He hesitated and went on, "Go back to when I was six."

The war has just started, Walters's family is living in San Diego, and his father is getting ready to ship out with the merchant marines. Before he goes, he gives his son a gift, a pair of roller skates.

"I cherished those things," he says. "I knew we didn't have any money, and it really meant something my father went out and bought them for me. I carried 'em around my neck when I was walking.

One day I'm standing two doors down from my house and this kid comes up to me and says, 'You're the new kid in the neighborhood. What's your name?'

"I say, 'You wanna be my friend?'

" 'Nah,' he says, 'I don't wanna be your friend.'

" 'You wanna play with my skates?' I don't know no better, see.

" 'Skates, huh,' he says. 'Yeah, give 'em to me'. He takes the skates. Throws one down, hits me on the side of the head with the other one. I still have the scar.

"I go running back into the house. I was terrified. I still remember the fear and what it did to me. I tell my mother. She's goin' crazy. She's holdin' me, motherin' me, babyin' me. My father comes home. I say, 'The kid stole my skates.'

"My father says, 'Norm, what happened? What did you do?'

"I said, 'I ran.'

"He says, 'Why did you run?'

" 'Because he hurt me.'

"And he says, 'Yeah, I know, but why did you run?' I couldn't understand what he was trying to say. I'm six years old. I stopped and didn't say anything.

"My father had tears in his eyes which affected me because my father is a very stolid person. He never shows emotion, which is why my father and I never had a love relationship. Feeling but not love. He says, 'What are you goin' to do about the skates?'

"I thought, 'Me? Why don't you do somethin' about it?' 'What can I do?' I say.

" 'You can go get your skates.' he says. 'I think you better go get 'em. If you want your skates, then it's worthwhile to go get 'em.'

" 'But he's goina beat me up.'

"My father says, 'There's nothin' in this life that's worthwhile that comes easy. The only way he's gonna beat you up is if you let'm beat you up. If you can't figure that out, you're not gonna get your skates back. Now why don't you get your skates.'

"I walk down the block. Go up to the kid and say, 'Give me my skates, my father said you gotta give me my skates.' The kid, he's eleven, he laughs at me, and he had this brother, a giant, blond Prussian kid, fifteen, sixteen years old, and they're all laughin' at me. We're standing in the backyard of this carriage house and there are some bricks on the ground. I grab a brick and hit'm with it and pick up my skates and run, fast as I can run. The other guy's cold cocked. He's laid out. You talk about fear—that was *real* fear. Yeah, I was scared. But I was so proud of myself. And I hold up the skates to my dad and says, 'Got 'em. See, I got 'em.' And I tell him how I got 'em.

"The kids were right outside the house, right outside the door. He says, 'Do you think that's smart? Bringing those people here, havin' 'em chase you to the house. What are you gonna do about it?' He just put it all on me. My father made me go out to those two giants and made me tell 'em to get off my property. I knew later what my father was trying to do.

"When I told 'em, it was so amazing to them, they left. They just turned around and left. Understanding fear and seeing myself overcome it was what I lived with all my life. The idea, it can only hurt you if you let it."

This is his inheritance. The belief that nothing worthwhile comes easy. To survive, you have to dominate by fear and force. In the end you can depend only on yourself, you make no lasting alliances, you ask nobody for help, you are beholden to no one. His very solitariness made him a high-priced piece of merchandise. In the organization, they learned that when you gave Norm Walters an assignment, he carried it out quickly and efficiently, unrestrained by fear, outwardly untroubled by questions of conscience. Norm Walters was valuable because he had no interior restraints.

After his dad shipped out with the merchant marines, his mother shipped him out to live with an aunt and uncle in the shadow of the West Side Highway in Manhattan. Nine people living in a fourth-floor walk-up railroad flat. Most of the time he spent on the street; at night there wasn't much to do in the flat. "My uncle was a bricklayer, a classic kind of alcoholic, but who was able to maintain his job. Every single night he'd get quietly smashed and he didn't give a damn about nothin'. He'd sit in his chair and go to sleep with a grin on his face. He was like a blob."

The street had more to offer. "By the time I was ten, I was in the street, hustlin', taking care of business, whatever. This is how I got involved with organized crime. Everybody I knew was into somethin': drugs, prostitution, stealin' cars, boostin' stores. The big things were prostitution and dope. I started running bags for a dealer, a white guy, in the neighborhood. He'd give me a paper bag full of stuff and there were tags on each one, double wrapped like a big cigar. At twenty-five dollars a bag it could keep a person loaded for two days——the dope was that good those days. My friend Iggie and I were both runnin' stuff, and one day he said, 'I wonder what the stuff's like.' So we found out, right? I poked my head into the wax-paper bag and snorted, and this stuff's so fine, it blew my head off. I was eleven. Before my twelfth birthday, I had a giant habit.

"The dealer I was runnin' for found out we were beatin' his bags. So he pulls me around the corner one day and throws me on the ground and steps on my hands." Walters leans across the table and shows me his hands. His knuckles are like chunks of anthracite. "That's how they got that way. He just broke my hands. Busted them. Funny thing is I didn't feel bad. He was only teachin' me a lesson. It wasn't unusual. It happens all the time."

From then on Walters would treat the setbacks, the threats of violence, the beatings, the stretches in the can, as the price he paid for screwing up. You screw up, you pay. Justice and injustice, fairness and unfairness, didn't enter into it. When he was fifteen, he got his parents to sign a form that said he was eighteen and old enough to enlist in the marines. "Korea was a lot of noise, a lot of blood. I thought I was a tough guy and that was the toughest job I could get. I got smashed in the knee once and some internal injuries, but the dope got me through. I couldn't have done five years in Korea without dope.

"The time I spent in Korea was as close to flying on my own wings as I've ever been. I was in the Raiders, like the Green Berets in Vietnam. I operated independently. I didn't have anybody sayin' to me, 'Set up that murder over there,' blah, blah. I did it on my own initiative—I had to decide how. I never questioned it. It was just an extension of the street as far as I was concerned. Somebody was gettin' down on somebody else and that's all there was to it. I kept that same mentality when I got out. I had no trade, except one. And they taught me that in the service."

People who knew of Walters's work in New York, Chicago, L.A., San Francisco, and Detroit describe him as "invisible." In the thirteen years he worked for one criminal organization or another, he was the businessman in the gray worsted suit carrying the expensive attaché case. He was careful to have only the most innocuous conversations on planes or in hotel lobbies. He was quiet, serious, and polite. "When I was in a situation where there was a possibility of something happening or I was supposed to be taking a look at a certain individual, there was nobody I could talk to. I had to be almost a nonentity. Everybody sees you, everybody knows you, but nobody knows you, and they can't exactly remember you after you're gone because you never really said anything, you never made an impression on anybody at all. Maybe that was the hardest part, to sit back and not affect the situation I'm in. To be a shadow."

It paid off. At his peak in the early 1960s, after a five-year apprenticeship as a ranger with the marines in Korea, after he was connected up, he was drawing $140,000 a year. He was married, had one son, and they lived in an eight-room house in a suburb of San Bernardino, California. "Everybody thought I was a good guy, a professional. I assumed that air too. I kept up with the Joneses. Mowin' the lawn, I even did that myself. The whole bit: plantin' a garden every year. Joe Suburbia." His wife was an X ray technician at a nearby hospital. They had met when he went into the hospital for an ulcer operation. "Gettin' an ulcer," he says, "wasn't that kind of a badge of success for a businessman in the sixties?"

His invisibility extended to his wife. For most of the two years they lived together, she did not know exactly what he did for a living. Something to do with managing investments. She knew he was good to his father; he put up money when his father's business was in trouble. "You gotta understand, this woman was so upright, so honest, all that bullshit, the United Crusade for Christ and that crap, that she never bothered to look. Women are willing to put up with anything if they're comfortable, if they don't have to worry about the dogs at the door all the time. They don't ask too many questions. I married her because she was pregnant at the time. I thought it was the right thing to do. Then she started throwin' all of the middle-class bullshit stuff at me. 'We have to go to the opera just to go, to be seen.' I'd enjoy the opera, but not just to go. I didn't enjoy Wagner, but if Wagner is at the opera, she'd say, 'We have to go to see Wagner.' To hell with that, just to be seen. At the end I told her she was just a dumb cow, and I kicked her out. Don't get me wrong. I established a trust fund for the kid. I'm not irresponsible."

Three times in his career he might have had second thoughts: once, already described, on the Lower West Side of Manhattan, once in the hotel elevator in the L.A. Hilton, once on a suicide job.

Five years after he's out of Korea he's on the eighth floor of the Los Angeles Hilton. He's standing in the elevator, it's two-thirty in the morning, and propped up against the elevator wall next to him is a dead man. "It was a freak, really. It should have been very, very clean, a very ordinary workday. It wasn't. The elevator door opened up and the night security guard is standing there starin' at me. It doesn't look too kosher. You gotta understand, the average person can't pull this off because of his fears, his lack of experience, his lack of ability, and his lack of prescience. But immediately I go into my routine.

"I acted like I was livin' in the hotel. I was just a guest who got on the elevator and didn't notice the guy. I didn't know if he'd had a heart attack or was just drunk. The dick and I looked at the guy, and the dick said, 'Well, I think he's been hurt.'

"I said, 'Oh.'

"He said, 'Yeah, in fact I think he's been shot.'

"I said, 'Oh, my God!' And I'm all outraged, shocked, scared. 'Is there anything I can do?'

"He said, 'There's a phone right down at the end of the hall. Why don't you call the desk and tell them we got trouble here.'

"I said, 'Okay, but who are you?' He gave me a name and showed me a badge. I actually went to the phone; he was watchin'. Dialed. As soon as I talked to the desk, pow, I was down the stairs. That's what I mean by manipulation, handlin' people."

He did have a thought as he drove down Wilshire Boulevard. "Suppose the day comes when I can't pull it off, when I sweat or stutter, or there's a little blood on my jacket, what then?" But he was able to shrug it off, drown it out, by turning the music up on his car radio. "I was on the top of the heap. When you think you're at the top, you don't look elsewhere. I might feel just a split second of ambivalence, but not more. How many people have the direction to do that? Even if I was thinking that way then, which I really wasn't, who could I talk to about it? When you live in a snake pit with snakes, if they wake up, you might be in trouble. Show an inkling of weakness in that world, and weakness can be fatal."

The third time, the suicide job, happened when the organization was split in Chicago, and a consultant, a professional evaluator, was called in to resolve the conflict. "I'm not a side man, I don't get into politics," Walters says. "I wasn't a soldier. Nobody owned me. They owned me but they didn't own me. I was just common property. After the job was drawn out for me, in my estimation, I told the man it was almost impossible to do. A suicide job, but I'm not into suicide, right? I told him, 'This is bullshit. I don't know who the harebrained asshole is who drew this up, but this is wrong. Nobody is gonna make it out of this.'

"He said, 'I was the harebrained asshole who drew it up. Let me tell you something, punk'— that's as far as he got." Walters pushed his thumb into the guy's Adam's apple. "He went right up against the wall. 'Tell these monkeys in here, back off. Anybody in this room makes a move, he's dead.' He croaks, 'Back off.'

"I said, 'If you ever talk to me like that again, I'll kill you. I do your work, I'm paid a lot of money for it. I'm a professional, the reason I'm working here is because I'm a professional, I don't need this kind of shit. I don't care if you drew this thing up, it's suicidal. I'm not goin' to do it.'

" 'Fine,' he says.

"I ask him, 'Do you understand that?'

" 'Yeah,' he says. 'Yeah, it's okay.' "

It wasn't exactly okay. That night as Walters was eating in a restaurant on the Gold Coast, four guys beat him to a pulp. "The one guy, he says, 'This is to give you a message. Never, ever forget who and what you are. Who you're responsible to. Who you have to answer to.'

"When they fixed up the broken bones I got my backs too. I made an awful lot of waves. A lot of people ended up not people because of this. I wasn't dysfunctionally angry, I was calculatedly angry. Much later I talked to the guy who did it to me. He told me his organization was very badly damaged because of what I did. He said there was nothing he could do, outside of offing me. And he couldn't do that because I was merchandise. I was valuable property. I was an investment to more people than just him."

The get-backs weren't enough. The idea that Norm Walters was nothing but expensive merchandise bothered him. "In any type of employment there's the buyin' and sellin' of people. In my case, the organization was the purchaser and I was the purchased. Even though I always thought of myself as an independent, I realized I was chattel or something; I couldn't choose my existence, that made me sick. How can a man rationalize that?"

He was now in his late thirties, he had served two stretches in prison, he had been using heroin for almost twenty-five years, and he started thinking about retirement. In his line of work, there was more to it than writing a letter that said, I resign, and collecting his pension. "I was concerned about how I was just all of a sudden gonna disappear. Because that's exactly what I would have to do, assume a whole new identity. It's not possible to retire and live at any visible level. Most people wait too long; they overextend themselves. I was very aware of that; I was always testing to see if I might be in any subtle jeopardy at all. All I wanted to do was retire to some small town, buy some property, semisecluded, no neighbors. That's what I had in mind. But I waited too long."

When you want to get out but stay in, when your mind's alert but your reflexes are slowing, when you start to think about what you're doing, the right and wrong of it, you get into trouble. He did. There was a bank holdup—"I was losing control, it wasn't professional at all, I was acting out of fear"—and a mob shooting he wasn't involved with but which brought the heat down on him. Next a sensational prison escape and the substitution of booze for heroin and the revocation of his parole and back to Joliet. There, in Joliet of all places, options opened up.

One day a group of sociologists visited the prison and interviewed him. He asked them if he could write a couple of articles for a sociological journal—one on the prison system, the other on heroin addiction. The second one titillated academia. "The common myth is heroin makes you dysfunctional. What I was writing was that it doesn't have to.

"It's the type of drug and how pure it is, the physiological makeup of the person, his social and cultural background, all those interesting things that make a human being an individual. I had to limit my heroin use to function. If I had to do a job, say it was a kind of a hairy job, a cowboy job, like a hit, I'd say, This is gonna be a tough one. I've geezed an hour ago, I'm gonna do this thing at seven tonight. If I geeze in another hour, it'll carry me, and I know from using it for years it's not gonna influence me. It's only gonna keep me straight. Then after the job, I come home and lay down, if I wanna lay back. But I don't lay back in front of the job. The job comes first. I have to function."

The articles created a demand for more articles, for speeches before criminologists and penologists. He earned a B.A. in prison and an M.A. in sociology after he was released. On the campus where he was a graduate student at forty-one, he met a woman who was teaching history whom he later married and who left him when the booze took over. The booze bought him a rotted liver and the surgery for his liver bought him a morphine addiction and the morphine bought him a revocation of his parole.

In the summer of 1976 Norm Walters was not working. He was living in Long Beach in a rooming house, attending AA meetings every Thursday night, and spending a lot of afternoons on the waterfront benches. Although he didn't have a job, he had obviously made some progress in the past eighteen months. He showed me a photograph taken three years before. It was a snapshot of a man who looked about fifty. The man I was talking to looked his age, which was forty-three. He had reached the breakpoint, but the next step was unclear. A few hours before we talked he had met with a local organization guy who offered him a job fronting a legitimate mob-controlled business. He was dangling. "In the last two years I've had to make up for the thirty years that came before," he says. "The process has been building and destroying, building and destroying. I'm afraid all the time. Just disoriented. I've had all these conflicting things: You're an academician, a prof, you're a dope fiend, a boozer, an excon, an exkiller. Push-pull. I don't know which way to go. So I'm trying to lay down. Before I make a move, I have to understand why I'm afraid, fear is so new to me."

And so old. The last time he really felt fear was when he was six years old and his father taught him how to beat it back. It was a costly lesson. Before he takes the next step, he has to discover what changed in him when he was six. "I proved myself then," he says. "I proved I was a man. Now, I gotta find out how to do that all over again."

When the family inheritance goes, something has to replace it. Something has to replace Betty Tallgood's farm which was the embodiment of her parents' faith and hopes. A new life-style has to replace the life-style set by the banking business of Cliff Jones's father and the real estate business of Joe Browne's father. Something has to provide the same coherence, discipline, and sense of responsibility that Sam Meyers enjoyed in his second home at the magazine. Norm Walters has to develop a new persona, a new social system to go along with his new interest in academia.

Not working becomes for these people a search for focus, for an organizing purpose. They may engage in a series of short-term commitments or develop one overarching principle. But they need something to replace the ruins of the family structure. Without a new focus, not working can be tough sledding; self-indulgence and pleasure seeking is sustaining for a while, but the face in the mirror keeps demanding: What am I? Most of us must eventually find an answer.

THE QUESTION OF PURPOSE

What am I? It isn't enough to say: I'm a nurse; I'm a bill collector; I'm a statistician. Lucille Roberts, David Solomon, and Carl Reiter want something more. They want, expect, demand that their work have some social purpose. They reached their breakpoint when their personal ethics and morality collided with the single-purpose ethic of profit and loss.[1] For many years they had suppressed their rising indignation at the social indifference of their employers. Then their consciences attacked; they attempted to introduce an element of social awareness in their jobs, found it was not possible, and quit.

We may think that it's a luxury to ask whether our work has a purpose aside from the salary, but in the 1970s, following an era shaped by social action, many Americans were asking that question. In 1973 the National Commission on Productivity commissioned a national survey to find out what workers thought about efforts to increase productivity. Seventy percent of the respondents said that the people who benefited most from increased production were stockholders. Almost the same percentage said the prime beneficiaries were corporate managers. Only 20 percent felt that employees "benefitted a lot." The commission wrote:

> The word "productivity" is in bad odor. . . . While there is unanimity among economists and policymakers that productivity growth is the key to our economic strength—the source of jobs and prosperity—most Americans, according to the polls, believe it is not they, the wage earners, who benefit from productivity gains, but rather stockholders or those who receive the profits generated by productivity growth. . . . Exhortations on the value of hard work do little to improve public understanding of the importance of productivity increases to national growth and often add to the atmosphere of mistrust.[2]

I think the commission may have misread the results of its survey. On the one hand, workers were saying that if I work harder and produce more, I ought to earn more; I ought to be rewarded for increased productivity. But I think they were also wondering about the social value of making more windup dolls. When sociologist Craig Little was interviewing out-of-work engineers and technicians in 1972, here's what two of them told him:

> I wasn't happy there. Actually, I'm somewhat content with my present situation. I've had a chance to do a lot of thinking about national issues since I was laid off. (Design engineer; previous salary $12,300; age 51; unemployed 16 months; wife working.)

> I was in a rut—going 'round and 'round. It was hard to move up in that situation. I'm devoting my life right now to working to implement my political philosophy (described as "very conservative"). I'm spending my time lobbying for bills in the state legislature. I want to deal with bigger issues that I could in the engineering job. (Senior electrical engineer; previous salary $14,000; age 46; unemployed 10 months; wife not working.)[3]

Little told me, "Although they could get into the work in the technical sense, they could stand back from the work, a sizable number of them, and say, 'I had an interesting time today, I had an interesting little technical problem to play with, but what in hell was that all about? I was building a missile to blow people up.' "

When people question their purpose in working, I don't think it's in a narrow ideological sense. Most of those I interviewed did not want to go out and implement their political philosophy; they were not explicitly protesting the product they were manufacturing. They were simply announcing: There's more to work than a paycheck. To work day in, day out, for twenty, thirty, forty years, you have to believe in what you're doing. It must have some purpose.

If work is part of a belief system, people often are prepared to make great sacrifices. When there is no discernible purpose in an individual's work, apart from increasing productivity, the smallest complaint—too much mayonnaise in the cafeteria tuna fish—becomes a major problem (and justification for a little industrial sabotage).

If the National Commission on Productivity is confused about why American workers aren't producing more for the greater good, they might consult Bob Schrank at the Ford Foundation.

"The most interesting kind of work for me was work that involved causes," he says. "When I was a union organizer, I worked much harder than when I worked in a factory, but I was part of a crusade. Crusaders always work hard. They marched across Europe hundreds of times because they believed in something. In Israel people had this fantastic belief. The Mormons had that when they built Salt Lake City. I think belief is your great motivator. I saw people who believed in what they were doing work tirelessly, twenty-four hours a day, seven days a week, year in year out, and they were happy doing it because they were working for something they believed. Making widgets, pushing paper—it's hard to believe in that. It doesn't have to be political work to inspire belief. Once there were salesmen who believed in their product the way Vince Lombardi believed in his football team. The products motivated these guys. Where's the belief system today? It's been replaced by a kind of cynicism. I'm only working to consume; I'm only working to get more junk.

"I don't even care about the work. It's just a means to an end; it's not an end in itself. When work becomes just a means, not something you believe in, if you can get the stuff without working—the junk—it's all to the better. You're ahead of the game."

The commission is invited to consult Carl Reiter, Lucille Roberts, or David Solomon. They all produced for their employers. But not anymore.

Carl Reiter: Repossessing

Carl Reiter and his wife and their three children, who are still at home, live four blocks from where he grew up. When Carl was a teenager in Greensburg, a German-Irish working-class suburb of Pittsburgh, it was right that you stayed close to your family and people of your own kind. It was right that you got married and had children. It was right that you got a job and you stuck at it and you supported your family. It was right that your wife stayed home and took care of the house and raised the kids.

The house looks right. The brick front and the picture window. There's a 1972 Ford parked in the driveway. The refrigerator is full. The kids are growing up: The youngest boy plays Little League baseball, the second child, a girl, is in high school, the third child is a freshman in college and she's getting very good grades, the fourth is a boy who's working, and the fifth is a social worker. But things have not turned out exactly the way Carl Reiter and his father, a cop, and his mother, a housewife, thought they would.

In the last twelve years, Carl Reiter, now forty-seven, has worked only sporadically; there have been periods of four and five years when he hasn't worked at all. In the Reiter household his wife, Maya, is the breadwinner. The oldest daughter, who has moved into her own home, has a baby. She is not married. The baby's father is a black man who is under indictment for pushing cocaine. Carl's oldest son works for a lumber company when he wants to. He's not sure he wants to work at all.

The Reiters are an attractive couple, easygoing, articulate, open, and very hospitable. I was very comfortable sitting in their kitchen, eating the meatballs and spaghetti for lunch, driving with Maya to her job in the accounting office of Bethlehem Steel, popping beers into the night with Carl. I wanted things to turn out right for them in the end, because up to now it hasn't been easy.

At first their lives fit the pattern. Carl went to Catholic grade school, public high school, served in the army for two years toward the end of World War II, and then returned home where he met Maya. He was twenty-two, in his junior year at a Catholic college, and Maya was seventeen and working as a secretary when they got married. After leaving college in the middle of his senior year, he served his work apprenticeship at an electronics

manufacturing company. The salary wasn't much
but it was enough to put a down payment on a
house. Then he was hired by the Progress Finance
Co. where he worked for the next thirteen years.
The starting pay was $39.75 a week. "I was happy
with what he was doing," Maya remembers, "because I thought *he* was happy with what he was doing. In my mind I thought there was a need for
finance companies," Maya said. "There are people
who need money and can't be served by banks. I
thought Carl was doing a service. Carl, I knew,
wanted to do a service."

"Yeah, I told her that," Carl says. "That was my
feeling the first ten years. There's a need for this
company. I started out by going on the road and
chasing slow accounts. If a guy owed five hundred
dollars the idea was to get him to come into the office and talk to the boss. The boss was supposed to
be this genius type who's gonna solve this guy's
whole problem. Show him how he's gonna get out
of whatever he's in. The boss could refer him to a
job or show him how to get on welfare. It was a
game more than anything else. Sure, there were
some guys who were trying to beat you out of the
money. But there was the type who did work
steady, who could never get out of the hole. He'd
make three or four payments and come in with a little problem. The boss would renew the loan. The
guy'd never get out of the hole. The boss had good
dollar sense."

"These were hard times for us," Maya said. "Carl
never came home."

"My first year the boss told me: We work hard
and we play hard. Playing hard wasn't that hard to

accept. A woman we'd go out to collect money from, maybe she was a con woman. Your boss would tell you, she's a no-good bastard. But when you talked to her you knew that wasn't really true. You did a hard job, it seemed thankless. And when the day was over, ah, the hell with it, let's go over to Jack's and have a beer. Funny thing is, when we were drinking all we talked about was business. It was like we were separatists, we had our own separate world."

Maya said, "I thought life was not too good. It took me a lot of courage to ask him if he would come home for dinner one night a month. We weren't a family. He played more than necessary. I never did bring it up, it was easier to go on."

He went on, not really questioning the business, not really questioning the game. After almost ten years with the finance company, he became the branch collection manager. With the title came the job of repossessing the property of people who defaulted on their loans. "I'd go out and see car dealers and get their business. That was the real boozy, entertaining job. We'd threaten people all over the place, but never, hardly ever, do it. I hated to think about that, the threatening business. I wanted people to like me, to like the company, to pay their money, and to smile. That was my goal. For ten years I thought that society needed something between the loan sharks and the banks. They never told me we were loan shark number two."

What doubts crept in were dismissed because he was making progress, making more money. They were living in a larger house. They had three children and a fourth on the way. Carl, as collection manager, had assistants who chased most of the accounts, which allowed him to come home earlier. The work was still something of a game. The time the old lady chased him around the apartment with a broom when he threatened to repossess her television set was a joke. The guys in the office roared when he told them. Strange. When he finished the last beer of the night and pulled on his pajamas and slid under the covers next to Maya, he didn't think it was so funny.

The family of migrant workers, that wasn't so funny either. A husband and his wife and their five kids. They were working on an apple farm seventy miles away. Carl had sent one of the guys in the office to chase them. It's four in the afternoon and Carl has been out with one of the local auto dealers and the first thing he sees when he gets out of the elevator are cardboard suitcases and laundry bags piled up in the hall outside his office.

"Charley, my assistant, comes in with this godawful story about this migrant camp and this family. The slavery and bullshit that went on out there. He wants me to hear the story from them." For the next two hours Carl watches the black man in overalls, sitting in front of his desk, clenching and unclenching his fingers, watches his wife and their kids all crammed together on the couch. The guy tells him how the whole family was trucked up from South Carolina, how he was promised so much money and hadn't got any. The worst thing the farm owner tells the family they owe him for room and board.

Carl listens and listens and finally he gets up and tells his assistant to grab the office manager before he leaves and borrow $150 from him. Carl hits the assistant for another $20, and he throws in enough from his own pocket to pay for bus fare and food money for the family so they can get back to South Carolina. Carl leans back in his chair after they've all gone and thinks: *Ah, shit, people aren't gonna be helped by loaning them money. If you're gonna help these people, you gotta help them get out of whatever the hell they're in.* "That was the beginning of my thinking," he would say later. "My thinking about getting out of this business."

Business deteriorated. The collections started to pile up. Company headquarters in Philadelphia was getting a little irritated. "I began to talk to the customers more. They became people, instead of part of the game they had been for ten years. I let the other guy in the office do all the collecting, and he'd make mistakes. I couldn't tell him what to do. I couldn't do it anymore myself." The word kept coming in from Philadelphia, sometimes low key, sometimes with more menace behind it: "Carl, you gotta cut this delinquency down."

"I wasn't a good candidate for the job anymore," Carl says. "I knew that."

He had always been healthy. Hardly missed a day in the first ten years. Now he was struck by a series of illnesses.[4] First it was a strep throat that wouldn't go away. It put him in the hospital for eight days. He ran a high fever. His throat hurt like hell. But the doctor couldn't find anything wrong with him. His boss would come to visit him every afternoon. "He was trying to find out how long I'd be in the hospital. He was always talking shop. At that point I didn't want to talk shop too much. In the hospital

I really had a chance to read a book once in a while; for me it was something different. I kept thinking, All my boss is interested in is getting me out of the hospital and working again."

Carl went back to work, but he wasn't feeling well. He'd get dizzy in the office. Then at night the chest pains. Sharp. Shooting across his chest. "I thought I was getting a heart attack. I thought I was dying." The doctor who couldn't find anything wrong with his throat couldn't find anything wrong with his chest, except that maybe he cut down on the Luckies. The pains were sharper. His workday became shorter. He would leave at two or three in the afternoon. The headquarters man from Philadelphia was showing up in Pittsburgh more frequently.

Carl Reiter will never forget the last time. "Out in the field, he was the kinda guy you think of when you think of headquarters. A cutthroat. This day the first thing he does when he comes into the office is take off his jacket and pull his shirt out of his pants and loosen up his tie. He starts chewing my ass out about everything. He keeps doing that for a day and a half. I could see, he wants me out of here. But he can't fire me, he can't fire a guy who's been working here for twelve years. Not without a real reason. But he's gonna push me out. I didn't need that much of a push. I thought the business world stunk. The world itself was rotten. The loan business was all a lot of bullshit. Putting the arm on everybody while you're smiling. Rotten."

Maya didn't want him to quit. She wanted him to wait and collect his bonus and accumulated commissions. He tried to go along with her. One Wednesday morning it fell apart.

"I got dressed as usual," he remembers now, his voice dropping almost to a whisper as he talks about that morning. "I went into the bedroom and all of a sudden I found myself sitting on the edge of the bed, crying like crazy. And then I knew—ah, shit, this is it."

He called Philadelphia and got through to a vice-president of the company. "I'm going to resign," he said, measuring each word. "Get somebody in here to take over."

The vice-president said, "Look, Carl, what do you want? We haven't got another branch to send you to."

"It's not that. I'm quitting. Period."

"So, what other company are you going to?"

It took a few minutes more for him to persuade the Philadelphia honcho that he was sincere, he just wanted out. When he got the message across, the company moved quickly. The next morning two guys from Philadelphia were there. They had cleaned out the safe, stashed the checkbooks. "Things move fast when a guy quits in the finance business. They want to make sure he doesn't write himself one last check. These guys were all smiles and happy. Carl, we want you to know you're gonna get your severance."

He went home and took a long nap. "When I woke up, I felt like I was in another world." What Carl didn't know then, what Maya and the kids didn't know, was that he had exchanged one kind of hell for another.

Lucille Roberts: The Cost of Indignation

Lucille Roberts is a gutsy lady. She has fought two major battles in her life. The first time she had to overcome her husband's fierce opposition to her working. The second time she had to overcome her own insecurity about stopping work.

Her first test came in 1962 when her husband lost his job as a salesman for an export-import firm. It was a terrible blow to him. He was a graduate of Harvard, the descendant of a long line of Boston Brahmins. They were living in Newton, Massachusetts then and their youngest child was five. "He was a sensitive guy. He had been with this company for fifteen years and had built up this territory.

"He had no illusions about the work. Some of the customers were pretty bad. We also had to entertain them. I remember a thousand martinis and me turning off the oven and taking the steak out and putting the hollandaise sauce back in again. I would also be briefed on who was coming, and Tom would more or less figure out their views on everything. Certain subjects, naturally politics, were taboo. With a big company representative you were immediately stamped a pinko if you opened your mouth about anything. Both of us realized it was a terrible dichotomy. We had strong feelings about situations, and yet we had to put on a mask with the people he worked for."

The first few weeks that Tom was out of work, he felt relieved. Then he had to go into town to collect unemployment insurance. It was an industrial town and he felt he was the only gentleman in the line.

The rest were bums. As a Bostonian, this hurt his pride terribly.

"Every day he'd go up to his room with a gallon of wine and lower the shades and chugalug. I can't remember a worse winter in my life. I begged him to let me go back to work. I had worked when we were first married, as a lab technician. I said, 'I'll scrub floors, do anything, we need the money.' He said, 'No, no. If you do that you'll just be kicking me in the teeth.' He felt completely purposeless, and I had the feeling he wanted to drag me right down in the same mess. And I didn't want to be dragged down. Also, he wanted me around to help bolster his morale when he wanted help. If I had a job, he'd have been completely alone in the house and he'd have to take care of the youngest child. I said, 'This is stupid. We don't have to worry about a baby-sitter for Hank now that you're home. You can know more about him as he's growing up.' He said, 'No way.'

"There were times when he was out of work that I wondered whether we should have been married at all. The crisis brought out tremendous differences in both of us. We seemed incompatible. Finally we reached a point of absolute stasis, and I said, 'Hell, I've got to do something for myself.' And I did: I got a job." Two days after she started working, he found himself a job teaching in an elementary school.

She continued to work at a variety of jobs, but primarily as a lab technician in hospitals and in laboratories owned by groups of doctors. Her husband died when he was forty-six. She was in her early forties. Social security, combined with his veterans' benefits, her salary, and some financial help from his family enabled the family to get by. In 1971 she sold her house in Newton and moved the family west to California.

The income Lucille's work brought in was vital, but that wasn't her primary reason for holding a job. "I was always looking for a sense of community, a genuine feeling of service in my work." In her youth a furniture factory closed down around her father in Grand Rapids. He was out of work for two years. The family had to move out of their apartment to a thirty-dollar-a-month flat two blocks from the railroad tracks. Her mother, who had been a secretary before she got married, took a job working for a real estate agency. "My father would come home after a fruitless day looking for a job and would either sit down and play the piano, and he'd play as a form of self-therapy, or else he'd be so tired he'd go up to his room and take a nap before dinner. But he never lost his spirit. Tell the truth, everybody was in the same boat, and that created a sense of cohesiveness. Nobody paid a baby-sitter. The neighbors just automatically did this for each other. When somebody was sick, neighbors cooked dishes and brought them in. We had a telephone. Maybe it was the only one on the whole block. The only reason we had it was my father kept thinking he'd get calls for work. But everybody used our phone. I remember running up and down the street with messages.

"That gave me security, but the greatest security was within our family. My father came from a big family, they all lived in Grand Rapids. On Sunday afternoon we'd go to visit his parents. We'd sit at the dining room table, and the dishes would be gleaming, the table looked so beautiful. They weren't rich, they were actually very humble. But the talk was gay and people laughed and everybody seemed concerned with each other. It was such a supportive family that I felt there was nothing that could happen in the outside world that could hurt me.

"I really only found that spirit once." Lucille was twenty-four, just married, and working in the laboratory of a public hospital in New York. Tom hadn't objected to her working then because they were just starting out and they didn't have children. It was 1948. "I can't remember a person who worked at that hospital who didn't really care about the patients. The whole liberal idea, the fight against any form of injustice, touched us all. We all had that bond in common. We would bring in things from our houses for the patients. One old lady refused to have her bedding replaced. She stuck by her guns and we all supported her. One administrator there was a typical bureaucrat. But there were so many young, eager doctors, who were alive and with it, so when the administrator passed down some stupid decision, everybody would oppose it. We made him the odd man out. We really had an open management at that hospital, but we didn't know what that meant. The sad thing's I never found a job with that same spirit. And it seems to get progressively less so."

Many jobs followed that one. She typed stories on a small-town newspaper, worked as an administrative assistant for a research consultant firm, and helped out in a community daycare center. Most of her paid employment was as a laboratory technician at various medical facilities. At the same time she was raising four kids, watching one become an auto mechanic, another a bank teller, a third go through a series of nervous breakdowns, and the fourth become a waiter in a restaurant in Monterey. And through all this time, with each job, she got closer to her boiling point.

She was working as a secretary in a plastics plant. When the workers struck, she was classified as management and told to stay on the job. For the first few weeks of the strike, she stuck it out—she needed the money. "One morning I got tired of passing the picket line. I overslept and picked up the phone and said the hell with it. I told my boss, 'I'm not coming in to work today or any day.' He was dumbfounded. He thought he was doing me a favor keeping me on the job, and he'd tripled my work load."

The hospital came next. "I was working thirty-six-hour shifts. Thirty-six hours straight. You get to eat at the end of twelve hours, and then after a while you were beyond being tired or anything else. You might drink iced tea or have another cup of coffee—and keep going, because that's all you can do. Finally I refused to work the third shift in a row. 'Look,' I said, 'let some young kid run around—I've had it. I'm going home; I don't need the money.' This set a precedent, and after that nobody would work the third shift. Then they began to reorganize the hours and shifts. I suspect they had kept these hours because the chief tech liked to work those hours and make the extra money. He and his assistant—both of them were pushing years, neither of them were progressing at all—wanted the system for the money. But we refused.

"How many people died because of that system I don't know. I hate to think about it, but here, I'm afraid, is a typical example. A Saturday morning I pick up a blood count for a guy and it's one third normal. He had a weird blood type, so immediately I'm on the phone calling the state police and they get him two units, but it's too late. He had begun to go down hill and he was dead in a matter of hours. The thing about it was they knew he had a low hemoglobin when he was admitted on Thursday—the lab reported it out—and nobody did anything about it. Nothing was done for that man. The lab was absolved because we had reported the low blood count, but what good did that do the patient? He was dead. How can you expect any kind of communication when the techs, the interns, the nurses are walking around like zombies, half asleep."

The lab was the next job. It was a private operation run by a group of doctors near Monterey. The good thing about the job was she could drive to work in less than ten minutes. There wasn't much else good you could say about it. "Numero uno: They wanted to make money. The crazy thing was that at least once a day I had some free patient—a family member of one of the doctors or office staff who got written off no matter what the test was. The doctors'd come to you and say, 'We didn't make as much money as we made last month.' I kept a daily log, and I'd say, 'I can tell you why,' and point out the names of all the free patients. The whole thing was just a money machine—run through as many patients as you can every day in as little time as possible. Order as many tests as you think the traffic will bear. Discourage Medicaid and Medicare because they can't collect as much. In general it's a racket. In the med-tech business the patient is really being screwed. All they want is their money.

"The summer I went to work in the lab, by eleven in the morning the temperature would be over ninety, and there was no air conditioning. One aide had already written to the state and said, 'This is a really bad situation. The reagents are deteriorating; certain tests are definitely thrown off by the temperature.' The state inspector arrived, wiping the sweat off his brow. And this cute little aide goes up to him and says, 'You know, this is one of our cooler days.' He said, 'Ohhhh.' He recommended that the place be air-conditioned immediately. A month went by and they made measurements and Mickey Moused it up and nothing happened. I fired off another letter to the inspector. The next day a few ladders appeared and a few holes were poked in the ceiling. But it took a total of six months to get the air conditioning in and functioning."

Lucille brought her anger home with her. "I'd tell the kids what went on during the day. I remember one of them saying, 'If you feel that way about working, well, why don't you quit?' I'd say, 'We need the money.' But I knew I had some economic independence; I wasn't going to be destitute. The kids weren't all home, I had some money saved, I'd get unemployment if I handled it right, I had my husband's vet benefits. I'd rent out a room in the house if I had to. I'd survive. I just couldn't stand being part of a system that was really wrong and not have something done about it. I figured I'd fought a hundred battles in my life. I'd written letters and kept files and journals, but I didn't want to be a part of a killing system. I wanted time to be interested in life, in my life. I wanted to concentrate on something I could make better."

One doctor had died and the support staff had to be reduced. Before she left for vacation in May 1976, she told the doctor in charge that if somebody had to be fired, she wanted it to be her. When she returned from Hawaii, she was out of a job for the first time in thirteen years. During the next year she kept a journal of her life beyond work. What follows are excerpts from her first two days of not working:

Here I am back from Hawaii with my tourist's tan, one uncashed traveler's check, and as of 11 A.M. this morning—jobless! I had a quick peek into the past while the business manager squirmed and sighed and finally signed my last paycheck. I'm grateful to leave with my glory still intact.

Sheila, my able assistant, was attempting to soothe an irate patient who was complaining bitterly about the bill for his last clinic visit. His doctor had ordered every test going, and I remembered staying late to process his specimens (without being paid overtime, of course).

As I glanced into the lab, I saw stacks of culture plates waiting to be read. I remembered how routinely physicians prescribed penicillin for infections, only later to discover from the culture and sensitivity reports that certain patients' particular germs were resistant to penicillin. Some of these poor guys would wind up with secondary opportunistic fungi and then be forced to down new courses of expensive drugs along with cartons of yogurt to restore normal flora again. . . .

Now I know how much I kept conning myself into believing that I loved the work but disliked certain job situations forced upon me. "Oh, hell, there are no perfect jobs," I said as I turned myself into an eighty-mile-a-day commuting automaton for three years prior to my last position. How else was I going to keep my house and kids together without being a pawn to a paycheck? I knew I was as bogged down in the morass of bureaucratic chaos as the bewildered patients were.

Mostly there seems to be a dearth of praise or appreciation for any work well done. . . . Competent people are insulted for their intelligence and ingenuity. Incentive is given a swift kick. Mediocre, security-minded employees live out their working days picking away at the good workers who threaten their jobs. The bright comers spend their days off looking for better positions and sometimes use their lunch hours for promising interviews. Seniority (senility?) earns more money and longer paid vacations, the latter being in some cases a real blessing in disguise.

I wonder if I really hated working this much, or is this a natural reaction to all the years I did work and was so damn busy on every shift that I never before had a chance to think about all these things?

I do remember the shock I received when I recognized the truth of my own words on a quiz at a parents' seminar of my son's class in human relations. There was a neat little list entitled, "Things I Like to Do." When I finished the last entry, I realized I didn't have time to do any of the activities I had listed. Whatta way to live—up at 6 A.M. to meet the car pool by 7 A.M. to beat the hospital time clock (40 miles away) at 8 A.M. I would arrive back home exhausted at 6 P.M. . . . Now I think I was crazy to do it. Another recollection haunts me: the Gestalt sessions in an encounter group. The more I switched positions with myself, back and forth between the two mes, the more I knew I disliked my work self and respected my home self.

David Solomon: The Moral Insulation of Numbers

David Solomon's father was appointed to Franklin D. Roosevelt's first administration. He was an agricultural economist and was later recognized as an authority on mobilizing government resources to feed the hungry, first in this country and then all over the world. He went to work for the United Nations and prospered. In 1961 he was told he would receive his diadem for an extraordinary career: a top-level planning position with the State Department.

He had already quit his job with the U.N. in Paris and was preparing to return to the United States when a newspaper reported that he had worked in the thirties for a government official whose politics had a leftish slant. After the story appeared, the

Kennedy administration withdrew the offer of the State Department job.

"My mother's interpretation," says David, "was that what the Kennedy administration did destroyed, not only his career, but his ability to work effectively. As it destroyed him, he became more and more dependent on her, just for his basic emotional needs. He became senile rather quickly after that. His work and his position was so central, so important, and he was so good at it, he never believed he had to use stealth to promote the ideas he had. It crushed him when people could not see what he had devoted his life to."

David went to Bard College and did his graduate work at the Woodrow Wilson School at Princeton. In college he studied economics and statistical analysis, and before he graduated he participated in a project to evaluate the quality of public health care in New England. In the next fifteen years he worked for various state agencies and consulting firms, always engaged in efforts to remind the ever-forgetful bureaucracy that there was another America out there.

"For all of my father's suffering, for all of the cruelty inflicted on him for imaginary crimes, I retained his faith that government could be a tremendously powerful force for good," David says. "If he had a philosophy, it was the belief in government intervention on behalf of people who had no power. I inherited that faith and it took me in the same direction he had gone—until it was no longer possible for me to believe."

In his last job, he worked for a research organization in Cambridge, Massachusetts. The company had a multimillion-dollar contract from the federal government to study the effects of long-term unemployment in several northeastern states. David's salary was $21,000. He quit that job in 1974, three weeks before his fortieth birthday.

"The person I worked for shed light on my father for me. Basically, my boss treated economics as a science of the quantifiable. This man was a nut on the subject. He was far less sensitive to human and social functions than my father. He seemed to rejoice in the moral insulation that quantification gave him. He liked numbers in lieu of people and their statements. God, the information we took from people's lives and how we used it in ways that were not respectful of the people themselves."

David's specific assignment was to analyze data about the personal experience of people out of work: What happened to people when they were out of a job? Why had they left their previous jobs? How did they use their time when they weren't working? The answers were not easily quantifiable, but according to David, the organization didn't bother to try. The fix was in. The questions were included originally as window dressing, but there was an understanding not to pursue them. "All the nuance was cast out of the research. They changed the meaning of the questions and answers so that it fit a government bureaucrat's preconceptions and could be used to make policy that was predetermined before the research began. The only thing they were ever interested in was how much government assistance would make somebody lose interest in getting a job. So much work was lost, so many lives were wasted in that experiment, so many thousands of people were screwed. Even now people ask me what did they find out and I just don't know."

It was not easy to quit. It took him about eight months to finally make up his mind. "When I finally left, I felt like I was outside the system that the research organization and that experiment represented. To stay at that job I had to buy a lot of good cognac, and to buy a lot of good cognac I had to stay at that job. And what happened in the end? The cognac was gone, the money was gone, my time was gone. And I had not felt very satisfied about what I'd gotten from those bastards, and they were not very satisfied with what they'd gotten from me. I thought they ripped me off and they thought I ripped them off. So they think I've failed them and I think they failed me—and failed all those suckers they manipulated in their research. So we're both right."

His father would have stayed inside, to try to change the organization. His father would have said, "No matter how little government does, it's better than doing nothing. By my intelligence, by my determination, I can make government do more, do better." David had thought many times of applying his intelligence and determination toward objectives that reflected his own interests, rather than his father's philosophy. But he hadn't had much experience in self-determination.

"When I was growing up and even later my mother was the family planner. My impression was she would come down in the morning after having lain awake for several hours, running through the options and opportunities for everybody in the family, and sort of lay out what we would be doing.

Those were wonderful things. It was not dumb or unrewarding. But they were *her ideas*, and it would be us, me and my brother and father, who would be implementing them. Where would we go on what day: Where would we go for vacations? I never gained the experience of making decisions for myself."

When David's brother, who was also raised in the cultural and political stratosphere of Washington policymaking, decided he wanted to drive a truck for a living, it eased David's own separation from the past. "My parents never demanded that I become a professional man, but the pressure was there. I felt I had to be a professional. My brother broke the ice on that one. He had a much harder time getting through school than I did. And he went into the army and married a girl from Tennessee where he was stationed and he had two kids and he always worked driving a truck. It was accepted that he had found the path that held his life together. Without that precedent, I would have felt a lot more pressure than I did, and I felt plenty. What he did supported my romantic idea of who I am."

It is a contemporary luxury, once only granted to gentlemen and ladies of leisure and idiosyncratics, to question the social purpose of work. Recall the 1950s and the voluntary suppression of doubt:

> The uneasiness, the malaise of our time, is due to this root fact: in our politics and economy, in family life and religion—in practically every sphere of our existence—the certainties of the eighteenth and nineteenth centuries have disin-

tegrated or been destroyed, and, at the same time no new sanctions or justifications for the new routines we live, and must live, have taken hold. So there is no acceptance and there is no rejection, no sweeping hope and no sweeping rebellion. There is no plan of life. Among white-collar people, the malaise is deep-rooted; for the absence of any order of belief has left them morally defenseless as individuals and politically impotent as a group.[5]

This, by C. Wright Mills, was written from a particular perspective, that of the Marxist sociologist. But it is a faithful representation of the temper of those times. If Mills were writing today, I think he would detect a change in the popular mood, particularly in white-collar precincts. He would find in the accounts of Roberts, Reiter, and Solomon, and a dozen others gathered in the course of my research, both hope and rebellion. And he would interpret their break with work as an act of principle and a commitment to belief.

These are people who worked a long time. They were not hotheads or habitual soreheads. In their jobs they had learned how to mute their dissent. When they could no longer hold their silence, they chose their words carefully, so as not to endanger their jobs. At the crest of their occupational climb, at the end of thirteen years for Reiter, fifteen years for Solomon, and thirteen years for Roberts, they detached themselves from what they considered meaningless and purposeless work.

They probably would have stuck at it twenty years ago. They would have carried their complaints home and vented them at the dinner table, as my father did for so many years. Then they would have answered the call of the morning alarm. The reason they don't now is that "new sanctions" have been granted them to express their dissent in the most direct and personal manner, in the one sphere of their lives over which they still retain control—in their work. They *feel* free to quit. They have received permission for "the new routines" they want to develop.

When they started work, the people I have described had a dim outline of the future. They would, through pluck and diligence (with a nod to luck and connections), rise in their occupations, raise families, and accept the plaudits of their contemporaries. Generally, the future wasn't any better formed than that, and it was even more clouded when they quit. They couldn't know whether the protest that led to their resignation would become a resource or a trap. They could remain forever shackled to their anger, assuming the role of victim and ascribing their misfortunes to a vengeful and implacable "system." Or they could harness their rebellion and direct it toward a personally—and perhaps socially—productive end. Then their indignation would become a resource the vehicle for attaining the objects of their desire. Victims, no matter how loud their cries of anguish and rage, wind up flat on their backs.

A LOSS OF FAITH

Many Americans, particularly older Americans, rested their futures on twin pillars of faith: the faith that you can make something of yourself through work and the faith that the principal institutions in American society will affirm, honor, and reward the individual's achievements in his work.

Work was a membership card that entitled the holder to all the privileges of a bountiful culture. I think this almost spiritual connection between personal industry and the larger enterprises of the American will was most clearly expressed in a conversation I had with a New York psychiatrist whose patients included a number of people who had stopped working for varying intervals. He said, in essence, "It's American to work. That's the way we fulfill ourselves. This is the outlet for our ambition and energy and skills. This is where we find our pride, our sense of accomplishment. There are a number of ways, but work is a very important way of defining our place in American culture."

Many people I met first embraced this faith at the moment, ironically, when the country seemed to be crumbling. They were people who had lived through the depression. Material riches were scarce then, but feelings of camaraderie and cooperation nurtured optimism. It seemed as if everybody was caught in the same mess; if everybody worked together, life would surely get better.

Despite periodic downswings in the economy and a rising rate of inflation, the twenty-five years after World War II rewarded the perseverance and courage of the thirties. In this season of renewal, Tom MacCauley started out with a dollar-an-hour job unloading cement bags and ended up a rich man; Billy Morgan started a family and became a cop, an occupation admirably suited to a man of deep Christian conviction; and Charles Braithwaite dropped out of college to enter journalism, a considerable accomplishment, since this was not an industry known for its recruitment of minorities.

As individuals they sprang from diverse cultures and pursued different objectives, but none would disagree with the sentiments of President Eisenhower, who kept repeating to his speech writer Emmet Hughes, before his first inaugural address:

> All these generalizations about freedom and history do not mean too much. What matters to the average citizen is—what can *he* do? A carpenter or a farmer or a bricklayer or a mechanic—what is *his* role? The individual—that's what counts. It's not just a time of crisis for the statesmen and the diplomats. Every individual has got to understand and got to produce. He's got to work harder than ever—and he's got to understand *why*.

The *why* was subject to various interpretations, but it could be reduced to a relatively simple formula in those years. Hard work equals more and more success. Hard work would generate *more* jobs, *more* clothes, *more* highways, *more* housing, *more* suburbs, *more* cars, *more* schools. The more would yield occupational status, social standing, material comfort, and upward mobility for their children. Recalling that period, Daniel Yankelovich identifies the car as the defining symbol of material progress. "You went from the Chevy to the Buick to the Cadillac," he says. "When you reached the tail fin, you'd made it." The Cadillac was more than a symbol of wealth, it was a test of character. It meant that the kids would have a V-8 engine to propel them down a clear road. "For most people these goodies were for one's children, not only for oneself," Yankelovich says. "Holding a job was not only the obvious means toward economic security, but it also fulfilled the male role in the family. It allowed him to fulfill his obligations to his wife and to his children."[1]

Of course the stretch between V-J Day and John F. Kennedy's inauguration was not totally trouble free. There were the leaking roofs and the sinking foundations, the bite for taxes and the cost of college tuition, the suburban set piece of the worker-husband and the chauffeur-wife that was not so set. At the close of the decade, Cleveland editor Louis B. Seltzer found a wide audience for his editorial about the American mood. Seltzer asked:

> What is wrong with us? It is in the air we breathe. The things we do. The things we say. Our books. Our papers. Our theatre. Our movies. Our radio and television. The way we behave. The interests we have. The values we fix. We have everything. We abound with all things that make us comfortable. Yet something is not there that should be. . . . Are we our own worst enemies? Should we fear what is happening among us more than what is happening elsewhere? . . . No one seems to know what to do to meet it. But everybody worries.[2]

They were beginning to lose confidence in the collective future. Hopeful in the thirties, triumphant in war in the forties, rising in the fifties, troubled yet vulnerable to the psychology of affluence in the sixties, and besieged in the seventies. Was it all a swindle? Had they been sold the Brooklyn Bridge? By 1975 the Yankelovich polls found that nine out of ten Americans "expressed a generalized mistrust of 'those in power,' covering . . . most national institutions." More than 70 percent of the populace voiced its mistrust of big business (up from 30 percent in 1968).[3]

The people we met earlier questioned the purpose of their work. The people we meet now share a more generalized anxiety. They feel dispossessed in their own country, evicted from the mainstream of American culture. They are not enraged. Only numb. They say, "What is going on in the country has nothing to do with me." The political structure, as well as the cultural and economic institutions, "appears vaguely irrelevant and disembodied or absurd."

This uneasiness is not confined to any particular class or social outlook or political ideology, and it cannot be dismissed as the griping of congenital malcontents. These are people who have exercised power in their work and shouldered responsibility. But they aren't getting their due. They were taught the value of experience, craftsmanship, and a record of accomplishment. Now when they read the newspaper or watch television, they feel left out. In their personal lives, they thought they knew their places. But their sexual roles, which once appeared immutable, have become anomalous. Who's supposed to make the romantic overtures these days? Who's supposed to pay the bills? Who works and who raises the kids?

"People have come to feel that those who work hard and live by the rules are being neglected, shunted aside, and exploited while those who flaunt the rules ... get all the breaks," Yankelovich writes.[4] "We now have a situation where more than four out of five of our citizens seem to feel that the unwritten contract is not working properly, that the rewards of society go to those who fail to conform while those who do conform are made to feel like fools for faithfully observing the rules of the game."

In their own manner, Tom MacCauley, Billy Morgan, and Charles Braithwaite were conformists. They bought the package. When they unwrapped it, it was empty.

Tom MacCauley: Death and Taxes

Tom MacCauley can turn a vertebra into fine powder with a slap on the back. Around Cascade, where he moved after stopping work, they say, "Big Tom does everything hard. Drinks hard, plays poker hard, even fishes hard." Old habits are tough to break.

In Denver when he was building and installing water and plumbing systems, when he was selling air conditioners, and when he was running his liquor stores, they used to say, "Tom MacCauley works hard." Now he works very hard at not working, which is not the easiest thing for a robust, energetic man of forty-two.

Nothing got in his way. A messed-up childhood couldn't stop him. ("We moved around like gypsies. I think I went to sixteen schools in twelve years.") A broken family couldn't stop him. ("My mother divorced my father when I was twelve. I think she remarried eight or nine times.") A cruel stepfather couldn't stop him. ("He was a bum. He'd beat the hell out of me. When I got big enough I beat the hell out of him. He wound up in jail finally. I thought my mother knew the score. I was sure she'd leave him when he got out of jail. Instead, she took off with him. She wanted me to go to New Mexico with them. I told her to go to hell.")

His first job was unloading cement from railroad boxcars. That paid a dollar an hour and lasted a year. When he got out of high school in Denver, he took a job selling automotive supplies to Gulf Oil stations. That also lasted a year, but it was important because it proved to him that he had a knack for selling. The next eight years were spent with Standard, a major manufacturer of plumbing fixtures and systems. He began as a receiving clerk in a warehouse in Denver, earning $105 every two weeks. After five months he went to Ace, the warehouse manager, and announced, "I'm going to quit if I can't do any advancing in the company because I don't plan on being a peon all my life." Maybe somebody else would have called his bluff but Ace Markham knew a comer when he saw one. He put him on the road, on the back road, through towns like Cripple Creek and Stovetop, dry gulch towns. It didn't stop Tom MacCauley: He was on his way.

"I had just got married and I told Sue that I wanted to be pretty independent by the time I was thirty-four. I just wanted to get a job and work my way to something, to my own business. I didn't have in mind then that I'd retire that young. But when I did it, it was a very big personal satisfaction."

In his years with Standard, Tom MacCauley became a master at the art of the salesman's shmooze. The shmooze got him his first big order. "It was a small town near Denver. I had to stand up in front of the town council and tell them why we should put in their water system. I was scared to death. What I told them was I lived near their community. I was a hometown boy. They bought it. What I got out of that was you were selling yourself, and it was just as important as selling your product. You have to sell yourself, your dependability and your service."

That and persistence and a growing self-confidence that conquered his uneasiness at never going to college brought him bigger and more profitable orders. But one day he told his wife, "Why am I doing this for Standard? They're not paying me what I'm worth."

To say that Tom MacCauley went on from there to open a partnership in an air-conditioning firm and to say he bought up a liquor store and all that bought him visitor's privileges to the country club in Denver and to say that in the clubhouse he was an insider-outsider, a guy without the right pedigrees but with the big handshake and the dollars, makes it sound too smooth, too easy. It was much tougher to make it in the business and social worlds.

"Sometimes I'd go to work at five in the morning so I could get things done before the phone started ringing. Sometimes I'd bring plans home at night to work on. I wouldn't work on them until the kids went to bed. I'd put in at least a fourteen-hour day. The business was seasonal. April to October was really busy. In the winter it slowed down; I'd try to spend more time with the family then, but it was real work to find the time to devote to your family."

Although he was often invited to the country club, he never wanted to join. "It seems that the people who really have money in Denver are nice people. The people who think they have money are the ones who are really bad. Those people were tough to live with. When I went there to play golf or for lunch, they would be cold to me—aloof. *I was the guy who put in the air conditioning for the club. A working man.* That's why I didn't join. Too many of these people."

Tom tapped into the boom years of the 1950s and 1960s. The dollars flowed in. On paper Tom MacCauley's worth was a hundred grand. Two hundred grand. He owned a small office building. A few other investments here and there. He had made good on his promise to be independent by the time he was thirty-five. He had run very hard, and every once in a while, he'd get a stitch, a stitch of doubt. He had never stopped before to question himself. So why now? Why question when he had everything he had ever wanted? It was just those two things. They nagged at him. They wouldn't leave him alone. Death and taxes. Taxes and death. He went to sleep at night thinking about them, woke up in the morning thinking about them.

Taxes first because that's easier to explain, easier for Tom MacCauley to understand, dollars and cents, you could add that up. Death was something else, like punching a pillow. Thirty-seven, never really sick in his life, and worried about dying. No, better to talk about taxes first, then death.

"You get to the point in business where we did, making so much money, that the government takes so damn much out in income taxes you have no incentive to do better. That's no joke. I can honestly say they drove me out of business. The more money I'd make—the great American thing: You make a lot of money—the more they'd make. I'd been audited every year since 1967. Never missed a year. One year I paid an accountant $10,000 to handle an audit. At the end of the audit, I wrote the I.R.S. a check for $26. The accountant and the attorney said they'd earned their money because they'd saved me $20,000, which was true. But something was wrong. Either I owe $20,000 or I owe $26. One or the other. I have to hire a smart talent to make it right. That's wrong.

"My attorney said, 'Tom, you'd better decide you have a 50 percent partner, the I.R.S. You better consult me before you buy or sell.' I said, 'Wait a minute, I'm an entrepreneur, an individual, I like doin' it, making deals when I want to. Now I have to consult my partner, the I.R.S. before I do anything?' I started analyzing what my partner's motivations were. And when I looked at the I.R.S. I realized they didn't want me in business. They were the great leveler. And, shit, I didn't want to be leveled."

His income is spread out now, derived mostly from rental of property he owns back in Denver and some other investments. It ensures him better than $30,000 a year for the next eight years and it cuts down on the tax bite. He still pays taxes, but somehow it feels better to pay for not working than for working. Death is different. It's harder to put the fear of death on the installment plan.

It started when his wife died. She was thirty-six. Three years before a routine examination had detected breast cancer. She had a mastectomy, but a couple of years later the cancer spread to her liver. The pain for all of them was awful, for him, for his wife, for their son and daughter. His wife died in 1975. At almost the same time his bookkeeper, whom he later married, was going through the same agony. One weekend her husband went off on a fishing trip and never came home. He died that weekend of a heart attack. She was then three months pregnant. When Tom left Standard, he went to work for a plumbing contractor, a man in his early fifties who had Parkinson's disease. Within six months he was dead. Tom's first partner when he went into business for himself died three years later of a heart attack.

"I saw that happen to too many people. Young people, close to my age. It kept building up. When I was thirty-five, it began to scare me. Sometimes at night I'd wake up sweating. Was I driving too hard? Would I wind up like them? What was the use of being independent when you were independent in the grave? I said, 'When I think I can afford to get out, I'll get out. I'll enjoy my life before I drop dead.'"

His investments and savings make Tom MacCauley a wealthy man, but in his life he has suffered the injuries of class. You're taught to have faith in the self-made man, he would say, so what happens when you make it? Doors get shut in your face. You go to a party and wimpy liberals blow enough hot air to keep the whole country warm all winter. As Tom expanded his business and prospered, he proved he could be successful, but he was rewarded with reproval. The significance of the death image is different for him than it is for Sam Meyers. Sam mourned the death of the family business, a productive and satisfying career reaching its end. Tom, in effect, has been pronounced dead by the reigning cultural and political and social establishments of America. When he talks about the social appurtenances that surround him—his comfortable house, his neatly tended lawn, his functional furniture—he describes them as "old-fashioned." "I guess I'm just an old-fashioned guy," he says. If you can't beat 'em, leave 'em. If American culture has left him to the embalmer, then he will leave American culture to its own slow death. A man like Tom MacCauley considers work his contribution to the social order. If it enriches him, so, too, will it enrich society. When his work and his values are deemed worthless, screw it, he'll stop working and keep his values to himself. He's the man who withdraws his savings when the bank teller insults him.

Yet he cannot secede entirely. He's still an American, a bitter American. In the year and a half since he stopped working, he and his wife have traveled to the Caribbean, Mexico, and Hawaii. When they're at home in Cascade, he will play golf two or three hours a day or go fishing. She will spend a lot of time in their house with the kids. She helps him keep track of his investments. In the evenings, they do crossword puzzles together. Whatever they're doing, the talk almost always turns to politics, to the politics of exclusion practiced by the fat cats and power brokers.

"I think we're getting ripped off by the government," Tom says, his wife agreeing vigorously. "The energy scare, I don't really think it's that bad. They want us to conserve here and conserve there, and the first thing Carter does when he gets in office is to give himself and all the congressmen a raise. Here they are saying they're going to give you a break, but at the same time they're screwing you someplace else.

"There's untapped oil resources all over the place, and Carter's blowing off that there's a shortage. He's going to stick you for buying a big car and put a five-cent tax on every gallon—and the oil people are going to get rich because the price of gas is going up. They all get rich, but not you.

"Nixon was a crook and he got caught. So we're not picking on Carter because he's a Democrat and a southern boy. I wouldn't care if he was a black Catholic. He's been bought. I'd like to take an ad on the front page of the paper saying Carter's been bought off by the oil companies. But they'd probably send the I.R.S. out to audit me. I know they'd give me a bad time."

His wife, Helen, puts down her knitting. "It makes you a bit bitter," she says. "We pay a great deal of income tax for our crooked government. I don't say they're all crooks. We've just seen so much of it. Even in the local county government. In the business world. Everywhere. I guess it doesn't pay much anymore to be honest."

Billy Morgan: The Power of Prayer
In 1719 Nathaniel Henchman, a Quaker minister, delivered the eulogy at the funeral service for a member of the Massachusetts Council. "Every man

has (or ought to have) a particular calling as a Rational Creature, wherein he is to abide and at the same time to follow his general calling as a Christian," he said.

If Billy Morgan had been there, he would have shouted a mighty amen.

He would have endorsed Max Weber's depiction of the Protestant ethic: "Not leisure and enjoyment, but only activity serves to increase the glory of God, according to the definite manifestations of His will. Loss of time through sociability, idle talk, luxury, even more sleep than is necessary for health, six to at most eight hours, is worthy of absolute moral condemnation."

In McAllen, Texas, where Billy grew up, the Protestant ethic was alive. He could see it from his school bus every morning, out in the fields where the Mexicans, who had been trucked across the border from Los Ebanos and Hidalgo and Nueva Laredo, harvested the lettuce and tomatoes in one-hundred-degree temperatures. They weren't engaged in idle talk or sociability, and they were clearly impervious to the temptations of luxury.

No lack of industry at home, either. Father was a salesman who plugged hard at whatever came along, insurance, sewing machines, encyclopedias. His mother prayed. "She was the one who showed me the religious light. The power of prayer. My father taught me the Christian value of work. He was a good, honest professional salesman. He would consider any kind of job good, as long as I liked it. He raised me thinking he would never be ashamed of me no matter what kind of job I had."

That simple faith in the coupling of Christian piety and honest work remained intact through high school and five years of Bible college. There were signs that his faith and industriousness were being rewarded. His parents didn't have much money, but he managed to pay his tuition by washing dishes and selling shoes in a department store. When he ran short, the checks came. "I never knew who sent them, where they came from. They were just there, in the mailbox. I had prayed and prayed for money to go to college. And it came out of the blue. I felt that it was a school God had directed me to go to."

The trouble was not everyone shared his belief in the redemptive nature of work, not everyone at the Bible college, not even his wife. Now fifteen years later and out of work for three years, in San Antonio, Billy Morgan remembers his wife's promise with a certain amount of un-Christian bitterness. "She wanted to get married while I was finishing my senior year," he says, staring at the pile of tennis rackets he has promised to string by the weekend. "She confronted me and said, 'Why don't we get married before you graduate. I know it's your last year in school and you need to raise your grades up and I'll work and support you.' The married couples we knew at the time, almost every married girl worked. The guys could concentrate on their studies, knowing they didn't have an awful lot to worry about as far as money."

She took a sales job in the store where he worked. "Halfway through the first day she came home with a horrible headache. She gets these from pressure, I guess. It got very, very bad. She'd go crazy about it.

She just absolutely hated it. I just hated her having something she didn't like, and at the same time I thought it was her responsibility for putting me through school for six or seven months. Finally, I said, 'If it's this much a problem just quit.' Then I went to work full time, forty hours a week, and I was taking a full course load. I almost completely ignored her for the next three or four months. I'd pay attention to her during the daytime—she was the type who'd want me to pay attention to her— and pretty soon she put pressure on me to have a baby. She said, 'Housewives should have babies also.' "

By that September both he and his wife achieved their goals. He was graduated. She was pregnant. There was one small complication. As an elementary education major, he had to return for another year to go through student teaching. The college insisted that he could not hold a job during this period. With a C average, he did not qualify for a graduate loan. "It was the first time I was very discouraged." What's more the mysterious checks stopped coming. The mailbox was empty. "I prayed a lot, I'm a very devout believer in prayer, but my prayers weren't answered."

He left college and they moved to San Antonio and stayed with her parents. "You'd think with a B.A. degree I'd have a good chance for a job. I tried for government jobs and construction jobs and business jobs. Everybody I spoke to said either I didn't have the right degree—they said I needed a business or engineering degree—or my grade average wasn't good enough or I didn't have enough experience."

After a year of looking, he found a job as a deputy sheriff, but what he never expected happened. Billy Morgan's faith was held against him. He worked in the sheriff's office of Boxer County for almost four years. They were not easy years. There were times, just a few times, when his faith almost wavered.

"When I got the job, I said to myself what would fit my faith, my values, better than a peace officer? When I became a deputy sheriff, I was known as Billy Good-Guy because the word got around that I went to a Bible college and nobody else would confess to having gone to one. I didn't cuss, I didn't drink, and they kept trying to talk me out of law enforcement. 'You're gonna have to learn to cuss,' they said. 'You're gonna have to learn to be a rough, tough person.' I said, 'That's great, but I'm not that type of person. If that's the type I have to be to be a good cop, I'll look for another job.' "

Billy Morgan did not change jobs, not right away, but he changed a little. The first change came in his home life. "Before my wife got married, she never knew what money problems were, never knew what problems in general were. She even stated that she thought marriage was like you see on TV—happy-go-lucky. No problems. When I was working the graveyard shift, I'd come dragging in at ten in the morning. Many times I was getting four or five hours sleep because she expected me to get up and change Frank's diapers or go shopping with her. There was bitterness inside, but I didn't speak up because I didn't want to cause fights with her. At home I was like at the sheriff's office: I was Billy Yes-Guy. It dawned on me one day, I'm tired of being Billy Yes-Guy. Why didn't I have enough guts to speak up? If she didn't respect my work, why should I respect her?"

Their marriage ended in 1970, and try as he might, Billy couldn't get it out of his head that it was his fault. "I really did not believe in divorce. And I felt *horrible* all the time. My mind was not always at work. I left work once, when my wife and I were first separated, I just couldn't control myself. I was crying. I was very lonely, very depressed. I didn't want anybody to see me that day."

After the divorce, he began to slip a little, and the ground that he was once rooted in began to slip from under him. He drank bourbon at the sheriff's Christmas party. When another deputy did something he disapproved of, he called him an "asshole—excuse the expression." Always proper in the way he treated suspects, Billy began to think of some of the citizens of Boxer County, not all to be sure, as "animals." "I would reach deep down for Christian charity, but there was no way of getting around it, they were animals."

The second big change came when he divorced the sheriff's office, or, more accurately, the office divorced him. He left his job temporarily in a dispute over a charge against him by a prisoner at the county jail. A minor charge. A charge that he says was refuted beyond doubt. When he reapplied, he was told that there were no openings. When he applied as a deputy in neighboring counties, he was told there were no openings. No openings anywhere for Billy Good-Guy.

He has worked only two of the last five years, so

now he sits in his pink concrete bungalow in a neighborhood of San Antonio that was once a back set for Western movies. Movies about guys with white hats and black hats.

Billy Morgan wears a gray hat these days. "I still pray," he says softly. "The difference is, sometimes I'm not sure now what I'm praying for. What I want. S'pose it's for peace of mind."

Billy stares through the dusty window at the chain link fence in front of the gravel lawn, at the stucco houses across the way, at the old Western hotel where the actors stayed when they came into town for the shoot-'em-ups. "Tell the truth, I once read about the work ethic, three years ago or so, when I wasn't working. It was all about what people expect out of employers, what employers expect out of employees. Why people quit jobs. I said, 'Boy, I can't think of any job I would really want to say at. If I could, I wouldn't work at all because all of them stunk. Really.'"

His source of income now is stringing tennis rackets, a job he does at home a few hours a week. "The only reason I'm doing that was to pay my bills. When I wasn't working, I started to relate to people who were being booked inside the county jail for theft, for stealing groceries. I had thoughts going through my head of stealing. If not for my faith in Jesus, in the prayers I was always sending up, I couldn't have made it. I didn't want to keep taking welfare. I hate that pressure from those stupid bill collectors. Everybody's always phoning you up. Truth is, society forces you into going back to work."

Truth is, Billy Morgan was always feeling things happened to him or didn't—he just couldn't make them happen, somehow.

Charles Braithwaite: Being Had

Charles, my friend. Charles, the romantic. Charles, always a lover but not always loved. Charles, the quintessential reporter, who would not tell me what the payoff to not working was, who instead told me, "Go out and cover the story, be a good reporter."

If you made up a list of Charles's passions, women and journalism would finish at the top. But jazz wouldn't be that far behind. Which roughly corresponds to my list.

There were differences, of course. Charels grew up in the Bronx. I grew up in Brooklyn. Charles's father ran an elevator. My father sold hats. Charles had a brother. I was an only child. Charles moved over to the tube. I stayed behind the typewriter. Oh, yeah. Charles is black. I am white.

His romance with journalism began in high school. He wrote an essay on: "Why I Want to Join the High School Paper"; the teacher gave him a 98 and said, "If you really want to join the paper, why don't you?" Charles accepted the challenge. He was the only black kid on the staff. "I felt a little odd." It didn't bother him that much. He was smitten.

A few months later he came home and told his father that he wanted to be a reporter.

"Don't do it," his father said.

"Why not?"

"You'll never get a job."

"Whadya mean?"

"It's a segregated business."

"So."

"So why not try the post office. At least there's security there, and they'll let you in."

He could not persuade Charles, who was in love with journalism, and he did not press the argument. In the Braithwaite household, the kind of work you did was less important than the fact that you worked. If the job wasn't great, next year you could get a better one.

"Labor was very crucial to my father. He worked as an elevator operator for forty-five years at Gimbels. When I was a teenager, I felt very uneasy about that, and then I realized—my mother explained to me, 'Well, papa keeps us going. What he does is not the best, but it's very basic to us all and we must respect him because of that.' When I was eighteen, I worked with my father. I worked right next to him, I ran an elevator at Gimbel's. I came to fully realize what he had done all those years. When you first operated the elevator it seemed like a great deal of fun, especially a fast elevator. Then I realized the tedium, the enormous boredom of it. And I grew to love him then, more than ever before. He had spent all this time doing this which enabled us, my brother and my mother and me, to do what we wanted to."

What Charles wanted to do was go to college. Which he did. And then he wanted to marry a girl he met there. Which he did. He left college before he was graduated when a friend found a copy boy job for him on a New York newspaper. Charles danced lightfully and gracefully through the 1960s. His wife and children were beautiful and extremely bright. So was he. "We were the magic family," he laughs dryly. "We were the original beautiful people and we did it without money."

In the iconography of New York journalism in the 1960s, he is remembered as much for his presence as for his work. He covered all the stories that were obligatory for a black reporter then: the civil rights demonstrations, the riots in Harlem and Newark, the black political establishment, Adam Clayton Powell and Basil Paterson and Percy Sutton and the disestablishment, Malcolm X and Stokely Carmichael and Leroi Jones. He did the routine ones also—the police shack and Barbra Streisand and Joey Gallo. I always thought he was most masterful when the story was over and he could pick it apart over a drink, describing the glide and slide that took him to the center, the moves he made, the clever ruses, the gentle art of telephone persuasion. I always suspected that his breadth of interest was larger that what he could write. But that wasn't so unusual. There are a lot of reporters who learn to write for space and save the best stuff for the bar.

If any black reporter had a shot at cracking the white palace guard of journalism, it was Braithwaite. That was what he was always drawn to—the big white news organizations.

"Journalism is a hustle thing. I bite off two inches when I can only chew one, but I figure by the time they catch up to me, I'll pull in the other inch. I knew I could do that best in a big vibrant shop where just because of its size I wouldn't fall into a very responsible position—at least not at first. But I don't want it to be too risky. I want time to weave and bob until I can land a punch.

"When I got into the business, I concluded I was suited for organization life. I never thought of myself away from a big organization, an overwhelmingly white organization. This is the kind of mood I put myself into. I think there's a neurotic touch to it, the pattern I go through. I enjoy it and I don't enjoy it, and in the process of not enjoying it, I kind of burn myself out getting away from it. I don't leave with grace and sensibility. I see myself as compatible with the organization, but for some reason my definition as a compatible person doesn't come across. They always say, 'You should fit in here, Charles,' but that never works out. I don't know exactly where the break comes. It's not a political thing, I don't think. I never try to impress my political ideas on a white organization.

"I've enjoyed journalism, not because I've been able to use it to practice my ideas, but because I've been able to be a very close-up witness to a lot of things that had to do with my ideas. It's sort of like going into medicine, not because you really help people when they're sick, but because you want to watch what happens. I never felt the relationship between my ideas and my work. I'd like to do that, but I don't know when that will happen."

There was little relationship between his emotional life and the white organizations he served. It is my conceit, perhaps not an entirely accurate one, that if he unbuttoned his blue blazer and showed what was churning underneath, he would have to stand stark naked before a white jury. So in the late 1960s, when he was working for a magazine and his marriage was failing and he was drinking too much, he hid, and they called him, with that glib cruelty that comes so naturally to word factories, The Shadow.

"I suppose I should have gone to somebody and said, 'Look, I'm very personally troubled and this is what's going on.' I never did that. I should have said, 'Give me a year off. I don't want the money. I just want the time off. I love you and I'll work for you, I'll come back and work even better, but give me a year off.' The company would have said, 'Oh, Charles, get out of here, go. Call us in a year.' But I couldn't bring myself to say that. All I could do was quit."

No one knows how the "company" would have responded if he had gone to it and bared his problems, but he didn't. That first time when he rejected the Braithwaite family ethic of work, work at anything, but work, he was out a year and a half. I don't think he suffered very much. He managed to come up with the money to provide some support for his two kids, and there were always good friends who provided rent-free houses and offered him temporary jobs to ease him through. By leaving the magazine he was not ending his romance with reporting. "I was still in love with journalism," he says. "I had left on a journalistic high. The period I spent at the magazine remains to this day the best time I had in the business. I just wanted to gather myself together in a personal sense."

Eighteen months later he was ready to return to journalism, but this time it was not as a note-taker. He went to work for a television news show as an assignment editor. When a story began to develop anywhere in the world, he had to make the decision whether it was worth moving camera crews, equipment, and correspondents to cover it. He was less a reporter than a technician. If he made a mistake—if the story, in the judgment of management, was not worth the expense—he was in trouble. The romantic had to learn to be an accountant.

In his first eight months he put together a couple of exciting stories that won high compliments. It was the right time to make a move, to pitch for a reporting job or for an assignment as a field producer. A friend of his at the station suggested that he go to the vice-president for news and tell him what he wanted. "Just tell him you want to move up in the world," Charles's friend said. "He'll understand—he knows you. It'll happen."

"You kidding?" Charles answered.

He never made the pitch. "I was really afraid," he says. "I was frightened. I was afraid about myself. Could I really pull the next job off? It was an illogical fear. They would have moved me into the next job gradually. But I didn't have the guts for going to him. There's another way of looking at it. I always fantasize what I would have done if I was still married. If I was there with her and the kids, I say to myself, I would have been much more agressive, I'd have really hustled for another spot. Maybe that's just a fantasy, an excuse."

In the next three years his relationship with the organization gradually deteriorated. He made some mistakes. An ambitious white mover and shaker took a dislike to him. There were a few confrontations over judgments exercised and not exercised. "At the station I was down on journalism. Fuck it, it's so much shit. I was fighting that thesis, I didn't want to feel that way totally, but that's how I felt. In that last year I was drinking like a dog. Dinner for me at that time was a trip to one of those Blarney Stone bars where I would just sit and drink scotch at fifty-five cents a shot. After 'dinner' I'd come back to the station and say, 'Fuck this shit.' A story would come over the wires. I was very casual about it. I knew I should have called somebody right away, but I said, 'Fuck it.' A few hours later the opposition would have it."

He worked it out so the station gave him severance pay while putting it on the record that the staff was being reduced, so he could collect unemployment insurance. Twenty-two years after he had written that high school composition on "Why I Want to Join the High School Paper," he took a walk. If the romance wasn't over completely, the fire had gone out of it. At eight o'clock on the last night, he turned to the guy he was working with and said, "I'm going to take this dinner break but I don't think I'm coming back."

Out the door, past the wire machines that once cued Charles to a civil war in Beirut, down the corridor where he had raced to take a piss because he was afraid he'd miss something while he was in the john, into the elevator where the chief had told him, "Great job last night, Charles, you're really coming on now," and out, cold turkey, into the night. "I know it sounds like a guy whose great love has just gone sour, but all I could think was, I've been had."

Different catalysts brought them to the breakpoint. Lucille Roberts and Carl Reiter express their indignation at the social indifference they encounter by quitting. Cliff Jones and Norm Walters pay off their family debts and search out a new system to define their purposes. Tom MacCauley and Charles Braithwaite secede from a social order that rejects their values. Martha Gorham, tired of changing jobs, decides to change her whole life—one more time. Robert Stern plans for a life of educated leisure.

I think if I described the impulses that drove them all from work, my father would have been sympathetic. He would have agreed, as a philosopher once said, that they were claiming possession of themselves. Although he found it difficult for himself, he emphathized naturally with everyman's struggle to be free. He would have understood, for he, too, had suffered the indignities of thankless work; he, too, had stooped under the burden of a crushing social legacy; he, too, felt estranged from the dominant institutions of American culture; he, too, craved a fresh breeze in the musty vault of a locked-in life.

After listening for a while, I imagine he would have been overtaken by reality. A pragmatic romantic, he would have asked two questions.

First: How do you support yourself and your family?

And second: So, what are the neighbors going to say?

As he asked, he would have been thinking back on his own life; on the $300 he still owed the hospital where he had been treated for his first heart attack; on a social insurance system that granted a pittance to the unemployed; on a union that knew nothing about supplemental benefits; on an employer who demanded you share the burden of work but not the profits.

I would have responded: You suffer from the afflictions of your generation—honesty and morality. There are others, though, who know no such restraints. They have learned to survive without working. What's more, they have been granted an official sanction, stamped by the authorities and licensed by the state, to pursue their freedom.

Maybe so, he'd say, but what about the neighbors? What would they think of a man who didn't work? Worse still, a man who decided not to work?

I'd put my arm around him and squeeze his shoulder. Look around, I'd say, look around and what do you see? Those that are still working count the days until they can stop. And those who have stopped are not despised. They are envied. Things have changed, daddy, since you put aside the dream of Sam Goody for the certainty of $92.50 a week.

And then I'd show him just how much things have changed.

A CHANGE IN CLIMATE

These persons believe that if desirable jobs are not provided, they have a right not to work for a living. . . . Society is responsible for their socioeconomic welfare.

—Susan Gray and Louis Bolce,
Fordham University

THE LICENSE NOT TO WORK

My father would have understood that our sustaining myths are not literal truths but what we would like to believe is true. Our belief in myths propels us forward in our own lives. If we believe that our government is responsive to our needs, we are prepared to respond to the demands of our government and to involve ourselves in the governing process. We pay our taxes; we vote; we attend school board meetings. If we believe the wars we fight are just, we send our sons to battle, with a catch in our throats but with a faith in the righteousness of the cause.

The same way with work. Our belief in work is richly embroidered with myth. We work because we believe this is how we can determine our future. We believe that our diligence is the great equalizer. Our immigrant parents rushed to the sweatshops, not because the textile mills and the slaughter-houses were joyful and cheering places, but because they were a place to begin. If you plucked enough chickens, you would be granted admission to the civilized order. You would put food on the table, send your children to school so they wouldn't have to pluck chickens, and flee the dirt for two weeks under the sun at Grossman's beautiful bungalow colony in the glorious Catskills.

To retain their force, myths must maintain at least the appearance of truth. If we can no longer suspend our disbelief, we begin to shop around for other certitudes. If we cannot find the justification for fighting, we stop sending our kids off to war. If we believe that government is unresponsive and un-interested, we cut back our support—and find a new accountant to make out our tax returns. If we believe that our work has little or no value, that our contribution is insignificant, that the only recogni-tion we will receive is a computer-issued paycheck, we begin to look for alternatives—for another job, or if our faith is totally shattered, for an alternative to working. We see it as a right, an entitlement, to seek an alternative. In their study of voluntary un-employment, Professors Gray and Bolce wrote, "These persons believe that if desirable jobs are not provided, they have a right not to work for a living. . . . Society is responsible for their socioeconomic welfare."

THE SOCIAL SANCTION

For more than two years I traveled the country talking to people who had stopped working and their friends and families. In some places I advertised in newspapers:

> Stopped working? Writing a book about people who have decided to quit. Would like to talk to you.

I met people on unemployment insurance lines; I pounced on them in supermarkets when they reached for their food stamps. Some people were suggested by friends. Once I had met one or two people in a community who had stopped, they insisted I talk to others they knew. For some people not working is a cause, almost a religious calling, and they wanted me to know they were not alone.

What do the neighbors think? What do other people think about someone who announces he isn't going to work anymore? What do they think about someone who collects money from the government instead of working for a living? How does not working affect people's marriages, their friendships, their standing in the community? I asked these questions everywhere I stopped, and one of my first stops was in the conservative heartland, where I expected traditional values to dominate. If the pulse of the work ethic was strong anywhere, it would be here.

Hillcrest, Michigan: A Conditional License

Hillcrest,* population 27,000; median income, $17,500. Hillcrest is a relaxed bedroom community near industrial Flint. Its past is represented by the faded red and green sign that has stood for years in the whitewashed railroad station near the town square. The sign reads:

HILLCREST
Work There
Live Here

We Prosper as Industry Grows

Hillcrest is divided into two social groups. The older residents, the original settlers, are cops and carpenters, polishers in the furniture factories and quality-control inspectors on auto assembly lines. These first- and second-generation Polish and Italian and German families lived south of the train station, south of the dividing line, Central Avenue. When they came here, they could still buy a house for under $30,000. In the summer their neighbors joined them for a barbecue in the backyard. If they had a little extra money, they vacationed in Saginaw, nice if you didn't mind the damn flies on the beach. When you walked into Janowicz's Dew Drop Inn, the bartender knew your first name, and that wasn't all he knew: He knew that your kid got picked up for speeding, and he knew that your wife threatened to kick you out of the house last week

---

*Hillcrest is not the actual name of the town.

when you dropped a bundle on the Lions. In Janowicz's bar they didn't cheer when Nixon said good-bye.

The newcomers settled north and west of Central. They came in the mid-sixties, and most of them were "knowledge workers." Teachers and librarians, researchers and computer analysts, mechanical engineers and statisticians, bookkeepers and actuaries. Many of them were WASPs, although there was a fair-sized contingent of Jews and a sprinkling of blacks. They drank their stingers and rob roys in the Commuter Café, preferred an evening at the Straw Hat Theatre to a barbecue in the backyard, and they drove Volkswagens and sometimes BMWs, if they could afford them, not Fords and Chevys. They voted for Johnson in 1968, split on Nixon in 1972. On Saturday night they defended busing; on Monday they sent the kids off to private schools.

Arthur Schwartz was a relative newcomer to Hillcrest. He and his family arrived in 1964. He bought a house in the white-collar district for $56,000. Arthur had been a tenured psychology professor at a branch of the Michigan state university system. I met him through a mutual friend who thought it would be interesting to talk to a man who once seemed to have the safest job in the world. It was safe until 1975, when the state had withdrawn funding from the human relations laboratory Arthur directed. Almost a year before I arrived, he had received a mimeographed form letter, with his name typed in, informing him that his job had been abolished. "It was a negative, legalistic type document that winds up with, 'And thank you for your long service to the college.' 'I felt like taking it and jamming it up the dean's rear end,' " Arthur told me.

After twenty-five years in the academic world, Schwartz felt he had been knifed, double-crossed by a callous administration that didn't give a damn about students or dedicated teachers. That's the way he told it, and the reason he told it that way was that it absolved him of guilt for not taking a job. He would not allow his virtue to be compromised again by the unprincipled university system.

The self-pity gave him a cover for not getting a job. He wasn't going to be hired because he was fifty years old. He wasn't going to be hired because he was Jewish and white, when "all universities care about is hiring blacks." He wasn't going to be hired because he was asking for a salary that rewarded his skill and experience. "They won't pay a man like me $30,000 because they can go out and get two twenty-eight-year-olds and pay 'em $12,000 each." He wasn't going to be hired because his creativity and enthusiasm and concern for students would disturb the established order of things. "One college I interviewed, the president just says, 'Yeah, I know a lot of the staff isn't working, but they're professionals and professionals determine how much work has to be done.' I know I frightened him because I represented a threat to the school's apathy and superficiality. You know why I'm laughing? I'm the kind of guy who doesn't belong in this century. I have long felt I should have been born in a more idealistic period. I believe in silly things like honesty and integrity. I believe in old hokey things like an educator is there because the students are there and not the other way around."

As if to prove his charges, Arthur Schwartz riffles through the stack of copies of applications he has sent to two dozen or more universities. The evidence is not entirely persuasive. Arthur Schwartz practices a small self-deception. He applies for a job he knows he is not going to get. In the tight academic job market of 1976, he is not going to be hired as a dean of students. In fact, he is deliberately putting himself into a noncompetitive position.

Schwartz has a secret life which he reveals over a chef's salad in the Commuter Café. Now I understand that crackling tension I first felt when he and his wife were talking about his period of unemployment. Now I understand his bluff prediction: "Even if I'm out of work for another year we won't starve, we'll survive," and his wife's rigidly controlled skepticism: "Yes, but . . . if you're sure." The secrets pour out. He wants to divorce the woman he's been married to for twenty-five years. She is in the middle of the latest in a succession of nervous breakdowns. One of his children has tried to commit suicide. He is having an affair with a woman who teaches at a Catholic college.

What, I ask, does all of this have to do with his not working? "I'm breaking out of my role, the husband, the provider. My wife'd want me to take any job, security is so important to her. By not doing that I'm separating myself from her, I'm declaring my independence. I can't say that outright, but that's what I'm doing. Otherwise, I'd be going right along, as I always went along with her. I'm breaking the news to her in two stages. One, I'm not going to go back to work like she wants. Two, I'll file for divorce."

He has received a few job offers—from an insurance company and an educational counseling service—but rejected them; they didn't pay enough, they were too commercial. Arthur Schwartz was not telling Sarah Schwartz straight out: He was communicating in code. He must send out the applications and vitae for jobs he cannot get and reject the ones offered him and hope his wife deciphers the code. Why the deviousness? Is it because the probity of Jewish family life demands it, brands as an outcast a man who breaks up his family in midlife? Is it because he himself cannot accept the loss of the high-caste mark of academic tenure? He couldn't come out and tell the community—friends, relatives, neighbors—in Hillcrest that he is rejecting work, tell this community that elected him to the school board and to the boards of a half dozen social service organizations, that his family life is a shambles. Arthur Schwartz is a man out in the cold, and he needs a cover in Hillcrest.

I remember sitting in his living room the first day I met him when he described the response in Hillcrest to his not working. His wife, a short, wiry woman, sat rigidly on the edge of her chair, her lips clamped shut in a thin, hard line, neither confirming nor denying what he said.

"Society is not condemning me," he said that first day. "It's been a supportive-type situation if anything. We're not starving either. We're living on unemployment, a few bucks that I can pick up here or there. A friend of mine has a cosmetics distributorship. He says the government allows him fifteen cents a mile for making deliveries. He asked me to make the deliveries and he'd pay me the fifteen cents. In effect, it's amortizing my car, and it's keeping me off the streets."

Did he spend more time with his family since stopping work?

"No, my daughter is a typical teenager who has mucho friends. She doesn't need me for her social life. With her, I don't think the situation has changed at all. In terms of *my wife*, it's about the same time." The woman he referred to in the third person as "my wife" said nothing.

Family expenses?

"We're living on unemployment, on my pension money. We used to periodically go out to dinner, and it just means we don't go out now. We don't go to the movies. I don't have a large wardrobe. I don't have to buy new clothes. I don't really miss anything. We've had kids in college for five and a half years so we never lived high on the hog. We used to go on vacation for a week every year, but living in this town, it's like being in the country, there's a lot of beauty for free. I just don't believe I'm ever going to starve whether I get a job this winter or next spring or whenever."

I turned to Sarah and asked her what her reaction was when he stopped working.

Sarah answered by saying to Arthur, "At first you thought there might be a chance they would accept you back into the college."

"Well, that was a *hope*. I didn't think so. My attitude then and my attitude since then is this family will survive. We're not going to starve. We'll just cut down on luxuries."

I asked him whether he had discussed his decision to stay out of work with his family. "No, I made that decision unilaterally." Sarah said nothing.

"Five years ago if this happened, I would have worried, I would have been uptight. Since this happened, it's made *me* personally evaluate what my needs are, what's important to me. I came to the conclusion that money is really a means to an end. This made it a less frightening reality than it would have been five years ago. It used to be important to me to get a car every few years. The important thing is I do not believe I've failed. I believe that the college, the university system in Michigan, has failed. I don't consider being fired a personal defeat."

I asked him whether in another eight months he would be willing to reduce further his living costs so that he wouldn't have to take a job he didn't want.

"What's your reaction to that, Sarah?" he asked. "Let's say in December we found ourselves with no money. We had to sell our house and had to use food stamps. Would you think I could afford to be selective? We have to speculate about it."

Sarah on the spot, said nothing.

"I figure," he went on, "that this family can afford to live—without considering the house—another ten to twelve months."

"Your unemployment expires," Sarah said.

"Yeah, but that doesn't amount to much. My daughter is on financial aid from the university. She'll also work during the summer."

"What about food stamps?" I ask.

"I really don't know if we qualify," Sarah said, in a barely audible whisper.

"No, we don't," Arthur said. "I went to apply, and they told me we don't. They won't give you any money if you have fifteen hundred dollars in the bank. If we were on food stamps, I'd probably go over to Morrisville or Lincoln township, rather than deal with the local merchants. I think that might be a residual effect of my feeling about the work ethic, maintaining myself. I know I'd never go on welfare. Never. The welfare mentality is one of the most disgusting things. I think even food stamps would bother me. Also, I don't like the mentality of the people you have to deal with to get the stamps. For me to be questioned about the truth of what you're saying ... they don't trust anyone. If you look at the people who are on unemployment, here, they're white. That's a complete reversal of the welfare line."

And how have the people in the community responded to his unemployment?

"I think," Sarah said, "because there are other people in the community out of work ... I don't think people would react negatively." Arthur: "I've gotten no negative reaction. In terms of the positive—people here are nice people. Not like Hillsdale Estates, where everybody is trying to outdo the next. A friend who fixed our washing machine, for example, didn't charge me anything because I'm not working. A lot of people here know about it. The entire faculties of both high schools know about it, and it hasn't affected their relationships with me as a member of the board of education. They're concerned, sure. People will go up to my daughter and say, 'How's your father doin'?' But nobody's criticizing me. Look, 14 percent of the homeowners in this town are unemployed. And now you can't buy a house for less than fifty thousand dollars in this town. I'd guess that 50 to 60 percent of the people who are working now were out of work once.

"If you had the time, you'd find out that not working is a common experience in Hillcrest. It's just something you accept. People accept me working or not working."

I spent the next two weeks in Hillcrest. I wanted to find out whether not working was as common as Arthur Schwartz said it was. I also wanted to investigate the ambivalence I sensed here. The community might not condemn the individual who stopped working, but did it approve? There would be support for someone who was thrown out of a job and who was actively looking for another one. But what would your neighbor say if you announced that you had had it up to here with work? In Hillcrest I had the feeling you needed an acceptable justification, an excuse like the one Arthur Schwartz had contrived—that he was just being selective, that he'd go back in a minute if the right job came along.

In south Hillcrest people don't bother much with cover stories. Maybe there's just no way to lie about not working. Life is too out in the open, too close to the surface to indulge in artifice. Here people know when you're applying for a job you're not going to get. People know when you're using not working as a wedge to get out of a marriage. At the same time, I found that not working was not as shocking a statement as I thought it would be. Nobody, working or not working, seemed terribly romanced with their work. The people I spoke to did not condemn others who had stopped. They might be looking forward to the day when they could stop. But they also worried about the future. They were anxious about what would happen to a relative or a close friend who didn't work. They had learned that it's possible to get along from day to day without working—many of them had gone through extended periods of unemployment themselves—but an uncertain future troubled them.

What follows are excerpts from a diary I kept during my two weeks in Hillcrest in the summer of 1976. My first entries concern the Antonellis, a family I met through an official in a local of the construction workers' union in Flint.

JULY 4—A quiet celebration with the Antonellis. Four generations are at the table. Joseph Antonelli is seventy-four, a retired watch repairman. Mike Senior is fifty-three, a supervisor for the phone company. Mike Junior is thirty-five. The last time he worked was nearly three years ago as a mason when a new bank building went up in Flint. Two of his five children, Cathy, ten, and Angie, eight, are also there. (The other three are celebrating the holiday with their mother.) During the day an assortment of aunts, uncles, and friends drop in for a plate of pasta, a glass of wine, and a chicken leg or two.

The celebration is subdued because Mike Junior has recently separated from his wife. Three months ago he came to live with his parents in their two-family house. Mike's mother, Marie, was not happy about it. "Let him stay with his wife and family," she told her husband. "She'll make him find a job. That's why he's coming here, so he won't have to work."

Mike Senior beat down her resistance. "Better than he moves into a boarding house. We're still his parents, no? In three years she didn't get him to work. So maybe we try."

That they accepted him back into the house in this tightly knit family-centered community was not surprising. But what Mike tells me that night as we wash dishes is: "They put a condition on it. I had to support myself. No freeloading. I had to pay rent, buy my own food. I say, 'Hey, I got no plans to work, right now.' And they say, 'Okay, but you still gotta come up with the money.'"

The next week Mike went to the Flint welfare office and applied for assistance. He brought with him a notarized statement, signed by his parents, attesting to his presence in their house and stipulating that he would have to pay $145 a month in rent.* He is now receiving the rent money from the state as well as $94 a month for living expenses. He also received Medicaid and food stamps, which he pays for out of the $94.

"Construction, it's a tight line," Mike Senior says. "It's not only his fault he's out of work. The way I look at it, he paid taxes, I paid taxes, so we get some of the taxes back. Yeah, we're not rich, but we could put him up, we could feed him, there's always a plate. Why should we? The

---

*Actually, he only pays his parents the sixty dollars they set as his rent payment. He keeps the rest of the money he receives from welfare for his personal expenses.

blacks, the Puerto Ricans, they get welfare, right? An Italian shouldn't?"

On that level, then, with reservations of course, the Antonellis have accepted their son's disinclination to work. They would like him to get another job, but they don't seem to be ashamed that he is on welfare or that they pushed him to get assistance. If they are concerned that the welfare money will tempt him to stay out of work indefinitely, they don't show it.

On another level, they do express concern. That concern is directed toward the future. This Sunday it's as if every rest home, nursing home, retirement home in the state of Michigan has opened its doors and disgorged the residents into the land of the self-sufficient. The Antonellis receive what seems like an endless stream of aunts, uncles, friends, friends of friends, old neighbors who have been let out for the July Fourth afternoon. "Mr. Lefkowitz, I want you to meet Louis Alfieri, he lives in St. Mary's . . . Mr. Lefkowitz, I want you to meet Anna Rossi, she went into St. Catherine's last year. She's doing well."

What totally amazes me is that these people are not gravely ill, they're not infirm, they're not senile. It's as if the moment you turn sixty, you're committed. I look at a sixty-two-year-old woman who suffered a stroke two years ago. She gets around with the help of a walker. She has a bit of a vision problem. Otherwise she seems perfectly fine. She carries on a lively conversation, eats her third helping of lasagna, and exhibits a facility for the lethally understated comment. After her stroke, her husband dumped her into the old-age warehouse. She and her husband are not poor and they are not really old. For a fraction of what it costs to maintain her in the nursing home, she could be cared for in her own house. "It's not too bad at the home," she says, "the people have something in common. It's just that the staff, they don't have much time for you. Seems like they're afraid almost to talk to you. You feel like you're a burden, inside and outside."

After an early dinner, the Antonellis and their relatives form a motorcade to visit all the nursing-home residents who were not let out for the holiday. These homes have a dreary uniformity—the fluorescent lighting, the television sets mounted on the walls in the rooms, the ever-present smell of disinfectant. We march through these premises carrying our offerings: foil-wrapped chicken and pasta. (Why doesn't somebody smuggle in a bottle of Scotch? Why doesn't somebody smuggle in a book?) The conversations are as cheerless as the furnishings.

"So, how are you feeling?"

"Oh, I can't complain. What's the use of complaining?"

"They treatin' you all right?"

"They changed the menu."

"Do you get enough food?"

"Enough. But who wants to eat it?"

On and on we go: through St. Mary's and St. Catherine's, through Alfred Hall and Hillsborough Retirement Home. When we have made our last visit, Mike Senior and Mrs. Antonelli drive me back to Hillcrest. Mike Junior is in another car.

"Do a lot of people wind up in these homes?" I ask Mr. Antonelli.

"A lot. It's a big industry here. The old family ways, they're not the same. When you get old, the family doesn't believe in taking care of you. You go to the home."

"That's why I worry about Mike," Marie Antonelli says. "What will happen to him when he gets old and we're gone? No wife, no money. I don't mind, he doesn't work. But I can't sleep sometimes. Will he end up in a welfare home? They don't feed them so good there. They rot there. I want him to have money so he can live in a nice home, where they take care of you."

"Ah, what's the use," Mr. Antonelli says. "Mike doesn't think about the future. Today, it's only today, he worries about."

I am about to fall asleep in the Antonelli's guest room when Mike Junior walks in, carrying a glass of coffee sweetened with anisette. "Got an eyeful, today?" he asks. "The nursing homes, some life? That's the whole point, huh. They think I should work and save my money so I can go to Alfred Hall and die watching color TV. Some payoff. Thirty years my father works for the phone company, and all he thinks about is when they're gonna put him in a home and will there be enough money to pay for it. Me, I figure a charity home, a private home, what the fuck difference is it. If that's what you work for, if that's how it adds up, I'll be fucked if I'm gonna work."

JULY 5—Mike and his father are standing in line at the First National Bank of Hillcrest. Mike had asked him to drive him to the bank so he could cash his welfare check.

This is the bank where Mike's father deposits his salary check.

This is the bank where Mike once deposited his salary check.

Now this is the bank where Mike cashes his welfare check.

Finally his father can't hold back any longer. "You were doin' okay. You had a job. Now you got this. I just wanna ask you: What are you gonna do when you retire?"

"Pop," he says. "You don't understand. I've already retired."[1]

JULY 6—Mike had shown me a letter he had received from the bank. It had said:

Michael C. Antonelli, Jr.
118 Morris Road
Hillcrest, Michigan

Dear Mr. Antonelli:

Next time you reach for your credit card to charge a big purchase ... stop. Take out your First National checkbook instead. Not enough money in your account? Look again. You have a cash reserve credit line of $500.... It gives you just as much *charge power* as any retail credit card ... maybe more.... Just as much time to pay it back ... maybe more. Yet your cash reserve costs less to use than a credit card. That's a fact. Compare the rates.... It's the best borrowing bargain you own.

P.S. You may qualify for a cash reserve credit line of up to $5,000. If you wish to increase your present line, please complete the application on the reverse side and mail in the envelope provided.

It was signed by Dan Vronek, chief loan officer of the bank.

Now I went to the loan department and Dan

Vronek was leaning back in his swivel chair and tapping his pencil on the desk. "Do we make loans to individuals who aren't working?" he said, measuring each word carefully. "Ten years ago I would have said almost never. Back then we'd ask the applicant for a copy of his last tax return. If he couldn't show a steady job with income of more than twelve thousand dollars a year, there was no way I could pass a loan. Unless it was a special case—the guy just had a bad year—it would get stopped automatically.

"That's not true anymore. I can't give you an exact figure, but 20 to 30 percent of our personal loans go to people who may not be working. Take a typical case. The man's banked with us for five years. Maybe his parents have banked with us for fifteen or twenty years. He has two thousand dollars in his account. We hold the mortgage on his house. Two years ago he paid off a car loan on time. His wife may be working, earning ten thousand dollars a year. The most important thing to us is: Does he seem stable? Does he own a house? Does he have a car? Does he have a family? Has he lived in the area for a while? Is he a good credit risk? That's the big thing. Nowadays, the easiest way to get a loan is to be in debt. If you pay cash, you don't have a credit record; it's very hard for us to make a judgment."

Would Mike Antonelli, unemployed for three years, qualify for a five-thousand-dollar credit line?* "Mike, why sure," Vronek said. "I've

---

*The bank letter was a computer slip-up. A few months before Mike had withdrawn his savings and put them in his father's account so that he would be eligible for welfare.

known his dad for years, a hard-working man. Mike, definitely. He's a very good risk."

JULY 7—Flint reporter says I should talk to P. R. guy at police department about cops who have quit early. The guy sets up a meeting with Ray Halligan, a big red-haired ex-cop who stopped working two years ago and now says he's retired for life. Halligan talks to me while building a swing in his backyard. His wife serves lemonade.

Halligan left the force after injuring his leg when he totalled his patrol car. He walks with a hardly noticeable limp. Since his injury was job related, he receives a pension that comes to three quarters of his salary. He also has applied for job-disability compensation from the state of Michigan. "I'm pretty sure I'll get it," he says. "How can they turn down an ex-cop whose patrol car was wrecked?"

He is thirty years old. He had been a police officer for eight years before the accident. Ray looks pretty fit. "The leg doesn't bother me much. I mean, I wouldn't want to chase a guy down an alley, but I can do pretty heavy work. I'm planning to build a cabin in the country, and I don't think I'm gonna have any problems with it."

I asked him if he had looked for another job after leaving the police department. "I didn't want this injury, but since it happened I thought I might as well take advantage of what comes with it. Why should I work when my income is more than enough to meet my needs? At least that's the way I feel now. If I get the state compensation, that's another three hundred dollars a month. I didn't make up the rules. The P.D. pays three quarters salary to anyone hurt on the job.

It's like insurance. I paid for it every week, and I'm collecting on it.

"Same way with the comp. If I'm entitled, I'm going to collect. I can use whatever's comin' to me. It doesn't hurt anybody. The city never hired anybody to fill my spot. When I was working, they had to pay my salary plus two dollars for every dollar I contributed into the pension fund. Now I'm retired, so they don't have to pay my salary and they don't have to kick into the pension fund. The day I retired the city started saving money. The money I get is from the pension fund, not from the city. Hey, they want guys to retire. When I leave, they unburden the payroll."

Since he was capable of holding another job, did he have any qualms about applying for state compensation? "It's an edge against the cost of living," Ray Halligan says. "When the cost of living goes up, my pension stays the same. I got a lot of years to go before I collect social security and a couple of mouths to feed, even though Mary's working now. The way prices of things are going up, I may not be able to make it on my pension alone. Anyway, why shouldn't I get disability? I'm disabled. It says so right on the paper, on the reports. I'm a disabled cop. I never collected a dime in my life on anything, except when we had the fire. I did have fire insurance and collected on that. But I worked eight years. Put in eight years. That gives me a right, hey."

JULY 9—"I was sittin' in the car with Ray, ten months, maybe a year before the accident, and I said, 'Hell, Ray, you don't really want to be a cop.' He didn't argue with me. I think that's the first time anybody said that to him. He just nodded." Bob Downes was Ray Halligan's partner in the patrol car for five years. He was not injured in the accident, but he has been reassigned to station-house work as a sergeant. "Eight years, Ray put in. He served his time." Downes continues, "I don't think anybody holds it against him he's retired. I couldn't do it, but it's his decision, I guess—not working, I mean."

Downes is thirty-nine and he's been a policeman for fifteen years. "My father was a cop, my brother's a cop. It's more than a job, it's a life. I wouldn't know what to do if I wasn't a cop. With Ray, it was a job. He was a good guy to work with, but he kept pretty much to himself. I had the feeling it could've been any job, construction or factory work. It paid his meal money. I don't think it really bothered him when his leg got hurt. I think he liked the idea he could call himself disabled. Me, it'd bother. I'd feel like I wasn't worth much, sorta used up. But I understand what he's saying. Everybody's out for their own. Everybody rips off what they can get, as long as they don't get caught. Nobody cares if Ray's got a free ticket, it doesn't hurt nobody. I guess I was surprised at one thing. He only lives a mile or so away from us, but he never called, not once, after he got off the force."

I stood on the train platform waiting for a train to Flint, where I would catch a plane back to New York. Most of the people I had met in Hillcrest— Arthur Schwartz, Mike Antonelli, Ray Halligan— had not met with retribution for stopping work. They continued to live, much as they always had, in Hillcrest.

Back in New York, looking over my notes, I realized that one theme ran through almost all of my interviews in Hillcrest. That was the banality of not working. In my father's time, the man who stopped working, even for a relatively short time, had severed his ties with the dominant culture. If he was not scorned, he would be pitied. In Hillcrest in 1976, there was no central controlling culture. Rather, several cultures—young and old, consuming and simple living, family centered and unanchored, ethnic and assimilated—coexisted on a level of rough parity. There was no center there or anyplace else I visited in America, no heart and soul of the country to tell you whether you were in or out. But there were many centers, sometimes overlapping, sometimes separate, but all relatively tolerant of each other's peculiarities and singularity.

To varying degrees, the significance and centrality of work had declined in all of these neighboring cultures. The unbroken string of workdays in my father's life was much less common than the stop-and-go pattern of work in Hillcrest. Most of the people I had spoken to there had taken time off before; familiarity had taken the fear out of not working. And it was not only the economic fear. To answer my father's question, in Hillcrest some of the neighbors might say, I think Joe would be happier if he got a steady job, but others would say, Joe's a good guy, a good son, a good friend whether he's working or not. Sam Schwartz was right when he said that in Hillcrest there was nothing aberrant about stopping work.

This seemed to hold true nationally. In February 1977 the unemployment rate was 7.5 percent or

7,183,000 people. When Harvard economist Martin Feldstein analyzed the statistics, he found that only a third of the unemployed had been fired or had their jobs eliminated. Adding together the number of people who had been fired and those who had been temporarily laid off, the total came to less than half of the unemployed. The rest were individuals who had left their jobs voluntarily (11.9 percent), people who were just coming back into the job market after a voluntary absence (27.5 percent), and newcomers to the job market (13.1 percent).[2]

A conservative national estimate is that 40 percent of the unemployed choose not to work. Moreover, the number of prime-working-age men who had left the labor force—they were not looking for work, they didn't want to work—increased 71 percent from 1968 to 1977.[3] And that's only the people counted by the government. How many millions more that have disappeared entirely from the work force is not something that the federal government includes in its monthly computer printouts. Eli Ginzberg, the economist, points out that "the number of job seekers who wanted [or settled for] less than full-time work [in the last twenty-five years] increased three times as much as the number of those on a full-time schedule."[4]

In Hillcrest many of the work-age men have held blue-collar jobs. Their work lives have been spotted with extended periods of unemployment. Layoffs in auto factories, cutbacks in construction work, plants consolidating their operations, automation—this was the built-in pattern of working-class jobs. They were accustomed to not working, and some of them looked forward to it. When thousands of workers were laid off by the auto makers in 1975 and 1976, Robert Schrank, drawing on his trade union background, expected a massive protest. "I thought there'd be a hundred thousand auto workers in Cadillac Square in Detroit," Schrank says.

But there were no protests in Cadillac Square. Schrank had forgotten to add up the numbers. The laid-off workers were receiving unemployment insurance checks in addition to union supplemental benefits that amounted to nearly 95 percent of their take-home pay for a year. Workers with advanced seniority *demanded* that they be laid off ahead of the younger workers. When Schrank talked to officials of the United Auto Workers, they said, "What protest? We can't find half these guys—they took off for Florida. They don't want to stay a cold winter in Michigan when they don't have to."

(In Hillcrest I had spoken to the deputy director of the state unemployment insurance office. "We know," he said, "that there's an increasing number of repeaters. People who collected for a number of weeks, say two years ago, and are out of work again. We don't know if they're caught in a cycle of employment and layoff or if they're fixing it so they can collect after working for a minimum number of weeks.

"Another interesting thing: People who switch their claims to other states and cities, like Albuquerque or Tucson or Miami, that's increasing. If you were cynical, you'd say they're leaving town for a vacation. If you were a trusting soul, you'd say they're going where the job opportunities are better, except there's no indication there are more jobs in those cities. Also, they do seem to come back to Hillcrest and reinstate their claims when the first robin shows up.

"One thing I didn't realize before I took this job is how deeply engrained the idea of not working is. It's sorta our national secret, everybody knows about it, nobody talks about it. These people have gotten used to being laid off, they've gotten used to closings. Before their boss told them when there wasn't gonna be any work. Now they decide when they feel they don't have to work. They control the decision.")

Blue collar or white collar, working or not working, I didn't meet many people in Hillcrest who were in love with their jobs. Maybe this is why Mike Antonelli wasn't tougher on his son; when I asked him about his work at the telephone company, all he said was, "It's a job." Maybe this is why Ray Halligan's wife didn't press him to find a job. When I asked her about her job as an inventory clerk in a discount drug and sundries store, she said, "It's extra money, it makes things easier, but if I had money coming in from the state and from a pension the way Ray does, I'd quit tomorrow."

Professor Eli Ginzberg defines a good job as one that offers above-average wages, fringe benefits, regular employment, and opportunities for advancement. Those kinds of jobs are scarce. In the last twenty-five years, he found, more than three out of every five new jobs were in retail trade or services where "many jobs are part-time and wages are traditionally low. . . . Between 1950 and 1976 about two and a half times as many new jobs were added in industries that provide below-average weekly earnings as were added in industries that provide above-average earnings."

It's not only earnings that make the difference. As a mason, Mike Antonelli, Jr., made good money—when there was work. But he got tired of kicking back part of every paycheck to his foreman and to his union rep. "What kinda work you did had nothin' to do with whether they kept you on the job or whether you got called the next time something opened up." Mike rubbed his fingers. "This is what counted." Ray Halligan made a decent living as a cop; he knew he wouldn't be laid off. Yet for a couple of years he had been looking for a way out. He complained about the ever-growing volume of paperwork, about the lack of appreciation for extra effort, about liberal judges who treated him like a criminal, about department politics which valued cost reductions and administrative procedure more than a good collar. That's why he says, "They didn't cry when I left. It means there was one less budget slot for them to fill. I mean, those guys stayed up at night worrying about how to speed up attrition."

No one I talked to in Hillcrest believed in the intrinsic worth of work. It wasn't endowed with a spiritually regenerative force that would make them better people. They did not feel spurred on to nab one more carload of juiced-up kids or to build one more perfect skyscraper or to teach one more terrific psych class.

If a wonderful job came along, they might be lured out of their mid-life retirement. But their attitude, which stripped the work-ethic myth of all its motive power, was that they were entitled to a job that was satisfying, and if they couldn't find one, they were entitled to take their leisure. Along with all the social benefits provided by a semiwelfare state, they tagged on a good job. Without it, they welcomed the benefit of government-supported retirement.

It took me a while to understand what the people in Hillcrest were telling me. One man who helped me was James O'Toole, the former Rhodes scholar who directed the Presidential Task Force on Work in America in the early 1970s and who, when I talked to him, taught at the School of Business Administration at the University of Southern California.[5]

As far as O'Toole knew, his father was a staunchly conservative man. He had always been loud in condemning welfare cheats, no-work bums who leeched off decent, hard-working taxpayers. A few years back O'Toole's mother died at her job. The next day his father stopped working. His father didn't have much money, only a small pension, and very little savings. A few weeks later his father applied for food stamps. In effect his father told him: "I've worked for so many years at a shitty job, I'm entitled even if those other bums aren't." It wasn't the work he disliked, he had always taken pleasure in working with his hands. But when he quit, his son found out that "his relationship with his boss was so damn shitty all those years. He would never admit it when he was working, but he did at the end."

His father's experience had special significance for O'Toole who has spent a lot of time thinking about the changing meaning of work in contemporary America. Here was his father, a man in his sixties, who had quit his job, applied for food stamps, and confessed after all these years that he despised his boss. On the other side of the generation gap, O'Toole was watching, with some incredulity, his brightest, presumably highly motivated graduate students at the business school proclaim their own independence. In 1975 and 1976 while the country was deep in a recession, a number of these students had rejected solid middle-level positions with General Motors.

"I spoke to a G.M. vice-president and he wasn't sure what the hell was going on," O'Toole recalls. "Here were M.B.A. students, the most business-oriented people you could imagine. And they were turning down good-paying jobs. He didn't know whether it was the idea of living in Detroit or that they didn't want to go to work for General Motors. Whatever the reason was, it just floored him."

O'Toole began asking his students questions. "Half, roughly half [of the students] are traditional. They are looking upward. They are prepared to work for a while to get a position they want. The other half, they hold new values. They could get a job in New York or Detroit, but they won't. And they won't talk about it. They keep it to themselves. Ten years ago, the job was the most important thing. Now something else: They feel they're entitled to a job with authority and decision-making power. But those jobs are rare. So they won't settle—they won't take a job that doesn't give 'em what they want, even though the salaries are there. You see, I've been raised with this idea, somebody's out of work, they're depressed. They feel stinko. That's changed. Once any job was a good job. Now my father, the students are telling me something else: They'd rather have no job at all than a lousy job."

The work-place problems O'Toole identified in the 1972 Task Force report have not vanished; he believes they have been ignored because the issues they raise are too unpleasant for management or government to confront. "Absenteeism is one way of looking at the whole question of job satisfaction. Are people finding ways to stay away from work? Well, it's almost impossible to get good, solid statistics on absenteeism. Companies don't want to collect the data, and if they do have it, they don't want to make it available. I suspect the rates are much higher than they'll admit. If a worker had a hangover, in another time, he would have dragged his ass in. Now he calls in sick, uses up the sick leave coming to him. Is it the hangover or is it his feeling about work? They don't want to ask that kind of question. An executive is being transferred. Rather than move his family to another city, he quits. Is he quitting because he doesn't want to move, or is he looking for an excuse to get out? We don't know the answers to these questions, and I think we're afraid to find out."

LIFE IN THE DISCARDO CULTURE

Punctured in the Midwest, the work myth was stabbed in the heart at America's psychological frontier, at the edge of the San Andreas fault. The deed went almost unnoticed. There were so many other psychological transformations underway that the more subtle dissociation of work and self evolved virtually undocumented. Compared to the innovations of the beat generation and Haight Ashbury, of the psychedelic laboratories and the self-growth and human potential movements, kissing work good-bye was as dramatic an event as a Rotarian clean-up-Main-Street campaign.

Of course, if you needed help taking the step, you could always take a course. A college in San Francisco gave classes on how to stop working until the teacher decided to stop working. Its place has been taken by a variety of organizations, not the least of which is one called New Ways to Work, which instructs candidates for change in such work-shrinking alternatives as job sharing and flexitime. Flexitime allows an employee to tailor his work time to accommodate really important interests— such as sailing. Job sharing, in which one work position is shared by two or more persons, is directed toward the same purpose.[1] In its brochure, the organization describes various situations where these tactics would be appealing. They are all listed under the heading: Adaptation to Change.

A writer, visiting California for the first time, once observed, "Change becomes the one predictable ingredient in the California bouillabaisse." The writer recalled meeting a graphics designer who said he was a member of the "discardo" culture where "it was bad form to hang on to things." One day the apartment house where the designer lived burned down. "He was surprised, but undisturbed.

His wife had just left him; it seemed somehow in the scheme of things that his belongings should now be pouring out of broken windows in the form of smoke and ashes."[2]

By the time I arrived, the irrelevancy of work, already firmly established in San Francisco, Berkeley, and Santa Cruz, had made inroads into the more conservative outposts of Sacramento and Arcadia, Seattle and Olympia, Salem and Cascade. And so when I appeared to inquire about what the neighbors were saying, to poke around in the social world of not working, I was greeted as an anthropologist excavating the ancient past.

Lucille Roberts: Minor Adjustments

On an earlier excursion west, I had placed an advertisement in a San Francisco newspaper. Lucille was one of the first respondents. For eight or nine months we had maintained a running correspondence. When I finally arrived in Monterey, I felt as if I were visiting an old friend. I was particularly comfortable with her because she hadn't discarded her eastern ways. She hadn't traded words for babblespeak. She hadn't lost the mocking irreverence I identify with the effort to stay sane after a thousand rush hours in the subway.

Lucille Roberts drove across the country from Massachusetts with her four children in 1972, as if she were "grandfather on a red pony." In the distance beckoned California, where she would "enter on a new life." She found some of what she was looking for: beaches, pretty country, a slower pace, independence, and a new set of friends. She also came upon a few less desirable cultural traits: the dread fear of a provocative thought, a masculine allergy to a strong-willed woman, and a million and one salvation cults. Lucille wasn't interested in salvation, only the freedom to show what she was made of. And for all the efforts to remake her in the estian image, she has remained herself. There is an eastern snap and crackle to her that the sun and sand will never polish smooth.

When I asked her how not working had affected her personal life and social relationships, she responded as my father would have. She talked first about money and then about the neighbors.

She was receiving $700 a month, from her unemployment insurance, from her late husband's veterans' benefits, and from the rent money a local student paid for boarding in her house. It was roughly one third of what she was earning at her last job.

Her house has a comfortable sun deck and looks down on the ocean. The house is filled with books and music. There's a fireplace in the living room and antique quilts in the upstairs bedrooms. The house hasn't changed because she's stopped working.

"I honestly don't feel I have less money than when I worked," she says. "When I think of what I've cut down on, I realize how little I'm missing. I still buy the basic staples—milk, bread, eggs. I gave up bacon for a while because I figured it's nine tenths fat and very expensive. Why should I buy it? And then one day I got really hungry for it and broke down and bought some nice lean stuff. It was expensive, but I figured in the time I didn't buy it I have saved the money so I could do it that one time. I try not to buy a lot of junk, especially canned food, stuff that's filled with sodium nitrate. I buy a lot of fresh vegetables. Before this, I didn't think about what I was putting into my stomach.

"There are all sorts of labor-barter things here. I latched onto a guy who fixed cars for the cost of parts. When I arrived at his place, his kitchen looked like it had been blitzed. While he was working on my car, I quietly cleaned it up. I still expected to pay him something. When he saw the kitchen, he said, 'I don't want any money.' I said, 'Well, you'd probably like a couple of six packs.' We settled on that. I think I would have been almost reticent in the East to ask neighbors and friends to help me with things like that—it's just not done. You feel a loss of pride. Back there I would never have used a clam bucket for the ice for cocktails. What a disgrace! Here, nobody notices.

"I think about how much I spent when I was working. The gas money, the wear and tear on your car. Now I dovetail my errands. I walk a lot more. When I was working, there was the lunch money— ten, twelve, fifteen dollars a week, depending on what I wanted to eat. Now I've stopped eating lunch. Actually, when I worked the night shift, I ate only two meals a day and I always felt good, and lost weight. When I wake up now, I have a cup of coffee, then when I really feel hungry, I eat brunch, at eleven, eleven-thirty. In the early evening, I have dinner.

"Clothes are not a big problem. I don't have to buy any new lab coats and the slacks that went on under them. The entertainments I have are relatively cheap. It costs me three bucks to play bridge and it gives me a little intellectual exercise. The swim club's only fifteen dollars a month. That I need and I won't give it up. I gave up garbage collection. It was a rip-off, anyway, and half the time they wouldn't come up the hill to collect.

"On the holidays, I send cards instead of gifts. Just the fact that somebody's remembered you counts. At Christmas time I went through all the things I had in the house that I wasn't using that I thought my kids could use. I had a set of lovely china and the silver was just getting tarnished in the drawer. So I split up all those things among the girls. I gave my son a half dozen teaspoons. He was hard pressed that month, so I gave him one month free board in the house.

"If there's a freebie going or a way to do something without spending very much money or a service you can get for next to nothing, I probably know about it at this point. The county health service has a free screening service for anybody over fifty, including X ray, blood pressure, blood count, cardiogram, pap smear. Even if you pay something in the clinic, it's a lot less than going to a private doctor. It doesn't bother me to go to a clinic. It might in Boston, you can spend a couple of hours at the clinic at Mass General, but here it's twenty minutes to a half hour, and the treatment's even better.

"My life isn't very different, at least externally it isn't, and people don't treat me differently, and that makes me comfortable and uncomfortable at the same time. You don't feel pushed here at all. You get into the lackadaisical thing and it's easy and pleasant and nobody upsets the apple cart, but you get to feel restless sometimes, a little worried that maybe you're wasting your life. Right now I feel comfortable; I don't know about the future."

Some people do nag her about getting a job. Eligible men are a little wary when they find out she isn't working. "Most of my close friends know I'm not working and also know by now that I may never want to work again. The longer I don't have a job, the more shocked most of the men are. They want to know, How do you keep yourself going? Are you going to make it? This is the end all and be all of everything. I tell them it doesn't bother me that much. I can meet my bills. If the time comes when I can't, I'll take some kind of job if I have to. One guy, who was kinda interested in me—he's an insurance salesman, a very gung-ho, outspoken, boy-let's-get-the-signature-right-on-the-contract guy—is absolutely horrified that I'm not making an attempt. But I think you have to have an understanding with a guy like that. I've tried to explain, I've reached the stage in my life that I've been in the job market all those years, I went out and did that, I have learned what I want to do, and I'm going to be honest with myself and do what I like to do. He's just going to have to understand that.

"A couple of girl friends will call every now and then and say, 'Is everything all right? Are you working yet?' And they're quite concerned. They have steady jobs, but they also have younger children. I think they're jealous, especially of the fact that I don't have to get up in the morning except when I want to. Strange, sometimes I'll go to bed quite early and get up quite early, and it's almost like I was working again. I tell my girl friends, if they ask, you can do what I'm doing even if you don't have much money. But you have to work out some plan. It'll work if they don't feel panicky about not having as much money as they did before because that's the sine qua non of the whole thing. Really. If you're constantly nagged by your own built-in feeling that I have to have this, I have to have that, where am I going to get the money, then you're going to be in trouble."

Tom MacCauley: A Touch of Envy

One of the advantages of wealth is that it magically transforms nonconformity into old-fashioned American individuality. In Cascade, Idaho, they wonder a little about Tom and Helen MacCauley, but in the end they accept Tom's retirement. They accept him because, although he doesn't work, he is very much like his neighbors, only wealthier than most of them. In this basically conservative community, his feelings of estrangement from the political system and the modish, socially chic innovations of trend-setting institutions fit right in. A lot of the people who live here on these spotless streets, who take pleasure from their hunting dogs and from the big cloudless sky, also feel they have been dealt out.

Phil Lewis, MacCauley's next-door neighbor, is an official in the Idaho state corrections system. Although MacCauley has stopped working at forty-one and he is a couple of hundred thousand dollars richer than Phil, his neighbor considers him a regular guy. "A straight shooter and a little bit of a hell raiser," Lewis said as he brought me over to Tom's house, which is no more opulent than Phil's. "He's not a guy who'll put on airs. He'll drink beer with you all night. Talk politics with you—and what's more, his talk makes sense. He's interested in you. He doesn't think he's special because he has a few bucks. What's he drive, a three-year-old Buick? Maybe people here'd be upset if he sat on his lawn smoking pot or throwing wild parties all night. But he doesn't live that way, he lives like us; maybe some people are curious he doesn't work. It doesn't mean that much to them anyhow."

While Tom and Helen feel accepted in this section of Cascade, they still sense that their neighbors are curious about them and a little envious. "They think Tom belongs to the Mafia," Helen says.

"I told them I do," Tom says, "to tease them. Some of them really think I do. At first I was really free, saying I was retired. Now I find that I just as soon hope they don't ask me, because I think it's sort of embarrassing to them. They feel envious."

"I think they think we're bragging," Helen said. "It doesn't impress us that much that Tom is retired. I get the feeling they resent it, the fact that they have to work and he doesn't."

"The guy down the block is in lumber, big money," Tom said. "He's let me know what he makes, and it's big money. But even him, I think he's a little envious. He's a nice guy and he tries not to show it, but you can see it in some of the things he says. He'll make cracks like: 'Oh, Tom can afford it, he's retired.' They're not vicious remarks, but I think there's a little envy behind them. A few people'll stop and ask me what I'm doing home. And I tell them, and they act like, what the hell, I can't be retired, I'm too young. Sometimes I think they believe I'm a crook or a nut or maybe sick. I just tell 'em

I've sold a couple of businesses in Denver and sold 'em on time, which means I can live off the income. They take it but you can see that it's sometimes a little hard to take, especially if a guy's coming home after a hard day and I'm out in the sun. It's hard to believe, I guess. It doesn't make that much of a difference. I feel I have as much acceptance here as I did when I was in business. People are always a little curious, a little envious if you're doing well."

Frank Morse: On the Frontier of Change

"Change. I didn't know what the word meant until I came out here." Frank Morse isn't talking about yesterday or the day before yesterday. He's talking about 1957. Morse, the architect who came to San Francisco in the late fifties straight out of Yale, got a job at General Dynamics, and in a few years chucked it all when he bought a $1,000 houseboat in Sausalito, has joined me for a drink at an open-air dockside restaurant, which is a ten-minute walk from his houseboat.

"Look at the people I was working with at the company," he says. "One supervisor was as interested in racing sailboats as he was in engineering. A technical writer doubled as a poet. The man in charge of model building wrote about sportfishing for magazines. There was all this switching around. Now remember, I had come here from New York and New Jersey. Back there the competition was in the air, you could just breathe it. There was a Sybaritic atmosphere here; I was here, and I grabbed for it. Maybe it just touched this vein of innate laziness in me. My life was just beginning, and there's the feeling that everything is always just beginning here. I felt I could get away with anything. Nothing I did was irreversible. When I stopped working, I comforted myself with the thought: I can always go back, I can always find a job if I want one. The thing I picked up fast on was the sense of wonderment. People here thought the most ordinary things were fascinating. They were fascinated that I was a Jew and an architect. They were fascinated that I would choose the houseboat and the sailboat over the company and the tract house, but they weren't judgmental. 'Isn't that interesting,' they would say and they meant it. That attitude made it a lot easier for me."

Sitting there in the restaurant, feeling the warm sun, watching the sailboats skate in the bay, nothing seems strange.

Frank is wearing an old pair of khaki shorts and a pullover shirt. A sweater is tied around his waist, insurance against the inevitable evening fog. At the table nearest us, two men wearing business suits are rummaging through their briefcases. Two elderly women are sitting behind us in their pale summer dresses and straw hats. Nothing strange that half the world on this June afternoon is sitting in the sun, watching sailboats, and sipping margaritas, while the other half is harvesting cotton, plotting corporate raids, or becoming famous. Eclecticism reigns in the zone of indifference.

Morse tells me about the job he took after he left General Dynamics. He worked for a one-man architectural firm. The architect, Frank says, was more interested in building private homes out of wood than the more profitable office buildings and apartments where he could have made big dollars. Morse worked for him on and off for a couple of years. The firm prospered, more architects were hired, the pressure heightened to finish work quickly and go on to the next project. "I started to spread myself thin. I wanted to remodel my houseboat, so I'd take some time off for that; then I bought the sailboat and I spent more and more time working on that. Other things interested me as much as architecture. The guy I worked for wanted me to stay on, but if my mind was going to be on other things, then he didn't. And he was getting busier and busier and hiring more people. I guess I would have stuck with him longer if I felt I was needed more."

We have been talking almost an hour, and Frank is uneasy. He wants to get back to the boat. "I'm sorry, but there's so much I have to do this afternoon," he says. What he has to do first is prepare for the meeting that night of the Houseboat Owners' Association, which Morse heads. The association is meeting to protest an increase in the city's anchorage charges. He has to tack flyers at every pier to urge the residents to come to the meeting. His boat is out at the end of the dock, and as we go down the narrow walkway, we can feel it shift slightly with the breeze and the tides. As he goes, he raps on the windows of the boats and waves to neighbors. In a sense, Frank Morse is the unpaid mayor of this floating town, and he keeps in touch with his constituency.

On the deck of his boat, he receives visitors. One man wants to know where he can rent a sailboat for a week. "You sail much?" Morse asks, looking at him, sizing him up. The man assures him he has, and Morse tells him to come back the next day.

"Maybe we can work it out." A neighbor comes by with a rumor that the city is planning to amend the housing code for the boats. "Soon," the neighbor says, "you're going to have to spend a hundred thousand dollars to meet the code." Morse nods sympathetically. "We'll have to do something about that."

The next afternoon when I return to his boat he's just as busy. His impatience shows as he answers my questions while hopping from the deck of his sailboat to the houseboat. "If I don't get this done before tonight, I'm not going to be in the race tomorrow." I assure him that I have only a few more questions, and he can concentrate on mending his sails without interruption. "That's all right," he says, "it's always something."

Today he has to pick up his oldest daughter at her school and take her to the dentist. His wife has called to say she'll have to stay late at the elementary school where she teaches art. Later he'll have to find a mimeograph machine to reproduce the notes from last night's houseboat association meeting. "The notes are dynamite. Boy were people angry. The city isn't going to get away with this." After that, the fish have to be thawed out and cleaned, and he has to start cooking dinner. "Friday's my night."

Before he can get anything done he has to absorb a piece of unsettling news. Mr. Harrison, who lives three boats away, yells over to him, "Frank, did you hear about the new people?"

"No, what happened?"

"They threw their garbage out in the water. Their *garbage*."

"They didn't do that."

"They did. You've got to talk to them."

Frank turns to me, shoulders hunched, hands jammed into the pockets of his windbreaker. "People buy a boat here and they think it entitles them to be bums. There are rules to everything. If people are going to live here, they're gonna have to learn the rules."

Although Frank Morse says he doesn't work, his life clearly has purpose and direction. It also has passion. His daily activities are neither mundane nor trivial; they throb with his love of family, community—and boats. His romance with boats is as ardent today as it was twenty years ago when he graduated from Yale with a degree in architecture. His voice rises to song when he talks about soliciting funds for a museum—a floating museum—of houseboats. His enthusiasm and commitment to what some might consider a hobby has given him status and position in his community. In the nonjudgmental environment of California, he might still be accepted without working if he were a quiet man who kept to himself on his boat. But involved as he is, he has become the nexus of the community; all the gossip, information, political and social developments are hooked up to his receiver. He has earned a prestige that he thinks he would never have achieved as an architect. "I consider myself a guy who was searching for gold and suddenly struck a very rich vein," he says.

First the good news.

In America we have learned to distinguish between the inner man and the outer position. Our experience with flawed leadership has taught us to judge the individual on other grounds apart from the title on his office door and size of his salary check. The psychological emphasis, so marked in this decade, has sensitized us to the importance of personal growth and interior development, which we know, from too many encounters with manic foremen and insecure executives, are not necessarily synonymous with professional advancement.

This accounts, in part, for why we don't demand that the strays return to the fold. Single men in their fifties may approach Lucille Roberts with caution because they don't believe that she doesn't want them as her meal ticket; at the same time, they respect her for what she is—a woman of character. Mike and Marie Antonelli worry, as most parents would, about their son's future if he doesn't get a job, but they don't excommunicate him because they trust him and they know that he never intended to hurt them. Only when we perceive not working as a disguised threat do we condemn the act. Sarah Schwartz has figured out what Arthur is up to. He's using his separation from work as a bludgeon. Her marriage and security are threatened by his admittedly "unilateral" decision.

It's good news that we respect character and can separate it from the job. Now the bad news.

We have, in our inventive American way, substituted the myth of freedom for the work myth. Once it was popular to believe freedom and independence were won by holding down a high-paying secure job. Now more and more people believe the key to personal liberation lies in their distance from work.[3] This myth bears about as much relationship to reality as the work myth did. Not working affords an opportunity to achieve personal goals. It doesn't assure the emancipation of our spirits. That depends on our motivation, on our purpose in not working, and on our psychological perspective.

A primary ingredient in the American version of the freedom myth is our mourning for lost adolescence. The merchants of sentimentality would have us believe that adolescence is all *Grease*, a joyous celebration of irresponsibility and scoring in the back seat. If we scrub away the romantic film, we see it for what it was—occasional achievements and exciting discoveries mixed with shallow truths, purposeless rebellion, conflicting ambitions, and clouded identity. Who am I? we kept asking as kids. What am I going to do with the rest of my life? Our adolescent answers were at best a guess, and all that guessing made adolescence a rather twitchy time.

Almost everyone who contemplates leaving work suffers, to one degree or another, from an attack of juvenility. A few actually try to live as they thought they did when they were adolescents. More common is a desire to act as they think adolescents and postadolescents act today. They don't mourn so much for the adolescence they left behind, but envy that extended not-working period that they think is the luxury of growing up middle class in contemporary America. Most of the people I talked to, particularly those in their thirties and forties, went to work while they were in high school. If they went to college, they had to work to pay their way. They feel they missed something—years of joyous irresponsibility.

They say, "Look around and what do you see: All those kids, who aren't really kids, who are supported until they're twenty-eight by daddy. They have nothing to worry about aside from getting a date on Friday night or conning the teacher into giving them a higher grade than they deserve. And me, me I grew up in Kansas, my father made me take a job in the dry goods store when I was fifteen, I escaped to New York after high school, which my parents never forgave me for, put in my time at the Barbizon Hotel for Women, started selling dresses, learned to smile when that fat buyer squeezed my knee, smiled all the way up to 25M a year and the vice-presidency. Dammit, I don't want responsibilities anymore. Dammit, I want to enjoy life like those kids."

One reason why a social stigma no longer attaches itself to not working is the widespread and deep-seated fantasy of being taken care of. Of being a dependent again. Of having somebody feed me, clothe me, tell me I'm the most wonderful son and daughter in the world. Of having somebody tell me everything's going to be all right.

It's a rough world out there, and most of us, briefly, feel the need for the security of the womb. The trouble is very few people in our social worlds are prepared to perform as surrogate parents. Quickly most of us realize that work stops but our responsibilities continue. Life outside of work is a free-lance existence. Not only are we responsible to our dependents, but, as free-lancers know all too well, we have to answer to ourselves. The self is a more demanding taskmaster than any boss; it's possible to fool a boss, but much harder to deceive oneself. The urge sweeps over us to reconstruct adolescence, to wallow again in dependency; yet our fantasies are constantly disturbed by responsibilities.

Not the least of these responsibilities are the bills which must be paid. No one's going to put the food on the table or take care of the mortgage.

No one but the government.

THE ECONOMIC FACTOR

Richard Cornuelle left his job as vice-president of the National Association of Manufacturers in 1969. He later wrote a book[1] describing his experience, which he said resembled in a way the experiences of a family whose boat had been sunk and had to live for thirty-eight days in a rubber raft until they were picked up by a fishing vessel. The father of this family said, "The successful castaway will devise means to survive which no textbook can prescribe for him. The spirit of comradeship is a far more important factor in survival than any imposed discipline. The system of self-rationing we used for saving water was much more successful than imposed rationing could have been." Cornuelle observed that the "family's survival was *technically* impossible—it could not have been managed. But they survived on unexpected reserves of determination and resourcefulness and love. They survived as if they were guided by an invisible hand."

Not working is casting away from a safe harbor. Survival requires resourcefulness and determination. It requires you to explore the depths of your ingenuity and to test the limits of your tolerance. This is true in more than the economic sense. You are cast into a new social world with its own set of personal arrangements, and much more starkly than ever before, you are forced to confront that nagging question of adolescence: What's my purpose, what am I going to do with my life?

Unless you are extremely well-fixed, the first and perhaps the most difficult test you face is financial. Some people plan carefully for their economic security before they leave work; others leave without conscious preparation. All of them have to decide how much they are going to give up in order not to work. They have to decide whether living outside the work world is more important to them than the comforts provided by their earnings.

Reining In

Reducing expenses to absolute necessities, however we each define necessities, is an educational experience. We learn our limits. We learn something else: that we can expand our limits, that some comforts we thought we could never live without are expendable.

When Charles Braithwaite left his television job, he approached the future as an athlete approaches the big game. He went into training. Cutting down was something of a sporting contest. Him against a materialistic culture. Him versus himself. Charles represents an extreme. He almost welcomed austerity, celebrating it as a rite of purification.

"The first year I was reining in," he said, "I was much more fascinated with all the twists and turns I make when I'm not working than I was with the politics of working. It turns me on. I love the scheming and conniving and the scrimping, all the things you have to do to survive.

"Stopping work I began to live as I was brought up. I rediscovered that it didn't take that much for me to get along. The cooking—I like to cook, but I never did it when I worked. When I'm at the stove now, I think of myself as a child. When I was a kid we lived on codfish and rice and chicken. So I started to eat the same way—cheap food. Cheap chops, chicken parts, potatoes, all you need is water in a pot and a knife to cut off the skin. Besides I don't eat that much. I get up in the morning, I must have juice, it's a passion with me, or a cold orange and coffee. That's it. Lunch for me is two soft-boiled eggs and a piece of cheese. A piece of tomato. Dinner for me is two cheap chops, a piece of tomato, a boiled potato. Or I could buy a can of red kidney beans, get some corned beef hash, put the beans on top, chop up half an onion, put on some hot sauce, and drink a glass of milk. The beans'll cost sixty cents, the onion ten cents, and I'm not gonna eat the whole can in one sitting. Half the world lives on that. You forget that when you're working. When you have to, though, you learn you can get along.

"My parents had a very few luxuries, few things came easy. There was a bottle of rum in the house during the holidays for our friends. It would be empty by New Year's, and I'd never see another bottle of rum until the next Christmas. I never learned that you had to have a bottle around all the time until I was grown-up. When I was working, I tended to drink too much. The bread was available, the tension was available. When I stopped, I just wouldn't have a bottle during the week. If somebody came up, well, they'd have to drink fruit juice. When the weekend came, well, maybe I'd give in and buy one. But part of the deal is proving you can do without. Reining in is a moment when better instincts come to the surface."

Charles cut down in other ways. He'd walk across town rather than take a bus. He'd use a library rather than buy a book. When he couldn't afford the rent he paid for his apartment, he moved to a single room in a residency hotel. I felt sorry for him, but he didn't seem to feel sorry for himself.

"I like to give gifts to ladies," Charles said, smiling. "I like to entertain women. Let's go dancing; let's go listen to music. I remember I went to a party and I met three fine-looking women. I was dying to deal with that. If I were working, I would have called up all three, staggering it out over the week. But I knew I didn't have any money, even for a couple of drinks, and then, when I was just moving out of the work scene, I couldn't do a Dutch date. It wasn't my style. It got me down I couldn't follow through with those women. But, you know, I thought, so what did I miss? It woulda been a kick for what, one night, two nights? I found that I could live without that kick and live better without it."

It was more difficult for Alice Lambert, a divorced woman with three children. Cutting down was painful, almost as painful as the last few months on her job.

When the black cultural affairs program she produced for a public radio station in Chicago was cancelled, Alice expressed her rage in a wheeze. She had a series of asthmatic attacks, the worst one coming on the last day when she was cleaning out her office. "Asthma attacks every two or three days," she says. "I suffer from asthma, but never like that and never in the summer. I could not associate it with the job. Not at first. I had the blood tests and the chest X rays and the sputum tests, and the doctor couldn't find anything wrong. The medication would ease the wheezing and then it would start up again.

"On the last day my friend puts me in a cab and I go back to the doctor. He knew what I was going through at work. He said, 'Wait a minute, lady. I know you have this whole work thing and I know how much energy you have. But is the job really worth this, or *any* job worth it? Is this something you always gonna be in?' I had to stop and think about it."

When I spoke to her she had been out of work for ten months. Alice remembered the time she had taken the bus to a job interview a few weeks after she stopped working. "I couldn't stop crying on the bus. Because the big question was: So, now what the fuck do I do? I want another job? What kind of job? Do I want to do that shit? I decided: No. I don't want that. I want time to think.

"I thought maybe six months from now I can take a job. I don't know that for sure, but maybe. Then I have to think, What's my life gonna be like when the kids are gone? Do I wanna work for someone for the next thirty years? At the age of forty, can I keep doing the checker number—jumping from job to job? I had to think not only about working but sit down and think about what my personal life was going to be like. What did I want from that? Did I want to stay single—what's that going to be like? If not, what do I do? Campaign to find a husband? Unbelievable! Do I want a husband? And what kind of a husband? And if I do, who the hell wants to marry me anyhow? I'm sitting there on the bus telling myself I need to think about all of this. And the money thing flies up in my face."

She didn't show up for the job interview. Alice got off the bus and returned home. Returned home to face reality: the money thing. "Ninety-five dollars in unemployment. No severance, no nothing—I don't have any money in the bank. When the money stopped from my weekly salary, the money stopped. Bills here, rent and all that stuff, the kids going to school, and ninety-five dollars. At three in the morning, I'd sit in the middle of the bed and say, 'Ninety-five dollars. Oh, shit.' I couldn't think of what the hell you do with ninety-five dollars. I had spent that on food and coffee—just beer and lunch money for the kids. When I talked to the kids, their reaction was, 'You're the boss. Bosses don't lose their jobs. How could you be out of a job?' I had to sit down and explain that to them. The next question was, 'Where are we gonna get the money?' My answer was, 'I don't know.' "

One thing she did know—not through welfare, not through food stamps. She had done too much in the last ten years to go on welfare. She had broken through the color line at some of the leading white women's magazines, she had helped organize and edit some of the top minority magazines in the country. To come that far and . . . She wouldn't do it. Alice had one conversation with her seventeen-year-old son about food stamps. She put it to him this way: If she got food stamps, would he go to the supermarket and buy food with them. His answer was: "Nooo. I will not do it. I will not go up there to the cashier and hand her stamps."

It seemed important to respect his wishes. Her own professional success had served as an example for him, motivating him to go to college. Alice had just changed that image, and now she had to try to make a seventeen-year-old understand what happens to a forty-year-old woman when the work connection is broken. She could not make him understand—perhaps she didn't understand herself—why an intelligent, healthy, articulate, and talented woman should go on welfare.

Alice Lambert was not working. She was not working by choice. She could not go to the finest department store to buy the best pair of shoes. She had to calculate whether she was going to spend her change on a bag of potato chips or buy a newspaper. She was poor but she would not think of herself as a dependency case. Her life-style had changed, but she had not become déclassé.

That much was clear to the landlord's lawyer and to the judge the moment she walked into the courtroom. Two weeks before Christmas the dispossess notice had come. She was required to appear in landlord-tenant court to explain why she should not be evicted for failure to pay three months' rent. It was nine in the morning when she appeared in the Calvin Klein skirt and the white silk blouse and the pearl necklace. "Everybody else had sneakers on and they looked like they couldn't pay the rent. I couldn't either, but I was damned if I was gonna wear sneakers."

The judge gave her a ten-day extension, and in that time she received a check for back pay from her radio job and a couple of friends loaned her some money. She squeezed by.

During the Christmas holiday an old friend invited her to spend the holidays with him in Los Angeles. Her friend was a successful black businessman. "We talked about sacrificing. He ain't ever gonna worry about a dispossess notice unless somebody bombs L.A. His whole thing was I was going to have to start knocking on doors or I could continue dealing with the dispossess, which he did not sympathize with. He didn't know why I'd want a dispossess if it could be done another way. My answer was that I would prefer to take the trauma at the moment, and even if after going through that a couple of times I decided to take a job, I'd rather do it when I'm ready to do it, as opposed to feeling I must do it so that I won't get the dispossess."

The cats chase each other through her living room. Her kids are in their rooms doing their homework. Alice Lambert is sitting on her white sofa, her legs curled underneath her. She throws her head back and laughs a deep, rich, throaty laugh. "No I couldn't do that welfare diddly shit. No, I can't take a job, not now at least. The middle-class dilemma. You leave work, but you don't leave your class behind. I guess I just have to cross the street by myself."

Sixteen months after she stopped working, Alice took a job.

People adopt the strategy that is most compatible with their life-styles, their family lives, and their views of themselves. Braithwaite believes his better side surfaces when he is living austerely; Lambert is prepared to make sacrifices, but not to the extent where they would be harmful to her children or would wreck her self-image.

The details of economic survival vary from person to person. When husbands stop working, some wives start. College-age children are asked to go to work to help pay for tuition; or they are transferred to low-tuition public universities. Life insurance policies are cashed in. People barter services and material goods. They move to less expensive apartments or sell their houses and buy cheaper ones. They share their living quarters or live collectively. They may take temporary jobs when bills are due, or they may raise money in other more ingenious ways. For example, in New York the dwindling number of rent-controlled apartments are considered prize catches. The four-room rent-controlled apartment that goes for $120 a month in a well-kept building has the same space and facilities as a decontrolled apartment next door that rents for $450 a month. One couple I met generated a tax-free profit of $3,400 by subletting their rent-controlled apartment for thirty-six months at a rate higher than they pay but less than the market value of a controlled apartment. At the same time they occupy apartments for people who are vacationing or traveling for work. They charge $30 a week for this house-sitting service. In a city where the fear of crime approaches terror, their fee is considered reasonable.

Each individual develops his own strategy, but one element is central to all but the very rich. That is government funds.

The Dole

It is an understatement to say that the government sanctions not working. It is more accurate to say that the government is not working's major underwriter. The original assumption behind government assistance was that it was intended for the poor. Today that is not true. In 1975 more than $100 billion was provided by the federal, state, and local governments under the rubric of social insurance.* That is, you do not need to be poor to qualify for these funds. By comparison, only $12.7 billion was directed specifically for the poor.**

Including in-kind programs that provide services such as Medicare, Medicaid, and public housing, but not cash, total federal assistance came to approxi-

*This includes among other forms of social insurance, social security, unemployment insurance, public employees' retirement, veterans' disability, military retirement, and workmen's compensation.

**Programs earmarked for the poor include aid to families with dependent children, supplemental security income, and general assistance.

mately $188 billion in 1977, or 45 percent of the entire federal budget. This amount represented an increase of 600 percent over what the federal government was spending a decade ago. In that period federal assistance grew at a rate two thirds faster than the rate of growth of the overall federal budget. *About half of all assistance went to the nonpoor, and even in those programs where applicants had to meet a means test, an estimated 15 or 25 percent of the money went to the nonpoor.*[2]

The biggest cash program is social security. The second biggest is unemployment insurance. In 1975 on a typical week, some 3.5 million people were receiving unemployment compensation and another 4.2 million had exhausted their benefits. Although the basic benefit period was twenty-six weeks, starting in the recession the period was extended to up to sixty-five weeks. For 90 percent of the people I spoke to, their first stop after they stopped working was the unemployment insurance office.

Lucille Roberts's husband had hated standing on line to collect his unemployment check. He thought it was one of the most demeaning experiences of his life. Now in Monterey, she's the one waiting in line to validate her claim for unemployment insurance. She is not distraught or ashamed. The following excerpts from the diary she kept during the year she was on unemployment suggest the attitude that unemployment insurance was something owed her, a stipend she was due. In this, she is typical. The majority of people I met believed (or pretended to believe) as she does, that they had contributed to the unemployment insurance funds through deductions

from their paychecks. In fact, in all but three states*
unemployment is funded by contributions from the
federal government, the state, and, to a much lesser
extent, the employer.

They believed that having once worked, they
were entitled to a paid respite of indefinite duration, regardless of whether they had been fired or
whether they had decided to stop working. (Often
employers cooperated with them and said they had
been fired, so they could collect.) People who endure work as they endure the dentist's drill, for five,
ten, twenty years, expect that somebody should play
big daddy, somebody should spring for the Courvoi-
sier to chase the pain. Government has volunteered
to perform that function.

From Lucille Roberts's diary

> *JUNE 1, 1976*—Reported to window C at the lo-
> cal state unemployment office. No questions
> asked, no interviews arranged with counselors,
> no nothing really. Just handed over filled-in
> cards about not working for two weeks and col-
> lected a check. The amount ain't what I used to
> collect twice a month, but in my present frame
> of mind, it sure beats working.

> *JUNE 14*—Unemployment line early this morn-
> ing. Talked with two other people who seemed
> to be my age.
>
> The woman I spoke with had been laid off be-
> cause her employers felt she had taken off an ex-
> cessive amount of time following her husband's
> heart attack. I wonder if situations have really

*New Jersey, Alabama, and Alaska.

changed since Henry Ford's remark, "Not on my time do you—"

The guy I talked to told me he knew he was driving his poor wife crazy. "Shit, I've tried to be constructive—I've done all the chores she used to nag me about, like taking out the garbage and that junk. I've done even more—painted the house inside and out. I put in a vegetable garden. I weed it and I water it . . . Now all I think about is chasing her around and going back to bed." I loved his honesty.

Nine years ago, when I first came to this state and was phased out of a government job when funds were cut, I filed an interstate claim. I had four kids, two of whom were in college then. Each week when I went to the unemployment office, I was interviewed, sent out on job possibilities, and came away feeling that someone definitely cared about my working potential. Right now, this same state doesn't seem to be hurrying anyone into a job. . . .

Registered for work and received a little identification card. During my brief interview there, the man who interviewed me had to look up special code numbers for my technologist's rating. He was adamant when I told him that I did not wish to be coded as a medical technologist. I wanted to be coded as an administrative assistant. No way. I was what I had been and that was that. I knew then as far as he was concerned, he had done his job as far as I was concerned.

JUNE 28—Picked up another unemployment check and realized that I had been on the dole for a month now. Already can spot newcomers from hard-core unemployed. Artist friend, Harry, who has been in these lines longer than I have, wants to do a serial cartoon of two people at various windows. First picture would show clean-shaven, well-dressed businessman—decent haircut, button-down collar shirt, tie, briefcase in hand, all set for a big interview. In contrast is slatternly hippie chick beginning to show pregnancy, her worn jeans bulging at every seam. Second picture, three months later, shows same guy with longer hair and mustache, wearing casual slacks and sports shirt. He no longer carries the briefcase. By this time the girl is very pregnant, dressed in sleazy yoke-top, too-short maternity dress, shifting her weight from one bare foot to the other. The final picture six months later—same guy, frankly doesn't give a damn anymore—he's wearing sawed-off jeans, puka beads, and sandals. Hair is shoulder length and his beard, mustache, and sideburns all blend, going gray. He burrows a pencil from another guy in line, fills out his cards, and collects his check. Meantime, the gal has had her baby and now carries it papoose style up to the window where she fills out her cards and receives her money.

After I deposited my check at the bank, I went to the beach. Water very cold, but good.

AUGUST 20—A sweet old klutz from the state job development office got her hands on my file. Dear Jane! She helps place all women over forty. She picked up the medical poop on my resumé and thought I might be interested in a pharmacy clerk's job. No way! Particularly as I am well acquainted with the little sweatshop drugstore she had in mind. Next she came up with a teller's job in the very bank where my daughter now works. I checked on the bank's policy of nepotism and called Jane back with the good news that two members of the same family could not work in the same branch office. Two days later, Jane really outdid herself. A charming little clerical job at a tourist trap, twenty miles from here with a pay scale so low that my tax-free unemployment checks look like an account executive's expense allowance.

JANUARY 18, 1977—Liza and I had lunch together yesterday. She has gone back to work after two years of unemployment. Now she feels the corporation owns her after one month's employment and she hates the feeling.

MARCH 1—Received my second V.A. widow's pension check today. Decided last December when funds were low to put in for a renewed claim. Have been given an award which is good until I exceed a salary of $4,500. With this money, my unemployment stipend, and the rent payments [from lodgers in her house], I feel I am practically on easy street again. The whole past year, now that I am beginning to relax and enjoy not working, has really been a great experience.

MARCH 29—My son has decided to leave college and work full time. We have had several gut-level talks about this. Actually, I want him to do whatever keeps him happy. There is no way I can exert the pressure on him or any of my kids that was placed on my husband and me. Our families took the old adjust or bust and made a real travesty out of the statement, and our lives too. I just want my kids to do what they want to do and to be happy doing it.

MAY 26—Last week I went to the unemployment insurance office for what I thought was to be my last claim check. The clerk at the window asked if I had earned $750 within the last year. I said no. In the first place my impression was that I couldn't earn any money and still receive unemployment benefits, and secondly, I thought she meant from mid-May 1976 to the present. She then wrote "insufficient earnings" on my file cards, gave me my check, and told me to come back this week for one more check.

Today I spoke with a different gal at the same window. When I produced my 1976 W-2 form proving that I had almost two quarters of pay, she did reassure me that I would receive retroactive checks . . . I wonder how long this new claim will be effective?

JUNE 8—Am making it so far this month with only the rent money and my V.A. pension check. My feeling now is to enjoy unemployment as long as it lasts, maybe get a foothold on some temporary work. . . . Positive thoughts, full steam ahead.

JUNE 24—I had a jolting return to the mundane last Monday at the unemployment insurance office. My new claim required a job qualifications review which was conducted by a thirty-year-old shmuck sitting behind the usual authoritative desk. He tried to threaten me into taking a job in my old field (lab technology). I kept my cool. At this stage in my life, especially after all the months of reflection, I knew for sure that a continuing career along laboratory lines would be the end of my physical and mental health, and I told him so. Then he argued that I was not looking in the right places for the kind of work I thought I wanted. I should relocate . . . My narrow-gauge, single-track interviewer finally shook his head, the male-chauvinist-pig bit, meaning, "Don't try to tell a woman anything."

JULY 10—I did collect my retroactive monies and have been told that I will have just one more check coming. Apparently the federal government has decided that employment is so improved in California that all of us on special claims will be laid off within the next two weeks, and that means me, baby, among many others.... Looks as if I'll have to compromise on some kind of a job or really go broke....

JULY 25—Today at 9 A.M. I collected my very last check from unemployment insurance. I certainly am not complaining—I got the most out of my and my employers' money, and I feel good about the longest vacation from work that I have ever had in my lifetime.

When Lucille Roberts writes, with some surprise that "this state doesn't seem to be hurrying anyone into a job," she is branding the unemployment insurance system for what it is: a middle-class cushion. For many people unemployment insurance is a necessity. They have been fired, laid off, or forced out of a job. They have tried to find other work without success. But there are also many people who use it to finance their separation from work.

The perversity of the system is that it seems to encourage the latter, while penalizing those who are really poor, who can't find work, who haven't learned how to play the game. In America we have an extraordinary capacity for blaming the victim.

The Rules of the Game

I am in Chicago visiting an old college friend. He is living with a woman named Marilyn, who had been the head buyer in the furniture department of Marshall Field's. In one letter to me he had said: "One thing puzzles me about Marilyn. When the alarm clock rings in the morning, she shuts if off. When she gets out of bed, it's ten or ten-thirty, and sometimes I don't think she gets in to the store before noon. Maybe she does such a good job for them, they don't care when she gets in."

When I arrived, Aaron told me, "Marilyn got fired last week. It wasn't unexpected. She understands that she really engineered it. Her boss had no choice. She was pushing him to the wall, but she wanted him to do it, she couldn't cut the cord herself."

I am standing in line with Marilyn in an unemployment insurance office in Chicago. There are four lines, grouped alphabetically, in front of the counter. This is not a depression bread line: A guy in the next line is wearing tennis shorts; he amuses himself by playing a tune on the strings of his tennis racket.

"Carlos, did Ricardo get home from the party Saturday night?" a guy yells from line A–F across the room to L–P. "He was bombed, man."

"Woke up Monday morning. He says to me, 'Am I still alive or am I in heaven?' "

The appreciative laughter ripples through the room, but Marilyn doesn't seem to hear it. "I guess I'm a little nervous. I hope my boss hasn't screwed this up. The store has a policy against letting anyone collect unemployment."

"What could they do? You were fired?"

"They could say I was incompetent. I don't know. Or I planned to quit."

The man behind us on the line is saying, "*Annie Hall.* The perfect expression of the irony of urban angst."

Marilyn adjusts her pearl necklace. She looks like somebody who's looking for a job. The tailored brown suit. The white blouse. Her black hair shining with Redken brilliance. She passes her book over the counter to the clerk, a man in his thirties, a man whose dark blue polyester shirt is two buttons open to show the gold link chain.

"How you doing," he says, reaching for his stamp.

"I'm fine," she says, "just wish I could find a job."

"You'll have to go next week to the professional placement service."

"Why, is there something wrong with the claim?"

"The claim's fine. The state just has to go through the motions."

"Fine. I hope they find me a job."

"Don't worry," he says, with a crooked smile. "They won't. Have a good year."

The bulletin board at the professional center lists jobs paying $200, $220 a week. The dates when the jobs were first listed go back two years. This is a center for people who had been occupied in the retail and wholesale sales trade. There are some older men here who had their shoes shined recently; as they wait their turn, they actually seem to expect that they will be placed in a job.

Marilyn was prepared for her interview. For the past week, she had clipped job ads from the Chicago *Tribune* and called the companies. After ten years of buying furniture, she knew which firms would not be able to pay the going rate for her position. She had also called a few friends in the business; in case the state checked, they would say she had made an effort to find a job but that they had nothing open.

"Let's see, your last job paid nineteen-five," the employment "counselor" says. "It's a little hard to find jobs in that salary range."

The soft magnolia smile, lustrous as the finish on any coffee table she ever sold. "Well, after almost ten years with the store, I wouldn't want to accept anything less, it would be a real comedown." It takes her a good five seconds to stretch out the r-e-a-l.

"I know, I understand," the counselor says; it's not the first time he's heard that. "The state can't force you to take a job that pays less. And I certainly wouldn't want to do that to you."

"You're very understanding," she says.

"Look, I have some contacts in the business. Why don't I check around. If I hear of something, I'll call."

"I certainly appreciate that."

They both know that he will never call.

The noon hour in the Loop. People pour out of the office buildings. The coffee shops are processing burgers, medium rare, at a hundred a minute. At places with linen tablecloths, at the Blackstone and the American Furniture Mart on Lakeshore Drive, at Diamond Jim's and at Chez Paul, deals are served up with the coquilles St. Jacques. "I-got-something-for-you. You-got-something-for-me. We talking ten thousand dozen? No, thirty thousand, let's do it right."

Everybody's going someplace. Attaché cases bump briefcases, bump models' portfolio cases. Even the panhandlers seem purposeful. Dacron blue slides into the cab, shouting directions to the driver before he's closed the door. Slinky red with shiny knees slithers out in front of the Continental Plaza, tip in one hand for the driver, tip in the other for the doorman.

Marilyn's going no place. "I wouldn't want you to tell your friend, it might upset him. I don't want to work. I don't want to do anything. I don't want to ever have to make an appointment again. I just don't want any responsibilities."

Not everybody is treated equally by the unemployment bureaucracy. If you're a thirty-two-year-old woman, articulate, dressed fashionably, wearing a professional smile, the treatment's very gentle. Across town where the state places clerical workers and typists, it's a lot bumpier. Susan Keegan has a couple of things going against her. She wears old jeans, a sweatshirt, and torn sneakers. She doesn't have a 250-watt smile and her vowels aren't perfectly formed. Her biggest problem is that the last paying job she held brought in seventy-five dollars a week for twenty-five hours behind the typewriter. It doesn't count for much that she has a 150 I.Q. and a master's degree in English Lit from the University of Chicago. They make her sweat for thirty-five dollars a week in unemployment insurance.

The first time she went to the center, she waited two hours before she was called. Then she was treated to a fifteen-minute lecture on why she had to improve her typing. "If you learned to take steno you could get a job," her "counselor" told her. "You have to have a career goal." Fortunately the only job available was in a run-down neighborhood. "I won't send you there," he said. "It's too dangerous for a woman."

The second time, she stopped at the center on the way to a restaurant where she waitressed off-the-books twice a week. Susan had just come from the University of Chicago where she was taking courses, and she was dressed again in her school clothes, sneakers and jeans, but in a shopping bag she carried a pair of dress pants and shoes that she planned to change into before she began working that afternoon. Susan put her unemployment book in the wire mesh basket on the front desk and sat in the waiting area. A few minutes later a woman came out from a back office and asked her if she was there for an interview. When Susan nodded, the woman said, "Follow me to my desk." Susan smiled weakly.

"Who told you to come at noon?" the woman asked.

"Nobody, I thought it didn't matter."

Holding up her unemployment book, the woman said, "It says here your appointment is for two o'clock."

"I'm really sorry. I didn't look."

"Well, there's nothing I can do for you now. Everybody's out to lunch. All the employees are out to lunch. I don't know why you even bother coming."

"Well, I can come back," Susan whispered.

The woman acted as if she hadn't heard her. "And look at you. Look at the way you're dressed. I don't consider you 'able' to work dressed like that. Who would hire you? You're filthy. Sneakers!"

"But I have clothes with me," Susan said, holding up the shopping bag.

"What? What did you say? Where? Let me see."

Susan started to take the pants out of the shopping bag. "What's the matter, you couldn't put them on? You were afraid you'd be ostracized? Is that it? You thought your friends wouldn't talk to you?"

She started to say something, but the unemployment interviewer cut her off. "Yeah, you bring clothes with you and you'll put them on and you'll be a wrinkled mess. What's the point?"

She breathed a long sigh. Finally, she threw the unemployment book back on the desk. "You *will* come back on Monday," she told her. By Monday Susan would know all the rules of the unemployment game.

"My generation was really scared of unemployment because we saw bread lines and we saw people hungry," Robert Schrank was saying. "That's the reason people like myself really worked hard to put an economic support system in place, which I think now has become its own opposite. We just thought it was a way to dignify people being out of work, but what it's turned into is a whole culture that eats on itself. I have two kids who are regularly out of work and they could care less. They don't worry, they get unemployment insurance, food stamps, they do whatever they have to do."

There are two cultures here that commingle. There is the unemployment culture, supported by government funds. And there is the shadow economy which generates income, unreported and untaxed, from an enormous variety of enterprises ranging from baby-sitting and off-the-books hacking, to building inspectors on the take and dope dealers on the make. Unreported income in the United States is estimated at $176 billion annually, about 10 percent of the gross national product. If 20 percent of this income is earned by people who are receiving some form of public assistance, more than a million and a half people are combining unreported income and public assistance.[3]

People do, as Schrank says, whatever they have to do. It's a little late in my life to sympathize with the banks, the IRS, the credit card companies, and the real estate management corporations, and I don't propose to defend them against the people who hustle them to finance their nonworking life-styles. My interest is psychological, not moral. The not-working hustler is carrying over the same Snopesism he reviled in the business world to his life outside of work. He's the same card sharp, except now his ace in the hole is the government. If I have to choose between hustlers, I prefer the unsanctimonious sort— the guy who says straight out: I'm hustling for a buck. Most not-working hustlers I met dressed up their scam with righteous indignation—"Those bastards are out to screw me so now I'm gonna screw them." But they weren't fooling themselves. Figuring the angle, working the next hustle had become their primary purpose in not working. This is what took up their time and absorbed their energies.

They don't necessarily wind up in the loony bin or the drunk tank. They enjoy themselves, and they can be amusing when they describe their latest swindle. (One night I attended a party thrown by a woman who had just received a cost-of-living increase in her unemployment insurance. She was beaming. "It's the first time I got a raise for doing nothing," she said.) It's just that they are a little sad. They have been derailed, like the serious composer who winds up writing jingles for a soap company. The most accurate assessment of the damage comes from Patricia Knack, a New York television-commercial producer who once wrote:

> What we may not know is the damage to the whole person, the real price of dishonestly being on the dole. It took me a couple of years to feel and recognize the price I paid. Physically, my energy was never lower. I felt listless much of the time.
>
> The afternoons were the worst: People were working and I was watching the "soaps" and eating. Mentally, I was in a fog, confused and wandering, not wanting to focus on what was happening in my life. Emotionally, I felt vaguely disturbed, unworthy, generally uncomfortable, very anxious and very guilty. I was half alive, unable and unwilling to fulfill my responsibilities

as an adult, to take care of myself, to give to my community. Worst of all, I was lying to myself and justifying my position.

Now, when I think back, it's so clear, but then it was so insidious.[4]

On the Hustle

Cliff Jones worked for more than ten years as an investment counselor. He understands money, how to get it and how to use it to get what you want. He has not worked for seven years. For seven consecutive years he has collected unemployment insurance from the state of Oregon. This may be a national record.

"You have to start with my own analysis," he says. "I didn't dislike Bank of America. For the most part they treated me fairly, but I knew what was going on, I knew the corners they cut, how they moved money around, how they bent the rules, and stayed inside the law. I knew about tax shelters and changing currencies, and foreign banks and private foundations, I knew all about that, shit, I helped make it possible for them.

"Looking down, I understood how the welfare system worked. I knew people were making choices, squeezing public assistance rather than taking a shit job. I wasn't outraged with them, that was how they wanted to live.* There were three things: Number one, work was bonkers; number two, the govern-

*Jones's views of cheating in the upper reaches of business and in the welfare underclass are by no means atypical. In a survey of 1,227 readers, the Harvard Business Review reported in January

ment was totally fucked; three, society was very childlike. They were looking for government to help and they weren't realizing the monster they were creating. Government was saying to me, If you're smart, you'll learn to use the monster. It was a kinda challenge, to harness the giant.

"I knew that if I wanted out, I'd have to pull it off. I didn't want to quit and say, 'Fuck, I gotta get another job.' I didn't want to spend half my time building up ways to get back in. I knew, twenty-four M's weren't coming in anymore, I have two kids to support, so how am I gonna do it?"

He did it by putting a few pieces together.

The first piece was putting himself in the most advantageous position when he left: "I got the stock options right, and I got them to terminate me in a way that would get me on unemployment."

The second piece was the application of his skills.

1977 that four out of every seven respondents said that they had experienced a conflict between what was expected of them as efficient, profit-conscious managers and was expected of them as ethical persons. The readers also found a serious ethical problem in communications, in honesty in advertising, and in providing information to top management, clients, and government agencies. "We find number (statistical) manipulation to have become a particularly acute problem," the magazine said. As for attitudes toward welfare recipients, they seem to remain consistently negative in polls taken over the last twenty-five years. For example a recent eight-state survey of more than nine thousand adults by the University of Southern California's Regional Research Institute in Social Welfare found that the attribute frequently associated with the working poor was that "They work whenever they can find employment." Welfare recipients, on the other hand, were described as people who "often have skills they are wasting."

"I always had an interest in politics and economics. I guess I got that from my father who was in finance. I sensed that the American dollar was getting in deep trouble—remember this is in 1970. I had everything I owned converted into cash and then I converted the cash into Swiss francs. In a week the dollar was devalued 7.5 percent. Two weeks later it was devalued again. Suddenly, I was worth much more than I thought I was."

The third piece was marijuana and its sale. He was living in San Francisco then, an investment banker who enjoyed the good restaurants and the expense-account bars. A genial guy, with a handlebar mustache and a beer gut, who bitched a little too much about work but wasn't above slapping a few backs and spending an hour talking about the Giants at Paoli's. "I became the man. I serviced the heads downtown. It was really simple; dealing in that environment there was almost no risk. Most of the time I'd get paid by check. I'd lay a lid in my briefcase, and fifty dollars would be sitting on the bar, or pay me tomorrow, or give me a check. They all had plenty of money. What's the risk? I'm working for the Bank of America. What do you think a cop's going to do on a first offense? San Francisco's an awful loose town. It's always been that way—its the most tolerant city in the country. Nobody was gonna blow the whistle. I tried to be sneaky because everybody says you're supposed to be, but I stopped that after two months. I found out you didn't have to skulk around—nobody cared."

The last piece was public assistance, which began with unemployment and later included welfare and food stamps. "An attorney friend gave me the state code on unemployment insurance, on A.F.D.C., and I became an expert on all those systems because I knew I'd have to be. Now it becomes a financial game for me. How do I get these systems to support my philosophy? Look, I've been on unemployment for seven years. Is that a short duration? When unemployment ran out, which it did once, there was food stamps. Once I had to work for a month to get back on unemployment. You read the unemployment code. I knew more about it than the people at the state office. I discovered something called the lag period claim; I don't want to go into that too much, you don't want to screw up a good thing. But the point is there's a way. Anybody can get these resources together.

"If somebody came to me and said, 'I really want to stop working,' I'd say, 'Cut down here, change this here, move this over here, explore this one, put that together, and in two years you'll have this and combine it with this, and there's your program.' Most people who stop working come at it from their emotions. I came at it from my intellect."

Cliff got up from his rocking chair and reached for his scrapbook in the bookcase that serves as the partition between his living room/bedroom and his kitchen. Pasted in the scrapbook was an old newspaper clipping, a story about a man called Cliff Jones—"The King of Liar's Dice." Jones was recognized as the fastest man with a pair of bar dice for a hundred miles. Jones told the reporter who interviewed him, "With liar's dice we can lie with what amounts to impunity. All that's at stake is the price of a drink, lunch, cigarettes, possibly some money, or just the right to be the first to speak to the girl at the end of the bar."

Now when Cliff lies, all that's at stake is his life.

Martha Gorham, who once administered a school district near Wilmington, Delaware, and later was an organizer for Hadassah, has not worked for almost four years. She lives in a three-story frame house near the University of Colorado in Boulder. Martha has her own large bedroom and living room. The kitchen and two bathrooms are shared by the ten occupants of the house. Her rent is eighty dollars a month.

In the first year she exhausted her unemployment insurance and modest savings. She then went on welfare.

"It was hard for me to accept that in the beginning, even unemployment insurance," she says. "I always felt I was lying. I was saying what they needed to hear to get the money. If they wanted me to say I was interested in working, that I'd take a job if I could get one at my past salary, I'd say that. I know everybody does that. But it was hard to do things, to lie, that I'd been taught were not right to do. It made it easier that everybody around me was saying it was okay to do it. Eventually, it was like going on stage and improvising. I had a basic script, but there was always that element of surprise. I'd dress for it when I'd go to unemployment or welfare—you have to develop a different costume and a different facial expression for each of them, it was the whole number. I put my heart and soul into it."

The combination of welfare and food stamps gave her $160 a month. "Once I overcame my resistance, the Jewish thing—you know, you don't take public money—I got hooked on it. I could make it a career. It was like, damn it, I bought the thing you said would make me happy and I did it, and I did it well and it didn't work, and you fucked me over, you fuckers, and now I'm gonna get you—now I'm out to get you—so that's how I rationalized it. I guess I did what amounted to a Ph.D. on how to get money from the government, and I really did my research, so I knew the questions—sometimes I had some-body on the inside who'd prep me—I knew what they'd ask me and I had the right answers. It's all a game. They try to hold the dollars and you try to get it from them. After a while you get to know the rules."

After two years her research turned up a federal program, Supplemental Security Income (S.S.I.) that provided cash for the aged, the disabled, and the partially disabled. Physically, Martha Gorham, a tall, powerfully built woman, was in fine health. "Then the light bulb went on. The psychiatric bit. At different times in my life when I was in a crisis, I'd go to a shrink and let them baby-sit me for six months or a year or whatever it took to get through the crisis, and I'd go away until the next crisis. The last job I'd had, there was a lot of tension, so I'd seen a shrink for a while. It took me about ten minutes to talk him into signing a paper that said I was suffer-ing from a job-related nervous disability. The best thing was I didn't feel guilty about taking the mon-ey, because I'd contributed to social security directly when I was working and now I was getting it back."

At the start, she received $265 a month, plus food stamps and Medicaid. More recently, her cash payments have risen to $320 a month to keep up with the cost of living. She doesn't have to report regularly as she did when she was collecting unemployment insurance or welfare. The check just arrives from the government every month. There's an additional check of $100 a month that goes toward the support of her two children who are being raised by her former husband.

At times she's tempted to take a job—"I get the feeling I'd like to be self-supporting again"—but she doesn't because "the thing I'm into is so fantastic, it's hard to give up. One of the great things, under this program you can work and make up to two hundred dollars a month; so if I need a little extra money, I can always pick it up. It's just such a nice cushion. I did get reviewed recently, and they said, 'When do you think you'll be self-supporting?' And I said, 'I don't know, I haven't thought about it.' They said, 'Well, how about six months?' And I said, 'I don't know—maybe.' If I still want to stay on it after another six months, I can do it. After four years you learn to figure a way."

The Joneses and Gorhams were in the majority among the people I met. They stand out only because of their candor and the elaborate planning they brought to their hustles. In this majority there were two subgroups. In one, people are forthright about their deceptions. They don't justify or rationalize what they are doing. When I asked them if they were troubled by hustling bucks from the government or any other sucker, if, in fact, it wasn't a little like working, they would smile at my ingenuousness. *Baby, it's a jungle out there, the smile said. I hustled when I worked, I hustle when I'm not. The hustle pays the freight. That's all there is to it.*

The other subgroup of hustlers tried to justify their actions. As Martha Gorham did, they defended their swindles by arguing that they had no choice. If they didn't protect themselves, they would be destroyed by a cruel and unjust economic system, so they were acting in self-defense. Then came another argument. "We might not like it," they'd say, "but the lie is here to stay. It's a fixture in our social interactions. If you stop lying, you make waves, you get everybody upset, you're the odd man out."

There is some truth in this. Sissela Bok, who teaches medical ethics at the Harvard Medical School, writes about doctors who lie to patients suffering from terminal cancer and about researchers who lie about their intentions when they infiltrate hospitals, schools, and religious sects to pursue their research. "At times they see important reasons to lie," she says. "In their eyes such lies differ sharply from self-serving ones."[5] The hustlers I met would call these officially sanctioned lies. They'd say, these people are just as bad if not worse than me. At least they have a choice: They *can* be honest about what they're doing. Their work would be made more difficult if they chose to be candid, but they could continue. If I'm honest, I'll get cut off. If I walk into the unemployment insurance office and tell the clerk

I'm not really looking for another job, I'll be punished for breaking the rules—for not lying.

There is an important demographic fact about all these hustlers. Most of them were under the age of forty. They grew up in a white-collar world where the wink and the shrug were the accepted way of doing business. Untruth, they had learned in their work lives, was part of making a profit.

Hustlers accept the proposition that the lie is the great facilitator, the grease on the wheel. Whether they hustle at work or hustle outside of work, they are very much in the American mainstream.

On the Straight

The ones who played it straight were not smug. They didn't condemn hustlers, but personally they felt they weren't cut out for it. The hustle was alien to their system of values. It conflicted with their beliefs, with their social training. They recognized that the Snopeses had taken control, that they would be considered fusty and old-fashioned. But they didn't see that they had any other choice.

Six months after Carl Reiter quit his job at the loan company, he was down to his last seven hundred dollars in the bank. He had his wife, Maya, and his kids to support. Every month he had to shell out for mortgage payments. He was aware that he could have worked it out with the loan company so that he could have collected unemployment insurance, but he didn't. "Part of it was the feeling that whatever trouble I was in, I had brought on myself. It was my decision to quit. Money, I thought about money a lot. Maya said, 'We keep taking the money out of the bank, someday it's going to run out.' But I held to this theory: You got all screwed up with the world, the world isn't what you want it to be, but you don't wanna make the government or anybody else pay because things didn't turn out the way they were supposed to.

"Maybe it was pride, just stupid pride. Some days, when I'd think about what I'd done, how everybody was suffering 'cause of me, and I wouldn't—or couldn't—do anything about it, couple of times I thought I'd just take off, leave the home. I thought of suicide, too. But that was ridiculous because I knew, the way things were going, I wouldn't even be able to do the suicide right. Ah, I thought, the kids deserve better than that. Even in this state I'm better than nothing."

It was not pride alone that kept him from going to the unemployment insurance office. There was his father, a man he revered and admired. One of the things he admired most about him was his honesty. His father had been a cop for more than thirty years. "All those years he was nagged by my mother," Carl says. "She'd always say to him, 'How can we get by on your salary? The Roths got this, Johnny's got that, what have we got?' There was a lotta money he coulda had on the side, but he'd never do that. It woulda made life at home a lot easier. He tried being a detective for a week, and he said he got offered ten bribes. He said, 'The hell with this, this is nonsense,' and he turned down the job and went back to the patrol car. He was not above takin' a shot of booze or a case of beer from the brewery at

Christmas, that was all right. As far as taking dollars to shut your eyes to something, to gambling or some racket, that wasn't his cup of tea."

The other strong influence on him was St. John's, the Catholic grade school where his character was tested and molded for eight years in the 1930s. He was taught there that suffering silently tested a man's Christian fidelity, that you worked out your problems by yourself, you solved them by an act of solitary faith.

At St. John's he had learned that if you remained silent and strong in the face of terror, you would win love and respect. Show weakness and you became a burden; once you were a burden, how could you ask love from God or a woman? "In the school, I was brought up with love and terror. Sometimes it'd make me feel guilty that I didn't make it easy for them to love me. I had started to stutter and that was my real big problem. When I read in class, the other kids would laugh. The nuns would help me with the words all right, but they were more carried away with suppressing all this laughter. Hell, I couldn't change the way I was.

"The sisters did their job. They taught you what you had to know: To make it to heaven you lived the just and honest life. Whatever you got, you got through hard work. You had to pay the price—you were going to get this award—but you had to pay for it."

When Carl Reiter stopped working for the finance company, he was Robinson Crusoe; his ship had gone down and he was alone on an uninhabited island. If he survived, he would do so through his own resourcefulness and desire to live. As he would not ask the nuns for special dispensation because he stuttered, he would not turn to those close to him—his wife, his children—or to strangers—the government—for understanding and support. (When Maya sensed his inner turmoil and tried to draw him out, he could not find the words. "He was so elusive," she would say later. "You know the man was suffering, but he wouldn't say it.")

He also carried within himself an uncommon code. It would have made life easier for his father to have accepted graft; perhaps Carl's mother would have stopped taunting his father. But his father would not compromise his standards of morality. When Carl quit the finance company, he felt as if he had crawled out of a sewer. To hustle money from the government would be diving back in again. What allowed him finally to speak, to share his sorrow and pleasure with other human beings, was the opportunity to atone for the years of contamination. Neither shrinks nor Thorazine, both of which he tried, brought him out of his isolation. What saved him was the understanding that he could help others who had suffered more than he had.

David Solomon knows the curves and twists of unemployment and welfare and the rest of the economic support system as well as anyone. In his last job, he had studied the effects of the system on the unemployed. So why's he hauling telephone books up five flights of stairs instead of standing on line at the local unemployment center? "Oh, it's very interesting," David says. "You learn a lot about architecture, you learn a lot about neighborhoods, the people who live in them." Interesting, sure, but not something David would choose to do—if he had a choice, which he feels he doesn't. In a few weeks he has to come up with the mortgage payment on the small house he owns in Cambridge, Massachusetts.

There had been times when the shadow economy was inviting; he knew he could have taken a job off the books or applied for welfare or qualified for food stamps or played some games with a bank. He didn't. Instead he chose to sell off a piece of property he had acquired long ago. He was still reacting to his work experience. David quit his job because he felt that his employers had purposely distorted and misstated the findings from a major research project to please the government agencies which had sponsored the research. The research had become, in his view, a hustle. What he didn't want to do was invent his own hustle.

"I didn't want to hustle anybody or to con anybody. I didn't want to be part of a rip-off anymore. It's not somebody else's book I'm trying to live, it's only unique to me. When I left work, it was to search for ease, for my personal ease. Hustling is not ease. When I get anxious now, about money or something else, I can say: Wait a minute. What is it you want to happen? How can that happen? Do you want to make the effort to make it happen? The thing I have learned is to disentangle these two things: what I want and what I have to do to get it.

"There is a voice now, which I never heard before, which is always asking me: 'Do you want to pay the price?' I found that by not working, by not fighting, by not hustling, by not having to reward myself for what I was giving up, I could hear that voice much better. I know now that was what I was looking for when I stopped working."

David felt, too, that to apply for public assistance would leave him vulnerable to yet another anonymous, indifferent organization. The public assistance bureaucracy, like the research organization he had left, would demand a piece of him in return for what it gave. His father had been abused by the government; after years of working for government agencies and nonprofit organizations, David did not expect them to be more humane than private industry.

He left his job because he would not subordinate his personal beliefs to the politics of work. He would not compromise his newly found independence to satisfy the demands of the welfare system. The welfare bureaucracy no longer practiced the gross abuses it once had. Yet, even today, once you applied for welfare or other forms of assistance that required a means test, you were put in the position of proving your poverty. The computers and clerks began to poke into the dusty corners of your life. You had to learn and repeat the answers that satisfied their curiosity. That required stealth, a staged casualness, the caginess of the thief. David would be forced to lie, to pretend that he could not work when he knew he could, to employ the stealth which his father had always disdained; it was too high a price.

After years of practice, dissimulation becomes second nature. Mixed with rationalizations and justifications, it's no longer a lie but a half-truth. It's a tough habit to kick, particularly when the supposed victim of the lie sanctions it. But the break with work is also a break with the past—and an opportunity to revise one's self-image. To open oneself to new challenges. To appraise work for what it was and to move on. The act of stopping work scrambles many past patterns of behavior. What emerges from this personal reorganization depends on the motives for stopping and the goals set for the time beyond work. If the primary motivation is to live out the fantasy of adolescence, it's unlikely that the non-worker will assume responsibility for his actions. In a new setting, he will continue the same old hustle.

A configuration of social and personal issues swept the people I've described beyond the break-point. On the outside, they were the beneficiaries of new social and economic permissions that were denied to my father's generation. Now they faced the hard part: to determine what they wanted and how to get it. The trying, the effort to find it, is in itself renewing. But the lift of a fresh start doesn't last. The only real and lasting change comes when each person realizes his most distant vision. And that is? If I had to put in one word what the people I met wanted, it would not be *happiness*. Happiness is too evanescent, too shallow, too much a child's Eden. No, I think the word is *ease*.

IN SEARCH OF EASE 4

Everyday affairs bind the time of all of us. A man's
time is bound from the moment he opens his eyes
in the morning until he quits for the day. . . . None
of that time . . . is his own because he has sold it to
the job. Sold time is bound and is governed by fear.
Time not so bound and is governed by fear. Time
not so bound, time that is not sold, is unbound and
is therefore free for empathy and love. Unbound
time has become so important in our culture that
we have given it a special name, "leisure," meaning
"to be permitted."

—Jules Henry,
Pathways to Madness

Leisure is not the attitude of mind of those who actively intervene, but of those who are open to everything; not of those who grab and grab hold, but
of those who leave the reins loose and who are free
and easy themselves—almost like a man falling
asleep, for one can only fall asleep by "letting oneself go." No one who looks to leisure simply to restore his working powers will ever discover the fruit
of leisure; he will never know the quickening that
follows, almost as though from some deep sleep.

—Josef Pieper,
Leisure: The Basis of Culture

Redwood hot tubs. Two weeks in Yellowstone Park. A year's sabbatical in Spain. A "singles" cruise to Martinique. A long theater weekend in London. A $180 "bliss trip" that promises such sensual delights as a champagne bath and a massage with a peacock fan.

Packaged refreshers.

That's not what Josef Pieper meant by leisure or what Jules Henry meant by "unbound" time. This is time appropriated, parceled out for pleasure, planned time, the conscious pause meant to chase the fatigue of mind and body before returning to the grind of labor. "No one who looks to leisure simply to restore his working powers will ever discover the fruit of leisure," Pieper wrote.[1]

Wait, he urged; stop and see what is happening to us. "The world of work is becoming our entire world; it threatens to engulf us completely and the demands of the world of work become greater and greater, till at last they make a 'total' claim upon the whole of human nature."[2]

Pieper, a Christian philosopher, looked into the faces of the workers who were reconstructing Europe after World War II and saw the "fixed, mask-like readiness to suffer *in vacuo*, without relation to anything." He found in the frightened eyes and taut lines of these faces no animating vision, no sense of wonderment, no desire for wholeness, no end in sight. "Man seems to mistrust everything that is effortless," Pieper wrote; "he can only enjoy, with a good conscience, what he has acquired with toil and trouble; he refuses to have anything as a gift."[3]

Work has afflicted us with intellectual sclerosis, he said, and a hardening of the heart. In a world preoccupied, driven by producing and consuming, there is little room for the nonutilitarian activity, for the passive, contemplative spirit. True leisure transcends the pragmatic, the *necessary*. It is a receptive posture, an attitude of "inward calm, of silence; it means not being 'busy,' but letting things happen." Inner calm and the peaceful silence brings the true renewal: "wholeness."

The "wholeness" to be discovered in the leisure state is both a mental and spiritual attitude, Pieper believed. "Leisure is a receptive attitude of mind, a contemplative attitude. It is not only the occasion but also the capacity for steeping oneself in the whole of creation."[4]

As I reread Pieper's book, *Leisure: The Basis of Culture*, which was first published in 1952, I am awed as much by his extraordinary prescience as by his eloquence and passion. A quarter of a century later, so many of the people I met who weren't working used his words to describe their experience. They spoke of each day, each happening, each serendipitous turn in human relationships as a "gift." They repeated, as if they had memorized his text, "I don't know why it happens this way, but when I really need something it is there, it's like getting a gift." They took their pleasures without first having to struggle and suffer for them. They talked of letting things happen without planning for them, without measuring each act in terms of its utilitarian value. They described their "passivity" without shame. Passivity was not weakness, but a state of receptivity, an openness to experience.

Wholeness. In all our conversations, it was the one word that was italicized. While most people did not associate wholeness with a religious experience, their accounts have a spiritual resonance as they describe activities that were commonplace and obligatory when they were working and are novel and refreshing now. Taking their son for a walk in the park. Developing a photograph in their darkroom. Attending the junior high school graduation of a friend's daughter. They had recovered their capacity for amazement, a quality they said they had lost in the work world. That was how they defined wholeness: the pleasure the prisoner takes in walking across an open field after years of being locked up.

The hustle is the opposite of wholeness—a form of self-imprisonment. Hustling amounts to an exchange of one form of utilitarianism for another, the struggle to work for the struggle not to work. Those who reject hustling as a life-style may never fully achieve the wholeness Pieper summons up—"steeping oneself in the whole of creation"—but they seem to be embarking on a calmer voyage.

How do they keep busy? What do they do with their time? I've often been asked these questions by people who do work about people who don't work. It takes me a while to answer because my mind's eye is watching slides. Click. David Solomon sitting by his window in Cambridge, beer can in hand, Miles Davis playing in the background. Click. Carl Reiter sitting by his kitchen table reading Thomas Merton. Click. Sam Meyers, the man who covered half a dozen wars and revolutions, walking slowly around his garden, inspecting the tomatoes. Click. Lucille Roberts drinking coffee and surveying the Pacific Ocean from her sun deck above Monterey. The short answer I give is that many people who have stopped working are redefining time.

There is a longer answer. The object of the exercise, I say, is not to keep busy, it is not to use time; it is to let time use you. That awareness of time is evocatively described by the anthropologist Jules Henry in his book, *Pathways to Madness*.

Henry's book is a study of the relationship of family organization and structure to mental illness. In an early section, he discusses bound and unbound time, and appropriate and inappropriate time. Time at work is bound time and is governed by fear. It doesn't belong to us but to somebody who pays for it. Unbound or free time is supposed to be reserved for love, but only if love can be fitted into the time allotted for it. (It's all right to call your wife from your office to tell her you love her, but whisper so nobody can overhear.) "All relations in our culture have a fixed or flexible time schedule and after twenty or thirty years we usually come to know how this works," Henry writes. "Some people do not learn." Henry's annotation for the late 1970s might read: Some people are unlearning how it works.[5]

Henry explains that in our culture time is freighted with so much anxiety (if you're late, you'll lose your job) that "unbound time becomes bound time." People will use up their so-called free time in guided tours, card games, theater parties, events that demand you arrive on time and leave on time, that have beginnings, middles, and ends. This is how bound time passes for leisure. Lucille Roberts, writing of her first few weeks of not working, describes the difficulty we all experience when we try to break the familiar if oppressive rhythm of bound and unbound time: "I like not being at the beck and call of an employer, but goddammit, I am conditioned to being screwed by a time clock. On the other hand, there's no one telling me to do anything I don't want to do, so why in hell don't I do exactly what I want to do? Why don't I trust my intuition?"

As days pass and she tentatively accepts her jobless status, Lucille says that she is "beginning to feel like an old windup clock, ticking slower and slower between windups."

She is not so much slowing down as redefining her time and flowing with it. What time offers, she receives; she does not demand, as she did when she worked, that it provide her with constancy and cue her to "appropriate" and "inappropriate" behavior. Throughout her lifetime, even as a child, she has been constantly reminded that time is not neutral. There's a right time and a wrong time for everything. We are rewarded for acting correctly, doing the right thing at the right time, and punished for the "inappropriate," as Henry demonstrates in *Pathways to Madness*.

In one illustration he describes how we hoard our time, even the time we spend sleeping. "In our culture sleep runs eternally away from us," he writes. "If we don't get enough sleep the rest of the week we can store it up again on the weekend and put in the sleep bank. An early phone call on Sunday is a bank robbery— he robbed me of three hours' sleep,' we say poisonously of a person who calls too early."

In other words, the early Sunday morning caller is guilty of the crime of inappropriateness. Culturally determined time dictates when we sleep, what and when we eat, and what we wear. The T-shirt the businessman wears to the beach Sunday afternoon must be replaced by the dress shirt when he goes to the board of directors' meeting Monday morning. When a Cliff Jones wears his hair too long to the bank in the late 1960s, he knows he's asking for trouble; showing up without a tie breaks the rules and in a way presages his break from work.

Henry describes a man driving to work in a snowstorm. He has to get up early because he knows it will take longer than usual to get there. His stomach churns as he waits for the lights to change. He stalls his car in his anxiety. Finally when he arrives, his secretary is already there and he has to rush to catch up with her. The businessman's "very capacity to foresee the stream of events affects his movements, his heartbeat, and above all perhaps, the mood of other people, " Henry says.

Now Lucille Roberts is putty, and time is the sculptor. Moving across the cultural border between working and not working, her definition of what's "appropriate" and "inappropriate" is being revised. It's as if she had escaped the gut-tightening spasm of anticipation before acting, the schedule of rewards and punishments to which she conformed when she was working. As she describes a visit to an old friend, she sounds at ease with her surroundings. She accepts the countryside as a surprise gift, unlike the person who can accept it only in those precious moments when he's away from work, and in Josef Pieper's phrase, assumes a receptive passivity; she is, at least for the moment, "letting things happen."

"I enjoyed my solitary drive through John Steinbeck territory, sort of reliving his *East of Eden* as I went along," she writes in a prose as unhurried as her excursion. "Only once before had I driven this route in fall sunlight, and I had practically forgotten how beautifully the road wends the wide valleys between the coastal mountains and the inner ranges. When Patty [her friend] returns today, she and I will walk the dunes at a nearby beach."

Returning to her own home, Lucille thinks not of what she has to do next, what she is expected to do next, but of the past before she began her career, of a time when life appeared relatively effortless. "Meantime I hear the blackbirds in the swamp behind my house and I am overwhelmed with nostalgia. I think of summers we spent at the camp back east, and there is almost a physical hurt to various memories. I see the children as babies, toddlers, humorous little people, and I remember all their funny sayings and especially the plays they put on for us parents, grandparents, aunts, and uncles. Now only my sister and I are left to remember the children as well as grown-up happy hours. When the kids were filed for the night, we went on with dinners and bridge games while the kerosene lamps burned low and logs crackled in the fireplace."

This return to the past is reminiscent of another time when she felt truly at one with her environment. That was during the depression. "The greatest security was within our family. . . . They weren't rich, they were actually very humble. . . . The talk was gay and people laughed and everybody seemed concerned with each other.... I felt there was nothing that could happen in the outside world that could hurt me." During the depression, career climbing and competitiveness were not possible because the jobs weren't there, so often people turned inward, to their families and their communities, for emotional security and cohesiveness. Now forty years later, in Monterey, she searches for empathy, a new connection with her environment.

She has not completely settled in, still resides in two cultures. One is the culture of unshaped time—her interior zone. The other is the external world of friends and children, people who live in a work-centered environment. She sees them pushing, striving, advancing, and at times she scolds herself for floating free. "I can't help noticing the vitality and the feeling of a younger group of people striving to accomplish things with their lives. In contrast, my beach town seems like a stagnant backwash and a senior citizens' haven. No wonder I have often felt as if I had retired too early in a superannuated vacuum."

The unbound present does not unfetter the future. The anxieties it produces are of a different order, however. Lucille Roberts lets time use her, but she still wonders, What's next? What happens when the free time ends? Wistfully, she writes, "I'd like to spend more time trying to find the right guy to support me. Awfully tired of coping with kids, cats, kittens, and dogs, to say nothing of jobs. Just need a nice relationship with a man appreciative of my real talents—like good in bed and the kitchen, plus some intellectual sharing and just plain old companionship. . . . I happen to like myself, as I am, but I'm beginning to wish someone or something would give me a push in the right direction. I have come full cycle in twenty-eight years [from the not-working young mother to the working woman and head of her household to the not-working woman alone] as opposed to the usual twenty-eight-day cycle for a woman."

Ease.

That's what breaktime, life without work, is all about. Inner ease. Settle up, settle in, begin a new life as a whole person. It's not as gossamery as it sounds.

Consider the parallels to work. The career ladder offers visible signs of progress: more money; a promotion to a position with more power and responsibility; a bigger office with a better view; an expanded staff and the testimonial dinner, although the last may be a veiled suggestion that it's all downhill from now on. The not-working ladder has its own standards of achievement; living on less and liking it; rearranging the family constellation so it provides more satisfaction to all the members; closer relationships with people you care about and doing things for youself or for others, rather than for an employer or a customer.

In one respect, the payoffs are similar whether they come in the work world or outside of it. Working people talk about security, satisfaction, a feeling of accomplishment, and the appreciation expressed by co-workers, family, and community. People who aren't working talk about personal well-being, self-awareness, differentiation, and the support and reinforcement they got from friends and family—their community. In both instances the rewards of effort are realized more in psychological terms than in economic currency.

When the issue of work dissatisfaction was raised in the early 1970s, the more innovative managers responded by trying to change the material conditions of the work life. Adventuresome researchers, such as Craig Little and Kenneth Root, realized that sure, people liked to work in a clean place, sure, they wanted to be rewarded and recognized for their efforts, sure, they wanted to be treated fairly, but what they really wanted was something to care about, something that bore their personal stamp, something that made them *feel* good.

And *now*, not *then*. They lived in the present, instead of anticipating the future. They were unwilling to postpone pleasure until their retirement years. They wanted to emotionally position themselves to realize their potential, to follow their intuition and not someone's orders. Whether they worked or not, their direction had turned away from Cadillacs and kidney-shaped swimming pools, turned inward. The inner seventies.

The satisfaction-now principle, accompanied by a skepticism toward guarantees of all kinds, relegated many traditional values to the attic. In 1977 Daniel Yankelovich published a national survey he conducted for the General Mills Corporation on the subject of changing attitudes toward raising children.[8] Forty-three percent of the more than twelve hundred families interviewed subscribed to the values of what Dr. Yankelovich calls the "New Breed." Summarizing his findings, he said:

> New Breed parents have rejected many of the traditional values by which they were raised; marriage as an institution, the importance of religion, savings and thrift, patriotism and hard work for its own sake.... New Breed parents question the idea of sacrificing in order to give their children the best of everything and are firm believers in the equal rights of children and parents. Compared to previous generations, the New Breed parents are less child-oriented and more self-oriented. They regard having children not as a social obligation but an available option which they have freely chosen.

He also notes that "Traditionalists" have been influenced by the new values and are "trying to reconcile these newer concepts with older theories and beliefs." The values of both groups are converging around these issues:

- "Both groups agree by a two-to-one margin that unhappy parents should not stay together just for the sake of their children."
- "A solid majority of both New Breed and Traditionalists agree that parents should have lives of their own even if it means spending less time with their children."
- "Unlike parents of former generations, today's mothers and fathers are strongly 'now' oriented. Over half the parents expect to receive their main pleasure from their children now rather than in the future."

While all the values of the New Breed are not shared by more traditional parents, these beliefs are in the ascendancy, not only among parents but among their children as well. The Yankelovich study found that children of New Breed parents were "more relaxed and well aware that their parents do not put the same emphasis on superiority in studies, sports, popularity and behavior as the parents of some of their peers."

One effect of this change in values is that many Americans now believe that they have a voice about how they are going to live, different options for any situation. They can hold a job or stop working. They can get married or not get married. They can stay married or get a divorce. They can have children or not have children. They can acquire possessions or discard them. As they make their choices, tradition, family, church, or community count for less than self-gratification. Walk into the department store and pick out what you can afford. Pick out what will make you happy. If you feel good it's the right choice.

Not all of the people who hold these values have stopped working, but the increase of these attitudes in American life has reduced the importance of working. And because these values are being communicated to children, it is even more likely that future adults will be less competitive when they do work, and be able to slip in and out of the work world without a feeling of great loss or failure.

The rise of self-interest and the demand for gratification in the present, reflected in the way we raise our children and how we organize our private worlds, have also left a deep imprint on the work world. In the boom years after World War II, individuals were expected to mesh with the company if they wanted to succeed. The emphasis was on adaptation, refashioning the individual personality to complement the corporate profile. The needs of the self were subordinated to the style and objectives of the corporation.

Now the individual is cast in a more effective role. He influences the corporation as he is influenced by it. The organization and the individual are interactive. One notable effort, Michael Maccoby's *The Gamesman*, conceives of the contemporary corporation as a *psychostructure* shaped by and shaping the variety of personality types who roam its interior corridors. In this scenario, Maccoby suggests a rough equity between the individual and the organization. How fast and high he rises in the corporation is regulated by his own attitude, his view of himself, and his inner needs as much as it is by his adaptability to the organization's psychostructure. Writing from a psychoanalytic perspective, Maccoby identifies four primary character types in the corporate world.[7]

The craftsman: "Within the corporate world, the craftsman is on the defensive, trying to preserve his integrity from the exploitive demands of more aggressive managerial types. Inside his protective shell, he does not let difficult issues penetrate, and he is unable to reach out to others who might share a new point of view."

The jungle fighter: "Cunning and secretive, with strong exploitative, narcissistic and sadistic-authoritarian tendencies. They wanted to dominate other people and be admired as superior beings."

The company man: "As much as they are motivated by hope of success, they are also driven by fear and worry, for the corporate projects and the interpersonal relations around them, as well as their own careers. Separate from the corporation, company men feel insignificant and lost. As part of the organization they have their spot at (or on) the cutting edge."

The fourth type, Maccoby believes, dominates the upper reaches of the corporation. The *gamesman* is "playful, industrious, fair, enthusiastic and open to new ideas. . . . More dependent on both others and the organization than he admits, the gamesman fears feeling trapped. He wants to maintain an illusion of limitless options and that limits his capacity for personal intimacy and social commitment."

The gamesman pays a price for his success, however. He must suppress the loving part of his nature. His head, rather than his heart, controls his behavior. He cannot afford to feel deeply, express stong emotions, or let his judgment be swayed by compassion. "Those who were active and interested in the work moved ahead in the modern corporation while those who were the most compassionate were more likely to suffer severe emotional conflicts."

It is at the breakpoint of emotional conflict that not working becomes an option. This option is exercised because there seems to be no other way to meet the needs of the heart and to achieve the human potential thwarted by the work organization. What happens after reaching the breakpoint is, of course, not entirely up to the individual. He has to contend with the reactions of the people closest to him. He has to withstand economic pressures. He has to live in a culture where most of the people continue to work.

How he manages these external conditions depends to a large degree on his internal makeup. After I finished the first third of my interviews, I strongly resisted psychological typecasting, which can lead to seriously flawed generalizations. We are not company men or craftsmen or gamesmen, but a combination of all of them. The jungle fighter in us is magically transformed into the gamesman at the right party in the presence of certain silky company. Yet against all my biases toward this compartmentalized form of analysis, I found myself drawn toward a psychosocial framework. The people I interviewed persuaded me.

As I listened to hundreds of hours of taped interviews, I discovered something I had missed in the personal encounters. The nonworkers hadn't changed so much their way of living as they had their feelings. They were facing up to problems that had been long buried while they had piled up layers of experience, grown up, developed new relationships, advanced in a career. They were reexamining their emotional responses in many situations: their fear of failure; their headlong flight from loneliness; their need for constant support and reinforcement; and their unquestioning acceptance of a life plan drafted by others.

I began to hear a second voice beneath the voice on the cassette. It was the inner voice, the voice that expressed feelings and emotions, the voice that did not explain but evoked. When I finished transcribing the tapes, I was left with a number of questions:

Why did people of roughly the same means react differently to the economic pressures of not working?

Why were some people able to handle unscheduled time and others overwhelmed by it?

Why were some people always referring back to their work experiences while others seemed to put their jobs and careers behind them after they stopped working?

Why did some people discover new interests and challenges beyond working while others swam in a void?

Why were some marriages strengthened and others destroyed when the primary breadwinner stopped working?

Why did some dramatically change their lifestyles when they left their jobs while others continued to live much as they always had?

Why did some go back to work and others stay out for years?

Charles Braithwaite had told me long before that he couldn't explain why he didn't want to work. "It's not that I can't explain," he had said. "I just don't want to." I think what he was saying that night when he got up from the table and left me with the check was: My words are not all that important. My emotional state is. If you want to understand me, consider first my feelings, my dreams, my needs. Then think about where I came from, what I struggled for, what I want now.

I began to group the character traits of the people I had interviewed within different psychological and social contexts. Beneath these headings I scribbled the key notes: emotional responses, fantasies, unspoken aspirations, and myths. My typology went as follows:

The Technician: Always adjusting—dreams of constructing the perfect machine—replaces rather than repairs worn-out parts—tinkers—intrigued by, yet fearful of long-term commitment—impatient—fascinated by newness—stays close to the original design—grace and style most important.

The Protester: Retains residual rage against work—measures progress by the degree of personal independence—suspicious of all systems—wary of marriage, family life, social organizations—interprets advice as manipulation, support as seduction—seeks reinforcement for the indictment of work—fears being trapped—feels victimized—an escapist without goals.

The Seeker: Once needed the company to validate competency and position—now seeks new system to provide guidance and self-worth—attracted to growth psychology or spiritual and philosophical discipline that affirms actions—the more imaginative seeker develops personal brand of humanism—requires external order and coherence—drift is frightening—must have stated goals—task oriented.

The Adventurer: At work resembled Maccoby's gamesman—once rolled for high stakes—stimulated by intrigue and risk taking—now losing appetite for game playing but stirred by challenge of psychic adventure—searching for most dramatic setting to do what others think is impossible—always testing himself against great odds—identifies contentment with stasis and atrophy—regards himself as a romantic in a pragmatic world—the last line of defense against the utilitarian mind.

These psychological attributes attached themselves to the individuals I had met during the previous two years. In my mind they did not represent a permanent psychological state, but a stage in emotional and social development. Some protesters evolved into seekers, and there were technicians who took a turn in the road that led them to gamble on adventure. I shut off the tape recorder and began to think about where their travels had taken them and what they had learned about themselves beyond the breakpoint.

THE TECHNICIAN

Meaninglessness. Homelessness.

> The individual is threatened not only by meaninglessness in the world of his work, but also by the loss of meaning in wide sectors of his relations with other people. ... The institutional fabric as a whole tends toward incomprehensibility. Even in the individual's everyday experience, other individuals appear as agents of forces which he does not understand. Furthermore, he is constantly in the situation of having too many balls in the air simultaneously. He has "too many choices" all the time. ... The typologies and interpretive schemes by which everyday life is ordered ... must be used from moment to moment to deal with vastly complicated and constantly changing demands. ...

The pluralistic structures of modern society have made the life of more and more individuals migratory, ever-changing, mobile. . . . In terms of his biography, the individual migrates through a succession of widely divergent social worlds. Not only are an increasing number of individuals in a modern society uprooted from their original social milieu, but in addition, no succeeding milieu succeeds in becoming truly "home" either. . . . A world in which everything is in constant motion is a world in which certainties of any kind are hard to come by. . . . What is truth in one context of the individual's social life may be error in another. What was considered right at one stage of the individual's social career becomes wrong in the next.[1]

In this analysis, three sociologists, Peter Berger, Brigitte Berger, and Hansfried Kellner, conclude that in America and other postindustrial Western societies the individual is becoming a nomad. Forever searching for a spiritual and social home, a place where he can rest his weary psyche, he pauses at one oasis after another—a job, a marriage, a community—but they always turn out to be just mirages.

When the nomad asks, "Where's home? Where do I find 'wholeness'?" the response is maddeningly ambiguous. Work is central, he is told; it is the defining experience. But how can that be the answer? Work, he has already learned, will not provide the "wholeness" he seeks. Work is the opposite of integration and coherence, just more empty, airless rooms, anonymous bureaucracies that lead to other bureaucracies where it is a crime to open the windows.

The technician thinks, perhaps I need a rest, a cool-out period. In their book, *The Homeless Mind*, the three sociologists write, "In order really to remove himself from the dominance of the 'world of work,' (the individual) must literally or figuratively 'go on vacation.' Such a 'vacation' always involves a deliberate and often very difficult effort to shake off precisely that reality that is foremost in the individual's work life."

Inevitably, the vacation ends. A week, two weeks and the worker is back to the same gnawing reality. It's like leaving a banquet hungry—he needs something more. His next move is based on two attitudes that, ironically, have helped him to get ahead on the job. The authors call these themes "makeability" and "progressivity."

Makeability: "What is involved here is a problem-solving approach to reality which is apprehended as 'makeable.' Life (including social experience and identity) is seen as an ongoing problem-solving enterprise."

Progressivity: "There is a tendency to maximize the results of the benefits of any action, a tendency that can be traced to the engineering mentality of technological production. This tendency produces a basic instability expressed in the notion that 'things can always be improved.' Combined with the concept of 'makeability' this leads to an 'onward and upward' view of the world. There is not only an expectation of recurring and ongoing change but a positive attitude toward such change."[2]

Among the one hundred people who had stopped working, the technicians were the largest psychological bloc. What identified them was the fact that they were always changing. It sometimes seemed that the reason for any one change was less important than the act of changing. They had migrated through a dizzying assortment of social worlds and occupational roles. They had lived poor and they had lived rich, but even when they attached a positive good to temporary poverty, they had a glass of white wine and a slice of Danish fontina to offer a guest. On the road to transformation, they had experimented with various forms of therapy and self-growth disciplines. Their sexual adventures were a kind of bloodless latter-day version of the *Decameron.* From monogamy to est; from open marriage to primal; from group sex to encounter groups—they always had to keep looking for the breakthrough.

Since these experiences, psychic or sexual, were unlikely to provide the magic key to "wholeness," they were relatively short-lived. Superficially, technicians resembled another personality type, the seekers, in their enthusiasm for new psychological and social movements. The seekers were different, though, because when they found a theme that engaged them, they were prepared to commit themselves. The technicians reminded me of snowbound travelers in an airport motel. They allowed themselves to become intensely involved with their fellow travelers because they knew they would be moving on when the storm passed.

On Martha Gorham's wall is a sign that reads: Today Is the First Day of the Rest of Your Life.

In 1972 this was an idea whose time had come, and no one was more ready for it than Martha.

August 15, 1972: Martha resigns from her job with Hadassah. Her children are living with her ex-husband. She is ready for a fresh start. The alternative life-styles of the 1960s had passed her by; then she was still building a career, raising her children, and paying lots of rent for a luxury apartment. Now she is ready to plunge into the alternative stream, to make yet another change.

First Esalen.

"After the first week at Esalen I was standing around the pool. One of the gals who was 'sophisticated hip' and worked in the office there said, 'Why don't you go in the pool?' I said, 'I don't want to get my hair wet.' She said, 'What do you mean get your hair wet?' I said, 'It looks terrible when it's not fixed, and I can't fix my hair myself.' So she said, 'Well, I'll fix your hair. I've got rollers and a blow dryer and I'll fix you up again.'

"When I came out, she made me put on this Indian madras kind of dress. Eastern kind of thing. I still have it. She gave me long earrings. I washed and I didn't use any makeup. We didn't curl my hair, just blow-dried it, and I looked in the mirror and it was another person. I couldn't believe it, you know, no bra. I looked so different from who I was used to looking at. I went into the dining room and I waited for everyone to be shocked, to stop eating. Nothing happened! I went up to the people in my group and I said, 'Don't I look different to you?' They didn't even notice the difference. I realized that it must be all in my head. That I had this image of how I had to look and that I would be perceived as so different."

Martha learns it's okay to be different. To dress differently, not to work. She knows no one will censure her. Her mother and father are dead. Her husband is remarried. Her children are gone. She doesn't have a job to dress up for anymore. She also learns that different doesn't necessarily mean happy.

She shops around. From Esalen she moves on to est, from which she learned: "That people are into symbols in this society and that doesn't nurture you. The message of est is that you shouldn't be stuck and be the victim of a belief system. Once you can get outside, you can choose. See, I was brought up in a belief system that I thought was universal. I didn't know it was just another belief system; I thought that's the way life is. It was all in my head. Like the fish that's in water doesn't know what water is until he's out of it. They also showed me my intuitive side. That I could sense things. I didn't have that. As a little kid, I was so sensitive that I closed down that part of me since it was too painful. I had a Western/rational/intellectualizing analytical head. That was the only way I knew how to deal with problems. I didn't know what I *felt*. It was like dynamite blasting open this closed part of me."

In the fall of 1972 Martha Gorham was existing on her savings—she hadn't yet tapped welfare or unemployment—and living in her expensive apartment in Denver. She was depressed: "I ate and watched TV. Twenty-four hours a day. There was no night and day. I didn't like anything on TV except movies. My old fantasy: I watched movies. I was really down and I didn't want to play in the world. I had left my kids and that was my crime. That's really the emotional thing I was dealing with. So I couldn't do anything good for myself. I was to be punished."

The particular punishment she chose was a middle-aged Army veteran who had been discharged from the military because he had a fast trigger finger. He asked her to share his apartment and she moved in with him, starting what she would later describe as her "skid row" period. "Here I was going through dollars like crazy and he said I could come live with him and I thought, well, I'll give him a lot of emotional stuff, I'll make him feel good about himself, physically and sexually. This was a guy who told me he loved to kill people—put a gun in his hand and he couldn't control it. I was in such a self-punishment thing that I sometimes thought, 'He'll shoot me and end my misery.' And I'm not the suicidal type. That was skid row. I'd hit the Bowery. What could be worse than a nice Jewish career lady living with some Irish Catholic alcoholic psycho."

At the crucial moment, her technician's mentality saved her. For that to happen, she had to arrange things so that she was up against the wall. She had to be able to tell herself that her needs, particularly the need to survive, were so imperiled that she had to make a change.

"He started hitting me for money. I kept telling him don't ask me for money. I have a big thing for money and I don't want to write any money off. When I said no, he cut me off physically, sexually, and emotionally. That was his way of punishing me.

It was hell and I wanted to move out. But he threatened me and told me I couldn't leave.

"I guess what kept me there so long was this schiziness he had. One part of him was this military killer, straight, conservative, uptight, controlled Nazi guy, and then when he got drunk, he was an absolutely marvelous, loving, gentle, poetic, and beautiful man. One night I suddenly got interested in him sexually and I must have been giving him some messages and he came at me. Here we are just living like enemies, not communicating, and I suddenly got turned on to him, out of the blue, and he came over and I refused it and then he hit me. He could have killed me but he didn't. He just hit me, not too hard, and I just lay there with relief. Then he hit me a few more times. Suddenly I—hey, I don't like this and I started fighting back. That's when I made the move, when I got out of the apartment."

Martha is not a cold-eyed technician, she is not bloodlessly mechanistic about her moves. As she gets ready to leave one social milieu and enter another, she maneuvers herself into a corner. Often she seems to make a change out of hostility rather than out of legitimate striving. Her husband had let her down because he couldn't meet her social and sexual needs. Her children have left her no choice but to split because they have become a burden. All her jobs, which she took with such hopefulness and excitement, inevitably disappointed her. If they hadn't disappointed her, she wouldn't have had a reason for moving on.

Martha doesn't deceive herself. She knows what she's doing. She knows that she provokes crises and that she is not simply a victim. Knowing that makes her feel guilty—about the affair she had before her divorce; about giving up her children; about coming on to the trigger man. ("After I left him I called him and told him he really didn't hurt me. I had to look at how much I provoked him. It was on an unconscious level, but it left enough of a shadow so I had to notice it.") Guilt is her self-inflicted punishment for not measuring up to what others expected of her, and maybe what she expected of herself.

It had been four years since she left her job with Hadassah. Outwardly, she had changed. She wore thrift-shop dresses (but kept her old business suits in the back of the closet). She lived in a quasi-communal arrangement in Boulder that didn't cost her much, allowed her some privacy, and kept her from getting very lonely, and she fixed her teeth at a free clinic. She had become expert at thinking small and collecting money from the government.

I am not sure she had changed inwardly. She was still making changes, leaping from reality to reality. Her enthusiasm for est subsided when she did some volunteer work for the organization and found it as rigid and didactic as any work organization.

In the end, she severed her ties with the est organization. "The est training acknowledges you as perfect and beautiful and complete. Then you go into the organization and they say, you have no rights. You do what you're told. You're a robot. We don't want to hear anything. And to *me*, who's been in administration, who knows management models. And here I am at est, and I came up against the same bureaucratic bullshit. . . . So I said to myself, I don't want to play by their rules. I don't have any power here. Why don't I play my own game and come up with something?"

From est to Synanon, which wasn't her game either. "That was a haven. In the beginning, the only time I left where I lived was to go to Synanon, where I was a volunteer. I worked for my food there. I peeled potatoes, whatever you do in the kitchen as a flunky I did. And then I quit Synanon 'cause they started to game me about work. I said, "I just want to live here and I'll pay you.' 'No,' they said, 'you got to go out and get a job. You can't work here.' So I said, 'I can't do that.' Work to me was just poison. 'I can't go back to that,' I said, 'that's like the lion's den.' Then they started gaming me, really hitting me. And I was too vulnerable to handle that kind of . . . so I stopped going to Synanon."

Deciding that she couldn't hack organizations, she considered going out on her own. She flirted with two schemes. One involved holding discussions with groups of high school students. "I was going to have them pick one thing they'd want to see changed in the school, and I would guide them 'cause I know the game, I know how you expand your purpose to include the school's purpose. I went around to high schools asking to do a rap group for free and nobody wanted it. I went to a volunteer center and nobody was interested. Maybe they knew I was subversive. I pursued it to a point and lost interest in it."

Martha had more success leading discussion groups on introducing experimental and innovative methods in religious education. A Jewish organization paid her $24 a night to do a workshop on the celebration of four major religious holidays. "It was effective," she says, "the teachers really liked it. That was very positive, but I couldn't sustain that somehow."

Her sexual style has been no more consistent than her work interests and psychosocial involvements. "Oh, I've gone to the orgies," she says. "I've been to the sex parties. I haven't been into whips and chains but group sex; I've pursued that because I'd been repressed in that area. But it's interesting to me that I seem to be going back to more conservative values because I've done it all. I'd really like a full relationship with somebody. I'd like to be monogamous. It's just what feels good to me now. I could change tomorrow."

If Martha Gorham has been fully engaged in anything in the last five years, it has been in persuading the government to sponsor all of her moves and experiments. It is doubtful if she could have done it alone, but she didn't have to. After her first six months on unemployment insurance, she heard about a group called New Moves.* "At first, it was really, really hard. I was into this self-punishing, denigrating trip. Then I found this group and that began my reeducation in terms of values. They said that it was okay to do that, to take money from the government, and they were middle-class, educated people that I could identify with. So now I had a new peer group.

*This is not the real name of the organization.

"Every Wednesday night in Boulder they ran this drop-in group. From them I learned to shop at thrift shops. Me? Secondhand clothes? I learned that that was okay. So it began to be almost a challenge as to how little I could live on. It wasn't hard to give anything up. The only thing that was hard was to do things I'd been taught were not right things to do. Like taking money from the government, like lying. I know everybody does that. But my ethical system is very high and very narrow, so it was hard for me to do those things. When this group kept telling me it was okay, I began to put my heart and soul into it. I got so hooked it became a career."

I mentioned to her once that I had met this guy in Oregon who had been able to capitalize on a loophole in the unemployment insurance regulations and collect for seven years without interruption. "My reaction," she said, "is that I'm not really interested because I'd like to be self-supporting again someday for my own ego needs." Then she hesitated and sighed. "But I don't know if I'll ever get out."

She took me through the house in Boulder, introducing me to some of the people who lived there. One was a former teacher; others included a fifty-five-year-old woman who had once sold classified ads for a newspaper and a twenty-three-year-old druggie who had kicked. The place was clean, almost hygenic. The bulletin board listed different chores and who was responsible for doing them and when they had to be done. It struck me as a dropout community without any of the sloganeering and counterculture posturing that I used to find in a place like that. When you walk into a communal house and there's not a single dirty plate in the sink or a ring around the bathtub, you know times are changing.

Back in her room, Martha was saying, "The thing I like about it is if I get depressed or want to be with people I don't have to go anywhere or have to call anybody. I just walk out that door—as long as that door is closed, unless it's an emergency, nobody bothers me—and if I want people I walk out into the kitchen and people are there. They don't lay trips on me and it's a very permissive, easygoing, laissez-faire kind of place."

Pause. "I could walk out tomorrow and not wince at all. Or I could stay here forever." Well, if it's so relaxed and all, why would she want to walk out? "Understand where I was coming from when I moved in here. I was coming from a rebellion place. I had done the other way, and I was angry: Fuck you, I'm gonna get you back. Then I realized I'm still being run by the system when I'm rebelling against it. When you resist something you're still being run by it. I also learned that the counterculture can become another establishment. I started bringing straight men home and I got all kinds of negative stuff. From here! At first I started being defensive, and then I said, 'What kind of crap is this? I mean, what's this, the new establishment? Instead of a tie and coat you gotta wear jeans? That's crazy. We're back to where we started.' So I put that out and they stopped hassling me. Now I don't feel I have a commitment to counterculture stuff 'cause that's like another establishment."

It's a long way from that first revelation in Esalen to the house in Boulder. "What's the counterculture anyway? Health food and jeans and no makeup and no bra. Big deal. I'm just sort of picking and choosing what I want. I want to work but not just work to work. It has to be something I feel good about. I really do like being paid; I like the money. I like luxuries. I like the freedom to buy. I'd like a color TV. I'd like to go traveling more if I wanted to. When I did it all the time it got to be boring. I'd like to have the choice to do that when I want to do that. You know buy some expensive clothes, something I like that costs a lot of money.

"I don't have to adhere to any system. Whatever feels good. I'm not excluding *anything*. Whatever feels right at the moment is okay. That's why I wouldn't wince if I got out of here. I'd be looking toward something else."

If somebody asked me to bet, I'd lay odds that Martha Gorham, the technician, was planning another change.

Be "creative," our culture demands. Don't just sit there swilling beer and watching the tube. Do something imaginative, innovative, ingenious with your life. Martha Gorham can't just change jobs or living conditions. She has to make a "creative" change and move to a "creative" place. She's not allowed to be satisfied or smug about what she's done in her life. She has to think "creatively" about the future. She can't have a good old-fashioned dish-throwing hair-pulling fight with her housemates; it has to be a "creative" confrontation. If you want to calculate the price we pay for converting accountants into poets, think about how messed up Norm Walters's life is since somebody told him he had the stuff to be a really "creative" intellectual.

A few years back he was a perfectly competent craftsman and his work carried his personal stamp on it. He didn't give you any of that mass-produced assembly-line crap. You wanted somebody killed, Norm would go out and do the job right. Was he unhappy? No. Did he feel unfulfilled? No. "I did enjoy a system of comforts and security that other people didn't. I had more independence than other people did. I was better off than other people were. Looking at what I had versus what I wouldn't have if I stopped, I thought that was better."

He thought it was better until the academics showed up and screwed up his thinking. He got his masters in sociology, kicked his heroin habit, attended A.A. meetings regularly, and married a college teacher. And what's that got him? "It's confusin', you know, confusin'," Norm Walters says, shifting his book bag from one shoulder to another.

"What's confusing, Norm?" I ask, stealing a french fry from his plate. He gives the woman at the cash register a few bills. Lunch is on him. "All of it. It's all confusin'," he says, picking up his tray and leading me to a table in the student cafeteria of Long Beach State College.

"Sorry I couldn't meet you last night, my homework took longer than I thought. I had to finish studying for a quiz today. Urban Problems in America. Sociology 202."

Sociology 202 gives Norm Walters a label: Norm Walters, college student. A way to fill up his time while he decides what he wants to do next.

"This is the right thing for me?" It's half question, half statement. "I mean, the life of the mind. In academia, I can realize my potential. Before, I could tolerate myself because I was doing a thing and I was having some success. But I didn't really like myself. Something was wrong. I had tremendous potential I had never really utilized until I got involved in academic work. It showed me a way. I got exposure to all those feelings of vague discomfort."

"Do you like yourself better now, in academia?" I ask. "These feelings of discomfort, they're gone?"

"I don't know, that's what's confusing. I know if I stick at this I'm not gonna be asocial. I'm not gonna be beatin' an old newspaper vendor to death just to steal his nickels and dimes. But, am I gonna be my own man? In organized crime I was chattel. But if I use my intellect I can be free, I can be respected for myself. Right?"

"Well, uh, Norm. It's a little bit of a business. Tenure. Promotions. Academic politics. Publish or perish. It's not entirely free, you know you've got to sell yourself."

"Yeah, I was thinking that. A few days ago in class I'm talking about drugs, what the life is like when you're comin' up, and I'm goin' on and goin' on, and I notice the teacher's not listenin' to me, he's shakin' his head but I know he's not listenin' cause he's glommin' the blond in the first row. So I say to myself, What is this? I mean back in the business when you talked you knew they were listenin' 'cause that's a well-oiled, smooth business. It was all business. This world, what is it—a game?"

"Well," I offer, "maybe you're taking it too seriously, Norm."

"You don't understand," Walters says. "I. Got To. Make. It. This. Time. Always before I could make these switches. Small-time hood. Big-time hood. Doper. Run a drug program. Get busted. Stretched out on the jones. Hold up a bank. All the time I'm outside of everything. I'm watching it, it's the only way I can function. Now I can't afford to be clinical. And because I'm not clinical anymore, I'm always afraid. I can't lose again."

"Why?" I ask. "Why's it so important? You decide you don't like the game, so you try something else. Maybe you go into business for yourself."

"Why's it important? Remember the time we were in the coffee house. How the waitress came over to you and asked *you* what *we* wanted. You were wearing old dungarees, you didn't have a shave, I had on pressed slacks and my best shirt, and she knew you had the power. The last couple of years, I've groomed myself to be as articulate as I am and I'm very articulate, but I wasn't always. I've picked people to attach myself to and picked their brains, anybody who had class, brains. Get a future going if I have any future. I want people to know I have power and it's not muscle or a gun, but it comes out of my intellect. That's why I went through all the trouble to get these credentials. In the academic situation, if you don't have credentials you don't belong.

"This sounds so snobbish," Walters says. He

cracks his knuckles. "I don't mean it to be that way, but the average intellect is like ... my mental processes don't work like other people's. Mine is much more rapid. But that's a problem. I am my own worst enemy—my assets are my deficits. Every work thing I'm in, it's like being in a den with a bunch of lions who want to eat me up and all I have is a whip and a pistol which are ineffectual. I'm perceived as a threat to most people I come in contact with. Truly. When I come into a job and start making my moves and start performing, the people start lookin' for the wrong moves. 'He's moving too fast. He's too damn good, we have to get rid of him.' I expect them to appreciate what I can do. Yeah, I expect many, many things of people they can't deliver.

"In organized crime I used my intellect to avoid the restraints, so I wouldn't wind up dead. I manipulated the situation. I was able to choose my existence, fit into any existence I wanted to. Now it's different. The thing I want to do, prison reform, alternatives to prison, a new attitude about drugs, all that stuff, I got to accept the situation, I can't manipulate it. I can't just use my mind to get out of the hole. I have to use it creatively. If I can use my mind to think creatively, I'll be able to understand why I'm afraid all the time."

I try again. "So you're afraid you won't fit in? You'll blow the situation, you won't get what you want?"

Norm stares off into the distance. "Not exactly," he says. "I'm afraid of the fear. When I was killing people, I could neutralize the fear. It wasn't the crippling kind of fear. I just had to be better than the next guy. This is different 'cause I'm afraid of what the fear is going to do to me."

Norm then tells me the story about the skates. How his father demanded that he beat up the kids who took his skates, how he's carried that family legacy with him all these years, how he's never trusted anyone and never adhered to the code of any organization, not even the Mafia.

When he's done, I understand why he's afraid.

He had disciplined himself to be a chameleon. He had slipped in and out of identities, in and out of marriages, in and out of danger. The moral and ethical restraints that applied to other people didn't affect him; he was able to write his own rules. (Even to the extent that the organization used him for delicate assignments while he was a known heroin user, a habit the mob would have considered contemptible and dangerous in anyone but him.) Every time he pulled off a job he was proving himself all over again to his father. All he had to worry about was living up to his father's standards.

Now Norm Walters is joining a professional tribe with customs, rules, values, and proscriptions. To belong and be accepted he has to subscribe to a community ethic. Walters can't go it alone any longer. He has to build alliances, accept support, and enter into collaborations. He is going against his father's dictum: You do it for yourself, you do it alone. The hardest thing for him will be to admit that he needs help. For forty years his father's approval sustained him. Now he will have to go elsewhere for approval and that's frightening. So he dangles, uses academia as a possible out. "I'm buying time. It's so different.

In the organization you had two types of people,"
Walters says, "the sheep and the wolves. All it was
was the ability of one to terrify or control the other.
I got good at terrifying and controlling people.
Now I have to get good at something else, at winning people over. I don't know if it's too late for
that."

Not everybody can afford to be a technician. It's a
privilege that comes with middle-class status. If you
grow up poor, particularly in a minority community, you grab at the job and hold on. Nobody told
you that the job had to make you happy. Nobody
told you that self-fulfillment ranks with freedom of
speech as a constitutional right. The pursuit of ease
comes down to a better job than your parents had.
You make progress when you can afford a decent
apartment or house and your kids don't have to
drop out of high school to get a job.

Almost all of the technicians I met came from
middle-class backgrounds. Their responses to
change and variation in their lives were strongly influenced by what social psychologist Kenneth Keniston calls the "second-chance syndrome." Keniston
directed a study commissioned by the Carnegie Corporation that documented the privations suffered by
children of low-income families. He found that even
when parents and teachers encouraged them, poor
children discovered very quickly that their opportunities were severely limited. "These kids are smart
enough to see that their world is full of smart people
who don't have jobs as good as white people," Keniston says. "By third grade a lot of people's fates are

sealed. . . . Their sense of the future, their definition of the future, is such that they believe they will
be in the same rank in society as they started in."[3]

For contrast, Keniston offers the case of his own
daughter. She suffers from dyslexia, a reading disability. "She was in a progressive school and her
condition got worse," he says. "The school was bad
for her, she wanted more structure. Because her
mother had credentials, we were professionals, we
were able to get her out of this school into another
school; we gave her tutoring, and her reading still
reverses, but she's reading pretty well now and
writing and her basic gifts are beginning to flourish.
I kept thinking about this, she's got two psychologists with Ph.D.'s as parents, you know, we have all
the right people around us, we have the information
to get the best medical people, we can send her to a
private school—well, what would have happened if
she didn't have these resources available to her.

"She had a disastrous three, four, or five grades in
school and then got a second chance," Keniston
says. "For the poor kid, the lack of a second chance
runs through his whole life. The poor kid makes a
mistake and he gets stuck. Whereas a rich kid who
has greater resources and the capacity to wheel and
deal in the world makes the end-around run."

Believing that there are always options and that
almost no decision or act is irreversible cushions the
shock of change. But choice and alternatives are limited sometimes by such external forces as the overall
economy, a changing job market in a particular occupation or profession, age, and sex. But there is always the idea that if you're not terribly old, if you

have an education, if you're white, if you're articulate, if you're reasonably well-groomed, if you read and are well-informed, you won't starve. There's always a ticket back, a second chance. Moreover, you can always take the end run. If you decide not to work, your parents might be upset at first, but they'll come around—that's what parental love is about, isn't it? If you're a man, your wife can find a job, you can cut back on expenses. Somebody is going to pick up the tab.

This is something the technician learns after the first or second or third social or work change. Now that society generally sanctions not working, the technician's status is not radically impaired when he quits. Martha Gorham is applauded for leading discussion groups in her communal house. Another technician does a little painting and his parents can explain his not working by saying, "He needs the time to paint." A woman volunteers to work with retarded children and her friends applaud her. It's a wondrous vaccine against despair, this idea that no matter what you do you can't lose.

The belief that you can always go back to an institution and earn $25,000 takes the danger out of change. Instead of do or die, change becomes do or do something else. The psychological confidence the technician exhibits through all these transformations is rooted in a new social reality. It is a reality that redefines work. Work is now straightening out your relationship with your mother, wife, or children. Work is deciding whether you want to go the TM or the transactional route.

Man's fate was once a wife who said we need a new refrigerator, a boss who said you have to keep producing, in-laws who said you need a new car. He accepted his lot as the Chinese peasant accepted his future in the hoe he dragged across the Mongolian plain. In the contemporary social reality of the middle class, fatalism has been banished.

Technicians have a view of the modern world that reminds the sociologist Peter Berger of "the activity by which a child puts together and takes apart the pieces of a construction set." As might be expected, they were the most likely to return to work after a few years and were also the most likely to leave these jobs when the novelty wore off and they had enough money to sustain themselves without working. They pursued ease by tinkering with their unfinished constructions. "I love change," says Martha Gorham. "What there is to learn about life excites me, and it can be learned anywhere."

THE PROTESTER

"The turmoil that was going through my head," Billy Morgan was saying. "What was I supposed to be doing on this earth? Do I always have to be in a job that wants me to do what I don't want to do?" I had called Billy to find out what had happened to him since we talked more than a year before in San Antonio. In that period he had worked as a home appliances manager for a department store and quit. Beneath the sadness in his voice there was something new—a tone of resignation. "It was a lot less traumatic than when I left the sheriff's office," he said. "I'd been through this before. My stomach was upset but it wasn't terrible. I thought, well, a job's a job. They don't give you a chance. You can't expect them to act humanely. I tell you, I felt kind of relieved when it was over."

There is a temptation to caricature Billy Morgan. His Bible quoting, his faith in the Lord, his self-description as Billy Good-Guy, Billy Yes-Guy, his put-upon manner all evoke the ninety-pound weakling who gets sand kicked in his face. But there is something touching about him. Religiosity aside, Billy Morgan is representative of the displaced person in a world of interpersonal war games.

He came out of a Bible school believing that there was a place for the good man who tries hard. In the next fifteen years, he learned that that was not always true. The graduate school he applied to held it against him that he had attended a Bible college. Law-enforcement work demeaned his faith. "When I worked in the county jail, I began to discover the average jail inmate would not listen to you unless you talked in his language. I was still Billy Good-Guy until somebody—my temper got to me—wouldn't do what I asked him to do. If I said, 'Fuck it,' or what, he did it. I'd usually feel guilty. I didn't like it; I hated being forced down to somebody else's standards. All I wanted was to be nice, 'Please, sir, this, sir, that,' but the animals of the jail wouldn't listen." The department store didn't want him; they wanted a machine. "You had to meet these quotas," Billy said, "But they never gave you a chance. There was always some new diversion: paperwork, bookkeeping, entertaining the big shot from out of town, customer complaints. How could you keep your mind on selling? They want a robot and I'm not a robot and no job is going to make me one."

He was as disillusioned by social relationships as by his various jobs. His wife never understood his needs, he says, never went the extra yard when he pleaded with her. After the divorce, there were other women who treated him as roughly. One took him for his money and left. Another took him for his emotions and left.

What makes Billy Morgan different from the technician is that he never distanced himself from his work and the other organizations he passed through. He was too transparent to fool anybody, and he was incapable of the detachment of heart from mind that makes for the successful strategist. He always cared too much to treat the loss of his job and marriage lightly.

It takes some planning to survive without working. Billy never planned ahead because he didn't believe that an honest, hard-working guy would be without a job. It takes some planning and emotional detachment to make it through a divorce. Billy didn't plan ahead because he never believed that a faithful, sincere guy would wind up in divorce court. The protester is the suitor spurned; all he has left is his bitterness.

The protester always has a tough time giving up work. Everyday griping at the job becomes a cry of betrayal at the moment of separation. It's like losing a parent or child. The sadness of loss is transformed into a protest against the unfairness of life. How dare they leave me? It doesn't make a difference whether the job was really unsatisfying; portraying it as a horror justifies leaving it. The outpouring of anger and resentment may persuade the outsider, but the protester knows the truth: The job meant everything. The job organized his time; it was the beginning, middle, and end of the day. Work was both process and goal; now the process is gone and the goal is vague. Like the others who stop working, the protester talks about achieving some form of personal ease. Yet his resentment blinds him to the possibility of adventure or discovery. He is trapped in a sealed container. Until he can find a way out, he cannot begin to hope for something better. "To wonder, to philosophize," Josef Pieper wrote, "means to hope." Without work, Billy Morgan and others like him are bereft of hope.

Carl Reiter is watching television. No, he's not watching. There are images on the screen, sounds. But he doesn't see, doesn't hear. He's trying to decide whether to have his fourth cup of coffee. He feels the leg muscles tightening, the cramp is coming on. He stretches his leg out under the table, bending his foot back toward him. Oh, shit. The pain brings tears to his eyes, he bites his lip, then the spasm passes. I should paint the garage, he thinks. Six months painting the damn garage, and still it isn't finished. I should make supper, I don't want to make supper, I have to make supper. Damn, I'm not ready for this role reversal business; damn, I'm not ready for nothin'.

One time after he quit the loan company, he tried for a job with a steel company. They wanted a bookkeeper, but he was turned down. The next day Maya went to the same company and was hired as a keypunch operator. Now she's getting bonuses, her friends from work are always calling. Carl's home, painting the garage.

Louise, Carl's oldest daughter, returns home from school. "Dad," she says, "can I spend tonight with Susie? Her mother says it's okay."

"I don't know," Carl says, "ask your mother."

"I have to know because I have to tell Susie's mother and mommy doesn't come home until five," Louise says.

"I can't say," Carl says. "You'll have to wait for your mother."

"Please, daddy."

"I'm gonna take a nap. Don't bother me now. I'm tired."

He walks into the bedroom and stretches out on the bed. He stares at the ceiling. Why's Maya out working, he thinks, and I'm a vegetable? Why's she doing things, why's she having fun, and why'm I a zero? Is she just tryin' to make me out a piece of shit? Why do I let her decide everything? Why do I have to be on the outside of everything? But how can I complain? She's bringin' home the money. She's supportin' the family. That gives her the right to make the decision.

I should tell Louise about stayin' over at Susie's. Louise is gettin' to the age where maybe it could lead to somethin'. I should say, okay, or no, you can't. Maybe it's a good deal, maybe not. I should investigate. Shit, I'm gonna get some sleep.

Maya comes home. Louise wants to know if she can stay over at Susie's. "Did you ask daddy?" Maya says.

"Daddy said to ask you?"

"Where's daddy?"

"Daddy's takin' a nap."

"For how long?"

"Since when I got home. Why is daddy always nappin'?"

"He's a little sick, Louise. I think we should let him sleep."

"When is he going to get better?"

"I don't know. I don't think anybody knows."

The Reiters are playing bridge with the Schmidts and the Robinsons. They have all known each other since high school.

"The old guy's gettin' out," says Max Robinson. "I don't know if he's bein' pushed or what, but he's getting out."

"Max is in line," Cora Robinson says. "Keep your fingers crossed, Maya. A five thousand raise. We'll be able to send the kids to the Catholic high school."

"And buy the camper," says Max Robinson.

"Did you know, Carl, I'm buying in to the new mall?" George Schmidt asks. "I'm gonna be a regular conglomerate, with the bar and all."

"Of course, Carl knows," says Ann Schmidt. "He's got the invitation for the opening. We're saving a bottle of champagne for you and Maya."

"Deal the cards," Carl Reiter says. "Just deal the damn cards."

"Shit, don't be that way, Carl," George says. "Something's gonna happen. Ya just gonna be five years behind the times when it happens."

"Look," Carl says, "do you guys have to talk

about work all the time? Is it such a big deal?" Carl makes intersecting circles on the card table with his beer can. Without looking up he says, "I'm foldin'. I'm goin' home an' take a nap."

Maya Reiter: "Even today, just bringing up how Carl's not working affected the family makes me panic. I would just as soon he had died. I didn't want him around. It seemed Carl had totally given up. And I guess I had lived with him long enough I didn't want a dead horse around.

"He made no decisions whatsoever. He took himself out of the picture. George Schmidt once said to me: 'This man is never going to work again.' At the time I was inclined to agree with him. Carl didn't care about anything. My oldest daughter cooked the first shift, my son took over for the second stint. They were the parents to the other three kids. Carl was just existing.

"Oh, yes, I thought about leaving. But I thought I was too important to Carl and Carl wouldn't be able to make it without me. I kept bugging myself by saying, if I could find a place where Carl would be comfortable ... I thought about renting him an apartment, but the money wasn't there. Even today it occurs to me often whether I should leave Carl. And then I think, no, I shouldn't. I still want Carl to do the most he can do. And I'm not sure he will. I think maybe I take too much of the burden off him. I don't know. We haven't talked about it enough. We don't talk about it. I'd throw out something at a time I knew he wasn't ready to talk. Then maybe he'd say something and I'd turn my back and leave the room. All this time, we never had a serious discussion.

"The thing that changed everything was the job. I got it at the end of the second year Carl was out of work. I think it hurt him that I got a job at the same company where he applied, because it was so hard for him to go out and even knock on a door. I was extremely lacking in self-confidence. I hadn't worked in so long—since right after high school, really—I thought I had nothing to offer and no one encouraged me to work. Gradually I came around to the fact that I'd have to go to work. That was the awakening time.

"I realized I was able to take care of our family. It never occurred to me before. When I was working I realized I could do very well without Carl; in fact, I was making more than he made at his best at the loan company. It was my money, and I decided as long as he wasn't working, he'd have to find a way to pay his bills. I had always resented terrifically the fact that when we didn't have money for anything else he had his beer and cigarette money.

"I loved working *with* somebody at the job, whereas I hated working *for* somebody, *for* Carl. There was such a feeling of pride, the fact that I was taking care of things. For example, Carl had said it was too much money to spend to fix our son's teeth at the orthodontist. I thought money was to be used. Carl didn't want to go see the orthodontist. He never went to see anybody's doctor but his own, and he was forever getting sick after he stopped working and he always thought he was going to die and we didn't have the money to pay for his doctors. Oh, but we did; we ate less. I knew it wasn't just a cosmetic thing; I knew the boy wouldn't have teeth by the time he was thirty if we didn't do something. I made sure the teeth were fixed. As soon as I began working, the problem was taken care of.

"Another thing, Carl thought the kids should be paid an allowance for the work they did. I thought they should be paid an allowance because they were our children. When it came to discipline over the kids, Carl thought he should still have the say. It did occur to me before I went to work that it wasn't right that I didn't have equity, but I couldn't do anything about it. Now that I was earning money I found some equity. The way we resolved the allowance question, the kids got it, but we tried to integrate Carl's thinking into it by asking them to do some chores, but not to get the money. I was in control. I had the money."

Maya Reiter's life proceeds in relatively steady progression. She has her job, her increasing earnings, her awards for doing a good job, her responsibilities for raising the children who are still at home. Carl's development is less even; he works part-time and tends to leave jobs abruptly when he is asked to do something he finds objectionable. He has worked at various jobs since he left the loan company, but he has never regained his enthusiasm for working. "I'd feel much happier if I knew his plan," Maya says. "Any goal at all I would like vocalized. Anything. Carl does not search out when it comes to working for his family. If a job is offered to him, he might take it, but then he's too fearful when it comes to using his capabilities to make a better life for all of us." Then Maya said quietly, "I think he has a valid path but it's different than mine."

It's hard to pinpoint the exact moment when Carl Reiter turned, when he reclaimed himself. All Carl knows is that some time in the late 1960s, he stopped protesting, stopped believing the world was terrible, and found something worth striving for. It could have been when he picked up a book by the Catholic writer and philosopher Thomas Merton. "If I was still in the finance business, I don't know if it woulda had the impact it did. Finance was a trap, but it was all I knew, all I wanted to know, except for some nagging doubts in my head," Carl says. "I suppose I was always against racism, against the Klan, against the Birch Society, but I didn't say much about it. The guys in the office, they were pretty loud, they were rooting for Joe McCarthy, they thought there was a communist conspiracy all over the place. I was very much against him, but I kept quiet.

"Then I picked up Merton. This makes a little sense to me. I had been a Catholic all my life but always the same thing, the churchy business. Merton talking about God, people and God, he opened up vistas. This was in the sixties and Merton was writing about social action, the Christian responsibility. I started thinking about that stuff."

One night he was playing bridge with neighbors, and in the middle of a hand he dropped an unexpected line. "I said, 'If you saw a guy lying on the road would you stop?'

" 'Shit,' the guy said, 'if you stop who knows what's gonna happen to you.'

" 'You serious?' I said. That was the last time we played cards with those people. We weren't invited back and we didn't invite them. I still can't believe that answer. Now I wave and talk when I see the guy on the street, but that's all surface bullshit. We never got deeper than that after that bridge party.

"The whole thing started to turn around. We went to a party across the street and a black-white thing came up, school integration stuff. We talked about white girls and black boys. I was astounded at some of the answers I got. People sitting on the fence. And I may have been going too damn strong the other way too. They just didn't want to get into it. During this time I was getting more and more rebellious, indignant."

It was like a fire storm. Once Merton dropped the spark, the forest was ablaze. In Pittsburgh in the late 1960s, there was no lack of social issues and no lack of people willing to take them on. One of those people was a former minister who was working as a community organizer. Reiter was introduced to him one night by his parish priest. Bill Montgomery was a round-faced bearded man who spoke slowly and softly. (He was the one who had suggested that I talk to Carl.) His style was to get people to talk about themselves, to find out what was troubling them, and to link these troubles up to larger social issues. His unspoken message was, You're not alone; the troubles you have a lot of people have. Why not get together and do something about them.

Carl, whose oldest daughter had begun to date a

black man, was a responsive listener. "First, Bill was talking about religion," Carl recalls. "About our responsibility to people who didn't have what we had. Then he talked about community organizations, what they could do. I opened up to him. I told him about my not working and it didn't shake him up. He was clinical about it. So what, he seemed to be saying, it's not a crime. He was cool on the surface, but you could tell underneath there was all this warmhearted stuff.

"What Montgomery did was make it all right to be myself. Montgomery was telling me, Be yourself or what you think you are. Like, Montgomery would interrupt a church service. He'd interrupt the service and grab the mike and ask the congregation to support a school breakfast program. Well, I couldn't do that, especially when I went into a Catholic church, so Bill said. 'Do what you're comfortable with.' So I made my contribution by writing about it in the church newsletter and I did other things that felt right."

For many years Carl had been silent. When he had been a senior at a Catholic college, his stuttering got so bad that he couldn't speak in class. He went to a brother who was supposed to counsel students, and the brother told him in effect, Don't pay attention to it and it will go away. Carl knew that it wouldn't go away, so he did. He dropped out of college barely a month before he was to graduate. At the loan company he kept quiet as his doubts about the business grew; he kept quiet until he couldn't handle it anymore, and he dropped out a few weeks before he was supposed to receive a $5,000 commission. (Maya prevailed on him to wait until he got the money.) In the five years he had been out of work, he had considered himself a cipher, less than a man, but he always remained silent. He would not talk about his troubles, not with his wife, his kids, or his friends. Suddenly he was talking.

A few days after he first met Montgomery he visited a psychiatrist who had been treating him at the public health center in Pittsburgh. "I talked to the doctor about idealism and Christianity, I told him my eldest daughter was going out with a black guy," Carl remembers. "He said, 'Either you have an awful lot of ideals or you're the most naive bastard I ever saw in my life.' That's when I got mad at him. I think he was happy I was mad at him, too, because this was the break-out-of-the-shell business. Fight back. And when I broke out, it starts to bother me that I'm not looking for a job."

He had been answering blind job ads in the newspaper, hoping that he wouldn't get a response. A few times when he was asked to come in for a job interview, he made it to the door of the company— and ran. Then one day he opened the door. He had answered an ad for a bookkeeper at a country club near Pittsburgh. "The guy wanted me to come in that afternoon. This was eleven o'clock in the morning. 'Yeah, okay,' I said. Shakin' Jesus. I borrowed a car from a friend an' went to talk to the guy. The more we talked the looser and looser I got. He went away for ten minutes to talk to his boss. He came back and said, 'If you want the job, it's yours. When can you start?' I figured I needed a day to catch my breath. I said, 'The day after tomorrow.' He says,

'Good.' That's how I went to work after five years."

Now he had not one but two jobs. During the next three years, he would work during the day at the country club and then work evenings and weekends with Montgomery, who was building a community action program in the downtown area. Reiter, who was always one to keep everything inside, discovered that he could be an effective organizer. He mobilized the residents to pressure the city to improve garbage collection. He talked medical students into providing public health services. He ran a community clothing store and later a church coffeehouse. The racial composition was 40 percent white, 40 percent black, and 20 percent Hispanic, a different mixture from what he had been accustomed to in his all-white, mostly German suburb. "I identified with all these people," Reiter says. "I was indignant when they were indignant, and I was indignant when they shoulda been indignant and they *became* indignant."

As his involvement with this new community deepened, his enthusiasm for his bookkeeping job waned. It wasn't the work that bothered him; he got so good at it that he was given a raise and an extra day off. It was that the social climate didn't agree with him, and remembering what happened to him at the loan office where he stifled his discontent for years, he started to think about quitting.

"Six or seven months into the job I knew it wasn't for a lifetime," Reiter says. "Here I was working at night with Montgomery and in the afternoon a woman comes into the club and asks me to make her a sandwich because she doesn't want to eat anything made by the black woman who works in the kitchen. I knew it was phoney. I knew I wasn't right there.

"What broke it was this lady came in to look at the microfilm chits her husband had been signing at the club bar. She wanted to check out what he was doing when she wasn't around. I knew he didn't want her to look at them and also knew what would happen if I told her she couldn't look at them. I made some sort of facetious remark: 'I wouldn't look at them if I was you.' And I laughed. She said, 'I'll do what I damn well please.' Who was going to argue with a statement like that from a corporate member? I gave her the chits.

"But I thought, that's kind of lousy. I'm taking on the role of God; this shouldn't be done this way. Kowtowing to these people. I'd get that kind of thing every day. Well, I wasn't gonna get sick again. I talked to Montgomery. And he didn't say no. He said, 'Do what you think is right.' I did. I quit."

As he reaches his fiftieth birthday, it is evident that Carl Reiter's goals and satisfactions are separate from the work that pays him a salary. Not long after he left the country club, he picked up a job at a hardware store. The job was not demanding, it paid a little, and it allowed him to continue his community work. Montgomery left Pittsburgh and new leadership took control of the organization he had built. "The new people decided they didn't need the suburbanites' help," Reiter says without bitterness. "They kicked me out."

Carl Reiter, the convert. First, the plugger at the

finance company. Then the bitter protester, to whom the world had done dirt, and now the seeker after truths, the committed believer. His strongest commitment today is to St. John's Church, in his community. "As small as that church is," he says, "I gave a commitment to it and I'm not gonna get pushed out. When I'm involved in something like minority housing or segregated schools, I'll hear one of the conservatives say, 'If he doesn't like it in Greensburg why doesn't he move out.' But I'm gonna stay here and fight."

He knows now that the job thing he does to pay the bills will probably never be as important to him as it once was. "Today, even if I were in the finance business, you're talking forty-five, fifty hours a week, how would I have time to play with this current garbage? I can't even work forty hours at the hardware store. I have too many other things to do, important things to do. It *is* serious to me, even if I say it with a laugh."

Sometimes he wishes that he had that period of protest, of blind flailing out, to do all over so he could have saved his family some of the anguish they went through, but he's not sure it would be any different the second time.

"When the pressure comes, you don't think about anything but yourself. You're more concerned about yourself than anything around you. You're also frightened to death because you know you're leaving out some essentials, like who's gonna buy the bread and how the kids are gonna feel. But in my case I was so carried away by myself somebody coulda said you're just thinkin' about yourself, and I

don't think it woulda changed anythin'. If I could
see it comin', and I think I could see it comin' next
time, I'd tell my wife right away. Lay it all on the
line, that's for sure. Get the kids into it too. We un-
derestimate the kids an awful lot. They'll pick it up
one way or the other. My kids picked up the stuff
when I was out of work. If your family is tight to
start with, cohesive, then I think they can weather
this stuff. I say that now 'cause nothin' happened to
my family. But in another family maybe the wife
would say, 'Enough of this crap.' But then again
maybe she was sleeping with Joe two years ago.
Who knows?"

I asked Carl about goals. What were his plans
now? What did he want to do in his fifties. "First,
the church. Then maybe change the world a little,
or Greensburg anyway. One goal I know I don't
have. That's the paycheck. Sure, I'd like more money—but we have enough. I know that to make money isn't the answer. And one other thing: No more
games. I played all the games when I chased the
loans. I was a great game player. It's not fun anymore."

I asked Maya about the future, her future with
Carl, the family's future. "It's just that there's no
plan," she told me. "If he said, 'I'm not going to
work for five years or maybe I'll stop in five years.'
Any plan, but I don't hear it.

"His work at church, thank God for that. This is
where I hold him in esteem. Carl wants to heal the
world. I want to work with the small family and let
it enlarge into the world. I don't understand him because I don't think anyone can heal the world if

they're not 100 percent themselves. I guess I've just developed a different way than he has."

I cannot win.

That sentiment is implicit in the protest, whether it's Carl Reiter's specific criticism against the loan company or Billy Morgan's more general sense of disinheritance. "I can scream all day," they say. "What difference will it make? I've voted the rascals out time after time; the new ones who get in are no better. I keep paying higher taxes; the schools keep getting worse. I organized a citizens' patrol to guard the streets; so I get ripped off in a different place by more imaginative thieves." The protest is too large to be squeezed into the program of a political movement. It may be captured temporarily by an enterprising demagogue, but as George Wallace found out, it could not carry him to the summit of power. To succeed, demagogues require the absolute trust of their followers. But the new protesters trust no one in power. They feel, as Daniel Yankelovich observes, "neglected, impotent, manipulated, taken advantage of, fearful that whoever is running the country does not care what happens to them."[1]

As I suggested earlier, work is the one sphere of their lives where they feel their protest will be effective. But why now and not ten or fifteen years ago? After all, *alienation* was certainly a vogue word in the sixties. I think they stayed at work then because their jobs contained the promise of economic security. As their salaries increased, as they took advantage of pensions and other benefits, they assumed an unending prosperity. In the 1970s they learned that they were wrong. They saw their savings gobbled up by hospital bills and college tuitions, their plans destroyed by inflation and taxes, their ambitions thwarted as the business world was reorganized and refitted with new technologies and strategies. They were getting old quickly.

When asked what concerned them most, the majority of Americans in 1975 expressed "a deep and pervasive anxiety about their future economic security—a recurrence of the old Depression-based trauma."

In the depression people were anxious because they were not working. In the seventies people are anxious because their work is not paying off in the economic security they expected. Fifteen years ago they might have compromised by creating a sanctuary where for a part of every day they could forget their jobs. In 1963 Jules Henry wrote, "In a society where most people work at what they have to do rather than at what they want to do, work is denied and even home becomes a kind of delusional reality . . . in the sense that it becomes the *only* reality, while work becomes a kind of phantasm. . . . The function of the American home is to deny the existence of factory and office."[2]

Today half and half is not enough. For in the absence of the dream of universal prosperity, a new priority has developed—the care and cultivation of the self. "The new values," Yankelovich says, "are organized around the theme of how to live rather than how to make a living. The stress is on self-fulfillment; freedom of sexual expression; less emphasis on duty, more on pleasure; a more relaxed attitude toward status as defining success in life; . . . introspection and the trip toward self-knowledge; . . . a greater emphasis on friendship and personal relationships; a rejection of formal social amenities and a more casual attitude toward authority."[3]

With this shift in emphasis from the economic to the personal, from the organizational to the individual, cutting loose achieves two important purposes. First, it affords a Lucille Roberts or a Tom MacCauley an opportunity to make a public statement of protest: I've had it, I'm getting out. The protester, as opposed to the technician, has not emotionally disengaged from his job. The reason he protested is because he gave a damn. He cared about his work; he wanted it to make a difference. By pulling out, the work protester stops contributing. He denies the company his talents, and he proclaims his loss of faith in the American Future by withdrawing his industry. This is not a symbolic act. He really *feels* he's doing something. He has stopped paying taxes, he has subtracted his labor from the gross national product, and either by choice or necessity, he will diminish his consumption. Now that's saying: Hell, no, I won't go.

There's another side to the protest, the private side. Stopping work is defending yourself. The crowded freeway that carries the protester to work every morning also brings him into a collective system where his personal needs are not respected (or so he believes), where his creative development is blocked, and where his self-interest is served only if it furthers the schemes and machinations of a suspect social order. Stopping work then becomes his personal expression of self-interest. Now I can concentrate on myself. Now I can advance. Now I get my turn.

You're not wrong if you detect a thirst for revenge in all of this: Not only am I pulling out, but I'm going to get back what I put in. Thus, a Martha Gorham: "The system fucked me over, now I'm fucking it over." (She's a technician, but that doesn't mean she's not angry.)

The bitterness usually passes rather quickly. It's useful because it adds authenticity to the protester's criticism of work and lends credence to his decision to disengage. As enamored as he was of his work, magazine editor Sam Meyers whispered a mild protest against the years of the arguous assignments that threatened his health and sapped his vitality. But he cut his protest short and went on to lead his new gentle life outside of work. For a few people, the protest is never ending. It is not the catalyst for healing but an insatiable and consuming demand for retribution against the culture of work, then against all of society, and, ultimately, against the protester himself. You broke the rules, goes the inner monologue, and you'll pay. And pay. And pay.

Earlier I discussed some people who are magnetized by the fantasy of adolescence. That urging is strongest when they shed the responsibilities of work. But after a while other responsibilities overtake them and they accept the fact that their youth is behind them. Louis Trotta never accepted that. He has been at war with himself throughout his adult life. A part of him recognizes that he is a forty-

one-year-old man with commitments and responsibilities to others. The other side is the id run wild—
the primeval roar of unchained youth.

There's one image from his childhood, an image
that he holds up as the symbol of perfect freedom.
Trotta grew up and still lives in the North Ward, an
incestuous and ever more threatened Italian enclave
in black Newark. When he was a teenager, he would
steal out of his parents' wood frame house on a midnight foray, and he and his pals would go to the
train station. "We'd run across the track as soon as
we'd hear the train noise," he remembers. "We'd lay
down underneath the tracks and the train would
roll over us. We'd play footsie with the third rail. It
was the wildest, freest time of my life."

For his friends, it didn't last. They grew up, got
married, had kids, bought houses, took jobs, and
moved to Pompton Lakes. Louis took that transition
into adulthood as a personal insult. "Here were
these people who were as wild as you can imagine.
If you could look into their brains, there was no way
in the world you could tell they would turn out the
way they did. I saw these devil-may-care kids turn
into the most abject, miserable fascist mentalities—I
can't even talk to them when I see them. I thought it
happened because of the social pressures—family,
the kind of job you had, the responsibilities you had,
getting a house and having to protect it. Protect it
from what? They all got married young. I remember goin' over to visit them and I was not made wel-
come. All I felt was fear and friction. You're goin' to
disturb my household. I don't want you near my
wife. You're a bad influence.

"I had this understandin' that when you had somethin' in your nature it just didn't go. And when I saw that it went, I was totally baffled. I said, 'This mother-fuckin' place did it.' The world. The way the place was. Twenty years ago I turned against that life. I totally rebelled against it. Once I made a move away it turned into a rebellion. Everything I learned after that was a total negation of that straight world."

A second image—not of freedom but of rebellion. He was twenty-six years old and he had a job as a construction worker. They are putting up an office building in downtown Newark. Louis is working on a girder on the eighth floor. "The foreman was no worse than anybody else. He was drivin', drivin', drivin'. It's one o'clock and I'm not feelin' good. The foreman's tellin' me I should work late. He's sayin', 'You're gonna leave the other guys short. They're gonna have to pick up your work.'

"It didn't matter to me. I didn't feel good; fuck 'em and all the work they had to do because I wasn't gonna be there—I didn't give a fuck. They didn't give me any reason I should care. I'm not committed to you fucks. I do it because my kid gotta eat. All I'm committed to is give me that fuckin' money so I can feed somebody. If I wanna leave, I'm the one who's gonna lose the money. Don't start comin' to me, tellin' me I left you short. You make more money if I'm not there. And if the foreman's gonna make you work harder, you're the fuckin' idiot, not me. You tell him to take a fuckin' walk. I'm workin' seven hours and gettin' paid thirty-five dollars and that's all I want to know. And if I worked five hours, all I'm gettin' paid is twenty-five dollars and that's all I want to know. The point is a boss won't stop before you fall. Then they'll get the last bit before you stop."

The foreman told Trotta to work another hour.

"I say, 'Shit, I am.'

"The guy says, 'You can't answer me back.'

"I say, 'I already did.'

"He says, 'I'm gonna speak to somebody about you.'

"I don't like workin' for you, man. You're not doing me any favors.'

"The other workers around me are sayin', 'Shhhhh.' An' I say, 'What do you want me to shhhh for? Fuck you, scumbags. You go lickin' after his ass. I'm not.' "

Trotta had to carry a four-by-four the length of the girder before he was finished. "The foreman was standing about three feet off the edge. Eight floors up. I walked toward him with the four-by-four in my hand. For an instant I got the feeling of bumpin' him with the four-by-four. It woulda took nothin' to do it. I woulda just have bumped him. I threw it down off my shoulder and walked away. I had reached the end. The next day I was gonna do something' bad and I was gonna get bumped myself. I said, 'What am I doin' here? What am I doin' this for?' "

He's had brief spurts of working since—truck driver, bartender, autoworker, carpenter, watch repairman, and one six-month job as director of a drug rehabilitation program that collapsed under political pressures. But when he walked out of that construction job fourteen years ago he rejected the idea of steady work. No occupation or trade engages him. The word *career* is not part of his vocabulary. All of this is a little hard to understand because Louis Trotta is not without lift and vision and intelligence.

There is energy in his sinewy muscular frame. His eyes are bright and animated. The coarse angry words he uses to describe his working experience soften to a gentle lyricism when he discusses the glories of the Italian Renaissance about which he is extremely knowledgeable. And it is evident that he accepts certain adult responsibilities: He is affectionate and supportive toward the woman who lives with him, deeply involved with raising his two teenage daughters, and tightly bound to his eighty-one-year-old mother.

Yet he has allowed his existence to be precision crafted in every detail by the twin images of a youthful freedom stolen by adult thieves in the night and the slavery of work. Therein the paradox of Louis Trotta: A life spent in protest against the denial of freedom and the slavery of work is given over to the worse peonage of all. For some twenty years Trotta was a stone heroin addict.[*]

Trotta's family wasn't rich; they weren't poor: They were lower middle-class Italian. His father, a bus driver, was an epileptic who drank too much. Louis's mother often sent him to fish his father out of saloons. His parents didn't understand why Louis

---

[*]In the last few years he had broken the habit, but he continues to be maintained on methadone.

was frequently truant from school. Their response was, If he doesn't like school he should find a job. As immigrants, they were not practiced in exploiting the social system. Louis says that they didn't think that a kid with a lot of unharnessed energy *could* get into college. If you didn't have a lot of money, you went to work. His parents didn't know about, or perhaps never considered sending him to, a tuition-free state college. In the early 1950s, in that Italian ward of Newark, if you weren't going to go to college, you got a job in construction; that's what half the neighborhood did. It was an honest, good-paying job, a respectable life.

If his family's class doesn't satisfactorily explain how he turned out, neither does the spread of drugs. The mob was not more concerned about the effects of the heroin trade in the Italian neighborhoods of Newark and New York than it was about selling in Harlem or black Newark. The mob wholesaled the dope. Pushers sold it to anybody who could afford it. And when the dope came into the neighborhood, how did Louis's parents respond?" "They prayed for us," he says. "For a long time they were completely and totally removed. They lived in another world. When they couldn't help but notice, they reacted mostly with hysteria, revulsion, and years and years of strife.

"One of the first things we southern Italian kids knew was gangsterism. The connected people, the big people who lived over in Fort Lee, were smart; they knew what the world was about. We all read books. Ericson and Frank Costello and Joe Adonis. They were hero figures in all ways. The ones who got thrown out of windows, the ones who wouldn't squeal—our heroes. Our attitude was *we* were using the blacks for cannon fodder. They would take all the chances and our people were too smart, too slick to get trapped."

Add it all up: the lower middle-class life, the immigrant innocence of his parents, his father's alcoholism, the inundation of drugs into what seemed to be a sheltered village, the adulation of the "connected people"—add it all up and the social argument falls of its own weight. Louis Trotta had a second chance. The Montanas who lived next door and the Profitos who lived up the block were not much different. Nicky Montana played with scag, then moved off it, went to night school, became an accountant. Mike Profito played chicken with the trains, calmed down, and did okay on Wall Street. Louis's own brother, Phillip, didn't exactly become a titan of industry but made out as a haircutter (today: hairstylist).

If you start with a different premise, if you don't accept the hypothesis that Trotta's future was predetermined by social conditions, but that to some extent he was as free as we all are, then a more realistic, less sentimental portrait of Louis Trotta, the prototypical protester, emerges. Louis Trotta becomes a more extreme version of garden variety Americana. A piece of ourselves, a New Breed man with a bad habit.

Louis says three things made him what he is: the deviant attitude of his generation toward achievement, the dark fraternity of the heroin brotherhood, and the pervasive resistance to authority that colored his life and more than a few other lives in the early 1950s.

"*I am not Italian,*" Trotta will say, emphasizing each word. "I am southern Italian." This is an important distinction to him because in his Newark neighborhood the northern Italians and the southern Italians regarded each other with as much warmth and camaraderie as the Swedes and the Germans.

Remember this and never forget it, Trotta was instructed almost from his cradle: The northerners are not to be trusted. They are cold-blooded mercenaries, schemers. They care nothing of traditions, they deny their birthright. Above all, they want to be Anglos. Rich Anglos. They call you brother and cut your heart out for a dollar. They are only interested in what success will buy them: televisions and new cars, air conditioners and washing machines. Their doctor-sons care nothing for the sick, only for the girth of their patients' wallets. Their marriageable daughters are trained at birth to bag a rich husband.

(On the other side of the ward, the northern Italians had their own opinions of the southerners. They were old heads. They dressed as if they were back in the old country. They still hung their wash out to dry on the clothesline. They talked big and took the sun in their backyards. Laziness, shiftlessness was bred into their bloodlines. They drank their vino and argued over Mazzini and Cavour and Garibaldi. Who was the greater influence, Leopardi or Manzoni? Who was the greatest living Italian writer, Moravia or Silone? Talk, talk, all they did

was talk. Where did they think they were anyway—
Puglia, Calabria? Why didn't they grow up and act
like Americans?)

Stereotypes, of course, but they held Trotta's
imagination when he was growing up and they hold
it still. From the south came the creative spirits, the
musicians, the painters, the poets. That soil nurtured people of conscience, political idealists, and
social reformers, and that legacy would be carried
on in America. When the sons and daughters of the
southern immigrants entered the professions, they
cared as much about performing a public service as
they did for fame and fortune. They became lawyers and surgeons, but they were also the people
who organized the seamstresses and meat cutters
and motormen. Today when Trotta sees a Cadillac
parked outside the home of a northern Italian family, he sneers, "Flash, just flash." On a street corner
not far from where he lives now, he and his friends
once rested a plank on two milk boxes and kept a
crap game running through the weekend. "The
southern kids took the money they made all week
and gambled it," he says. "The northern kids were
the bankers, they loaned the money out."

This responsibility, to succeed with honor and
with grace, had been borne solemnly by one, two,
three generations of immigrant families. Then the
string snapped. "Before that in six blocks alone, one
avenue, they made something like two bishops, one
monsignor, unbelievable," he says. "Lawyers, neu-
rosurgeons. Up until 1950. The generation after
that—nothin', that's it." As he looks back on the
time, he thinks that maybe part of the reason was
that while the immigrant kids, the kids born on the

other side, had something to prove, a reason for struggling, the American-born kids had it made in a sense. "The southern immigrant kids had lived on ideas. If the kid could paint, he had status. If he did arithmetic, he had status. The immigrants had a history of unions, socialism. The Americans wanted the money. The ones born here were dauphins. They wanted to drive around in their cars stoned. One out of five of the foreign-born kids had a flashy car in the family; four out of five of the American kids had flashy cars."

The idealism that had spurred earlier generations of southern Italians had soured; in his parents' lives he saw no hope, just weariness, disappointment. What was the point to the struggle, anyway? "My father had been involved with the unions. I was grateful for his struggle, for making it possible for me to get a job. Teach me a trade, and I'm goin' to get a raise, earn a livin', function. I was grateful for that. I was grateful for some people in the past I never knew. But I also knew that the unions had botched up. They didn't make a difference anymore. I learned quickly how unions work: I knew there was a lot of graft, that business had co-opted the unions. I didn't have any illusions.

"My mother worked, my father worked, and at night they sat at the table and each talked about the job and it was very hard to listen. My mother worked forty-seven years, my father worked for twenty-eight years; they paid the bastards with their blood, their bones. When I went into the job, I went in with hate. I said, 'Now they're gonna have to pay me back for my mother and father. Unless I collect for them, nobody's gonna.' I wasn't wrong. My mother she's eighty-one years old. Nobody gave her nothin' yet and nobody ain't ever gonna give her nothin'. You know when she retired in 1971, after forty-seven years sewin' dresses, *forty-seven years,* she had to fight with the union for three years to get her lousy fuckin' pension."

Louis is telling his friend Mike about his first job. Louis: "It was this department store down on Broad Street, downtown. I was fifteen. They had me packin' shirts in boxes. I did so good they wanted me to sell, but as soon as they gave me the floor to work I quit. I wasn't gettin' any other pay, and the responsibilities increased threefold. I had to work harder and they were stricter on the floor."

Mike: "That was your stepladder."

Louis: "What stepladder! They're payin' the same amount of money. You think rewards; I don't. I think you're gonna be taken advantage of at any level, that's the way I look at it. I wasn't goin' on the floor and show 'em for a month before they gave me a raise."

Mike: "Would you become president of the company if you stayed? You mighta."

Louis: "If you're into that ... if you got a plan maybe it's worth goin' along. But if you just comin' in every day, and they're gamin' you, they're takin' your balls."

If his family had not lacked for food and shelter, they did lack, and conspicuously so, happiness. He foresaw that his life, as a carpenter, would not be happier. The evening blues and the morning shakes. At best, work was an hour's labor for an hour's pay;

if he wanted happiness, he'd have to find it some-place else.

Listening to Louis and Mike talk is to be there when the web unravels. To understand what changed between their parents' feelings about work and their own attitudes. To understand the differ-ence between them and older workers. To antici-pate what Louis's children will be like. Mike is a tall, strapping twenty-nine-year-old, an ex-con and a heavy drug user. He works sporadically as a meat cutter and packer for a supermarket chain in New Jersey. The day he came to see Louis he was high (or low) on pills. I could have edited their conversation, but I chose to leave it intact, pretty much as I re-corded it. It doesn't fit together like a measured joint—it explodes all over the place. But that's the way it should be. Their whole lives have been one blast after another.

Mike: "Your World War II guys are crazy. They're sixty-seven and they don't want to retire. They don't take their breaks. They'll do anythin'. The boss says jump off the fuckin' roof, they'll do it. That's why I can't hold a job. I go to work with these guys and they want you to pick up three-hun-dred-pound things. I won't do that. These guys live their jobs. Most of the guys who work in the slaugh-terhouse, the highest thing is alcoholism. I figure that's their only identity—their job. I don't get it."

Louis: "I had a principle, I'd work my ass off, I would, but I didn't want to be fucked with. I didn't want anybody to think they're doin' me a favor. The older guys think it's a favor to 'em, they're workin'."

Mike: "What I don't get is the older guys bustin' their nuts. They get this whole thing of rush, rush, rush. They go along with the bosses and all they care about is production. Used to be cuttin' meat was an art. They're takin' that away. You're cuttin' a few loins of pork, and you're doin' it nice, right, it takes you more time. They don't want that. They want it rushed out."

Louis: "Almost all the times I worked I thought they wanted to steal your mind. I always valued my mind. The best thing I got is my mind. If you want me to sit there and do this thing, you're takin' my mind away. The worst was when I worked at the Fisher body plant on the assembly line. I was petrified, terrified of the place. Noise, workin', yellin', pushin'—work fast, oh, God! The cars run on the tracks and you got a gun and you put the aluminum on the side of the car, oh shit. Broooom. Broooom. Broooom. In the whole fuckin' plant, there ain't enough money to give me to do it. I did it three different times; I never lasted more than three weeks. When I got enough money, I got out."

Mike: "Whyn't the older guys get out? The family thing, you think?"

Louis: "That, yeah, but it's an attitude. Maybe the depression and hard times got the earlier generation to work. We were like the conquerin' babies. We didn't have no hard time. Our only objective was leisure time. The people before didn't know what the word meant. When I was seventeen, I went to the navy—a year and seven months, either that or go to jail—and when I got out I was gonna do nothin'.

"My parents were scared of the government. Me, I wasn't scared. I figure the government's gonna pay me back for my parents who were too scared to ask. Unless I collect for them, nobody's gonna. I said to myself, I don't like the way you're runnin' this place, I don't like the way civilization is. You not lettin' me change one part. Well, then, you got to feed me and clothe me. And they fed me and clothed me as long as my demands weren't great. I took from the Americanos. The Americanos, they were the ones with power. Me, I was Italian, I was just gonna take as much as I needed. That was what I worked at—havin' 'em support me. So I went to college."

Mike: "You went to college? Why'd you go to college?"

Louis: "It gave me seven hundred dollars a month* from the government and the state, veteran benefits, S.S.I., and grants."

Mike: "Y'learn anythin' you didn't know before?"

---

*College grants and loans are a popular, if hidden, source of support for some nonworkers. The National Direct Student Loan provides up to $10,000 to students. Of course, you have to pay the money back—if you're scrupulous about that sort of thing. In addition in New York State there is the Tuition Assistance Plan, an outright grant based on need which pays as much as $1,800 a year; the federal Basic Educational Opportunity Grant, providing a maximum of $1,600 a year; the Supplemental Educational Opportunity, which gives grants of $200 to $1,500 a year to undergraduate students from families with incomes of less than $9,000; the Guaranteed Student Loan program, jointly administered by New York State and the federal government and providing up to $2,500 a year for undergraduates. The beauty of these loan and grant programs is that the nonworker can continue to collect from other public assistance programs, such as unemployment insurance, veterans' benefits, and workmen's compensation.

Louis: "Oh, sure. I learned it gets you ready for the shit you're gonna get when you go to work. I used to thank God, I was thirty-five, thirty-six years old, so I knew what was goin' on. I asked a lot of questions. A lot of time people have a hard time explainin' things to me, and I force them to explain. Teachers resented it. They take it as a challenge. I got into this thing with a philosophy teacher. I asked him a lot of questions one day, and he tells me at the end of the class, 'Don't come back next week.' I told him, 'This is a philosophy course—or what? Are you teaching the catechism or is this a philosophy course?' The guy says 'No, get out of my classroom.' I said, 'That's a violent thing. I might come up and punch you in your mouth.' I said, '*You* get out.' The way the kids in the class acted, it was like the worker who gets on the good side of the boss by goin' against the other workers. Ultimately, the kids who were against me would get some of the teacher's power and control."

Mike: "They didn't care about their own dignity?"

Louis: "Dignity, what's that?"

Mike: "Some college did this study. What's the number one thing the worker wants? It was credit for the work done; second, salary; third, dignity. The way things are, they don't want credit and they don't have any dignity. How do you have dignity packagin' this shitty meat. Your kids could be eatin' it. The veal cutlets are killed as soon as they're born, instead of being fed. They're ripping people off, chargin' three times what it should be. The ground round sirloin, they put any kind of red beef in the package, and the difference in price is sometimes twenty cents, sometimes fifty cents a pound. The chickens. The water is free and they're chargin' you fifty-nine cents for water. They inject the chickens with water and they spray chemicals all over them. It's so fucked up, and the guy who cuts the meat and packages the meat, he knows what's goin' on. He's gotta be ashamed. I was so pissed, I went to unemployment and they're askin' me about the store, and I was goin' crazy, like telling *them* not to eat meat. I couldn't put up with it. I had enough money to quit, so I told 'em. I didn't play the game, I didn't care."

Louis: "I still think salary's got to be the main thing."

Mike: "Dunno. You ever been workin' and a guy with a suit comes into the room. Don't say nothin'. Just looks. That's *terror*. You don't have no dignity then."

Louis: "For the old guys, not us. Nobody scared us; the guy with the suit, we said fuck'm. The old guy'd be scared. The cop scared us; he had a gun. Nobody else. Maybe we just kept lookin' for a guy to scare us, and we couldn't ever find him."

Mike: "Whadabout the kids? You got two girls grown up. Are they gonna be like us? Or different?"

Louis: "I tell my kids everyday if you go to work you're gonna die. Youre gonna get old before your time. The older girl (twenty) she's a worker. It's her nature, nothin' I can say'll change her. She's goin' to college now. I made a point of tellin' her when she was young: 'You're workin' class. You have no chance of gettin' outside your class except for two things—an education or be lucky. You're gonna become a housewife, you're gonna be shit on. Your husband's gonna abuse you, dominate you. If you don't want to depend on love, you gonna have to go to school.' My younger daughter (sixteen) doesn't want to go to school, she doesn't want to go to work. She's got my blood. I worry about her. She's gonna have to go through it, but I'm here to watch her. But just havin' my blood's bad.

"The kids saw that I didn't let them down. They know there's been situations where they needed someone to watch their backs. My kind of character comes out in the worst of times. If there was a fire in this house and the building was burning down, I'd be a good person to have around. But if things were running smoothly I might cause disturbances. I'm there when they need me. The rest is bullshit. In the last three years, they completely understand. They got the clothes, the color TV. They're not lackin' nothin'. I tell 'em why I'm not workin'— they gotta face it. They can't go around makin' bull-shit stories about their father—my father does this, my father's got this job like everybody else does. They know the truth and they know I don't care if they tell the world about what I do.

" 'Cause I didn't work, I enjoyed spendin' time with them. I talked to 'em like human beings. I didn't go da da da. Now, I sleep in the parlor. When they're gonna come home late, they call me. They don't have to sneak back, they don't have to lie to me. They just tell me they're doin' it. I don't bull-shit them, they don't bullshit me."

Mike: "No shit."

Louis: "No shit."

There's only one missing piece in all of this. It's there, underneath every word, ticking, a thousand pounds of TNT. Dope: the ultimate scrambler. The most authoritative studies of addiction emphasize the depressive effect of narcotics on the central nervous system. Since addicts seem to have an acutely sensitive reaction to psychic pain, the drug reduces their anxiety. The primary characteristics of the addictive personality have been described as "a fearful and negative outlook toward the world; low self-esteem and a sense of inadequacy in dealing with life, an inability to find involvement in work, personal relationships and institutional affiliations rewarding."[4]

But this profile isn't true for every addict. Norm Walters, for example, used heroin for twenty years and seemed to function smoothly on his job. I'm not sure heroin was Louis Trotta's defense against his "inability to cope with life"—that he used it to numb awareness. I don't think he has tried to avoid "novelty and challenge." But what it did for him was prolong adolescence indefinitely. Heroin was his substitute for playing with the third rail. For some addicts heroin deadens pain and blacks out the drama of daily existence. Not so for Trotta. Heroin *was* his pain and heroin *was* his drama.

When he got too old for the North Ward youth gangs, he switched his allegiance to the drug confederation. He was making a deliberate and conscious choice. He needed a stage to mount his protest, and the hit-and-run, slash-and-crash guerilla theater of chasing scag gave him one.

"Drugs gave me excitement, somethin' to do. Livin' dangerously filled up a void. Every human bein' likes that. Violence exists in every community, but in the drug community there was more cuttin's and fightin' out in the open. The human body craves excitement. You have to get it wherever it is—else the body starts dyin' and the spirit starts to die. You know you're alive. It's a test: If I'm good, I'll get out of danger; if I'm not, I'll get caught. When you get out you know you're happy. You were able to function, you faced danger. My body would go through violent upheavals. It shook and quivered. Which I needed. I'd rather be in a war than in a good, stable, successful society. All the time excitement: You get arrested, you get beat, you run away from the police. When you cop and people try to rip you off, the balls you have of goin' into a neighborhood where you don't know nobody, the coloreds, you cop and get away—that's a tremendous amount of excitement.

"When I had to work, drugs got me through it. It gave me somethin' to look forward to. Friday was the big day. I binged to Monday mornin'. God forbid you asked me to do somethin' over the weekend. I put my time in over the week. Weekend comes I'm gonna do what I want to do; when Friday afternoon came, I got mine." Sometimes he didn't wait for the weekends. "I was always tired when I worked. I'd be coppin' at night, chasin', runnin' down alleys, lookin' for the score. I didn't have much left over for the days. All the time drugs came first. At certain points I couldn't go to work if I didn't get fixed. I've left jobs right in the middle to go get a fix. By then it didn't matter to me—I had no loyalty to nobody."

The most intrepid jungle fighter tires after one too many campaigns. By 1969, when he was thirty-two, the excitement of the heroin war began to pale. "I began to see that the drug scene was like the work scene. There was the same push-pull, the same abuse in both societies. In one society my payment was a paycheck; in the other it was a high. The violence in the drug community was never creative. It came down either to robbin' somebody or protectin' yourself; you weren't changin' anythin' by violence. For a long time I had chosen the high over a paycheck, but the people were the same. And it ate at you in the same respect. It bothered me. It upset me. My body trembled and I didn't like it anymore. There was excitement in drugs, a community in drugs, strife, but it wasn't givin' me anythin' anymore."*

Before I met Louis I had heard a little about him from Elisabeth, the woman who lives with him. She filled in the details of his marriage and his addiction, his stretch in prison and his two years in college, his brush with the Black Panthers and his interest in Marxism. As I waited to meet him at the bus stop, I tried to picture what he'd be like. Was he the guy who came out of the garage in a grease-smeared sweatshirt? Was he the guy with sunglasses who kept circling the street in a battered old Ford? Was he the son of the old lady who gathered greens in the weed-choked lot across from the bus stop? When I saw the figure approaching from a block away, I knew it had to be him. The Maquis on a mission behind the German lines. He wore a maroon

*Methadone is his main drug now. "It's a graph that goes up and down. It gets to some points that I say, 'God, I have to get off this.' There are other points that I say, 'I'll live for today.' "

beret cocked to the side, an Eisenhower jacket over a black turtleneck, a pair of fatigues, and work boots. But it was the walk that gave him away. He marched toward me, arms swinging at his sides, eyes straight ahead, the gunfighter waiting for me to draw.

When we shook hands he sized me up with the wariness of an addict meeting a new connection.

My first impression was accurate only to a point. His pugnacity and volatility have not diminished. He still despises work to the extent that he will not allow Elisabeth to talk about her job when she comes home at night. (She goes to college and works part-time as a bookkeeper.) Poker-faced, he will talk about her as one talks about an investment in the stock market. "She's gonna go to law school. When she gets out of school, it'll be like a bank account. I'll never have to do anythin' again. She'll take care of me. She'll have a law degree and that'll be worth somethin'."

But he doesn't treat her as an investment.

One night after we had been talking for several hours, Louis kept glancing at the clock on the wall. "We'd better go and meet her," he said. "I don't like her to walk from the bus alone." We hurried downstairs and in the distance we could see her getting off the bus. Louis broke into a run. In the gathering darkness of the Newark moonscape, they embraced each other fiercely. An arm around her shoulder, he led her back to me, with the relieved look of a parent whose daughter had been out too late.

They had met four years before, two outlaws in America. Elisabeth had been through heroin and methadone and then was deep into cocaine. Since high school she had worked at secretarial and book-keeping jobs; her most recent position was as a credit manager, an irony that did not escape her since her one bust was for passing bum checks to pay for her heroin habit.

"I'm twenty-seven years old," she told me. "I'm spending all my salary on coke, taking methadone and using coke—what is all this? I met Louis and I admired him. He was a dope fiend and all, but he had something about him, he was in control of himself. How come I'm such a scatterbrain, I can't take control of myself? I'm always going off with one deviant or another, people who were known as the baddest cats going in the neighborhood, people who beat me, who rip me off. Louis pointed out to me: What am I getting out of work? Now I have this coke habit. He said, 'You worked for the last nine years of your life and what do you have to show for it—a bunch of holes in your arm and a coke habit.'

"He said, 'Quit your job.'

"I said, 'What quit your job. How can I?' Any other man I was involved with wanted me to work. Yeah, go to work. They didn't work. Now, Louis is not threatened by me not bringing home a salary. This is something different. He says, 'Look at you, you're a complete wreck, you've got mental problems, and the only way you can work is shoot dope or coke or something. You're not going to live past thirty at the rate you're going.'

"He said I hadn't learned anything since I was sixteen. One night he made up a list of ten items. Things that if you're alive in this world you should know something about. He said, 'Talk to me about any one of these topics.' I said, 'I should know this but I don't.' My education had been stifled. All my energy had been spent on working. Boy, I'm dumb.

"It took me a month and I went to my boss and gave two weeks' notice. It was hard for me to do. I had to work up to it. I was trembling, afraid the boss would yell at me. The boss agreed to say I was laid off so I could go on unemployment. That was the best six months of my life. I had to get up in the morning to do something for myself, to ride my bicycle, to exercise, to read, to discuss current issues. Suddenly, I'm alive, hey. Louis influenced me to stop taking so much methadone. I cut my dose down and my whole life opened up. All of a sudden I was there and awake. I had been sleeping for ten years."

Louis, recalling that period, said, "The first thing I did was make her stop work. I wanted her to realize she could live without workin'. She had faith in me. She was like a little kid who was totally trustworthy of her father. So she stayed out of work for six months. But she's not like me. She's a worker. She gets gratification from it, and I didn't want to take that away from her. I just wanted her to understand she didn't have to. When she understood, it made her feel much better about workin'."

I spent time with Louis on several occasions. Each time he would bring up his family, his kids and his mother, and Elisabeth (she was part of the tribe now). I remarked that he seemed to have a deeper attachment to his family than many men who were working. "That's right," he said. "In American culture we destroy the concept of family. In hindsight I realize that I wanted to destroy my family, too, when I was younger. Now it's the most important thing to me. I've got to keep it together. Elisabeth's grandmother is in a home and we have to help take care of her. My kids—I need to give them a good place. My brother, he's divorced—if I can get a big enough house, he'll come. The house is a powerful base. When you have the house, the outside can't touch you."

When I repeated to Elisabeth what he had said about family, she said, "That was one of the first things that attracted me, he loved his kids. The fact that he was living with his mother, he had this thing about the family, which struck home to me. That was something I always wanted and it didn't work out. Here was a guy who was living with his mother, they fought like cats and dogs, but at least they would get things out. She's an inspiration to me, an eighty-one-year-old woman doing the cooking, washing, and the shopping for a household of five people."

The nest has softened him. His scattershot protest is more selective now. He can differentiate between legitimate targets and too-convenient symbols. In the past he would have attacked Elisabeth's father, a retired cop, just because he was a cop. Now he sees him as an individual. "When I was in the can, I'd ask the other prisoners, 'If somebody came and robbed your home, what would you do?' They'd say, 'I'd call the police.' I'd say, 'You mean after they busted your door down and smashed your face, you'd call them?' I couldn't comprehend it. But I've grown. Elisabeth's father is a cop. I've learned from him that they're human beings. I didn't have that idea all my life. I had too many violent confrontations with police to think otherwise."

He has not mellowed so much that working for somebody, working for pay, is an acceptable goal. "I'd trace out these ideas: in two and a half years, I'd be worth a half million dollars. Everytime I made that script, I'd get to the point I didn't want to be there. I'd say, 'Fuck it, man, I don't want to waste my time with that one.' I'd get another idea. Then I'd say, 'I don't want that one—I don't want twenty-six trailer trucks. I want to write and read.'" But he can imagine earning money from pursuits that involve him. He loves athletics (he learned to play tennis when he was thirty-six and made the college tennis team) and dreams of attracting funds to build a sports complex for teenage kids. Louis spends a lot of time in the neighborhood candy store, and he thinks about writing about the different personalities who hang out there. He once even talked about selling real estate to help Elisabeth pay for law school tuition.

Louis Trotta remains a protester. The world is divided, in his scheme, between the fat people, the *popolo grasso* ("the ones with power") and the skinny people, the *popolo minuto* ("who got no power").

Something's changed though. After almost twenty years of abusing others and punishing himself, he finds he needs Elisabeth, he needs his kids, he needs his brother, he needs his mother. And the circle keeps widening. Man without work, he is discovering, cannot survive on protest alone.

THE SEEKER

The peacock screams at dawn.

And every fifteen minutes after that.

Cliff Jones sleeps on.

Cliff Jones's housemate, Marianne, sleeps on.

His buddy, Joe Browne, sleeps on.

Joe Browne's wife, Ellen, sleeps on.

I am burying my head under a pillow, silently screaming back at the peacock. The country life is wonderful, but give me an alarm clock to a peacock anyday. You can shut an alarm off.

Credit for the peacock goes to Browne and Jones. Six years ago they put together this "creative paradise" on the banks of the Willamette River near Salem, Oregon. Jones had worked as an investment counselor with Bank of America, Browne as a successful real estate broker. With Browne's money ($262,000) and Jones's liar's dice panache, they founded what Browne likes to call a "getaway center," and what Jones describes as a "halfway house." Jones says, "Stopping work changes one half of people's lives. In this place we thought they could decide what they wanted to do with the other half."

Vain, querulous, graceful, beautiful, and totally independent, the peacock would be their symbol. "The peacock is a very human bird," Jones says. The sign on the front gate was Browne's idea. It says: Go Slower. The physical centerpiece of the new community was a massive fifty-two-room resort hotel, built in 1914 and adorned with a marble staircase and mahogany trim. Until the depression, the hotel was a spa for the very rich. There were other attractions: the natural sulfur baths, the towering pines, the rushing Willamette, the rugged yet arable countryside. The owners abandoned the place during the depression, and it remained deserted until the start of World War II when the government converted it into an interrogation center for high-ranking prisoners of war. The hotel was outfitted with trap doors, false panels, and two-way mirrors. After the war, the resort became an albatross. It passed through a succession of owners whose plans for it never materialized. In 1971 when Browne took out a mortgage on the hotel, the neighboring cottages, and the surrounding two hundred acres, this was a ghost town, haunted by memories of the Kaisers and the Hearsts and repentant German generals.

Jones and Browne wanted to construct a bastion against the storms and furies of contemporary culture, an oasis for people who wanted to go slower. Instead of pluralism, the revolving door of changing realities, they wanted to create a unitary overarching social system. Instead of the rigid, compelling timekeeping of the work world, they hoped to create a rhythm of time that followed individual need and inspiration. Instead of a pragmatic, rational approach to problem solving, they would rely on spiritual faith. Browne and Jones had their own spiritual interest, but they didn't ask the other settlers to adhere to it. "My idea was this was going to be a center of peace and quietude," says Browne. "The idea was expressed by the sign at the gate: Go Slower. I came here right out of the business world. I wanted to give people who had made the same kind of change the time to play Bach at night, to enjoy the sun and wind during the day."

To that Jones adds: "I'm really a romantic idealist. Thoreau, with *Walden*, was, cheez, much more of an influence on me than anybody else. I had spent my life either getting anxious about the future or recriminating about the past. The idea behind this place was instead of becoming something why don't we be something. What we are. That was the idea that guided Joe and me. But to tell the truth, when I moved out here I had no idea where this would take me."

Compared to some spiritual seekers I had met, Jones and Browne were refreshing characters. I didn't have to fight to keep my skepticism intact; they weren't interested in proselytizing, only in telling their story. The sermon they preached was: You can stop working if you want to—and survive. Comfortable in the world of deals and wheels, they came out here to enjoy themselves. After five years of not working, they retained enough detachment to laugh at their own pomposity. They took pleasure in the sun and wind, but remembered where they could buy a bottle of Jack Daniel's.

They balanced each other nicely. Jones prided himself on a measured sloth. His little house was filled with books and papers and overflowing ashtrays. He changed his sweatshirt and washed the dishes when inspiration seized. No mantras interrupted *The Late Show;* no early morning meditations broke his peaceful snores. Browne was more meticulous. And richer. His house, three times as large as Jones's, was a strong candidate for this year's Easy

Livin' Award. Open and uncluttered, wood and pine softened with just enough paintings and hangings. The dishwasher hummed efficiently; Bach sang softly from every corner. Everything was in order; the ashtrays sparkled, the kitchen counter glistened, and the medicine cabinet mirror told more than it had to.

Jones and Browne didn't have much to complain about. They had stopped working as relatively young men (Jones at thirty-three, Browne at thirty-two), but they didn't remember the corporate system as a snake pit. "I'd always done a good job, I never had job problems," says Jones. "I was getting the brownie points, but they didn't seem to have all that much meaning. If I had stayed around longer and got into a place of power, I might have been able to change things. But I'm a romantic idealist. Staying inside to change the corporation was intolerable to me. A pragmatic realist should fit in very nicely in the corporation if his goals are compatible with the organization's."

In 1970 he met Browne. They discovered not only that they shared the same spiritual interest, but that they both enjoyed a good crap shoot. It was time for Browne to take a gamble. If he sold his business, he would have enough capital to live comfortably without working for four or five years. He was tired of paying off the I.R.S. and was ready to try country life. Browne told his new friend about this lovely piece of real estate he had been watching for eight years. "It could be our Sistine Chapel," he told Jones. "We could make it so that anybody who walked in there would leave higher." Jones didn't need that much persuading; he had already quit his job and was living off his grass dealings, his stock market investments, and his savings. "Sounds like a place where I could be a little more free," he said. Browne put in most of the money, Jones contributed a smaller share, and together with a third friend, they closed the deal. As a sweetener, Browne threw in the peacock.

Jones and Browne were systems men. Jones once designed telecommunications systems. He knew that for information to be used effectively it had to be organized carefully, communicated rapidly, and updated frequently. Browne's real estate corporation was the model of a business system—responsibilities carefully delegated, functions delineated, power distributed. Now they had to design a system to organize their "creative paradise." Anarchy was confusing. Absolute freedom was too dangerous. Permissiveness was all right, but lines had to be drawn. "The only efficient method," Browne decided, "was a benevolent dictatorship."

A Day in the Life: May 1973

9:00 A.M. Thirty people have moved in. A belt maker from Santa Cruz, a reformed prostitute from Portland, a college dropout from Madison, Wisconsin, a kitchenware salesman from San Francisco. Some people have brought their children with them. Browne and Jones meet to discuss whether there should be any standards for admitting new residents.

"I think anybody who'll take care of their house and help out with the work," Joe says.

"Right. Anybody," says Cliff. "We have to re-member it's not who they were, it's what they are that's important."

9:30. Marianne, Cliff's housemate, takes off for her bookkeeping job. Cliff tries to decide wheth-er to read a mystery novel or a spiritual tome. Settles on the mystery.

Joe is building his porch.

11:00. Jones has business in Seattle, but he doesn't have a car. He sold it when he gave up working. Then a friend comes by with a gift—a '65 Ford. "If you can make it run, it's yours." With a beatific smile, Jones later tells Browne: "See, if you just let things happen and don't wor-ry about it, they'll happen."

"Here, I wanted to show you this," Browne says to Jones, taking a card out of his wallet. The card reads:

Joseph Browne
Caretaker

"We're not landlords," Browne says. "We're not going to charge rent. We'll just have people barter their work for the rent. All we are is care-takers. The land will always be here. We're just taking care of it for a while. And then we'll leave."

2:00 P.M. Ellen Browne returns from shopping at the general store. "You know," she tells her husband, "they're a little suspicious about what's going on here. Maybe we should show them we don't have horns."

"I've been thinking about that," he says. "Why don't we talk to the other people and see if there's any interest in putting a Renaissance fair in August. We could raise some money for the mortgage payment, and it'll be a great way to introduce ourselves to the neighbors. Let's talk to the others about it tonight."

4:30. Jones stops by the hotel where three newcomers are rewiring the electrical system. "Is there any state or county code we have to follow?" one of them asks. "Or can we do it any way we want."

"Hell, it's our place," Jones says. "We can do it any way we want as long as it works."

Browne asks Jones if he wants to work on the new water tank. "Oh, let it wait for tomorrow," he says. "I feel like reading awhile."

6:00. Everybody's at the barbecue. Homegrown corn. Fresh tomatoes. Kegs of beer. Guitar music. "I feel we're a community," Ellen says. "It's a terrific feeling."

A young woman comes up to Jones. "I've decided to live in a tepee. Do you mind?"

"You don't have to ask me. If it's what you want, you do it. That's all that counts."

A Day in the Life: December 1977

The tepee is empty. The woman who lived there has long since moved away. A light snow falls, blanketing the mounds of garbage that no one has bothered to burn for a week. The snow whips in through the cracked windowpanes in the old hotel that no one has repaired for a year. The peacock spreads his fan and offering one last indignant scream squeezes under Browne's porch.

Spread out on Joe Browne's coffee table are a checkbook, bills, letters, and a telegram from

Dallas. Browne, as always, is crisp, hair neatly cut, mustache trimmed, plaid shirt freshly ironed. But he feels a little frayed. The mortgage is due again. Each time it gets harder, soaking up more and more of Browne's savings. Browne looks at the foreclosure notice. One hundred and twenty thousand dollars owed on 130 acres. "You want me to collect the rents this month?" Jones asks him. "The same as last month: the trailer $200, the houses $175?"

Browne nods. "It doesn't make much of a difference," he says. "You know, Cliff, the rents are a washout. They don't even cover the expenses. We've tried sixty different ways. The craft fairs, the festival, the fruit and vegetable market. Forget the mortgage, we can't make the twenty-thousand-dollar nut to keep the place up."

"I guess we could try something else," Jones says.

"I've been thinking about the offer from Dallas," Browne says. "I've been out for five years. I don't really want to go back to work. But the developer who wants to hire me is going to pick up a quarter of the mortgage, plus my commission. I can't think of any other way. Anyway, it's only for six months."

"Well, sure. It's a squeeze," says Jones.

11:00 A.M. It's a long walk. Every step feels like a mile. Two times this year I've had to make this trip, Jones thinks, and I hate it more each time. He is going to tell a young woman she has to leave the place. It seems that the woman has been stealing cars. For the last few nights, her friends have been racing their hot rods through the compound. "I know that's your number," Jones tells her. "Your number is your number, but we didn't put this together for your number. You have to leave because we just don't want you to bring heaviness down on this place."

Noon. Jones and Marianne are reviewing the last few years. (I'm in the corner of their living room.)

Marianne: "When Cliff dropped out, he set it up so he could live comfortably for two years. If he told me it was six years the day he quit, I might have gone . . . I don't know about that."

Jones: "There was anxiety for me but not economic anxiety. It was the change in my head. It's very simple for a hippie not to work—they never have. It's a lot easier to go from Madison Avenue to running an inn up in Maine. You just got to put another business together. I was putting a new consciousness together, developing an entirely new system. The anxiety is what do you do at the end of two years. What's the next move. What happens with the rest of your life?"

Marianne: "I learned you don't have to have a lot of money to exist. Before I thought you have to have certain things. If you didn't have a microwave oven, it was terrible. We geared down our material possessions."

Jones: "Look around at our material possessions. Remember what I had when I started."

Marianne: "We just geared it down to a smaller scale. [Laugh.] Instead of twenty-five hundred square feet, we're now in six hundred square feet."

Jones: What makes it a little hard is not that many people understand what you're doing. The farmers around here are almost totally incompatible with me. There are a coupla kids around that are pretty good people. But most of them think it's a kinda funny place. They're a little afraid of us. We bought a big piece of property. We look funny and never seem to work. They're not sure what they're gonna find. It's a small town they live in. I think they probably think I'm a little nuts. There's bound to be envy—there's a place in everyone that wants to be a little more free, if that isn't overridden by a desire to be secure. . . . That's why the world's so nuts. Instead of being freedom directed, we're security directed."

Marianne: "I understand. But I'm stuck in security. I feel less free than you do."

2:00. A conversation between Browne and his wife, Ellen.

"Everybody's got an ace in the hole," Browne says. "Cliff's got three aces in the hole. His kids are raised by his folks. They provide the clothes, this and that. Marianne has always been working. She buys all his food for him. He has her car. He has an investment in this place and he pays no rent and no electric bill. He's been able to get his nut down to where unemployment or welfare can cover his life-style. His life-style is not suffering at all. But he'd made certain sacrifices that I don't want to do. He went on unemployment, welfare. There are subtle prices you pay for that. An invasion of your privacy. Privacy is the most important thing for us. I don't want to pay that price. I don't want to live in a tepee."

Ellen laughs uneasily. "Cliff is clever. He'll always come up with something. If Marianne splits, he'll find another lady."

5:00. Browne is sanding a table on his enclosed porch. Jones is drinking a can of beer. I ask them why they put up the high iron gate at the entrance way to the grounds. Gates are a barrier; freedom and locks seem contradictory.

"When we moved in, the county told us these

houses were very old. They said, 'You've got to tear down all the wiring and everything else and you have to do it our way,'" Cliff says. "We tried to do it their way and it didn't work. Then we started doing it our way."

"All the building here is absolutely illegal," Browne says. "If we leave the gate open, the county can come in at will and see anything they want. If we leave the gate locked, they have to get permission and it would take them two years through the courts and they wouldn't be successful. The county looks for something to do. We don't want inspectors to come and see what's happening. We don't need that.

"Seclusion has become very important to me," says Browne.

It is almost midnight and I'm about to go to sleep. Outside there is total silence, not a sound disturbs the crystalline purity of the night. Then: the screech of burning rubber, the roar of motorcyle engines. Pow. Crack. "Shit, who's bombing us?" I yell.

"Ah, it's the fuckin' local kids," Jones says. "They're doin' their little firecracker number. Showing off for their girl friends that they can scare the weirdos."

The next morning a new sign has been posted on the gate, alongside the Go Slower sign. It says: Anyone Who Enters Here *Must* Lock the Gate Behind Them.

June 1978

Moving time. Browne has shuttled between Dallas and Salem for the last six months, putting together a condominium deal. There is a new

Mercedes parked outside his house, compliments of the developers. Joe and Ellen and their children are moving to Big Sur. The property will be bought by a group of Iranian investors. The arrangement provides that Jones and Marianne can continue to stay in their house, or they can leave and recover their original investments.

"It's been a seasonal life here," Joe Browne is saying. "There's never been any hurry. There've always been projects: the barn, putting the kitchen on the back of the house, the gardening. I came here because it offered a total system different from the work I'd done. I was here for the life-style, the farming, to raise the children, the weather. Now, I'm leaving. I can't believe I'm leaving.

"The first few years it was very vital. There were always a lot of kids for my kids to play with. Then somebody would leave—usually people stayed for a year—and somebody'd come, and they didn't seem to have that interest in the place. Only recently has there been a problem occupying my time. Since I got back in the business world, I've been thinking about something else. The last six months have given me a perspective. I see what place business has in my life and it doesn't mean avoid it at all cost. For a while I said I'd never go back to the city and fight those people. Now I'll never say never.

"I just told the guy I was working for I'll probably drop out again in another three, four months. Why am I not continuing forever? Because it's a rat race, that's why. It's the thing about making money, to have to make money, to have to pay taxes, to have to buy something else. The guy in Dallas bought me the Mercedes—sixteen thousand dollars. If I want that car, I have to continue doing that number. I don't want the car that bad. I know what it's like to not put miles on a car. I've found that out in the last five years. I like that. I don't want to lock into that making money thing again.

"This was a five-year phase, and now we're moving on. When we came out here we needed a life-support system because we weren't working. Now I'm working and what we need is more seclusion."

"Don't forget to tell him," Ellen shouted from the kitchen. "Don't forget to tell him we're taking the tepee with us."

Jones was not following Browne into the work world. Not for a while anyway. He was curious to see what an Iranian landlord was like. When I stopped at his house to say good-bye, he was shoveling a potful of pork and beans onto a plate. He had laid odds I'd never want to leave. Now, incredulously, he said, "You're not going to stay?"

"I don't think I can," I said.

"Then that's right for you."

"What's right for *you*?" I pushed him.

"What I learned here was I could manage the bottom line. I could keep body and soul together. If I tried to do that by myself maybe I wouldn't have. Maybe I needed other people to help me—Marianne, at least, Joe. I am scared, you know. There are times I think, will I be eating dog food at fifty-five? Those thoughts occur. The fear of the unknown is a very scary thing. Yeah, but when I go into an elevator in a downtown building, it really makes me cringe. I go oooooh. I know I can't do that. Just say when you write the book, the upstate returns on Cliff Jones aren't in yet."

I was reaching for the door when Jones sprayed the room with beans. "Remember," he bellowed.

"Remember what?"

"Remember it's guys like you who work who let guys like me not work. You finance me. If enough of you lived like me, it'd make my life a lot more difficult.

Doe's Eating Place in Greenville, Mississippi, is quartered in a tumbledown old house on a back street in the black part of town. Any of the Formica tables in the two small dining rooms provide an excellent view of the smoky kitchen where black women prepare and serve the finest steaks and ribs in America. Doe's fans include the presidents of the United States and France and many lesser pols. I was a little surprised when Betty Tallgood suggested that we meet there. The last time I had seen Betty she was sitting on the porch of her farmhouse in the delta, telling me that now that she had sold out her farm to the pickle company all she was good for was rocking in her rocking chair. Now the fifty-year-old woman in a flowered hat and a print dress left a crowd of whites who had been waiting for an hour gaping with envy as she was led to a table. "Guess they know me at Doe's," she said. "I come here a lot when I got business with the white folk. They think it's down home."

"What happened," I asked.

"I got tireda rockin'," she said.

"Now, really."

"Oh, I always had a head for figures."

"Come on, Betty."

"I jes' decided. I wasn't takin' my body over to Chicago. My son didn't need any more bossin', and I didn't need all the noise they got up there. I didn't need any more sittin' and knittin', neither. Case you didn't notice, I got 'nuf back in the sittin' area right now. I wouldn't want you go tellin' everybody in Sharkey, but I was never much for the church business. All the eulogizin' all the time. I worked with the ministers back when we were straight'n'n' out the voting rights business, but that was then. That was somethin'. Well, now, I thought, Betty Tallgood's not much for the choir and she's not much for the gospel, but she's good for somethin' isn't she. But I didn't know *what*, 'til Mr. Williams came along and said, 'Betty, you know anybody'n keep a ledger?' "

Asking Betty Tallgood to keep the books is like asking Fats Waller to back up Lawrence Welk. "Mr. Williams said come on in every second Tuesday and take a look at the books. First look I had, I said, 'Mr. Williams, you keep on like this there ain't be nothin' to put in the books, nothin' but owin's.' "

The Sharkey-Twilight Farmers' Cooperative, a legacy of the civil rights movement in the Mississippi delta, was sinking fast. Members were selling their okra and cotton and cucumbers on the sly, leaving the leftovers to be marketed by the co-op. A dozen different black co-ops in the delta were competing with each other for the sliver of the market that remained when the white farmers finished selling their produce. Agricultural products, particularly fertilizer, cost the blacks twice as much as what the white farmers paid because statewide white manufacturers refused to give credit to the black growers.

"The first meetin' was held in Mr. Williams's barn. Six members and me. Mr. Williams said, 'I want you to meet our new volunteer, Betty Tallgood, who's a gonna give us a report on our books.'

"I said. 'This is a very short report, 'cause there's nothin' in those books. Who you kiddin'? You foolin' yourself if you think this is any kind of organization. I know you all my life. You helped raise my sons and I helped raise your sons. Y'all can farm, but you sure can't co-op. You been stealin' out in the night with your trucks sellin' what you can and then comin' here and easin' your conscience with a twenty-dollar membership. I seen more cooperation in the Klan.'

"Mr. Williams, he didn't say nothin' when I finished, 'cept, 'Now do we have any new business.' I think he was thinkin', I got me some volunteer."

A slab of meat arrived that would have made a vegetarian salivate. "I was doin' it as much for me as for them," Betty Tallgood said, ignoring the food. "I wasn't about to farm, an' I wasn't about to mother, an' I wasn't going' to work for nobody 'cause I never did an' I wasn't goin' to start then, but I needed somethin'. So I had to do somethin' now 'cause I had no 'scuses."

What she did was persuade the black farmers—and a few more open-minded whites—that they could make more money working together than working separately. That is supposed to be the first principle of cooperativism, except no one had bothered to observe it before in Tallahatchie County.

She got them to sell their crops together. She got them to pool their farm machinery and trucks. She organized a league of all the co-ops in the delta. She persuaded them to hold back selling until the price went up. Gently she reminded the less enthusiastic members they could always go it alone if they didn't want to cooperate. ("Gentle?" Mr. Williams told me later. "Mrs. Tallgood is one of the finest women I ever met, but I don't think you'd say she was gentle.") She recruited a neighbor's son who had recently graduated from an ag college and sent him north to seek funds and technical help from the foundations. "We got some money but the advice didn't go too far. We got some stubborn heads down here. I didn't want to go tryin' to change everything right away."

How did the white buyers react to this newfound unity? "They didn't like it one bit," she said, finishing off the fries. "They couldn't cheat us no more, so they didn't like it. But they couldn't do nothin' 'cause we always had a man down there watchin' the sortin' machine. No more of that Grade A for Mr. White Man and Grade B for Mr. Black Man. We all gettin' the same grade for the same quality, at least most times.

"Now I wouldn't want you to go 'way thinkin' I'm sittin' here like a picture star or somethin'," she said. "We done all right, but one bad season we'd be back like before. When I go 'round to the members and show 'em the ledger book an' they see that black ink, they say, 'We makin' it, we 'bout makin' it now, Miss Betty.' But a couple of months I go 'round and show 'em some red, they be thinkin', I'm better off on my own. In 1964 it was justice we was talkin', it was rights we was talkin'. Now we talkin' dollars. Harder now. Back then they didn't expect the rights, they been so long jest stayin' alive. When they got them, well, it was a miracle. Praise the Lord. Money, they come to expect it. I tell 'em we can slide right back down, an' they shake their heads like they know what you're sayin', but one year the price is off, they'll be on their own. Their heads think that way. You have to keep after 'em. Keep raisin' the spirit."

And how long would she have to keep at them? "Oh, I'm jes' startin', jes' learnin'. Someday we'll have the whole South, the county's only the beginnin'. An' the whites, too, they plowin' the same dirt. Oh, it's a long road. We jes' makin' it now."

At the end of the evening, I asked her about her son. The last time we talked at her home, it was right after she had sold her farm. She had said that she missed him terribly and that she wished he'd visit her more often. "I still miss him," Mrs. Tallgood said. "I wish he could see what we's stirrin' up here. He's a good boy, even if he lives in the city. He worries 'bout me and I get letters from him all the time, packages, you should see the packages. I tell you a secret. I'm such a po' mother, I feel jes' awful sometimes"—her eyes flashed—" 'cause I hardly have time to answer."

In their thirties, forties, and fifties, Jones and Browne and Betty Tallgood found themselves released from their past debts. They no longer felt the compelling need to prove themselves to their parents and families. Now what? How do I fill the vacuum? What do I really want? "Unless you know the answer to that question," says David Solomon, "you're dead."

Some years before he stopped working, Solomon suspected that he could capture life more fully through a range finder than he could through a bar graph. The economist's tools, the elements of his profession, seemed to screen out emotion. The camera, on the other hand, was a subtle instrument. It was capable of nuance and suggestion, but with a sensitive eye behind the lens it was also capable of embrace, of sensuality, of intimacy. Above all, what David desired beyond work was the intimate connection. His goal was to transcend the moral insulation of professionalism.

"On my last job, when I was doing statistical research for that unemployment project, I started taking pictures. I had them in boxes, in my desk drawers. When I stopped working, I thought, that's unique to me, and if I keep at it, I can also find what's unique to other people. Taking pictures I was meeting my own requirements and nobody else's. I had to understand what I was looking at, what I recorded, what I did with that record. As I began responding just to my own requirements, I found I could hear myself much better; I knew what I wanted out of my life. I never took a picture with the intention of selling it. I think that would change the image. I'd be thinking of what other people wanted."

His photographs are wonderful. They are artful in their seeming artlessness. The old man at the bridge. The girl clasping her books, head bowed in thought, amid the swirl of Harvard Square. The short-order cook chewing a toothpick as he takes his leisure in the doorway of a beanery. David would say that there is a connection between the freedom of not working and the quality of his photographs. He has no deadlines. Weeks and months pass between pictures. He will spend days thinking about what he wants to shoot. He has no compulsion to put together a portfolio, to sell his photographs, or even to show them. (Others, however, insist that his new work come out into the open. It has appeared at a Cambridge gallery, and a few friends have insisted on buying some of his pictures.) "I refuse to learn that end of the tube, the marketing," he says. "When I think about that I get fucked up about what I want to do for myself."

The goal is his defense against the austerities of not working; when he is tempted by memories of good brandy, he considers what he would have to give up to buy it and finds it's too high a price. He did work that one time, delivering phone books. "If I didn't have a goal, I don't know if I could have done it," David says. "I might have felt ashamed. But I discovered that I didn't have to be ashamed; I wasn't humiliated doing that because I had something else to go for."

David is as vulnerable to financial anxiety as any man of modest means in his early forties who has worked most of his life. To pursue his objective, he has sold some possessions that he would have liked to retain. "I panicked in an economic crisis, it scared me. But my feeling is that if I hadn't had something to sell, I would have figured out some other way because I had the goal. The goal, you understand, is not photography. It's living my life in ways that allow me to be myself.

"An illustration of how that's changed me is in my relationships with women. When I was working, there was something missing behind the things I would say. I'd talk about events in my life but not so much the meaning of the events. I'd talk about the events that I thought defined who I was. Milestones and all that. And women would come back with the question: 'Who are you?' I'd say, 'Jesus, I thought I covered that.' Everytime I heard that question it was such a wallop.

"I used to think I'd better hang on to my feelings because I don't know how she's going to respond to them. There was a reason I felt that way. I remember as a child I would 'play' with my father. I felt that he was very consciously imitating real playing. He could not remember any time in his own past when he really played to have a good time. It would have been a lot nicer if he could have just thrown the ball instead of making it so orchestrated. I didn't like it—as a kid I was feeling that distance. I always felt there was a huge difference between what he could show from his experience and what I felt I needed—which was the immediacy and the emotional response to what was going on. Now I feel that what I do speaks to what I am. My feelings are not something I have to preserve because if I expressed them I wouldn't have them anymore."

David Solomon seemed to have come through the not working experience in fine shape. When I first met him he had been out of the work world for two years. When I spoke to him a year later, his confidence had grown. It was appropriate, I thought, to ask him, What would you tell somebody who was considering leaving work? "I'd tell them, sure you're giving up something, but what for? If you change direction, what are you going for, what do you want to happen? It's necessary, of course, to identify what are tolerable risks. How would you raise money in a crisis? But that's really secondary. You have to have a reason for stopping work beyond not wanting to work. If you have no purpose, you're just as vulnerable as when you're working."

Clear-eyed seekers came closest to finding inner ease outside of work. They were the least vulnerable to the ambiguities of unformed time; they were not boxed in by anger; they were not driven to change, to experiment, to innovate. And they were the most determined to remain out of work. It takes strength to unburden oneself of the past, to define one's purpose, and to pursue it in an unfamiliar environment.

Some people stop short of their goals. They are never quite certain of their purposes and never completely disengage themselves from their work roles.

Lucille Roberts resembles other seekers in that her primary motivation for working was to fulfill her responsibilities to her family. Her work and the income she brought in sustained them, particularly when her husband was out of work. When he died, she became the sole support of her four kids. She was equal to the test.

A month after she stopped working in May 1976 her son graduated from high school and one of her daughters graduated from college. Her two other daughters were self-sufficient. "Suddenly no more dependents for this mama," she wrote later, "and what beautiful timing it is, I must say." And she added pensively, "Keep thinking of my sister's remark about my writing: 'A page a day for a year and there's your book.' This present span of time really is my golden opportunity, but the only writing I'm doing is this journal of my impressions and adjustments."

Throughout her journal and in my conversations with her, I had the sense that writing was not a goal but a nag, a scold. Something she ought to be doing rather than something she wanted to do. After editing a friend's paper for a college assignment, she reflects, "Whatever happened to your favorite old dream? Remember—you, all nicely put together in a great outfit, peddling your poems to various far-out presses."

Six months after she stopped, Lucille wrote, "I really think that the only thing I want to do is write, and I suppose I'm bugged by the old bohemian picture of starving in a garret, especially when my unemployment insurance runs out. Somehow, just can't seem to square myself with the fact that I'm not working.... Why do I even bother running around looking for half-ass jobs when I can write full time in the comfort of my own house? I keep thinking about all the artists who up to the time of the Industrial Revolution and its dehumanization rarely doubted their abilities because they knew they were of value as productive men. Maybe, some-

time, another Renaissance will occur. Then products of aesthetic worth will be placed in value above
the present computerized nonsense of materialistic
possessions and paychecks."

The contrast between Lucille and David Solomon
or Betty Tallgood is instructive. Recognition is important for her, less so for them. If Solomon's photographs are appreciated, fine; if Betty improves the
economic position of farmers in the delta, fine. But
their nonworking time is precious because it frees
them to develop their personal ease. They knew
they had to find it by themselves. They didn't depend on the judgment of a sitting jury; what was a
job, after all, if not the suppression of uniqueness to
win the affirmation of the paymasters. Whose wine
do I drink? Whose song do I sing? Not mine but the
foreman's. Not working was a chance to sing their
own song.

It was not a goal or purpose that preoccupied Lucille, but what Cliff Jones once called "future anxiety." Will she be loved? Will she be appreciated?
Will she have enough money to survive? (While Lucille was by no means rich, she had as much money
as most of the other people I met.)

A month before I visited her and almost a year
after she stopped working, she wrote me, "Strange-
ly enough, just as I had joined the cadre of people
you know so well, who have decided they really
don't want to work anymore, many exciting possibilities of jobs in new fields that interest me began
to open up."

Much of her journal is taken up with her anxiety
about finances and with her anger at past employers. But there is hardly a mention of what she wants

to do with her not-working time, what lies beyond the Monterey beaches, the swimming club, the growth groups, and the weekly meetings of Parents Without Partners. After I spent four days with this endearing woman, she sent me a copy of her journal. The last page was dated July 25, 1977:

> I certainly am not complaining—I got the most of my and my employers' money out of it, and I feel good about the longest *vacation* from work that I have ever had in my lifetime. . . . The phone was ringing as I unlocked the door, and I rushed to answer it. I couldn't believe my ears! The county was calling to offer me a job! So I will go back to work August 1st. I made myself a cup of coffee, lit a cigarette, and sat down to think about my fantastic luck.

In March 1978 I received her last letter:

> I loved my job with the county and was sorry to have it end in December. . . . Once again I was on unemployment, and this time I had to wait a full month before the governor of this state signed a bill which entitled me to benefits. I only collected a week's worth, because out of necessity I took the first job offered which was as a medical transcriber. How broke can you get? I am still working at this job which frankly is the shits, but it does pay much of my bills, and since I am now living alone without renters, I can't complain too much. . . . Meantime, I remember the weekend you were here as a lovely little island in time.

Her time away from work was a "vacation," an "island in time." I hope someday she will return to that island and find there her true ease.

THE ADVENTURER

Now I understand why Charles Braithwaite refused to tell me his reasons for not working. He was right. At that time I wouldn't have understood. How do you explain to your friend that you're looking for something you've lost when you're not certain what you've lost? How do you describe what you're looking for when the objective is a blur? Anyone who knew Charles well in the last few years before he stopped working was able to recognize the symptoms of his malaise. Those mornings when you're not sure you have the courage to get through the day. Those afternoons at work when habit dictates action; when you ask, How many times have I done this before? Those nights in bed when the body next to you is every body and you grope for the name and the words are lines from a tired script. The symptoms of melancholia. Tired. Bored. Lost. Frightened.

In public his recitatives about the daily happenings in the newsroom got longer and longer, as if embellishment could substitute for the missing theme and climax. With women he went through the motions of engagement. After a while the thrust and parry turned nasty. What I once thought was contempt, but now knew was self-contempt, coarsened the silky gestures, the courtly compliments, the rituals of affection. "I was angry," he said after one long boozy night. "I don't know what I was angry about, but I was angry."

On my travels in 1976 and 1977 I met a number of men and women who were looking for a hard place. They took their ease in struggle. At work they had been hard-driving high rollers. They had invited risk, courted danger. But the edge was gone, work no longer challenged them. Outside of work, they looked for adventure. The greatest adventure was taking control over their own lives. Many of them had long felt that they were losing dominion—not only in work, but in the private sphere as well. Against the grain of the culture, they set out to exercise autonomy over their personal worlds.

Paradoxically, it was their achievements in the business world that persuaded them they could claim possession of their private lives. Their characters had been tested in a variety of high-pressure situations. A supervisor of nurses in the intensive care ward of a Philadelphia hospital. An undercover narcotics investigator in the New York City Police Department. A Chicago politician who defied the Daley organization for fifteen years and kept getting elected. An Oklahoma oil company lawyer who quit when he discovered that the company had been derelict in the death of a wildcatter whose head was blown off in a well explosion. If there was one philosophical position that characterized them all, it was that of an organizer for the farm workers in Texas. For fifteen years he had played hide and seek with the Texas rangers. Three times he lost and three times they had to fish the buckshot out of his body. He admitted that he had provoked the attacks to dramatize the repressiveness of the farm owners and the police, but that wasn't the only reason. "I enjoyed the battle," he said. "I'm not one of those guys who organize from the office. I need the danger. That's when I'm most alive."

Out of work they were still on the firing line, only the challenge was different. To make their own rules. To fall back on their own resources. To test their courage, ingenuity, resilience. To do it on their own.

And in their own way. Climb Kilimanjaro. Sail off in a forty-foot boat for parts unknown. Build the perfect harpsichord. Read every major work written in English since 1600.

The technician is intrigued by newness, by change for change's sake. The protester strikes back at the injustice he found in work. The seeker prospects for an inclusive system to house all the realities and fables of modern life. The adventurer has a different interest. He wants to establish his significance against the indifference of the contemporary culture. By acting he wants to prove he exists. Society goes its way, the adventurer his.

To reestablish his legitimacy, the adventurer follows certain rules:

- He must act alone. He will not be guided by external systems or psychological disciplines, not by gurus or masters, not by experts or friends.
- It can't be easy for him. It's not a true test if you stack the odds in your favor. If you're

building a harpsichord, you don't order any outside parts; you construct them all yourself. If you're sailing off into the wide blue, you don't hire a crew. You have to sail the boat yourself or with friends.

- No set agenda. What happens happens. The adventure is not fitted to a purpose. The adventurer may discover many things in the course of his experience. He doesn't want to limit his time, circumscribe his space, define his relationships, or establish ground rules. He wants the experience to take its own shape. The adventure is in accepting surprise and accident. Planning robs adventure of its mystery; it's cheating.
- The experience is all that matters. The adventurer is a new frontiersman without a frontier to cross—except for the limits of his endurance. At the end there may be death or catatonia or the discovery of unknown emotional resources, but he cannot know that at the start. All he knows is that for something to happen, for his life to take a new turn, he has to give himself over to the experience.

When Charles Braithwaite left his television job that night in the spring of 1976, he was disappointed. The journalist's life had not fulfilled its promise. He wasn't bitter, his parting had not been acrimonious; if he looked at it honestly, the station had been more than generous. Somebody, he thought, just should have said something sooner; they should have told me that this wasn't a marriage, me and the organization. He knew this was probably a rationalization, but he couldn't help feeling that he had been politely deceived. He had imagined that a black man with ability and an independent turn of mind could fit into the organizational structure. He should have known better: Organizations act with their minds not their hearts; they prize obedience over independence; they don't bend their rules for a white guy and certainly not for a black guy who thinks independently. But a reporter would rather admit illiteracy than confess innocence. He'd rather believe that he had been the victim of an ornate swindle, than admit he was naive.

"Okay," Charles says, "I'm out of step. Maybe they were wrong, maybe I was wrong. That's over with. Now where do I fit in?" In those first months when he was cutting down, when he was pitting the hedonistic side of his character against the puritan side, he would meet strangers on his walks, in the library, in the park. The protectiveness, wariness he always felt when he was working gave way to a more open, receiving temperament. There were no appointments to rush off to, and he no longer had an official (working) identity to maintain. If people had time for him, he had time for them. From those chance encounters, more stable, continuing relationships evolved. On Sundays, during the summer, he would picnic in the park with people he had met during the week. To these events, each bringing their own contribution, would come "bag" ladies who lived on the street, musicians who had no set hours, students, retired men and women, recently arrived immigrants who had not yet learned that in New York you don't talk to strangers. "Those Sundays would be mini-festivals for me," he said. "It was a party where nobody knew each other, but everybody had this one thing, they were unencumbered."

With the gains, there were losses. Charles had to give up certain fantasies. When he was working, he took vacation trips to the Middle East and later to the West Indies. In the first few months after stopping work, he talked incessantly about going to live in the West Indies. Ten minutes into the conversation: "We'll get our bikini suits and do the beach. . . . I have this friend and she's got a swimming pool in her living room. . . . Oh, Bernie, the West Indian women'll go crazy when they see you." He'd double over with laughter. "Rum and sun and those crazy women. We'll go tomorrow morning."

After that period passed, he'd look back on the dream of the West Indies and say, "That was just a kind of dream. I could have gone but there was no plan. I was talking about fifteen different things; the West Indies was the nicest thing. I couldn't make a decision." I think he made a decision: He'd stay and fight. Resettlement in the West Indies was a plan that would prematurely shape the adventure. In one sense he would fulfill the fantasy: He'd transplant himself to the West Indies without leaving New York.

Writing was another option he rejected. Writing for himself or for publication was too closely associated with work. It required intensity, effort, and concentration. Writing would challenge his mind and his intellect, it would test his talent, but his adventure was elsewhere—in the challenge to his character. "I think about writing," he says. "I even get to the point where I construct the plots of novels, the outlines, but I throw them away. It may be I'm afraid to write unless somebody is telling me to. But I also think I do my writing through observing. When I don't work, I see things I wouldn't see otherwise.

"When I'm going somewhere, I see people on their way to work. The awkward makeup, the nervousness. I don't feel contempt for them, just a kind of compassion, and relief that I'm not doing what they are. I started out as a person who associated people at work with assembly lines, and I never had a chance to experience that. But you can get on the subways in New York and see that same thing. Apart from the real struggle of getting to and from work, there's a real tension. One day I was on the train and a black guy was carrying an awkward package, something he was delivering for a florist, and the way he was holding it, he obviously cared about it. A guy standing next to him was angry at him for crowding him. I wanted to step in, defend the man with the flowers. I'm very humble in the midst of that enormous effort to survive. It surrounds me, especially in New York, which is such a passionate place and which is so passionate about work. I feel like an island, like a reporter observing it. The writing is in my mind, in my eyes."

I said earlier that Charles had shown an uncharacteristic contempt for people I thought undeserving of contempt. I believed then he was angrier at himself than the people he was skewering. A year or so after he stopped working, his gentleness returned.

My mother took ill and was hospitalized for a few weeks. Charles visited her two or three times a week. He brought gifts of West Indian home cooking. He sat at the side of her bed, holding her hand, listening to her complaints, forcing her to laugh with promises that they would run away together— to the West Indies, of course. "Oh, Ann," he'd say, "you'll be the queen of the island. Once the men there see you, you'll never go home. They won't let you." My mother, who was sixty-five then and more than slightly overweight, forgot for the moment that she was sick. When he'd leave, she'd say, "He's crazy, he's just wacko. I wish more people were like him."

Her second night home from the hospital he showed up at her apartment with a group of friends. "If you're going to the West Indies, you're going to have to learn to dance," he said, limboing the length of the living room. Embracing her, he said, "You've got the steps, all you need is the motion." She held him at arm's length and said, "Why don't you let an old lady enjoy her misery?"

Suddenly (it seemed sudden to me, but was probably more gradual for Charles) he was capable of intimacy. He gave and he received. He found a woman who had two children. It was an attachment that grew slowly, after a few false starts, and it was a lovely thing to watch. She suffered from a serious sight impairment that for a while threatened her teaching career. Charles guided her through that. Charles helped her raise the two teenage children with patience and gentleness. Shrugging, he accepted all of their reprimands for not working. Mother and children were very sober about work, very earnest about achievement. Charles was not wounded by their reproaches because he knew they arose out of concern and love. In the end, mother and children accepted Charles as he was, an explorer unearthing a long-buried humanity.

"Not working gives me an opportunity to be generous," Charles said once. "I feel I have this generosity all the time, working or not. When I'm not working, it's more evident. It's not a justification for not working, not a penance. It's what I'd like to do all the time if I could. We should all work four hours a day, so we'd have more time to be generous with each other. When I'm being generous, I'm really being generous with myself. I'm giving myself a gift.

"When I was working I could be very bitter. I wasn't loving myself. I was saving all my time for Saturday, Saturday night. I was thinking about Saturday all the time. I have the time now, the freedom to be generous. I think that's what people envy, not that they're dissatisfied, as I was at my last job, but everybody wants to make that gesture or thinks about that gesture. But because they're working, they have to squeeze it in, they have to mesh it with their labor, they're never really free because they're always so close to poverty, they were raised in the South Bronx or Brooklyn, or they see the man down the block who's poor, and they have to work harder so they don't slip back."

As he changed, I changed. I stopped trying to persuade him to go back to work. I stopped trying to set up job appointments for him, stopped suggesting people he should call. My effort to talk him back to work had made him edgy—although he said he understood why I was doing it: "My good friends will say, 'Charles, I hope you get back to work again,' because they know the details of my life—that I'm not helping my kids and they know that bothers me. Or they may think a lot of me in terms of what I've done at work. People who care will know the details, and they'll know I haven't forgotten the details."

Charles was unbinding himself from work, unbinding time, releasing suppressed kindness and generosity, enjoying himself and others. Why should I insist that he fulfill my image of him? Was I some kind of father who demands that his son live up to his expectations?

He planted himself in a culture partly of his making. It was West Indian, it was family, it was aspiring, and it was accepting. Charles liked to say, "It's quietly un-American." Although there were certain shared understandings, the restraints were essentially self-imposed and the punishment self-inflicted. You didn't get fired for not showing up when the family expected you to (you might be reprimanded), but you had to confront your own guilt for upsetting and frightening people who worried about you.

He brought to that culture his gaiety and his intelligence and his kindness, and it rewarded him with tolerance, humor, and affirmation. His contributions were not financial and neither was the support it extended to him; that was one reason he called it un-American. And so he received the fruit of his adventure. He had found a culture where he existed, a culture that was not absurd or irrelevant, a culture that evolved out of the experience, out of the adventure.

Such triumphs should be celebrated. One June morning I went to the junior high school graduation ceremony where the daughter of the West Indian woman was to deliver the valedictory address. Charles wore his working outfit: a sports jacket and slacks, a white shirt, and a canary yellow tie. He bustled about snapping pictures of the family and then sat back to watch the longest graduation ceremony in American history. I don't remember the exact words the girl used in her speech, but I'll never forget the substance. All that morning, she said, various graduates had received awards. Some for academic excellence, some for "good citizenship," some for athletic prowess. But, she asked, why weren't the students who had simply tried hard rewarded for their effort? Why wasn't one student honored for his struggle to overcome kidney disease? Why wasn't one student honored for working after school to help support his family? Why wasn't one student honored for just being a good friend? Who set the standards for achievement? Who determined what was outstanding and what was mediocre? The school authorities were sufficiently impressed with her speech (and thundering oratory) to invite her to repeat it at a meeting of the district school board where, I understand, it was received with subdued applause.

That early summer night we celebrated on the balcony of a Manhattan apartment house. We ate friend chicken and plantains, and we drank rum and fruit juice. The girl bore her celebrity lightly, the mother carried her pride gracefully. Braithwaite washed the dishes, poured the drinks, and proposed the toasts.

I sat next to the graduate. "Did you write the speech all by yourself?" I asked her.

"Most of it," she said. "My English teacher helped out."

"Didn't Charles help?" I asked.

"With the grammar," she said. "Only the grammar."

Charles stuck his head out onto the balcony. "Well, that's what an editor does. He helps the writer."

"An editor who doesn't work," she humphed.

"An editor who doesn't work," Charles agreed. And laughed.

The phone rang. "I want to go back to work," Charles said.

No money. Tired of standing in line for food stamps. Tired of the temp jobs, answering phones, playing security guard. "I still feel the affection," he said. "I care for people in my way. I still think of the fine moments in the afternoon and the spring in New York. But I don't want to be a burden. I don't want to survive on charm because the loveliness will wear out and I'll become a prostitute. My view of myself loses logic when I'm not working. I feel to some extent worthless. I'm edging back toward news, toward the sex and danger of that."

Charles reported to me weekly. He was sending out letters, making phone calls, and preparing audition tapes for television stations. Uneasily, because I had learned long before not to push work on him, I made a few suggestions and he listened, took down the names and phone numbers. One night he was excited that a station had answered his letter and hinted a job might be available. The next day his reaction was downbeat. "Oh, that one. I don't really think I want to work for them."

Reentry was difficult. He had spent three years in voluntary obscurity; how was he going to account for the period between 1975 and 1978? "Who knows I'm alive?" he said. "How do I explain what I've been doing?"

I told him that I thought a tougher problem was his own equivocation about returning to work. "Not equivocation. Chaos is what it is," Charles corrected me. He had left work with his faith in journalism shaken, his ardor dampened. Journalism is an occupation that demands a suspension of disbelief. It has to be played with an exaggerated enthusiasm. If you ask about its purpose, if you question its ethics, if you wonder whether it will fulfill your aspirations or allow you to express your ideas, you're done for. Performance relies on instinct and reflex; you can no more question the premise of an assignment or a story than a lineman can stop to question his purpose before he tackles a runner. After three years of introspection and reflection—"When I'm not working I spend a lot of time dreaming"—could he again operate on instinct? Would "sex and danger" blast away that dangerous habit he had developed of thinking about what he was doing with his time and why?

Work had some benefits. It would give him a weekly paycheck. It would provide him with a fixed position with some power and some responsibility. It would tell him where to go in the morning, when to have lunch, what to wear, and how to modulate his voice.

Work also had some drawbacks. Gone would be the chance encounters in the street world. Gone would be the challenge of the unexpected, the gamble of living by your wits, existing on two dollars a day. The real risk, though, involved his character. Would he become like the people he had watched on the subway? Would the tension of work sap his generosity, drive him back to the bottle, fill him with the anger and the self-contempt of three years ago? And what of the woman he had cared for since he left work and the children he had helped raise? "Nothing would change," he said; his feelings toward them would stay the same. But would they? He knew that in the past he had acted differently toward friends and lovers when he worked than he did now. He couldn't be sure, not really sure, that the old dance wouldn't start again once he heard the music.

The debits and credits wouldn't balance. Nothing balanced. Not sure whether to start again or to stay where he was, he did what so many others who were considering reentry did. He decided he would take nothing less than the perfect job: the job with the right pay, the right amount of freedom, the right appreciation for his ability. And that, he understood, meant no return. "I'm looking for the perfect job," he admitted, "and I know I'm not going to get it."

As of this writing, Charles had not gone back to work. I don't know whether he will ever resume his career as a journalist. If he does return, I don't know how long he'll stay. But I don't cry for the loss of his humanity. I rejoice in the rediscovery of his humanity.

The payoff from not working is a fresh look at yourself. When Charles began his adventure, he entered into a lasting conspiracy against entropy. He experienced the exhilaration of keeping mind, body, and spirit intact outside the cultural mainstream and the business world, he questioned the pernicious givens of the past, and he called forth, amidst scarcity, fresh reserves of kindness, generosity, and empathy. What a thrill to discover anew these qualities just at the moment when he thought he would be stuck in cement for the rest of his life. He is more at ease within himself and with those around him than at any time I have ever known him.

Q. AND A.

How long did they stay out?

On the average, the hundred people I talked to stopped working for a minimum of two years.* By the time I had finished the book, slightly more than 60 percent (sixty-two people) had returned to work. Of those who returned, ten had been out of work less than eighteen months; twenty-two had been out for more than three years; and thirty had been out for more than four years.

The 40 percent who did not go back averaged, in

---

*I lost contact with two people.

1978, five consecutive years without working. Twenty-two people had been out for more than eight years, seven people for six years, and nine people for less than three years.

Who stayed out longest?

A majority of those who hadn't returned were between the ages of thirty-six and fifty-one. People in this age group also tended to stay out longer than people in their twenties and early thirties.

Those who stopped with the purpose of pursuing a particular goal (seekers) and those who regarded not working as an unplanned, free-form experience (adventurers) stayed out longer than those who viewed not working as another link in a chain of experimental life changes (the technicians) and those who had quit as an act of protest.

When I began my research, I had expected that the wealthier a person was the longer he would stay out. I found the reverse to be true. People with individual or family income of less than $20,000 averaged more than three years out of work. Those whose income exceeded $20,000 averaged between two and three years. To some extent this is attributable to the support provided by unemployment insurance and other social insurance programs. The shadow economy, offering a variety of temporary jobs with unreported income, is another leveler. A third factor is the scarcity of good jobs for nonprofessionals.

Husbands stayed out of work longer than wives. Single women stayed out longer than single men. Married people without children stayed out roughly as long as those who had children. (I would have expected people with children to return sooner. That they didn't suggests a shift in attitude toward investing in children. Many of the people I spoke to believed that their children would not suffer if they reduced family expenses. In fact, they argued that their children would benefit from a more modest life-style.)

How would they feel if they had to go back to work? How had their attitudes toward work changed as a result of not working?

Their answers are not easily quantifiable. The most common response was: "I'd do it for the money, but it wouldn't be like starting a career. I'd work to get past a rough spot or for a change of pace. I'd stay for a while if it was interesting, but I'm not going to get married again to a job or a career."

Lucille Roberts went back to work, if only temporarily. At the end of her journal she describes her feelings about working and not working, and what she says is typical.

I began to think about a guy I once met years ago in the unemployment lines. I thought at the time he was a real ski bum, but after we went out for a drink together, I learned otherwise. He was an aeronautics designer for federal agencies. He was also canny enough always to land an assignment that gave out just about the time the snow began in Aspen or Squaw Valley. Then he collected his unemployment and went skiing. Whatta way to go! Maybe, I should be so lucky!

5

PAST ANXIETIES, FUTURE ANXIETIES

In the year 2000 . . . those whose basic attitude toward work is that it is totally abhorrent or reprehensible . . . will find it possible to avoid employment entirely. . . . Many Americans from "normal" [i.e., not deprived] backgrounds will adopt the position that work is an interruption, while many formerly in the lower and economically deprived classes will increasingly shift to the positions which reflect more work-oriented and achievement-oriented values. On the other hand, the man whose missionary zeal for work takes priority over all other values will be looked on as an unfortunate, perhaps even a harmful and destructive neurotic. Even those who find in work a "vocation" are likely to be thought of as selfish, excessively narrow, or compulsive.

—Herman Kahn and Anthony Weiner,
The Year 2000

For some time the market has been glutted with books that predict the future in alarming detail.

Personally, I considered much of the speculation fanciful, something like buying a ticket at the planetarium twenty years ago for the first tourist excursion to the moon. I don't think so anymore, and I want to add a few of my own futurist scenarios to the list.[1]

November 12, 1999

Katherine Morris, sociologist, fifty-three-year-old mother of four children, tenured professor, and a leader of the women's movement, explains why she decided to stop working, why she became a "hermit."

"You're looking at one person who concluded after ten years of a really dehumanizing pace that I've used up myself. Partly that's because I entered the labor force after many years of raising children, and I had so many ideas that I couldn't wait to unleash them.

"We still had three kids at home, and teaching for the first time, writing the dissertation, well, the strain was fantastic, but I wanted to do it. It was a whole new sphere. But of course it just kept escalating. And it gets to the point obviously where it gets out of hand. There were certain external considerations: I had a mastoid condition that left me deaf in one ear and with a permanent loud noise in my head. I figure that at least 20 percent of my energy goes to just dealing with that. So apart from the fact that I'm growing older, I have a lowered energy level. Also another thread that has woven in and out of my life is that I had always been trying to find the time for reflection and making more of a wholeness of life. 1996 was my year for that. I built a little hermitage behind our family cabin where I lived mostly alone for a year. Now I'm getting ready to do that again—for much longer than a year."

When she left work in 1996, she undertook a set of delicate negotiations with her husband. "Certainly he felt threatened by it. As a teacher, in some ways he could relate much better to my professional activity than to my hermit's side. He was really very proud of all the things I'd done. How did I explain it to him? I said that people as they grew older continue to differentiate. Whatever there is in you has had time to develop.

"This knowing about the process of inward growth is something I constantly rediscover and wander away from. When I decided to stop working, I felt undeveloped, that there was a kind of growing I hadn't gotten around to. I valued having time for doing that kind of growing.

"The children helped a great deal in the discussions between William and myself. They accepted what I was doing, and they understood that mom is mom and dad is dad. They are all worried about how to help dad accept the fact that my stopping work isn't the end of life and going on the shelf. For him it's a loss of legitimacy. For me it's simply an affirmation of me. It's freeing myself up to set my agenda and not in an irresponsible fashion. I don't feel there's anything socially irresponsible about wanting to stop when you need to. My husband travels a great deal, he's at the college only intermittently. So we're apart a lot. When I spent a year alone we were prepared to negotiate and stay in touch. That's pretty much the way it is now."

September 12, 2016

Fred Lewis, a $29,000-a-year sales representative, meets with the chief staff psychologist of the Mc-Naughton agricultural machinery corporation.

"Well, Fred, have you thought some more about your plans?" asks the psychologist.

"I appreciate the advance notice," Fred says. "It's still a little strange to think of myself as retired at forty-two. But the kids'll need me around more since Jane was made a vice-president. I've also thought a little about gentleman farming. You know, before I moved into sales I was in product development. Always thought it would be interesting to drive one of our tractors."

The psychologist says, "I'm glad you're being sensible about things. When we first started retiring staff because we were changing our product line or we were decentralizing the operation, people got really upset. They said, 'I've been here fifteen years, I've done a good job, why are you throwing me out on the street?' They didn't understand we can't wait for somebody to reach fifty-five. We need new blood; as the company changes we need people who fit in with the change. It's not a question of age anymore, it's a question of compatibility."[2]

May 10, 2009

A notice is sent to nine division heads, fifteen group heads, and twenty-four middle-level executives at the Markland Corporation, the third largest office equipment manufacturer in the world. The notice says:

> At our quarterly executive sales conference the following policy was established:
>
> Current projections indicate a 19 percent sales reduction in the winter-spring period. This will necessitate an administrative reorganization in line with a revised sales strategy. It will also be necessary to effect temporary staff reductions. As in 2007, during a similar period of reorganization, administrative and supervisory staff in the sales division will be offered the following options:
>
> 1. Full employment for a total of six months during the next eighteen months, plus continuation of benefits.
> 2. Ten-month furloughs at a rate of one third current salaries.
> 3. Limited consultancies to plan as needed for the anticipated expansion effort once market conditions improve.
>
> We wish to reemphasize that this adjustment is temporary. Following this period of reorganization we expect you to resume your full-time positions.

September 5, 2017

Tom Johnson, a senior at the University of Southern California, is majoring in "leisure marketing." To fulfill his course requirements he has taken among other classes: Leisure Life-styles, Social Dynamics in the Retirement Village, and Sexual Roles in the Nonworking Family. Tom is an excellent student. Last semester he received an A for his final paper on "Demographics of Not Working." In his report he pointed out that the average life expectancy is seventy-two years for men and seventy-seven years for women, and that on the average men will hold a steady job for eighteen years of their adult lives and women twenty years. He also noted that the average work week had been reduced to twenty-four hours. He concluded with this projection: "We have seen an accelerated rate of change in three areas: in automation and technological innovation; in the number of temporary and ad hoc business organizations; and in the use of short-term specialists for specific problem-solving assignments. If these patterns are sustained, we can expect the average number of working years to drop below ten by 2050."

Tom, himself, is looking forward to a short and successful career. After college, he will join Sunland Leisure Consultants, one of the fastest growing leisure firms in California. His father is president of the company, and he has told Tom that he expects to retire in five years at the age of forty-six. Tom hasn't broken the news yet, but he plans to do better than the old man. He plans to retire at thirty-five.

I am cheating. These scenarios are not fanciful and they are not speculative. They belong to the present, not the future. This is America today.

Many corporations, especially those relying heavily on new technology and information systems, have become, in Alvin Toffler's term, "adhocracies." They respond to changing market demands by restructuring their organizations and by substituting temporary, transient problem-solving teams for a permanent work force. It is estimated that these constantly adaptive organizations, which include government agencies and advanced technology corporations, will employ 65 percent of the American working population by 2001. Business organizations "can be expected to become increasingly kinetic, filled with turbulence and change," Toffler has written. "We are moving from long-enduring to temporary forms, from permanence to transience."[3] Already many corporations have a policy of extended "sabbaticals" as market conditions change. Like a football coach, they shuttle the "offensive" and "defensive" teams in and out with each swing in the market. Sometimes these sabbaticals are of indefinite duration, in which case they are called "early retirement."

A number of corporations have also begun to retire employees when they show themselves to be incompatible with new management or a new strategy. On a profit-and-loss basis, it's probably cheaper to pension an employee in his forties than to keep him when he's outgrown his usefulness. That is, if profit and loss is the bottom line.

The employee is not insensitive to corporate "turbulence." He reserves his loyalty for himself, for number one. When work problems no longer challenge him, he searches out other challenges. "He is willing to employ his skills and creative energies to solve problems," Toffler says, "but he does so only so long as the problems interest *him* [Toffler's italics]. He is committed to his own career, his own self-fulfillment."

With so many women entering the job market, their defections have not received much notice. But as more women rise on the organizational ladder, they are likely to encounter many of the frustrations experienced by men. They are certainly no less interested in self-fulfillment than men are. Katherine Morris* knows when enough's enough. So will other women. And, as she notes, they have had more experience than men in living outside the company. Not working isn't as frightening for them as it is for some men.

Not everyone is an adventurer, not everyone is up to the test of freeing time and seeking "wholeness" by themselves. They will need guides to direct them through the straits of not working. Thus, a new academic discipline is created. Four hundred colleges now have majors in leisure studies, and in more than a hundred colleges, classes are offered in "leisure counseling." As one observer wrote recently, "Only through that intensive educational background . . . is someone then 'qualified' to help the rest of us poor recreational rabbits through the briar patch of alternatives for our free time. This they are doing for a fee."[4]

So the circuit is complete. Business lets the worker know he's not going to be around forever. Government assures him he will not starve without working—unless he's a short-order cook, in which case he's going to have to take the first job that comes along. And the universities train their students to counsel the workless millions on how to

---

*Katherine Morris, whose name has been changed here, was one of the people I interviewed for the book.

spend their free time, with the emphasis on spend.

We can estimate the length of the working life of the average person in the future. We know where his loyalties will lie. We have an idea of how he will spend his time away from work. What we can't plot mathematically is that one small element we call character.

Many ingredients go into the making of character. Our genes, the circumstances of race, sex, and class, the emotional development that occurs in our lifetimes, all that and a thousand other building blocks. Yet somehow character is more than the sum of the parts. Human alchemy creates a distillate that is our private ideal, the resolution of our inner monologues. Character is our personal conception of what we are at our best. If we give ourselves over to the search for that ideal, we can transcend pettiness and banality, overcome the serious and not-so-serious reverses we inevitably suffer, and enlarge our lives.

In this book I have described people who held on to that ideal and others who lost sight of it. The ones who sustained their visions rediscovered their capacities for generosity, reclaimed their "uniqueness," and renewed their commitments to the mass of humanity. They were not saints and their lives were not filled with ecstasy, but they were advancing on that long road toward "inward calm," toward their ideal self. There were others who never seemed to have time to contemplate their goodness. They rushed headlong toward the next infusion of instant happiness, they rolled over anybody who stood in their way, they were exponents of the me-first principle. For them there was no breaktime. They hadn't given a damn about anybody else when they were working, and they didn't give a damn about anything but their immediate gratification when they stopped.

We can speculate at length about character in a culture where the bonds of work have broken. We can conceive of a selfish society preoccupied by the "more childish forms of individualism" and the more "antisocial concern for self," Kahn and Weiner write in *The Future Meanings of Work*. Or if we are optimistic, we can imagine the rise of the "cultivated gentleman" who renews himself outside of work.[5] But I don't want to engage in general speculation.

I want to speak personally. I want to talk about my father and how I think he would have lived beyond the work ethic.

My father's character was flawed, too, by lack of faith in himself and in the rightness of his instincts. He gave in to the earn-more buy-more compulsion. He was always fearful that he would sink back into the past, back to the Lower East Side, back to the immigrants' ghetto. Crossing the bridge to Brooklyn brought him closer to an outward respectability. He could afford a new sports jacket, a heated apartment, and an occasional vacation. He could afford it—barely.

Suppose he was living in a time when the anxieties of class and respectability had diminished.

How would he live? First of all I think he would live simply.

It pains me now to say that he wanted to live a simple life because for so many years I didn't (or wouldn't) understand that. I thought he didn't care sufficiently to provide all the good things in life for his family. It took me a long time to realize that the good things weren't necessarily the expensive things. In his terms, simple living meant stripping away superificiality. If your entire effort was devoted to making money and satisfying the craving for the next novelty in Bloomingdale's window, how could you get to the bottom of things, to issues of substance? You didn't need a pine-paneled rec room to ponder why white men hated black men or rich men manipulated poor men, or why politicians promised one thing on election eve and delivered something else, something they had promised their sponsors on election morning. You could discuss such matters anywhere—on the stoop, in the cafeteria, on the street corner, on a couch pockmarked with cigarette holes. The ideas were important; the setting meant next to nothing.

There is a concrete example of what living simply meant. My family held out longest on our street before buying a television. Partly it was because of cost. My father hated the idea of three years of indebtedness to pay for it. But his basic objection was to television, the analgesic. He was a man who loved to argue issues head to head. (*Argument* was a bad word in our family. "We're discussing," my mother would insist, "we're not arguing.") Conversation was his Dexedrine. Therefore, television had to be a mortal enemy. He resisted it because he knew it would steal his one great pleasure—human intercourse. But he gave into the screeches and whines, bowed to the social pressure, and bought a sixteen-inch box. Later his face fell apart as guests raced from the kitchen table to the television. Trailing them into the living room, he'd stand in the doorway watching the dots for a half hour. They he'd go to sleep.

By birthright he was a plugger. He plugged at selling hats. He plugged at making money. He plugged at satisfying the demands of his class. By conviction he was an idealist. It was in the nature of his character to change the world. To change it through his goodness and kindness. His personal war was fought between class and character, between what he was expected to be and what he imagined he could be.

What he was expected to be. There was a terrible moment in my childhood that I will carry with me always because it forced me to witness the destruction of his spirit. It had to do with my bar mitzvah. He wanted to celebrate the event with the religious rituals in the synagogue and a modest party at home, bringing family and friends to the apartment for coffee, cake from Kramers' bakery, and a few bottles of schnapps. My mother insisted (with my sad-eyed collaboration) on renting a hall, hiring an orchestra, inviting two or three hundred people (most of them strangers), and spending a few thousand dollars that we didn't have. In this way my confirmation confirmed the Lefkowitz's class standing. If you really cared about your only son, you would show it by putting the bucks on the table— right where everybody could see them.

They saw them. Three hundred people came on a Sunday afternoon. The orchestra played. I repeated the same canned speech I had made the day before in the synagogue basement. Toward the end of the afternoon the women went to the bathroom to change their shoes and the men came over to me and stuffed my pockets with the envelopes containing their gifts. The sports gave me thirty dollars; the real sports fifty dollars; the *shnorrers* fifteen or twenty dollars. My father took me aside and whispered, "Give me the money." I gave it to him. As the last guests were leaving, he sat alone at a table in the back of the catering hall. With madness in his eyes, his hands trembling, he ripped open the envelopes and heaped the checks and cash on the table. When he was done, he looked up at me and sighed. "I think there's enough to pay for the hall," he said.

What he could have been. There's another moment that expresses his character, himself at his best, living the truly good life. He had a group of friends who shared his political convictions. One Christmas Eve, when I was four or five, a member of the group showed up at the door dressed in a Santa Claus costume. All I remember about the man was that he stuttered.

"M-m-merry," he struggled, then gave up, dropped a huge sack of toys at my feet, and ran, laughing, down the stairs. The toys were all second-hand. They had been collected from my father's friends. Puppets without arms, trains without wheels. But they were priceless because they were a gift of joy, they came from people who cared about me and my parents. I have never had a happier Christmas, and sadly, neither did my father. On that one night, he had found his home.

To imagine him alive now, unconstrained by the traps and snares of his immediate culture, is to ignore those influences that directed his inner life. But beyond environment there is character. I think his character, his image of the good and full life and what has to be done to live it, was more suited to the present and to the next twenty-five years than it was to the 1940s and 1950s. His prime years were spent in a struggle for survival and identity in a consuming, aspiring culture. I think his values would have been more appreciated in a milieu, where according to a 1978 Harris poll, the majority of Americans desire to live "simply." He was born too early.

Today he would have still felt responsible for the welfare of his family. A respite from work would not have been an excuse for desertion. But he would have been open to sharing that responsibility. In his time, a man was marked a failure if he encouraged his wife to work. For many years he discouraged my mother from getting a job, although we needed the money. Today I'm sure he would have told her: Go out and work if you want to, it'll help all of us, and, who knows, maybe you'll like it.

Two anxieties ate at him. One was economic, the other political. As a young man he had been interested in left-wing politics, but it was a vicarious involvement, mostly talk. He signed a few petitions and contributed a few bucks. This haunted him throughout the McCarthy period and after. For years he stayed awake at night waiting for the knock on the door. In the 1960s, when I was being considered for a government job, he was sure that his infamous past would be revealed and that it would ruin his son. A few years before he died he had saved enough money so that he and my mother could take a vacation in Europe. When he applied for a passport, he read the line that started, "Are you or have you ever been . . ." and pulled my mother out of the passport office. They never left the United States.

Today I think he could have practiced politics, not the dream politics of the 1930s with the iron conformity of Stalinism, but his own brand of citizens' involvement. He could have picked from a smorgasbord of movements and interests: government-supported abortions, anti-nuclear power, welfare rights, economic development in poverty areas, union reform. His real gift was as an organizer. As a salesman he was a master of the gentle sell; he intuitively knew what people cared about and what they wanted. In his work, he was limited to what hats people wanted and how much they cost. Today he would have found out what people in a public ward of a hospital or in a nursing home wanted and helped them to get it. This is not pure conjecture or a son's homage to his father. In his twenties he managed a political campaign for his brother who was running for office in New York. His brothers still talk about how he welded together an improbable coalition of Jewish immigrant families, junior mafiosi, Irish truck drivers, and poolroom no-goods, and almost pulled it off. (His brother narrowly lost, but then again the local machine counted the votes.)

I can't say for sure that's what he would have done with his time away from work. He was a restless, curious man. He wanted to know what was going on, what was going on in the life of the man sitting next to him at the luncheonette counter, in the life of the woman feeding the pigeons in the park. Somehow, somewhere he might have found a place for his restlessness in one of the many restless cultures in this country.

My father was a seeker and therefore never a cynic. He believed that through numbers and organization and shared concern outsiders can achieve some equity. He would have gladly served as Betty Tallgood's assistant, her special emissary to the white pickle kings of Mississippi. I think he would have probably continued to work for long stretches; he found the give-and-take of the marketplace exhilarating. But he would have been free, living today, to experiment with other tonics, because the investigatory consciousness is respected. He wouldn't have had to forfeit his respectability to seek his vocation or to take a vacation from work.

But he wouldn't have done that at the expense of others. He had no patience for indolence and he was not selfish. Two days on a beach in Jamaica and he would have gone off to find the Rastafarians. He would not have ripped off the system to pay for his weekend in paradise. What's relaxing about being a thief?

He still would have worried about whether he had enough money in the bank to sustain himself and my mother in their old age. He would have brooded about his effectiveness. He would have had moments of doubt about whether he was doing the right thing, whether his effort was going to make a difference in the lives of people he cared about. I think he would have been concerned that he was raising people's hopes without certainty that they would be realized.

Maybe because I was a witness to them and a victim of them, I think his past anxieties were fatal. The anxieties of future man seem, by comparison, progressive disturbances—creative anxieties, if you will. I doubt whether my father would have found perfect peace, total ease, in his breaktime. But, hell, he would have come closer, and so would have I.

NOTES

1: INTRODUCTION

The introductory quote is from C. Wright Mills's *White Collar* (New York: Oxford University Press, 1951), p. xx.

1. The description of Joe Gould is taken from Joseph Mitchell's collection of pieces published under the title *McSorley's Wonderful Saloon* (New York: Grosset & Dunlap/The Universal Press, 1938–1943), pp. 68–86.

2. One origin of this book was the year I spent as a program evaluator for Manpower Development Research Organization, a nonprofit organization established to place the long-term unemployed in experimental work settings. In that year I met people who hadn't worked for a very long time—high school dropouts, former addicts, welfare mothers, and ex-convicts. Their backgrounds were diverse; some came from poor families, other from middle-class homes. I began to realize they represented a foreign culture that did not recognize many of the practices and customs that govern the work world. My conversations with them were my introduction of the culture of non-working America.

2: BREAKPOINT

The introductory quote is from *The Future of Work*, ed. Fred Best (Englewood Cliffs, N.J.: Prentice-Hall, 1973), p. 15.

Naked in America

1. The most incisive analysis of the changing meaning of work is found in the studies and research of the social psychologist Daniel Yankelovich. The results of the 1971 survey of college students appeared in the *Work in America* report by the Special Task Force to the Secretary of Health, Education and Welfare (Cambridge: M.I.T. Press, 1973), p. 44.

2. Yankelovich's comments and the survey on work and leisure are from his study "Work, Values and the New Breed," scheduled for publication in 1978 in the book *Work in America: The Decade Ahead*, eds. Clark Kerr and Jerome Rosow (New York: Van Nostrand, Reinhold). Professor Yankelovich also discussed these and other subjects in my interview with him.

3. *Work in America*, p. 3.

4. Dr. Osherson's characterization of work is from an interview with him. He is a member of the department of psychiatry at the Harvard Medical School.

5. A thoughtful discussion of work and its changing definition throughout history is found in Peter Berger's essay, "Some General Observations on the Problem of Work," in *The Human Shape of Work*, ed. Peter Berger (New York: Macmillan, 1964). The quote is from p. 212. Writing in the early 1960s, Professor Berger suggested that work is perceived in three ways: as a means of fulfillment, as an oppressive condition, and as a "gray" area in which the individual neither thrives nor suffers, but endures. That "gray" area is expanding, he says, because of the evermore specialized division of labor and because of the private expectations people bring to their work.

6. Paul Goodman's quote is from his book *Growing Up Absurd: Problems of Youth in Organized Society* (New York: Vintage, 1962), pp. 34–45.

7. The preliminary discussion of the personal significance of work was drawn from the interviews with people

who had stopped working and from the following books: Mills, *White Collar*, pp. 215–225; Frederick Herzberg, *Work and the Nature of Man* (New York: New American Library, 1966), pp. 187–212; Ely Chinoy, *Automobile Workers and the American Dream* (Boston: Beacon Press, 1965), pp. 12–22 and the introduction by David Reisman; David M. Potter, *People of Plenty* (Chicago: University of Chicago Press, 1954), pp. 32–72; Abraham M. Maslow, *Motivation and Personality* (New York: Harper and Row, 1954), pp. 33–47.

First Person Singular

1. Warren Bennis's quote is from *The Temporary Society* by Warren C. Bennis and Philip E. Slater (New York: Harper Colophon, 1968), p. 128.

2. Dr. Harry Levinson, a clinical psychologist, is a major figure in the field of industrial psychology. I am indebted to him for his analysis of the psychological effects of a break with work, particularly the feelings of persecution and entitlement expressed by such people as Martha Gorham. Dr. Levinson's comments are from my interview with him.

The Passing of the Work Myth

1. This expression of official concern by Bavarian officials at the emancipation of journeyman workers is from historian Edward Shorter's "Toward a History of *La Vie Intime:* The Evidence of Cultural Criticism in Nineteenth-Century Bavaria." Shorter's study appeared in *The Emergence of Leisure,* ed. Michael K. Marrus (New York: Harper Torchbooks, 1974), pp. 41–43.

2. The quote by historian Herbert G. Gutman is from his book *Work Culture and Society in Industrializing America* (New York: Vintage Books, 1977), p. 4. Gutman's study focuses on the discontent of blue-collar workers in the nineteenth century and the early part of the twentieth

century. His discussion of the inability of capitalists to impose decisions on their workers because they lacked popular sanctions is particularly instructive.

3. A stimulating discussion of the puritan ethic and its political significance is offered in *Fall from Grace* by Milton Viorst (New York: Touchstone/Simon & Schuster, 1971). A more picaresque portrait of life outside the work ethic in the nineteenth century is presented in *Darkness and Daylight or Lights and Shadows of New York Life* by Helen Campbell, Thomas W. Knox, and Police Inspector Thomas Byrnes (Hartford: A. D. Worthington, 1893).

4. Robert and Helen Lynd, *Middletown: A Study in Contemporary American Culture* (New York: Harcourt, Brace and World, 1959), pp. 73, 80–81.

5. "The Function and Meaning of Work and the Job," *American Sociological Review*, April 1955, pp. 191–198. The authors, Nancy C. Morse and Robert S. Weiss, are members of the University of Michigan's Survey Research Center.

6. Mirra Komarovsky's study appeared as *The Unemployed Man and His Family: The Effect of Unemployment upon the Status of the Man in Fifty-Nine Families* (New York: Dryden Press, 1940), pp. 14, 23–48, 92–114.

7. Literally hundreds of books, magazine articles, studies, and newspaper stories that consider one aspect or another of the changing meaning of the involvement with work were written in the period from the mid-sixties fo the mid-seventies. A list of those I found most useful, grouped under various subject headings, follows.

Overview: Books

Jerome M. Rosow, ed., *The Worker and the Job: Coping with Change* (Englewood Cliffs, N.J.: Prentice-Hall, 1974). This is a collection of papers submitted at an American Assembly Conference in November 1973. In his introduction, Rosow, former assistant secretary of labor, writes that in

1973 an estimated eleven million people expressed dissatisfaction with their jobs. "More and more the American work force is seeking more from work than money alone." While values outside of work are changing dramatically, customs and practices at the workplace resist change. "The organizational hierarchy persists, communication moves through formal channels, participation is limited or nonexistent, opportunity for self-expression is often counter-productive and conformity by employees is required.... Absenteeism, turnover, grievances and strikes are indicators of the surface abrasiveness of the workplace.... Poor product quality, growing customer dissatisfaction, wasted materials and climbing labor costs are other evidences."

The contributions by Yankelovich, economist Eli Ginzberg, journalist Agis Sapulkis, and Peter Henle, former chief economist of the Bureau of Labor Statistics, are especially illuminating.

Work in America, the report of the task force to the Secretary of Health, Education and Welfare, discusses a number of topics including changing attitudes toward work; sources of dissatisfaction; blue-collar blues, managerial and white-collar discontent; and the positions of younger workers and female workers.

Harold Sheppard and Neal Herrick, *Where Have All the Robots Gone?* (New York: Free Press, 1972). This is perhaps the most comprehensive study of new work values. The authors drew on data from a 1969 study of 1,500 workers by the University of Michigan and on their own study of 400 white male blue-collar workers who were union members. They found that workers over the age of thirty were troubled by the lack of possibility of promotion and inadequate wages. Younger workers expressed dissatisfaction with "their lack of opportunity for self-development." Sheppard and Herrick urge the elimination of certain dull, repetitious jobs because "in the new epoch, workers will not accept monotonous and dead-end tasks as readily as we believe workers in past decades did."

Studs Terkel, *Working* (New York: Pantheon Books, 1974). These interviews with working men and women present striking evidence of the depth and pervasiveness of the discontent with work in America.

Ronald Fraser, ed., *Work 2: Twenty Personal Accounts* (Harmondsworth, England: Penguin, 1969). Among the English workers who contributed first-person accounts of their lives are a teacher, a bricklayer, a toolmaker, a miner, and an atomic energy researcher. In his concluding essay, Alvin W. Goulder writes, "Men's resistance to work is ingenious and ancient and the complaints about it are familiar and traditional. Yet in reading these reports I also thought I detected the emergence of a somewhat new sound, the still muffled sound of a slow and steady leak in the well-engineered world of work; an emerging awareness that work, as many know it, is nothing less than the wasting of life."

Michael Aiken, Louis A. Ferman, and Harold L. Sheppard, *Economic Failure, Alienation and Extremism* (Ann Arbor: University of Michigan Press, 1968).

A. Zaleznik, *Worker Satisfaction and Development*, (Boston: Harvard University Division of Research, 1956). I have included this book by Professor Zaleznik because its study of work and social behavior by a group of factory employees foreshadowed many of the work-ethic issues that emerged in the 1960s and 1970s.

James Robertson, *Power, Money and Sex* (London: Marion Boyars, 1976). Robertson, a former high-ranking British civil servant, writes, "It was a profound shock to discover after ten years of rewarding—indeed exciting—work in Whitehall that so many of the stock criticisms of it were justified. There appeared to be literally thousands of people—real, live, individual people like oneself, many of them potentially able or once able—whose energies were being wasted on non-jobs . . . whose capabilities and aspirations were being stunted and who were gradually reconciling themselves to the prospect of pointless work until retirement."

Elliot A. Krause, *The Sociology of Occupations* (Boston: Little, Brown, 1971). Krause is particularly effective in investigating interpersonal and intergroup relations in the work setting, and he offers a tough-minded analysis of a number of white-collar occupations.

Peter F. Sprague, comp., *What Do You Do For a Living?* (Princeton: Dow Jones, 1974 and 1975). These profiles are taken from stories that appeared in *The Wall Street Journal.*

Overview: Periodicals and Newspaper Articles
Daniel Yankelovich, "Turbulence in the Working World: Angry Workers, Happy Grads," *Psychology Today*, December 1974, pp. 80–87. Yankelovich discusses the changing definition of success, the reduced fear of economic insecurity, the spreading psychology of entitlement, and the growing disillusionment with the cult of efficiency.

Michael Maccoby and Katherine Terzi, "Character and Work in America" (a report that was part of the Project on Technology, Work and Character at Harvard University, 1974). They consider the effect of the character that is maladapted to work and find that "American workers as a whole are most dissatisfied with their jobs when they do not provide interesting work, opportunity for self-development and resources to carry out the job."

Peter Swerdloff, "Learning to Love Unemployment," *Esquire*, December 1972. "Young people with a lifetime of busy success behind them have discovered that slothfulness can be fun. . . . What should be tragic has been for many educational."

"Is Hard Work Going Out of Style?" an interview with Eli Ginzberg, chairman of the National Manpower Advisory Committe, *U.S. News and World Report,* August 23, 1971, pp. 52–56.

Raymond Livingstone, "Unemployment—The Story the Figures Don't Tell," *U.S. News and World Report,* November 18, 1974. The author, an authority on employment trends, writes, "We have inculcated our young people with the idea that it's their right to have a job that is interesting, that has status, that has security and that they enjoy doing."

Richard M. Pfeffer, *"When the Niceties Go: The Worker as Commodity,"* The New York Times, April 30, 1975. Personal account of how factory workers and teachers are treated as commodities.

Robert Lindsey, "Some Who Believe in a Not-Work Ethic," *The New York Times,* June 1, 1975. Interviews with people around the country who have voluntarily chosen not to work.

Stuart Fischer, "Jobless But Happy," *The New York Times,* January 23, 1975.

A. A. Spekke, "Work and America's Third Century," *Intellect,* September 1976, p. 105.

J. B. Fukumoto, "On Having a Meaningless Job," *Mademoiselle,* December 1975, pp. 20–21.

Eric Hoffer, "What Have We Lost," *The New York Times Magazine,* October 20, 1974, pp. 37–42.

Richard Todd, "Notes on a Corporate Man," *Atlantic,* October 1971, pp. 83–94. This is perhaps the best magazine piece I read on the emotional distance of the middle manager from his work.

Blue-Collar Worker: Books

Interest in the disaffection of blue-collar workers increased when employees of the General Motors Vega plant in Lordstown, Ohio, struck in 1972 against what was described as the fastest assembly line in the world. In that plant cars moved past the workers at a rate of one every thirty-six seconds. When the pace was slowed down, the workers returned, but their protest became an instant symbol of "widespread rank and file rebellion against the dehumanizing effects of automation," as a March 7, 1972, *New York Times* editorial said.

While a number of studies and articles were prompted by the Lordstown strike, the following books provide a useful background for understanding the general condition of blue-collar workers.

Stanley Levison, *The Working-Class Majority* (New York: Penguin Books, 1975). Particularly Chapter 2 on the discontentments of work, Chapter 5 on the influence of unions on the working class, and Chapter 7 on the future of blue-collar workers.

Richard Sennett and Jonathan Cobb, *The Hidden Injuries of Class* (New York: Knopf, 1972). Particularly Chapter 5 on freedom and the discussion of "desirable jobs"; pp. 121–125 on sacrificing for one's children; and pp. 236–240 on dreams and defenses.

Donald W. Tiffany, James R. Cowan, and Phyllis M. Tiffany, *The Unemployed: A Social-Psycholgical Portrait* (Englewood Cliffs, N.J.: Prentice-Hall, 1970). This is a useful study because it discusses people who remain unemployed at a time when jobs are readily available.

Harold L. Sheppard and A. Harvey Belitsky, *The Job Hunt: Job-Seeking Behavior of Unemployed Workers in a Local Economy* (Baltimore: Johns Hopkins Press, 1966). This study, which includes both blue-collar and white-collar employees, considers why the unemployed reject certain jobs, how their attitudes toward work change as time passes, and discusses their anxieties about returning to work.

Daniel Bell, *Work and Its Discontents* (Boston: Beacon Press, 1956). Still the most vigorous and stimulating discussion of work in America, particularly pp. 46–56 in which Bell discusses automation, relationships between workers, and "job enlargement."

B. J. Widick, ed., *Auto Work and Its Discontents* (Baltimore: Johns Hopkins Press, 1976). A sober discussion of contemporary issues, especially those concerned with union movement, skilled trades, and "exaggerated and misleading" claims of alienation and job satisfaction.

Ely Chinoy, *Automobile Workers and the American Dream* (Boston: Beacon Press, 1965). A landmark study of "auto-town." "The lack of interest, hope and desire was so widespread among the workers interviewed that it must be considered the 'normal' reaction to the circumstance in which they found themselves."

Blue-Collar Worker: Periodicals and Reports
The Winter 1972 issue of *Dissent* contains an excellent collection of pieces on "the world of the blue-collar worker." Particularly noteworthy are: "A Steelworkers' Local in New England" by Thomas R. Brooks; "The Tensions of Work" by Jack Barbash; "White Workers/Blue Mood: Labor in the Post-Industrial Society" by Daniel Bell; and "The Life of White Ethnics" by Irving M. Levine and Judith Herman.

Frank Friedlander, "Importance of Work Versus Nonwork among Socially and Occupationally Stratified Groups," *Journal of Applied Psychology* 50 (1966). Author finds that blue-collar workers valued the work context— feeling of job security, working relationship with supervisor, technical competence of co-workers, more than the actual content of the work itself. White-collar workers attached primary importance to the intrinsic content of their work.

Stanley Seashore and Thad J. Barnowe, "Behind the Averages: A Close Look at America's Lower-Middle-Income Workers" (Proceedings of the Twenty-fourth Annual Winter Meeting of the Industrial Relations Research Association, 1971), pp. 358–70. This study of 1,095 lower-middle-income workers found that the "blue-collar blues" were most intense among "hardhat" workers under thirty, without dependents, and among "matriarchs," women who were primary wage earners in a household with one or more dependents. But the researchers concluded that the "blue-collar blues are endemic in the whole of the work force and rest only slightly upon demographic characteristics."

A fascinating series of studies was conducted by the research department of the Oldsmobile Division of General Motors. ("Oldsmobile's Action on Absenteeism and Turnover: Control Program Report," unpublished, November 1971). The researchers asked foremen and workers to account for the causes of absence and turnover. Foremen in one study said turnover was caused by the workers' youth and inexperience, low qualifications, "welfare-state" values, and the fact that their jobs were too easy to get. Workers, on the other hand, said they left their jobs because of poor working conditions, unwarranted use of discipline, and their own lack of influence in the plant.

William Serrin presents a depressing portrait of factory work in "The Assembly Line," *Atlantic*, October 1971, pp. 62–73. "These days there is unrest in the auto plants once again. Roughly 40 percent of the automotive work force is under thirty. And many of these young men and women say their jobs and their lives are dull and unrewarding. . . . Many of the older workers, largely in their forties and fifties, are also angry and dissatisfied. They want to quit but say that they can't afford to; they wait to retire."

Richard E. Barfield, "The Automobile Worker and Retirement: A Second Look" (Institute for Social Research, University of Michigan, Ann Arbor, 1970). This work follows an earlier study in which Barfield found that "at least for certain mass-production-industry workers, early retirement is both strongly desired and (initially at least) largely enjoyable." In this second study, he says, "Inferring particularly from the apparent continuation of high levels of satisfaction among auto workers who have been out of the work environment for several years, it does not seem possible that the expressions of satisfaction in retirement on the part of most auto workers derive primarily from simple relief at having escaped a bad situation. We remain convinced that, for many people, the satisfactions of a life free from the demands of work are both persuasive and abiding."

Rick King, "In the Standing Booth at Ford," *Skeptic*, May–June 1976 (reprinted from *Washington Monthly*, 1975), p. 24.

Jack Horn, "Bored to Sickness," *Psychology Today*, November 1975, p. 92.

J. Gaylin, "Why Blue-Collar Workers Avoid Psychiatric Help," *Psychology Today*, October 1976, p. 34.

D. D. Braginsky and B. M. Braginsky, "Surplus People, Their Lost Faith in Self and System," *Psychology Today*, August 1975, pp. 68–72.

George Strauss, "Worker Dissatisfaction—A Look at the Causes," *Monthly Labor Review*, February 1974, pp. 57–58.

"Blue-Collar Blues," *Newsweek*, April 29, 1974, p. 90.

"Job Blahs: Who Wants to Work?" *Newsweek*, March 26, 1973, pp. 79–89.

"Boredom Spells Trouble," *Life*, September 1, 1972, p. 30.

Blue-Collar Worker: Newspaper Articles

The following stories from *The New York Times* on blue-collar workers helped guide my research.

March 9, 1976, p. 59. Describes the chronic unemployment in Quinebag Valley in Connecticut since textile mills began moving south thirty years ago.

August 22, 1976, p. 15. An assessment of current unemployment rates that allow the unemployed to be more selective about taking a job.

April 27, 1975, p. 51. Describes how for many in East-port, Maine, with the decline of commercial fishing in the region, unemployment has become a way of life.

February 1, 1975, p. 29. Long-term unemployment in Oswego County, New York.

February 8, 1975, p. 1. The impact of unemployment on a twenty-six-year-old auto worker.

March 6, 1975, p. 28. Widespread unemployment in Seattle following the Boeing layoffs.

March 4, 1975, p. 16. Describes conditions in the Hunts Point-South Bronx area where the unemployment rate is more than 25 percent.

August 14, 1975, p. 1. The difference in wages received by college graduates and the non-college educated is narrowing.

October 13, 1974, p. 143. Discusses the situation of 25,000 unemployed Vietnam veterans in New York, of whom 7,000 are on welfare.

November 24, 1974, section 3, p. 1. Although the number of unemployed was expected to increase, workers were likely to be much more selective than workers in the 1930s about taking a job.

June 15, 1973, p. 74. Describes the chronic unemployment on most Navajo reservations.

January 21, 1973, section 3, p. 14. Discusses survey of worker discontent in seventeen factories from New England to the Southwest, including more than 2,500 sewing machine oeprators.

The Social Effects of Changing Attitudes
Toward Work: Books

From an English perspective, the most interesting contemporary analysis of the effect of job and occupation on married life was *The Symmetrical Family* by Michael Young and Peter Wilmott (New York: Pantheon Books, 1973). The authors, who are co-directors of London's Institute of Community Studies, analyze the relationship of work to family life among the different classes in various communities in London and its suburbs. They consider the relationship between leisure time and class, the effect of family connections on job status, work and the social chemistry in different communities (including some neighborhoods that might be described as "gray areas"—zones of indifference). While the authors find the attachment to work is still strong, particularly in the upper classes, they also observe: "For working-class men the job was less often . . . their central life interest. The main reason seemed to be that they had less control over what happened to them at work. . . . They less often had a say in the day-to-day organization of their working lives. They were more often paced by the machines they served. . . . Middle-class people generally had more autonomy [p. 154]."

Men and Women of the Corporation by Rosabeth Moss Kanter (New York: Basic Books, 1977) is a perceptive discussion of many of the concerns and issues that led the people I met to break with work. Her description of people who are "tokens" in their work organizations reminds me of Frank Morse, the Yale-educated architect who was hired to do nothing; her portrait of the employee whose aspirations are depressed resembles Billy Morgan, the sincere but thwarted policeman; her discussion of people at a dead end who withdraw from their work relationships applies to Charles Braithwaite and Martha Gorham; and her observations on the severing of commitments is relevant in different ways to Lucille Roberts, Tom MacCauley, and Cliff Jones.

Early in my research I read an unpublished draft of a paper Mrs. Kanter wrote for the Russell Sage Foundation: "Work and Family in America: A Critical Review and Research Agenda." The research questions she posed gave direction and focus to my own research. The themes in her paper that I found most pertinent to my own work included: the organization of family as a "bureaucracy"; the function of suburban living as a separation from the work place; the spillover of family intimacy into work relationships; and the effect of different work patterns (such as frequent business trips) on family life.

Robert W. Smuts, *Women and Work in America* (New York: Schocken, 1971).

Rhona and Robert Rapoport, *Dual-Career Families Re-examined* (New York: Harper Colophon, 1977).

Lynda Lytle Holmstrom, *The Two-Career Family* (Cambridge: Shenkman, 1972).

Robert Seidenberg, *Corporate Wives—Corporate Casualties?* (New York: Anchor, 1975).

Simple Living Collective of the American Friends Service Committee in San Francisco, *Taking Charge: Personal and Political Change Through Simple Living* (New York: Bantam, 1977).

The Social Effects of Changing Attitudes Toward Work: Studies, Articles, and Newspaper Stories

The enormous increase in the number of working women has generated a vast amount of comment and reporting on work and family life, role changes, and new family and social arrangements. Here are some sources I found particularly relevant:

"Women in Blue-Collar Jobs" (A Ford Foundation Conference Report, 1976). The conference considered among other subjects the gap between salaries for men and women, how job titles affect equal pay, the obstacles that prevent women from assuming leadership roles in unions, and the attitudes of working-class women toward daycare centers.

Beverly Johnson McEaddy, *Women Who Head Families: A Socioeconomic Analysis* (Special Report: U.S. Bureau of Labor Statistics, Government Printing Office, 1976).

Roger Morris, "The New Family," *Context* (a publication of E. I. Du Pont de Nemours & Co.) no. 1 (1977), p. 12.

Myra A. Peabody, "Fifteen Years at a Defense Plant," *Humanist*, September–October 1973, pp. 18–21. A splendid account of the ups and downs in the General Dynamics plant in Groton, Connecticut, from 1956 to 1971.

Susan R. Orden and Norman M. Bradburn, "Working Wives and Marriage Happiness," *American Journal of Sociology*, no. 74 (1969), pp. 392–407. This is an analysis of personal interviews with 1,600 married men and women in Detroit, Chicago, and Washington. The study describes the tensions that result when wives enter the labor market out of economic need rather than choice.

Paul Wilkes, "Jobless in the Suburbs," *The New York Times Magazine*, June 8, 1975, p. 13. This portrait of a New Jersey family was important to me in a way I didn't anticipate when I first read the piece. Quite by accident I came to know this family, and their experience helped guide me in my later interviews with families throughout the country.

"The Hazards of Change," *Time*, March 1, 1971, p. 54. This article describes the stressful effect of changes, based on the research of Dr. Thomas Holmes, professor of psychiatry at the University of Washington. Work changes, he found, were on a middle level of stress, while the most serious life changes were the death of a spouse, divorce, and marital separation.

"Women and Success—Why Some Find It So Painful," *The New York Times*, January 28, 1978, p. 14.

Two *New York Times* articles in its series headed "Men and Women," November 29 and 30, 1977, provided useful background information on work and family. The first discussed the implication of the increase in working women, and the second considered the trend toward sexual equality.

The Effects of Institutions on Work Attitudes

In my research I was very interested in how various institutions, schools, churches, military and fraternal organizations, influence our values toward work. Since almost all of us went to school in America, I spent considerable time investigating the impact of formal education on work values, on career choice, and on the idea of success. The following books and studies were helpful in my preparation for the interviews.

Edgar Z. Friedenberg, *Coming of Age in America: Growth and Acquiescence* (New York: Random House, 1965). Friedenberg's most telling observations concern the absence of individual style in high school (p. 32); the lack of dignity and privacy in high school (p. 47); the emphasis on power rather than legitimacy (pp. 47–48); the social basis of decision making as divorced from political principle (p. 139); efforts to persuade a dropout to return to school without considering the reasons for his decision to leave (pp. 164–175); the adaptation of the protestant ethic to the school environment (pp. 187–188); depiction of education as an economic lever (pp. 194–195); and the need to organize and control leisure (p. 251).

David C. MacMichael, "Occupational Bias in Formal Education and Its Effect on Preparing Children for Work" (Menlo Park, Cl.: The Center, 1972). The author, a senior social scientist at the Educational Policy Research Center of the Stanford Research Institute, describes how schools transmit an "overwhelming bias for white-collar occupations requiring lengthy formal education and certification" and how this bias frustrates many poor and minority children. He argues that the old middle-class ethic "may no longer be appropriate to the emerging economy."

Leonard L. Baird, with chapters by Mary Jo Clark and Rodney T. Hartnett, "The Graduates: A Report on the Plans and Characteristics of College Seniors" (Educational Testing Service, Princeton, New Jersey, 1973). This survey of thousands of students graduating in the class of 1971 found that opportunity for leadership in work, interpersonal contact, interest in job activities, providing service to others, and independence are work values that are more important than job security and at least as important as income.

Regis H. Walther, "The Socialization of Youth for Work" (prepared for the H.E.W. Task Force on Work in America in 1972), describes some of the behavioral styles developed early in life that are applicable to work, including self-management, problem solving, reaction to aggression, relation to authority, and interpersonal style.

Robert Schrank and Susan Stein, "Yearning, Learning and Status" (The Ford Foundation, October 1970). "The rising educational attainment of the work force is a positive but also disruptive factor for change. When higher educational levels are not met immediately by greater opportunity and challenge, increasing demands and restlessness should be expected in the work place."

Norman Adler and Charles Harrington, eds., *The Learning of Political Behavior* (New York: Scott Foresman, 1970). Joseph C. Grannis's chapter, "The School as a Model of Society" (pp. 137–148), describes different models of schools the "factory" school, and the "corporate" school. Grannis argues that none of these models adequately deals with the concerns of inner-city students.

"Education and Careers,' an interview with Alvin Toffler, *Dialogue* 7, no. 4 (1974), pp. 36–45. "I believe that the educational system in the United States, Britain, France, Germany, Japan—all of the rich nations—is basically a system very carefully designed to produce people who will fit into an industrial culture. It does a very good job. . . . We still think that success in later life requires a great deal of routine processing, that work will be boring . . . that work will be difficult. . . . All of these things are breaking up. Students are resisting the pressure for obedience. They won't accept the authority of their elders. They don't want to do routine work ... and they are at least questioning, if not in open revolt against, the idea that economics is the most important thing in life."

Brigitte Berger, "People Work—The Youth Culture and the Labor Market," *Public Interest*, no. 35 (Spring 1974), pp. 55–66. Professor Berger's thoughtful piece considers the demand for "meaningful" work, the aspiration to upper-echelon white-collar jobs, and the constriction of the white-collar labor market. If desirable jobs don't exist, she argues, government may have to invent them in the form of what she calls "people work." By this she means government agencies and programs that purport to serve the interpersonal and psychological needs of groups and individuals—a "huge psychological soup kitchen."

David Gottlieb, "Youth and the Meaning of Work" (Manpower Research Monograph No. 32, Department of Labor, 1974). This study of 1,800 college seniors, who graduated in 1972, finds significant differences between the graduates and their parents. "Students see themselves as being far less concerned than their fathers with earnings and security and much more concerned with the nature and purpose of their work. ... The first priority will be to one's self, one's family, and one's closest associates. ... There appears to be an emerging work ethic which places a much greater demand upon work. The expectation is that work can and should be of greater significance to the individual and of greater value to the society."

8. The most comprehensive examination of the human resources movement, which is directed toward increasing job satisfaction through various work-place experiments, is Ted Mills's "Human Resources—Why the New Concern," *Harvard Business Review*, March–April 1975, pp. 120–134. Another proponent of human resource development is Stanley E. Seashore of the Institute for Social Re-

search at the University of Michigan. Professor Seashore's paper, "Social Change and the Design of Work Organizations" (Presented in the Pierce Lecture Series at Cornell University, April 23, 1975), points out that when innovations are introduced in the work place, "many workers would for the first time be confronted with a demand that they become aware of and knowingly choose their own values and motives, rather than taking them as given. . . . It is to be expected that historic, traditional and cultural factors will cause many to resist change and to reject the risk involved in an added degree of responsibility for choice and self-determination." He adds, however, that "objectives of efficiency and economic growth are losing their exclusive primacy. The individual motives of duty and necessity are weakening in industrialized societies. New and varied criteria are being advanced for assessing jobs, job environments and the associated control and reward systems." A more skeptical position is taken by Mitchell Fein, a consulting industrial engineer. Writing in the *Humanist* (September–October 1973) pp. 30–32, Fein says, "There are no job-enrichment successes which bear out the predictions of the behaviorists, because the vast majority of workers reject the concept. . . . Perhaps not recognized by behaviorists are the moral issues they raise with their proposals to redesign work, such as: intrusion upon a person's right to personal decisions; exploitation of the workers' job satisfaction for company gains; distortion of the truth."

9. Little's study was published in the *Sociological Quarterly*, Spring 1976, pp. 262–274 with the title: "Technical-Professional Unemployment: Middle-Class Adaptability to Personal Crisis."

10. The quotes attributed to Little are from my interview with him. Little is now associate professor of sociology at the State University of New York at Cortland.

11. This discussion of Professor Root's study is drawn from his paper, "Workers and Their Families in a Plant

Shutdown" (Presented at the American Sociological Association Meeting, Chicago, Viking September 1977). Other quotes are from my interview with him. His formal position is professor of sociology at Luther College in Decorah, Iowa.

12. This discussion is drawn from the Gray and Bolce study, "Job Desirability and the Right Not to Work," that was scheduled for publication (*U.S.A. Today*, vol. 107, September 1978, pp. 44–47) and from my interview with Professor Gray. A shortened version of the article was published in *The New York Times*, December 5, 1977, p. 37.

13. All the quotes attributed to Schrank, unless otherwise indicated, are from my interview with him.

The Family Business

1. For a fuller discussion of the "family business" see Dr. Levinson's book on the Midwest power and light company: Harry Levinson, Charlton R. Price, Kenneth J. Munden, Harold J. Mandl, and Charles M. Solley, *Men, Management, and Mental Health* (Cambridge: Harvard University Press, 1962).

2. Jules Henry, *Culture Against Man* (New York: Vintage, 1965), p. 350.

3. "Farm Population" (Current Population Reports, Department of Agriculture, September 1976).

4. The linking of death and work has, of course, a more concrete explanation. Many work places are hazards to workers' health. Colman McCarthy, writing in the *Washington Post*, September 19, 1978, p. A-21, says that federal officials estimate that there are 390,000 cases of occupational disease every year, 2,200,000 disabling injuries, and as many as 100,000 deaths.

The Question of Purpose

1. For a discussion of the conflict between individual ethics and principles and the profit motive see Richard E. Walton's paper on the innovative restructuring of work in

The Worker and the Job, ed. Rosow, p. 145. The physiological effects of an absence of interest and commitment are considered in Jack Horn's "Bored to Sickness," p. 92.

2. Second Annual Report of the National Commission on Productivity, Washington, D.C., 1973, p. xix.

3. Little, "Technical-Professional Unemployment," p. 265.

4. Reiter's illnesses appear to be related to the stress of his work. In their paper "Work and the Health of Man," Bruce L. Margolis and William H. Kroes describe different stressful conditions that they correlate with coronary heart disease. These include "role ambiguity," "role conflict," and "responsibility for people," all of which seem to apply to Reiter's position with the finance company. Their study was published in *Work and the Quality of Life: Resource Papers for Work in America* (Cambridge: M.I.T. Press, 1974), pp. 133–144.

Other major studies in this field include "Occupational Stress and Health" (September 1977) by sociologists James S. House and Mark F. Jackman at Duke University, and Professor House's "The Effects of Occupational Stress on Physical Health" in *Work and the Quality of Life*, pp. 145–170. See also Kathy Slobogin's "Stress," *The New York Times Magazine*, November 20, 1977, pp. 48–112.

Maccoby and Terzi write in "Character and Work in America," p. 120: "The kind of work a person does may fit his character and thus be satisfying or it may clash with character, thus causing dissatisfaction and suffering. What happens when character is *maladapted* to work? There is abundant evidence that the loss of 'Satisfying' work may result in emotional and/or physical symptoms of illness, particularly depression."

5. Mills, *White Collar*, p. xvi.

A Loss of Faith

1. This is from my interview with Yankelovich.

2. Eric Goldman, *The Crucial Decade—And After* (New York: Vintage, 1960), p. 218.

3. "The Status of Ressentiment in America," *Social Research* 42, no. 4 (Winter 1975), p. 761.

4. Ibid., p. 763.

3: A CHANGE IN CLIMATE

The introductory quote is from Gray and Bolce's study, "Job Desirability and the Right Not To Work," *U.S.A. Today*, vol. 107 (September 1978), pp. 44–47.

The Social Sanction

1. The differences between Mike Antonelli and his parents are interesting because they suggest an important generational split in blue-collar values. In 1964 when Dr. Mirra Komarovsky studied sixty working-class couples, she found that although they were earning middle-class salaries, their values and customs reflected their working-class roots. In his attitudes about security, employment, and marriage, Mike Antonelli, Sr., adheres to traditional ethnic working-class beliefs. (One exception is his approval of his son's application for welfare.) His son, who has always worked in blue-collar jobs, expresses feelings about self-gratification, living in the present, marriage, and work that are closer to Yankelovich's "New Breed" than they are to his father's values.

2. Professor Feldstein's analysis is taken from Lenny Marx's "Confessions of an Unemployment Cheat," *Washington Monthly*, May 1977, pp. 23–36. Professor Feldstein's views on distortions in the reporting of unemployment rates were also quoted in the DuPont Company's publication, *Context*, no. 1 (1977), p. 2–7 in an article titled "How Can We Get More People Working?"

3. "The Great Male Cop-out from the Work Ethic," *Business Week*, November 14, 1977, pp. 156–166.

4. "The Job Problem," *Scientific American*, November 1977, pp. 43–52.

5. O'Toole's remarks are from an interview I conducted with him.

Life in the Discardo Culture

1. Flexitime has become increasingly popular in this country and is a relatively common practice in Norway and Sweden. In the mid-1970s more than 3,000 American firms employing about a million workers had instituted forty-hour four-day work weeks. Job sharing has been adapted by firms and government agencies in San Francisco; Palo Alto; Madison, Wisconsin; Boston; and Loveland, Colorado. Some employers have reported that hiring two workers for the salary of one increases efficiency, cuts absenteeism, and raises productivity. New Ways to Work, which pioneered the concept, has received a federal grant to help support the program.

2. Ted Morgan, "The Good Life (along the San Andreas Fault)," *The New York Times Magazine*, July 4, 1976, p. 17.

3. C. Wright Mills wrote in 1951 that "the old middle-class work ethic—the gospel of work—has been replaced in the society of employees by a leisure ethic, and this replacement has involved a sharp, almost absolute split between work and leisure. Now work itself is judged in terms of leisure values [*White Collar*, p. 236]."

The Economic Factor

1. *De-Managing America* (New York: Vintage, 1976).

2. The statistics on government assistance are taken from the Welfare Policy Project conducted in 1977 by the Institute of Policy Science and Public Affairs of Duke University and the Ford Foundation. The specific source is Professor Lester M. Salamon's report: "Toward Income Opportunity: Current Thinking on Welfare Reform," pp. 1, 14–19, 24, 115–136.

3. These figures concerning the underground economy are taken from my 1976 report to the Ford Foundation, "Organized Crime: A Discussion Paper." As the article "The Underground Economy," by Peter Passell in *The New York Times*, April 15, 1978, indicates, the estimates of the underground economy range from $100 billion to $195 billion. If only one tenth of the $100 billion is earned by those counted as unemployed, then a million "unemployed" workers may be receiving a tax-free income of $10,000. Passell writes, "We seem to have achieved an uneasy, hypocritical peace with our economic underclass, providing inadequate education, job opportunities and welfare assistance, while allowing it easy access to the subterranean economy."

4. "The Personal Cost of Cheating on Unemployment Insurance," *The New York Times*, February 19, 1978, p. 17.

5. "To Lie or Not to Lie: The Doctor's Dilemma," *The New York Times*, April 18, 1978.

4: IN SEARCH OF EASE

The first introductory quote is from Jules Henry's *Pathways to Madness* (New York: Random House, 1971), p. 14.

The second introductory quote is from Josef Pieper's *Leisure: The Basis of Culture* (New York: New American Library, 1963), p. 41.

1. Ibid., p. 44.

2. Ibid., p. 70.

3. Ibid., pp. 32–33.

4. Ibid., p. 41.

5. This and the following discussion of culturally determined time, bound and unbound time, is from *Pathways to Madness*, pp. 11–17.

6. "The General Mills American Family Report 1976–77: Raising Children in a Changing Society" (conducted by Yankelovich, Skelly, and White, Inc.).

7. *The Gamesman: Winning and Losing the Career Game*

(New York: Bantam, 1978). This discussion of craftsmen, jungle fighters, company men, and gamesmen is drawn from chapters 2 to 6.

The Technician
1. Peter Berger, Brigitte Berger, and Hansfried Kellner, *The Homeless Mind: Modernization and Consciousness* (New York: Vintage, 1974), pp. 182–184. My discussion of "makeability" and "progressivity" was enhanced by an interview I had with Peter and Brigitte Berger. In fact, I am indebted to them for adding to my understanding of the technician type.
2. Ibid., pp. 112–113.
3. These quotes by Kenneth Keniston are from my interview with him. The Carnegie study cited here is Keniston and the Carnegie Council on Children's *All Our Children: The American Family under Pressure* (New York: Harcourt Brace Jovanovich, 1977). In an earlier book, *The Uncommitted*, Keniston described some of the reasons why college graduates had become disaffected with work in the 1960s. He attributed their disaffection to the vanishing relationship between the worker and the product he produces; to the lack of challenge in many jobs; and the high premium on coolness, detachment, and the repression of emotions on the job.

The Protester
1. "The Status of Ressentiment," p. 762.
2. Jules Henry, *Culture Against Man* (New York: Vintage, 1965), p. 384.
3. "The Status of Ressentiment in America," pp. 774. After this article, in 1978, Yankelovich found that the percentage of Americans holding these "New Breed" values now constituted a majority of the American people (52 percent). In his 1978 study, "Work, Values and the New Breed," Yankelovich wrote, "In the New Breed we see the beginnings of an ethic built around the concept of

duty to oneself, in glaring contrast to the traditional ethic of obligation to others. . . . The New Breed also press for greater freedom for the individual . . . freedom to enjoy life now rather than in some distant future; freedom to elevate one's own desires to the rank of entitlements; freedom to give one's own ego more room in which to maneuver; freedom to pull up stakes and move on without having to pick up the pieces."

4. This description of the addictive personality is based on an article by Professor Stanton Peele, "Addiction: Relief from Life's Pains," *Washington Post*, October 1, 1978.

5: PAST ANXIETIES, FUTURE ANXIETIES

The introductory excerpt is from Kahn and Weiner's *The Year 2000* as excerpted in Best, ed., *The Future of Work*, pp. 151, 152.

1. For additional discussion of these and other future work scenarios, see Richard J. Schonberger's "Toward a Greater Flexibility," *Humanist*, September –October 1973, pp. 35–37.

2. Some futurists predict that the common retirement age for white-collar workers will be forty by the year 2,000 (*The New York Times*, February 19, 1976, p. 40). Among the major corporations that have instituted early retirement policies are: Kimberly-Clark, Lever Brothers, Ford Motor Company, I.B.M., Dow Chemical, and Westinghouse. With the increase of profit sharing and pension plans, employees do not appear to be resisting early retirement. One oil company president reported that in 1968 80 percent of the company's managerial staff waited until the mandatory retirement age of 65; by 1978, 80 percent of the staff was retiring early. The proliferation of part-time work has also played a large part in the decision to retire early. In the mid-sixties, one out of every eight workers worked part-time; in 1977 it was one out of five.

In 1970 Eugene Jennings described the emergence of

the "mobicentric man" in the corporate world. For him, Jennings wrote, "movement is not so much a way to get someplace or a means to an end as it is an end in itself." When the corporate employee "cannot go up, he enjoys a ride to the side. For him success is represented less by position, title, salary or performance than by moving and movement."

3. *Future Shock*, as excerpted from Best, ed., *The Future of Work*, pp. 66–77.

4. The quote on leisure studies is from Ellen Goodman's column in the *Washington Post*, September 16, 1978.

5. *The Year 2000* as excerpted from Best, ed., *The Future of Work*, pp. 141–154.

INDEX

For a complete list of books available from
Penguin in the United States, write to Dept.
DG, Penguin Books, 299 Murray Hill Parkway,
East Rutherford, New Jersey 07073.

For a complete list of books available from
Penguin in Canada, write to Penguin Books
Canada Limited, 2801 John Street, Markham,
Ontario L3R 1B4.

ALL THE LIVELONG DAY
The Meaning and Demeaning of Routine Work

Barbara Garson

What do employees do all day in a tuna-fish cannery or a Ping-Pong plant? How do keypunchers, auto-assemblers, and insurance clerks keep from going crazy? To find out, Barbara Garson traveled around the country for two years, spying out the games, the devices, people use to restore meaning to jobs drained of meaning in the name of profit. She found resentment, humiliation, even sabotage; above all, she found that people "passionately want to work." "This is a loving book. It celebrates man's vitality and ingenuity under intense pressures designed to turn him into a machine"—*Christian Science Monitor*.

LOOKING FOR AMERICA
A Writer's Odyssey

Richard Rhodes

Several years ago, Richard Rhodes left home and job to look for America. What he found—"landscapes, patterns, technologies, the beast in the jungle, the masks of men"—was a vision of America that any American can share. *Looking for America* exposes our natural riches as well as our man-made problems. It examines the famous as well as the unknown: Ted Kennedy, Gerald Ford, and J. Robert Oppenheimer, as well as an old skywriter, the Osage Indians, and a freight-train engineer, among others. It confronts issues that appear in today's headlines: suburban values, pornography, drugs, ecology. Above all, it explores "the real wilderness, the only one that has ever challenged us, the wilderness of our own brains."